I was born by th[...]abe in arms yet when my mother brought me to the square before the Cathedral to watch. And so I suppose that I, too, could say I saw the Maid, but I will not say that I have seen what I do not remember. Those that did see say she still walked proud as any lord, even in the chains that bound her down. She was dressed in finest fur and velvet, brooched in gold, a gift from the Prince so that she need not appear in rags, though of course the boots the Prince had sent did not fit her feet as they had become, and so she walked barefoot across the square.

All the monks were there; they formed a circle around the pyre and chanted hymns while the Abbot set the torch to it. They say he hanged himself that night—I say he would have done a good deal more good in the world if he'd hanged himself that morning.

I think others have seen the Maid since, though I have not. She does not come to all women—nor to men at all, for all her concern is with us. And so we bring her such gifts as we can, and our prayers, and she does what she can for us.

But I have come to know that there is something she wants from us, too.

She comes to tell us to live without fear.

DAW Books Presents
A Reader's Guide to DARKOVER,
one of Marion Zimmer Bradley's
finest creations

THE FOUNDING:

A "lost ship" of Terran origin, in the pre-empire colonizing days, lands on a planet with a dim red star, later to be called Darkover.

  DARKOVER LANDFALL

THE AGES OF CHAOS:

1,000 years after the original landfall settlement, society has returned to the feudal level. The Darkovans, their Terran technology renounced or forgotten, have turned instead to free-wheeling, out-of-control matrix technology, psi powers and terrible psi weapons. The populace lives under the domination of the Towers and a tyrannical breeding program to staff the Towers with unnaturally powerful, inbred gifts of *laran*.

  STORMQUEEN!
  HAWKMISTRESS!

THE HUNDRED KINGDOMS:

An age of war and strife retaining many of the decimating and disastrous effects of the Ages of Chaos. The lands which are later to become the Seven Domains are divided by continuous border conflicts into a multitude of small, belligerent kingdoms, named for convenience "The Hundred Kingdoms." The close of this era is heralded by the adoption of the Compact, instituted by Varzil the Good. A landmark and turning point in the history of Darkover, the Compact bans all distance weapons, making it a matter of honor that one who seeks to kill must himself face equal risk of death.

  TWO TO CONQUER
  THE HEIRS OF HAMMERFELL

THE RENUNCIATES:

During the Ages of Chaos and the time of the Hundred Kingdoms, there were two orders of women who set themselves apart from the patriarchal nature of Darkovan feudal society: the priestesses of Avarra, and the warriors of the Sisterhood of the Sword. Eventually these two independent groups merged to form the powerful and legally chartered Order of Renunciates or Free Amazons, a guild of women bound only by oath as a sisterhood of mutual responsibility. Their primary allegiance is to each other rather than to family, clan, caste or any man save a temporary employer. Alone among Darkovan women, they are exempt from the usual legal restrictions and protections. Their reason for existence is to provide the women of Darkover an alternative to their socially restrictive lives.

THE SHATTERED CHAIN
THENDARA HOUSE
CITY OF SORCERY

AGAINST THE TERRANS
—THE FIRST AGE (Recontact):

After the Hastur Wars, the Hundred Kingdoms are consolidated into the Seven Domains, and ruled by a hereditary aristocracy of seven families, called the Comyn, allegedly descended from the legendary Hastur, Lord of Light. It is during this era that the Terran Empire, really a form of confederacy, rediscovers Darkover, which they know as the fourth planet of the Cottman star system. The fact that Darkover is a lost colony of the Empire is not easily or readily acknowledged by Darkovans and their Comyn overlords.

REDISCOVERY (*with Mercedes Lackey*)
THE SPELL SWORD
THE FORBIDDEN TOWER
STAR OF DANGER
THE WINDS OF DARKOVER

AGAINST THE TERRANS
—THE SECOND AGE (After the Comyn):

With the initial shock of recontact beginning to wear off, and the Terran spaceport a permanent establishment on the outskirts of the city of Thendara, the younger and less traditional elements of Darkovan society begin the first real exchange of knowledge with the Terrans—learning Terran science and technology and teaching Darkovan matrix technology in turn. Eventually Regis Hastur, the young Comyn lord most active in these exchanges, becomes Regent in a provisional government allied to the Terrans. Darkover is once again reunited with its founding Empire.

THE BLOODY SUN
HERITAGE OF HASTUR
THE PLANET SAVERS
SHARRA'S EXILE
THE WORLD WRECKERS
*EXILE'S SONG

THE DARKOVER ANTHOLOGIES:

These volumes of stories edited by Marion Zimmer Bradley strive to "fill in the blanks" of Darkovan history, and elaborate on the eras, tales and characters which have captured readers' imaginations.

DOMAINS OF DARKOVER
FOUR MOONS OF DARKOVER
FREE AMAZONS OF DARKOVER
THE KEEPER'S PRICE
LERONI OF DARKOVER
MARION ZIMMER BRADLEY'S DARKOVER
THE OTHER SIDE OF THE MIRROR
RED SUN OF DARKOVER
RENUNCIATES OF DARKOVER
SNOWS OF DARKOVER
SWORD OF CHAOS
TOWERS OF DARKOVER

(*forthcoming in hardcover from DAW Books in Summer 1996.)

RETURN TO AVALON

A Celebration of Marion Zimmer Bradley

EDITED BY

Jennifer Roberson

DAW BOOKS, INC.

DONALD A. WOLLHEIM, FOUNDER

375 Hudson Street, New York, NY 10014

ELIZABETH R. WOLLHEIM

SHEILA E. GILBERT

PUBLISHERS

For Marion Zimmer Bradley
a great mistress of magic;
and
Don, Elsie, and Betsy Wollheim
who helped nurture it.

CONTENTS

Contents

INTRODUCTION
JUST LIKE A REAL PERSON

by Diana L. Paxson

A number of years ago, when our children were young and none of us were on diets, we used to have Sunday afternoon tea parties at Greyhaven. Marion would come up the hill from Greenwalls (her house about ten minutes away), accompanied by her daughter Moira or some of the young women who at various times lived there. My sister-in-law Tracy Blackstone would cook up some goodies, and I would make endless cups of English tea.

Conversation ranged from costuming to conventions to whatever we were reading or writing at the time. At that point I was just getting established as a writer, and, as I recall, Marion was starting to work on *Mists of Avalon*. On the occasion I am thinking of, Moira, then about thirteen, had brought along a friend named Jeannie, who had been in and out of Greenwalls for several years. Jeannie had just started devouring the Darkover books.

Somewhere around the third pot of tea, it suddenly dawned on Jeannie that the books she had just been burbling about so ecstatically had been written by the woman she had known only as the mother of her friend all these years. She stared across the table, eyes widening, as Marion admitted that she was indeed "The" Marion Zimmer Bradley.

"But ... you're just like a real person!" exclaimed Jeannie.

*   *   *

Eventually, we picked ourselves up off the floor and stopped laughing. But the incident was typical of the problem people have sometimes had in reconciling Marion's physical presence with her impact as a writer. For years, people expected her to be a six-foot-tall Amazon with flaming red hair, and were disconcerted to be introduced to (in the early days) a petite woman with long blonde hair and, later, a motherly looking woman with short hair. Naturally blonde, her hair has grown paler, but it is still essentially the same color as it was when I met her thirty years ago.

A real person ... ? I suppose I've had more opportunity than most to know.

I was originally introduced to Marion by Ed Meskys in 1965, when she was still living from one advance to the next, even though the Darkover books had already attracted a devoted following. I slept on the floor of her Guest of Honor suite at my first convention (Westercon in 1967). In 1968 I married her adopted brother Jon De-Cles, and became part of an extended family whose ramifications have been confusing fandom for years.

So I have known her in her private persona as a sister-in-law, trading children's clothes and recipes and sharing all the concerns of a family. But I have also been privileged to know her in the same way as a number of other writers—as a mentor.

A creative writing course in college had traumatized me out of writing anything for ten years, but after knowing Marion for a while it finally dawned on me that real people could write stories that I actually liked to read, and I tried again. It is probably fair to say that if it had not been for her I would not be a writer. When I finished my first novel, she was kind enough to read it—and criticize it. When I stopped crying, I rewrote it. Several times Marion helped me through the birthing pangs of my stories until I began selling, and bought them from me when she began editing anthologies of her own.

Family connections and proximity made this easier, but I was by no means the only writer to have realized it was possible to make a career of writing and learned how to do it from Marion. Others include Mercedes Lackey, as well as Jennifer Roberson and Deborah Wheeler, whose first story sales were to Marion. Reading the introductions to the stories she has published in her anthologies, one is struck by the many which are first sales, especially when one notes how often those writers have gone on to make names for themselves in the field. Unlike many editors, Marion has been willing to work with aspiring writers, commenting on successive versions of a manuscript until it turns into a salable story.

Even before she began editing anthologies, Marion had been developing her own theories about what makes a good story in comments on panels at science fiction conventions and later in writing workshops. In a nutshell, it goes: "Joe has his fanny in a bear trap and gets it out." After struggling unsuccessfully to force my own work into the mold of "literary fiction," this concept burst upon my awareness with blinding impact. The reason I liked Marion's stories better than I did those in *The New Yorker* was because Something Happened—they had a Beginning, a Middle, and an End. It helped that the protagonists were usually people with whom one could have some sympathy, but the important point was that in an MZB story people had real problems and solved them, in the process learning something about themselves and the world.

This is the philosophy that has guided her as an editor, and that has enabled her to launch so many other careers. It should be pointed out that this approach to story-telling is not original to Marion, though she has made brilliant use of it. She says she learned it from Don

Wollheim, founder of DAW Books, and it was the support of Wollheim, whom she came to look upon as a father, than enabled her to keep writing this kind of fiction and to publish her anthologies. In a field that periodically denies its roots in entertainment and sets out to become Respectable, DAW's books in general and Marion's in particular have been a refreshing, even essential, refuge.

This is not to say that the kind of writing MZB fosters is fluffy or "escape fiction" (though it can distract a troubled mind). Without being pretentious about it, Marion's work has addressed some important issues. And it is in this, I think, that her real significance as a writer lies. More than anyone else I can think of, Marion has focused on areas that are of vital concern to different groups of readers and written about them with an understanding that leaves one with both hope and understanding. In the early Darkover books she presented psychic and paranormal phenomena in a way that showed people who had actually experienced such things (if not as dramatically as they do on Darkover at least enough to make them fear for their sanity) that they were not abnormal, only unusual, and that one could learn to manage them without going crazy.

As the Darkover series developed, she began to write about homosexual relationships (this was before it became fashionable), providing role models and acceptance for another subset of the reading audience and educating the rest. Though she swears that she is not a feminist, in the seventies, Marion started exploring the problems of being an independent female in a man's world through the "Free Amazons." This led to the formation of an actual organization, the Guild of Free Amazons, which has provided a great deal of moral support for women who are trying to establish an independent identity, especially in parts of the country where the "feminist revolution" never arrived.

This sense of the importance of the female perspective, especially of its spiritual side, was expressed most powerfully in *The Mists of Avalon,* a stunning example of a book that said what a large group of people most needed to hear, at the time they needed to hear it, in a form which they could understand. Having studied the Arthurian legend rather extensively in college, I had believed there was nothing new one could possibly say on the subject. Marion proved me wrong. The book became a surprise best-seller, not of the variety that is in all the bookstores one year and all the secondhand stores the next, but the kind of classic that people reread and give to their friends. It has been selling steadily since it first appeared and has been published in translation all over the world.

This ability to tune in to the "zeitgeist" transcends style and structure. It no longer matters whether the writing is consistently exquisite or the structure elegant. It is the vision, the psychological truth, the sheer emotional impact that lifts the work above any number of "literary" masterpieces to a level at which even the academics must accept it.

Is the author of such a work a "real person"? After *Mists* was published, Marion was disconcerted to encounter people who expected her to look (and act) like Morgan Le Fay. She was particularly bemused when people asked her how much of *Mists of Avalon* was "channeled." Her secretary Elizabeth Waters provided her with a classic riposte—"I'm not a medium, I'm a large."

And yet, there is a sense in which it is true, not only of Marion, but of every writer. When her fingers are on the keyboard, she is not thinking about tonight's dinner or the electric bill, she is living in a world in which Joe can get his fanny out of that bear trap if he will only try hard enough—and use his brain. She exists in a place where tragedy has meaning and even death can be a triumph, where people make mistakes and learn from them, and where those who have been misfits all their lives discover their true identity. In such a world, wisdom can flow through the fingertips to magically appear upon the page. Marion has said that sometimes she understands what her books are about only after she has written them.

The rest of the time, yes, Marion Zimmer Bradley is ". . . just like a real person." I love her anyway.

FOREWORD

by Andre Norton

Every field of fiction writing has its giants, those whose works are beacon lights to others striving hard to give the readers stories which have reality, impact, which are made to make one think, lead one to explore—to reach out in stretches which seem to be more than one can achieve.

Marion Zimmer Bradley has not only created worlds which will last for generations to come, but in turn she has reached out a hand to draw after her those who long also to find a voice, and tell an earnestly constructed tale.

Through her anthologies and her fantasy magazine she has opened wide the gate for so many who are now proving to be worthy daughters-in-letters, and for this, as well as for her own great gift, all of us must give her honor.

I discovered Marion's work years ago when a paperback, *The Colors of Space,* caught my eye. And thereafter I hunted down every title of hers I could see. From this beginning seed came finally such full flowering and splendid results as *The Mists of Avalon,* the Darkover tales, and others beyond listing.

To be a woman writer is to stand up and pay full homage to Marion Zimmer Bradley, both for what she has accomplished and what she is—unique and timeless.

TO LIGHT SUCH A CANDLE

by eluki bes shahar

In the town of Rimmon, at the opposite end of the square from the great cathedral, there is a statue of the Maid. The custodians of Holy Mother Church do not like it that the statue is there, for is it not proper that there should be statues only of saints and great men? But the Prince of the City, who was with the Maid when she helped the King to his throne, melted down his own cannon to cast it and pulled upon the ropes that set it into place with his own hands, so the statue remains. He is, after all, the Prince of Rimmon, and they merely the Lords of the Life Hereafter.

If you ask any among those who toil in the Cathedral and the monastery beyond what it is that they do not like about the statue, they will not tell you the truth, though it is a matter of public record. They will complain about how the statue's back is turned upon the Cathedral, which is true. The statue is very like the Maid in life, after all.

You must look up to see her—not because she is large, like the statue of Saint Tiresias the Judge who stands between the Cathedral doors, for our Prince made her bronze effigy just the size she was in life—but because she stands upon a great granite stone; a block as thick and as long as a man's leg, that it would take a team of oxen and a length of chain to shift. The stone is burned, and shiny with fire, and if you look closely you can see the stub of an iron bar, broken off close by her right foot.

The Prince has fixed the statue to the stone with mortar and long bronze spikes, so that who moves the Maid must move the stone as well, and though the Bishop would dearly love to see her gone, he dares not do so much as turn her to face the Cathedral. He is, after all, only the Bishop of Rimmon, and our lord is the Prince of Rimmon, who loved the Maid. There have been disputes between the Prince and the Bishop in the past, and the Bishop walks softly, lest our Prince forget again that he is a godly man. And so the Maid's statue remains.

When I was a child, I loved to hear tales of her. She died almost before I was born, but my mother saw her when she came to Rimmon to summon the Prince to fight the Goddams so that his King might rule. When she was gone in wine, my mother would say just what the ballad-sellers do, about how young the Maid was, and how beautiful. When she was sober, she would say one thing more: that the Maid was unlike any woman my mother had ever seen, for she was not afraid. We women live with fear; it is our bread, that men in this one thing our servants prepare daily for our meat. But when the Prince laughed at the Maid, standing before him in her smock and country clogs, and offered to set her upon his destrier, she did not flinch, but set herself upon its back without his aid, mastering horse and man together with that one gesture. The prince's stallion had a foul temper—the prince rides his get yet, and last year one of them trampled a child—and the Maid, being lately from the country, could never have been on a horse's back before. But gracious and mild (say the ballad-mongers; me, I don't believe that of her) she set her foot in the stirrup. It is a well-used tale, belonging to the part of the Maid's story that everyone knows.

It cannot be that she rode well, and the back of a

horse is a very high throne—not so high as a rooftop, though it seems higher; I who have been a-horseback say this. I think it was her fearlessness that made him love her; she laughed at him, you see, and bid him dismount, and leaped upon the horse's back as though she were birds-nesting in her family's orchard.

She was not afraid.

Or so my mother said while she was alive, and may well be telling the story to Our Lord and all His holy angels now. And it would be well for them to believe her as I do, for though my dear mother had her faults (and they were many, and I gave coin to the priests when she died), she did not have the wit to tell of a thing she had not seen, and where else would a woman like my mother ever have seen a woman who looked into a man's eyes and was not afraid, unless she had seen the Maid when she came to Rimmon?

So I believe that she did.

The rest of the story is the story that everyone knows—how our Prince went away with the Maid and how the other nobles followed the Maid and rose for the King, and how the Goddams were driven back across the water and the King ruled once more. Not many know the rest—I have heard it said by travelers that at the victory celebration angels from heaven came down and bore the Maid off to Heaven to wind knitting wool for the Blessed Virgin in Paradise, which would be a sad repayment for all her work indeed—but here in Rimmon we know the truth, whether we want to or not, though princes rarely ask what the people want.

It must be a great thing to be a prince, and have the whole world turn a woman's face to you, but when the Maid had the power of a great prince and rode upon a prince's horse, I do not think she saw the world so. She was brave, and saw the world through a hero's eyes. I think we all were men to her.

But she will always be the Maid to the women of Rimmon; a woman, and one of us.

It is a great heresy, but sometimes I wonder: would it have been so wrong for the Maid to sit where our lord the King now does? The King, they say, is a frightened man: frightened of his sons, and of his son's wives, and of the Goddams who will not stay in their own lands, but are always coming back to ours. I think the Maid would have laughed at the Goddams, and then they would have stayed home.

But so the tale of the Maid goes, and it has three parts. The women of Rimmon know the part of the Maid's story that even princes do not tell. We are the ones who leave the flowers at her statue's feet, and the knots of ribbon. That is what truly angers the Bishop; that we bring her gifts. We would bring her gold and incense if we could; as it is, we bring her what we have.

But I shall tell the Prince's story next, for more people know it, though even that is not many. The great lords live forever; the Prince of Rimmon was a young man when my mother was a girl, and even now when I am old he is not so old. There is gray in his hair (I have seen it), but he rides to the chase (his horses are devils) with a fury that leaves his sons behind. Old men do not have this fire, and so I say that he is not old. Perhaps he will not die; perhaps it is fear that uses up our lives, until we are smothered by the rites of Mother Church as a candle flame drowns in hot tallow.

But I speak foolishness because I would not tell what happened next; the Maid's tale as it is known to the Prince of Rimmon.

The King entered into his holy city, and all the great lords came and swore fealty to him there. Because it is the city where Our Lord's Mother died in exile, weapons are forbidden within its gates and enemies must meet upon its streets without quarrel. Where else could a king

over such great lords take their oaths without war? Yet
while the Goddams held the city, the King could not
command his princes, for they had not sworn to him.

There is a long ballad, as true as any other, all about
the siege of Holy Marcei, and how one by one each lord
slipped away from the fighting to slip into the city and
lay his life upon the knees of his king. It is pretty, but
in Rimmon we speak of what happened afterward.

When the Goddams were driven out by the King and
his lords together, a feast was held in Holy Marcei. The
Maid was there, though she did not wish to be. It was
not the King who compelled her, but the Prince of Rimmon, who had been the first to look into her eyes and
follow her. It was at that feast that Holy Mother Church,
coming late to the King's service once the battle was
done, swore that the victory was due to her prayers and
everlasting rituals.

I do not think the Maid would have argued with them;
all the stories tell of her as a great general, and a great
general does not fight when there is no hope of victory.
But the hall was full of fighting men, flushed with wine
and bloodletting, and at the back of their minds every
one was the anger at paying a tenth of all they owned
to the Church each year, when the Church had done
nothing to throw the Goddams out and more to keep
them in. That great hall full of men mocked and argued,
and shouted the Bishop of Marcei down from his place
when he would pronounce the Church's tardy blessing
upon their cause—is it any wonder that by daybreak the
Maid had become a witch and a sworn enemy of the
True Church?

They brought her back to Rimmon to burn her.

I do not think that is what our lord the Prince of
Rimmon intended. It is true that a heresy trial must be
held in a cathedral, and that Rimmon is a cathedral town.
Perhaps they wished to chasten our Prince as well, for

his championship of the Maid, but I have lived all the years of my life in his city, and I do not think even a Prince of the Church could bend the Prince of Rimmon so far from his own will, save through the threat of death and Hell which they could not hold over him while he stood before the King's face.

No, I think that he meant to save the Maid by forcing them to hold the trial here. Perhaps he thought that they would let him pardon her. Perhaps he thought they would fear him.

But if they did fear him, they feared the Maid more. They brought people from her village to swear that as a child she had been pursued by the spirits of the air; to swear that her mother lay with an incubus and so the Maid was, herself, half-demon. Her victories, cheered as miracles when she won them, now became evidence that Hesperus, sinful Lord of this world, favored her.

She held, it was said, evil influence over the King, though how this might be when she had not seen his face since the night of the banquet, I do not know. I do know that the King never asked how it was with her, nor placed himself between her and the Church—and it is not I who says so, but the Prince of Rimmon, who has told us all this story.

And so the trial went on. A full year, it took them, to seal the Church's case against her, for they had no confession of her. The Prince stood in the room each day as they questioned her and would not be moved. The first man they brought to draw her upon the rack he killed. The second was a priest, and so the Prince could not lay hand upon him, but the priest died untimely of bad wine and after that they could find no one who understood the drawing engines.

And so they hardly questioned her at all, but they would not have gotten her to lie no matter what they did. I said before that she was a good general (the King

on his throne bears witness to this truth) and she knew
that they meant her to die. They said it was for heresy,
and our Prince says it was for jealousy, but I think that
she had looked them in the eye, and once she had it was
that Holy Church must kill her if it could not make her
kneel. The Church is a prince above the princes, and
even the Prince of Rimmon must bow his head and stop
his tongue when she speaks.

And Holy Church has tender ears, suited only to the
hearing of soft words. The Maid, for all the ballad-singers
say she was meek and mild as the Mother of God, spoke
truth as hard as ice in the waterbucket on a winter morning, and that she was about to die did not improve her
temper. The Prince had followed her because she was
not afraid, and for that same reason Holy Church
burned her.

That he did not stop them—he, who had done so much
for her asking—was for his life and lands: had he broken
into the Cathedral and taken her, Holy Church would
have taken all he owned and hunted him outlaw, and
burned them both in the end. Yet the Maid would have
done even that, were he imprisoned in her place, though
it is true she had not so much to lose as he, having only
her life and her youth and her strong body. Or so the
Prince of Rimmon has said.

I think he must believe it; though it is an easy thing
to remold a woman's character after she is dead, she
rarely becomes so noble that she is a rebuke to living
men. But so it was that he withheld his hand on that day,
and ever after Holy Mother Church has walked softly in
Rimmon, lest the Prince should forget his prudence.

I was born by the time she burned, though a babe in
arms yet when my mother brought me to the square
before the Cathedral to watch. And so I suppose that I,
too, could say I saw the Maid, but I will not say that I
have seen what I do not remember. Those that did see

say she still walked proud as any lord, even in the chains that bound her down. She was dressed in finest fur and velvet, brooched in gold, a gift from the Prince so that she need not appear in rags, though of course the boots the Prince had sent did not fit her feet as they had become, and so she walked barefoot across the square.

The Bishop looked in vain to the Prince for the loan of his men-at-arms; it was novices from the cloister who brought her out of the Cathedral dungeons and across the square, and who bound her to an iron stake set in a stone and piled all around with dry, well-seasoned wood, so that she would die by fire. It is a slow and painful death; if you are ever sent to the stake, make sure they cut the wood for it no sooner than the night before, so that the smoke will kill you quickly.

All the monks were there; they formed a circle around the pyre and chanted hymns while the Abbot set the torch to it. They say he hanged himself that night—I say he would have done a good deal more good in the world if he'd hanged himself that morning. But I am only a woman, and do not understand how the world is run.

That day was like a feast day without joy. There was a dais for the important personages of the town, swagged in purple and set up high before the church doors so all could be seen. Our Prince was there, and the Mayor; Rimmon's Bishop and that of Holy Marcei and even a Cardinal from Avinyon. Some say Rimmon's citizens were forbidden to attend the burning, but that would be an edict that even Holy Church could not enforce, and so I do not believe that the Bishop made it. Besides, the Prince would only say the opposite, and there was enough bad blood in the town now without an open fight.

I have seen burnings since—dry wood ones, too—and so I know what my mother saw on that day. The skin turns black—at first that is from the smoke only, but then the fat seeps up through the flesh and burns upon

it until the skin glistens black like a piece of coal. Then
the skin splits, shrunken in the heat like the green hide
it is, and the blood comes out brightly, washing it clean
for a moment. The blood hisses as it falls into the flame,
and boils dry on the skin sometimes before it can run
down. Sometimes the bones burst also, especially if they
have been broken recently, and that is a mercy, as it
makes the dying quicker.

They say that the Maid sang hymns, or was silent in
the face of her enemies, but I do not think anyone can
keep silent on a pyre of seasoned wood. I know she did
not repent, for they would have strangled her before they
burned her if she had, even at the last, when the priest
came to ask her for her confession. But she was
burned alive.

When she was dead, they took all the pieces of her,
and burnt them again inside an iron box until there were
only bones. Then they ground the bones in a mortar and
scattered the dust outside the city, so that the Maid
should not partake of the glorious Resurrection of the
Body that is to come someday for all of us.

And one year from that date the Prince and his artifi-
cers came to the square where the Maid had been
burned, and set up her image in bronze upon the fire-
charred stone, where I have seen it every day of my life.
When the Prince dies, perhaps his son will let the Bishop
melt it down, as His Reverence yearns so to do. Perhaps
he will not. Who can say, of a boy come into his
patrimony?

This is the story of the Maid, as the Prince of Rimmon
knows it. He told it all to us on that day, and had a
ballad-singer to write it, too. But for him it ends here.

The women know more.

It is not something we speak of. Maria the Washer-
woman did, once: she was lashed at the doors of the
Cathedral and set outside the gates for the night in pun-

ishment. She was not seen again—not even bones, though the wolves hardly ever bother to drag them far.

But Maria spoke, and we heard, and the Bishop acted, and we saw, and now we do not speak, for Maria has said all that ever need be said.

Maria saw the Maid upon the road, she said. Maria was driving her pig to the forest to forage: the Church had the pig after, and I trust they had joy of the bacon. She saw the Maid upon the road and spoke with her, three days after she was burned.

Maria did not tell us in Rimmon what they spoke of before His Reverence caused a bar of hot iron to be laid upon her tongue, and had she lived she would not have been able to after. It does not matter. What she told us was enough, and though some do not believe, none of them are women.

I think others have seen the Maid since, though I have not. She does not come to all women—nor to men at all, for all her concern is with us. And so we bring her such gifts as we can, and our prayers, and she does what she can for us. I think God the Father still watches over her, and that is why she does not do more.

But I have come to know that there is something she wants from us, too.

She does not come to tell us to endure, for we know that lesson already. Nor does she come to tell us to have courage, for that is simple foolishness. We live always with fear and yet choose to live; how can we not have courage?

She comes to tell us to live without fear.

This is the Maid's story, the part that is only known by the women of Rimmon. That she has come, and what she asks.

It is a hard request to make of poor women, but she reminds us by having lived that it is possible. We know her life and her childhood as well as her own village does, for did not Holy Mother Church bring them here to testify of it? And we know that she was neither angel- nor devil-begotten; but a mortal woman who was not afraid.

And if we know also by her death that those who do not fear are killed for it, we know that we will die any- way, for the convenience of men and their pride. To die for a reason of our own making is good.

To live without fear is good.

This knowledge I have lived with all the years of my life; the knowledge of the Maid's life and the knowledge of her desire. I am an old woman now, nearly forty. I have borne twelve children and buried them all, and there is a pain in my belly as if hot iron were laid there. Someday soon I will die.

But before that day I will go to the village square and face the Cathedral. I will put my foot upon the block of fire-blackened stone where the flowers lay, and raise my- self to kiss the Maid upon her cold bronze lips.

And then I will go forth through Rimmon's gates, to tell the world the tale of the Maid as it is known to the women of Rimmon, and to speak of a world where women are not afraid.

THE GRAIL OF HEART'S DESIRE

by Judith Tarr

I

The young knight knelt on cold stone. The night whispered around him. Candles flickered in the gloom, casting soft light on Our Lady's altar. She smiled down upon it from her plinth of gold and porphyry: a serene and beautiful Lady in a blue gown, mantled in night and crowned with stars.

He was a very young knight. Only the night before he had lain on these same stones, clad in nothing but a thin white robe, praying that he might be worthy of the honor and the order. Now it was all his, and a blossoming bruise to mark it: a hard fist, his lord had, and gloved in steel, dealing the buffet of the knighting as if it were a blow in battle. He had rocked under it, and his eyes had gone dark, but his knees had held. He had not dishonored his name or his house.

They were feasting in the hall, drinking to his name. He had left them after the wine of Gaul had gone round, but before they brought out the cask from the holy city of Sarras. The little that he had eaten and drunk, after three days fasting, had left him weak and ill and faintly ashamed.

He had gone where men go when they are ill with feasting, but afterward his feet had carried him not back to the roar and reek of the hall but to the cold silence of the chapel in which he had been knighted. No one else had come here. No living thing stirred. There was

only the stillness and the candles' flicker, and the Lady's
soft and secret smile.

He bowed before her. His heart was full; he trembled.
Out of his trembling he shaped a prayer. "Lady," he
said. "I am your knight, your servant, the least of your
children. Grant me great deeds. Make me a knight above
all others, the splendor of my order—but never for myself. Only and ever for the glory of your name."

He fell silent. He had not dared to pray so while he
kept vigil before his knighting. It had seemed too proud
a thing then, and he too terribly unworthy. But in the
pride of his new knighthood he ventured it.

The Lady smiled. Her smile made him bolder yet.
"Lady!" he cried, "Lady, grant me visions. Even—oh,
Lady, if you are generous, or if it pleases your fancy,
grant me the vision of all visions. Grant me my heart's
desire. Show me the Grail."

His breath caught in his throat. He was not the first
to ask such a thing—he knew that; he was young and
much too bold, but he was not an utter innocent. But he
knew also what price they paid who demanded such
things of God or of His Mother. They could seek lifelong
and never gain sight of their desire. That was only for
the pure of heart.

He could not judge his own heart. He could only ask
out of the fullness in it, the giddiness of wine after too
long fasting, the high light exultation of what he was and
could be, now that he was a belted knight.

The silence deepened. The candles flickered. The
Lady smiled.

He lay on his face before her. He had been too brazen.
To demand of her what she was blessed to give—what
she gave only of her free will—

Something, some shifting in the air, brought him again
to his knees. He lifted his head slowly and gasped.

It hung above the altar, aloft on air as all the tales

told. It shimmered with another light than that of earthly
candles: white light, light of heaven, brighter than the
sun yet not a brightness that blinded. Rather, through it
one saw more clearly, to the heart of all things that were.

He stretched out a hand as they did in all the stories.
And as in all the stories, it drew away before him, never
nearer but never farther: always the same, visible and
yet unreachable.

Seek, the air sang. *Seek, and ye shall find.*

Exaltation bore him from the chapel, full into the arms
of the crowd of feasters. They had marked his absence
at last and come hunting him, to carry him back to the
wine and the revel. He resisted, but his knees were weakened, his head dizzied with visions. They bore him away
on their shoulders, whooping and laughing, baying like
wolves.

The hall was a vision of temptation, a foretaste of hell.
Reek of wine and ale, sweat and perfume and raw human
flesh. Wanton bare-breasted women with their hair
streaming all uncovered. Men tumbling them wherever
they happened to fall, on table or bench or floor. Limp
forms slumped in corners, drowned in wine. Red and
streaming faces, gaping mouths, snatches of bellowed
song.

Some of the youngest and most debauched caught
sight of the new knight borne in among them, and began
to chant his name. *Edmund! Edmund! Edmund!* He
struggled against the hands that prisoned him. His cap-
tors only laughed.

"The lion entrapped. The unicorn in captivity." It was
a sweet voice, almost too sweet for a man's, as the face
was as beautiful as a girl's. But there was nothing girlish-
sweet in those narrow dark eyes, or any love either, or
anything like charity. The smile was edged like a blade,
brilliant and deadly. "Oh, a unicorn, verily, our modest

maid: the image of virgin purity. Come now and be a man."

A true saint would have drawn himself up, even bound, and spoken noble words, words of unflinching self-sacrifice. Edmund was not a saint. He was only a new-made knight who had committed the sin of pride before the Lady in her chapel. He twisted, arched, kicked hard, broke free. And bolted, scattering revelers.

Not the worst shame, but the least becoming a man and a knight, were the tears that stained his cheeks. He ran like a child from the throngs that tormented him, ran and hid, while they hunted through the castle for him, yelling his name. But they never thought to look in the sacristy behind the chapel, in the cold still dark and the scent of wax and incense.

Long after the yelling had died away, when even the roar of carousal had grown muted, he emerged rumpled and shivering from his hiding place. His jaw was set. He had scraped the tears away. He knew what he must do, and do swiftly, without hesitation.

He was but a very young knight, of a family with great honor but few resources. It had taxed his father to the limit to provide the lovely new armor and the beautiful bright sword and the treasure above them all, the incomparable, the extraordinary, the dove-gray stallion whom God had shaped to bear a knight into battle. There was just enough left for a palfrey, a plain serviceable chestnut with a heavy head and a walleye, and a mule to bear the armor. Retinue he had none, except the one blear-eyed servant who sat up on his bed of straw and croaked, "What—"

"Up," said Edmund in a new and knightly voice. If it cracked a little, then Alfgar knew better than to remark on it. Edmund dragged him to his feet and shook him properly awake. "Up, fool! We ride on errantry."

"But," said Alfgar. "His lordship—your duties—you were to—"

Edmund raised shield against the stabbing of guilt. He was sworn to an earthly lord, but first he had sworn to the Lady as all knights did, to worship her and serve her and to do as she commanded. She had ordained this quest, he was sure of it. Had she not shown him the Grail? Had she not then cast him into the cesspit of hell, and taught him thereby to turn his back on worldly pleasure?

He said none of that to Alfgar. A servant need only know that his master commanded and he must obey.

Alfgar was schooled in obedience, but his schooling had never extended to his tongue. All the while he readied to ride, he muttered under his breath, but clear enough for Edmund to hear. "Drag a poor man out of bed before the crack of dawn, tell him he's running out in the dead of winter, and a blizzard coming, I wouldn't be surprised, and what Earl Richard will say when he sees how his new chick keeps his oath, I don't even like to imagine, except I'll get the stripes and he'll get a tongue-lashing and a few months on bread and water, see if he doesn't, not to mention what his father will say when—"

Edmund happened, just then, to catch him with a buffet on the ear. "Swifter, fool! Time's a-wasting."

"I'll say," said Alfgar, but he caught Edmund's eye. His lips clamped shut. He quickened his pace infinitesimally.

It was gray dawn and bitter cold as they rode from the postern gate. Alfgar had muttered, but Edmund had been adamant. Edmund rode the palfrey. Alfgar perched on the mule atop the packs and bundles of armor and provisions, and led the dappled stallion in his fine wargear, covered now against the wind and the cold and, as they wound down the steep track from the castle, the snow that began lightly to fall.

Edmund was warm in leather and furs and heavy mantle, gloved and booted against the worst bite of the cold. But warmer than any of it was the fire in his heart. He was a knight riding upon errantry, a knight out of the tales, a knight of the Grail.

Alfgar, wrapped in every scrap of clothing he or his master owned, shivered and grumbled. He was a thin man, a bony, gangly stick of a creature, and his heart had no fire to warm it. He had to trust in earthly craft, in the art of hearth and campfire.

There were no tales, Edmund thought, that burdened a Grail knight with so paltry a companion. True knights of the quest rode alone, or met with fair damsels who guided them to their desire.

"And what's a knight alone going to do for dinner?" Alfgar demanded when Edmund was so unwise as to speak his thoughts aloud. "Who's going to find and cook it, and who'll clean up after it? Will he dirty his pretty hands tending the animals, or dig the pit for the jacks, or God forbid clean and mend his own trews? No, he won't. Nor will the pretty damsel, and that's not a wager, that's fact. Stories don't tell everything. There's armies of servants behind every knight errant, you just see if there isn't."

Alfgar, by chance or by design, was much too far away for a buffet. Edmund settled for ignoring his existence. The hammerheaded chestnut plodded on through deepening snow, in wind that rose from icy gusts to a freezing gale. But there was a fire in his heart and a vision before him, a vision of light, splendor, purity. He was going to find the Grail. There was nothing else in the world, no snow or cold or hunger, and no guilt, either, that he had left without a word of farewell, and without his lord's leave.

II

"The Castle of the Grail," said Edmund in tones he had learned from an archbishop, rich and orotund, "is a mighty fortress, a monument of beauty and strength, warded with dragons. Only the pure may enter, pure of body and of spirit. Only the blessed may walk in its halls, hear the music of its choir, look upon the thing that it guards. Treasure, Alfgar. Treasure beyond any in the earth."

Alfgar was not listening. He had caught and killed a pair of rabbits; he was cleaning them for the spit. Edmund had assisted by setting him free to take his little bow and hunt, after he had tended the horses and the mule and set up camp in a clearing of the wood into which they had wandered. Edmund did not know its name. It might be Broceliande; it might be Lyonesse, or Ys—but Ys was sunk beneath the sea.

They had been wandering for a month and a day, from winter into deeper winter. Spring should be near, but here the winter was strong, the snow chest-deep on Edmund's destrier, the cold as bitter as ever it had been when they left his lord's castle to seek the Grail. The fire in his heart had sunk to an ember, as fires will with time and weariness.

He had caught himself, once or twice, on the verge of turning back. These were not the days of errantry. Knights no longer rode on quests. Even the glory of Crusade was departed, the Holy Sepulcher lost and the knights of the Lord driven away from Jerusalem. His own lord was a purely secular man, a noble fighter to be sure, but with little in him of either grace or devotion. He served the overlord who best suited his convenience, turned his coat as it pleased him, and reckoned himself well worthy of heaven for all of that. Did he not give great gifts to Mother Church, and succor all its prelates, and give alms to such of the poor as would best serve him?

Edmund, sent to him to learn the arts of knighthood, had fought a long and bitter battle to preserve his own soul. This he counted a victory. He had had a vision of the Grail. The Lady herself had sent him on his quest.

And if it meant that he traveled more as a fugitive than as a knight-errant, if he dared not present himself for guesting at any lordly house but must hunt—or leave Alfgar to hunt—for his dinner, then what did that matter? Alfgar saw to it that the horses were fed, which from the magnitude of his snarling and surling was rather more difficult than feeding his master. But beautiful gray Gyrfalcon must not suffer the pangs of hunger, however little might be left for the mule or the palfrey.

Edmund would stoop to tend the destrier. The other beasts were common creatures; he left them to Alfgar. But he looked after the great gray warhorse with his own hands, picked out the big feathered feet, brushed the silver-dappled coat. The feathers of the feet and the trailing thickness of tail and mane tangled terribly in briars, caught burrs and would not let them go. And Gyrfalcon had no speed, which belied the swift hunter of his name. But he was a destrier from Alemannia, and he had cost a whole year's revenues from Edmund's father's lands. He was the only right and proper mount for a knight.

Edmund said so, while Alfgar spitted the rabbits and rubbed them with herbs from a packet in his purse and set them over the fire to cook. "I shall ride into the Castle of the Grail," he said, "on my gray warhorse, in my armor and my panoply, for the honor of my house. Our Lady has promised me so."

"Oh, has she?" Alfgar muttered. The words were barely comprehensible: his teeth chattered appallingly. Perhaps after all he had said nothing.

Alfgar had a froward tongue and no grace, but two

things he had that persuaded Edmund to keep him: he
was loyal, and he could cook. The rabbits when he was
done with them were quite acceptable. Edmund, generous as a knight must be, ate only half of the second, and
left the rest for his servant. Then while Alfgar tended
the fire and saw to the horses, Edmund knelt to pray as
he did every night, running through the whole office of
Vespers; and when he had done that, he rolled himself
in blankets and furs and went to sleep.

There was a stone under his side. It was viciously
sharp, like a knight's mailed toe, and it seemed to have
the capacity to move. It thrust against him, rolled him
onto his back.

He looked up blinking in the cold gleam of dawn. A
shadow loomed against the sky. Shoulders as wide as the
king's own castle; high fantastical shape that must be—
was—a knight's helm.

Edmund sat up, or tried. His hands were caught behind
him. Bound. He stared at the knight, whose visor was
lowered, concealing his face. He wore no arms, no sur-
coat, only armor, black without sheen, no glimmer of
paint or gilding. He was nameless, faceless, a shadow
knight.

He did not speak. He raised his fist and deliberately,
with precisely calculated force, smote Edmund into the
singing dark.

It was dark in truth when Edmund roused. He was
cold. No fire was left in his heart, nor did one burn
anywhere about him. By the pallid light of the moon he
saw the clearing in which he had been camped. The snow
was all trampled and fouled. There was no fire in the
hearth of stones that Alfgar had made, only ashes, and
those stone-cold. The horses and the mule were gone,

and all that they had carried: armor, saddles, the remnants of provisions.

Edmund sat up. His hands were free. His head ached fiercely. Memory came and went in snatches: firelight, darkness, a shadow on shadow that was a knight in black armor without device.

A groan brought him about so swiftly that he reeled. Alfgar sat in the snow, his head sagging between his bony upthrust knees. His face was nigh as white as the snow. "Ah," he groaned again. "God and Saint Frideswide. My head feels like a paving stone with an army tramping on it."

Edmund's skull was in no better case, but he was a knight; it was his honor to be impervious. "We have," he said, "been set upon by bandits. We've been robbed, Alfgar."

"What, you just noticed?" Alfgar raised his head gingerly, as if he feared that too swift a motion might jar it from his neck. "They were good Christian robbers, I see. Didn't strip us naked and slit our throats."

Edmund sucked in a breath. "Isn't it enough that they took everything else? Everything!" His hand closed on air where the hilt of his dagger had been, the little one with which he cut his meat. They had taken it and his sword, even the lance that had been such an inconvenience on narrow forest tracks, slung from the mule's packsaddle and catching on every branch and bramble.

Alfgar failed to be properly impressed. "We're alive," he said, "and as warm as can be expected. That's not bad for a pair of wandering fools."

Edmund leaped, but Alfgar was faster than he looked, or more fortunate. He scrambled out of the path of Edmund's spring, and kept scrambling, till he was on his feet and loping among the trees.

Edmund watched him go. He was not even angry. Everything was gone. Horses, armor, weapons, servant—

provisions, too. Everything. He had nothing in the world but himself.

Alfgar was nearly out of sight. The forest was as black as the robber knight's armor. The moon pierced the branches, but fitfully. Alfgar was a shadow among shadows, the gangling fool transformed by moon and dark into a spirit of the wood.

Wood-spirits had no love for humankind. They would lead a man astray, lose him deep in the thickets, and leave him to die.

Edmund crossed himself with something akin to fury. He was a man of God, beloved of the Lady. No creature of the night could harm him. And his servant was escaping; and that, after all the rest, was purely intolerable. He fell into a staggering run, pursuing the shadow that was—that might be—that he prayed must be Alfgar.

He was lost. It was a great blow to his pride to admit that, but Edmund was an honest man, if a fool. Alfgar had been running on a track, and Edmund after him. But somehow in the shifting of moonlight and cloud, Edmund had wandered astray. Alfgar was long gone. Trees closed in. There was no stream to follow, no path, only the darkness and the dry grate of branches in the wind. Clouds, having danced hither and yon about the moon, drifted across it, covering it. The air was heavy with the scent of snow.

He stumbled against the bole of a tree and clung, shivering convulsively. "Lady," he whispered. He could barely hear himself above the chattering of his teeth. "Lady, if you love me, remember what you promised. If I die here, how will I ever find the Grail?"

If she heard him, she made no answer. He sank down where he had stood, huddled against the tree. He welcomed the dark when it came, the slow sleep that was, so it was said, the easiest death of them all.

III

Warmth was pain in a body so long racked with cold.
Light stabbed eyes that had looked too deep into the
dark. Voices roared in ears attuned to silence.

Edmund flailed against them. Hands gripped his arms.
Memory leaped to the chapel in his lord's castle, the
baying laughter of the knights, the hall with its visions
of hell. Sight's clarity did nothing to dim the memory.

He was lying on the softness of cushions in a broad
high space. The ceiling was black with ancient smoke,
but the carvings of its beams and panels were visible still,
strange twisted shapes in the light from high louvered
windows. That was no ceiling he had ever seen, even in
a church—least of all in a church. But what lay below it
was all too familiar.

They were feasting in the hall, high table and lesser
tables, people crowded together, wine going round, and
song, and the golden glimmer of a harp. The harper was
a woman, and a fair and shameless creature she was, too,
with her hair streaming over her white shoulders, and
her gown barely covering the tips of her milk-white
breasts. She sang in a voice like the cry of gulls or the
wailing of the wolf in the wood, eerie and wild yet
strangely beautiful. The words were none that Edmund
knew.

He crossed himself by purest instinct. His heart beat
drum-loud in his ears.

None of it vanished before the Lord's sign, least of all
the harper. Her gown was as green as beech-leaves, her
hair the color of old bronze. Her eyes he could not see:
they were lowered as she bent to her harp, long lashes
on white cheeks.

He lay alone amid the revelry, in a corner that was
almost quiet, and warm: a brazier stood on a stand—
bronze, like the harper's hair. There was a table near it,

and a jar, and a cup that held nothing but clear water. The taste of it was melted snow.

Whoever had brought him here had bathed him and stripped him of his ice-stiffened clothing and wrapped him in a soft warm robe of wool lined with silk. It had no color, no ornament or embroidery. It was simple white, and belted with plain leather. It made him think of a novice's robe. But this was no monastery.

It came to him that he was not the only one so dressed. They all were in the hall, all but the harper. It seemed to be their livery.

It was the only thing of purity about them. He saw man sitting beside women and woman beside man, arms wound about one another, lips locked in a long and utterly earthly kiss. Or a man sat with a woman on his knee, his hand on her breast, her hand where Edmund blushed furiously to see. Or a woman drank deep of wine, and fed it by the goblet to the man whose head lay in her lap. And the harper sang in her voice like wind and gulls, in that language which Edmund had never heard, but he knew what words it must sing. Words of earthly passion; songs of the flesh, and naught in them of the spirit.

A saint would have done battle with songs of his own, the order of the mass, the march of the Psalms. But the only verse of Scripture that came to him was distressingly apt to its subject.

Thy two breasts are like two young roes that are twins, which feed among the lilies.

It was an allegory, the priests said so. Christ's love for his Church. Passion of the spirit, shaped in the image of flesh.

Here was only flesh. Nothing of the spirit. Nothing at all.

The harper had finished her song and set aside the

harp. The revelers gave her a moment's silence, with an
air of great tribute. Then they returned to their reveling.

She left the stool on the dais, lifting her gown to step
down. Edmund glimpsed white ankle, and a slender foot
in a green shoe. The heat that flared in him was nigh as
hot as the fire that had burned in his heart, before time
and cold had dimmed it to ash.

She walked toward him through the oblivious revelers,
stepping lightly, her gown still lifted above the woven
rushes and the dogs that sprawled across her path. They
were gazehounds, lean and wicked-headed, all white, but
their ears were as red as blood.

And truly, thought Edmund in a kind of despair, what
else could they be but hounds of hell?

The lady of the harp came to his corner and sat on
the bed's end, all but touching his feet as he huddled
there. Her voice in speech was much less eerie than her
singing, a rather ordinary if enchantingly husky voice
speaking words that he could understand. Her accent was
odd, lilting and strange, but clear enough for that. "Ah,"
she said as if pleased. "You wake. It's long and long
you've slept, and great the need of it, from the look
of you."

"What—" Edmund stammered. "How—who—"

Ah, he thought. Fool. He should be praying, invoking
holy names to banish this that must be fever-dream. Or
worse: he was dead and in hell, and this was his
punishment.

"No," said the lady. "Dead you are not, nor dreaming,
but quite alive. We found you in the wood when we went
a-hunting the snow-white deer. You were blue and cold,
but life lingered in you yet. We brought you here, tended
you and warmed you. It was in our minds that harpsong
and firelight might rouse you more pleasantly than the
silence of an empty chamber."

He crossed himself. She watched gravely, with her

head tilted somewhat to one side, as if in curiosity. Her eyes were darker than her hair, the brown of oak-leaves in autumn, but with a glimmer of green.

He turned his own eyes away from her. She breathed temptation. "I . . . thank you," he said out of hard-earned courtesy, as a knight should do even before the Devil himself. Or herself, with her white breasts and her rose-ripe mouth. "And through you I thank the lord of this place, whoever he may be." Even if he were the lord of hell.

Out of the corner of his eye he caught her smile. "The lord of this place is thanked, and well so, since I am that one. You may call me Elen. I welcome you to Mont-salvat."

His teeth clicked together. "Montsalvat! But that is—"

"Yes," said the lady whom he was to call Elen, who called herself lord of this place. This hall of debauchery could not be the Montsalvat of which he had heard: Montsalvat the holy, Montsalvat the blessed, the Castle of the Grail. Its lord was a man, that also the tales said, and he was a knight of blinding purity, a mighty warrior against all temptation, who had healed the maimed king and taken his throne, and guarded the Grail in its hidden shrine.

The lady, this Elen, smiled as one smiles at a child or a charming fool. "This is Montsalvat," she said, "and I am lord of it. Or lady if you please. These are my people, my knights and paladins." Her hand took in the hall, the music and the laughter, the singing, the wantonness of man and woman at the feast together.

"This is mockery," Edmund said in sudden fury. "This is the devil's laughter. This is not—you are not—"

Her smile was gone, but not in anger. She sighed, shrugged, rose. "It is what it is. As am I. Will you join in the feasting? Or would it please you better to gather your wits in solitude?"

"The devil, too, may ape the forms of courtesy," said Edmund.

"Alone, then," the lady said. "Come, follow me."

He had thought that she would summon servants—imps of hell, perhaps, with human faces, but under their robes the click of a cloven hoof. There were servants enough, to be sure, but every foot was humanly shaped and humanly shod; and none came to the lady's side, nor did she beckon any.

She led him in her own person through a door behind a curtain, up a steep stone stair lit with lamps along the wall, down a passage similarly lit and into a chamber as warm as the corner below. It had a hearth and a chimney, and a fire roaring. He saw little else at first, in his haste to warm his bones. Only slowly did he recognize the bed in its curtained alcove, the tall carved chair with silken cushions, the chest under a linen cloth, the cups and the wine atop it. It was in all respects a proper noble bedchamber.

She bowed him into it, wished him a soft goodnight, and left him there. She did not offer to seduce him. Nor did she come creeping back long after, while he lay awake with the lamp still burning, coverlets drawn to his chin, prayers tumbling over one another in his head and babbling out of him.

His terror came to seem a weak and foolish thing. He lay in a castle with a somewhat unfortunate name, guest of a lady who happened to be exceptionally fair. None of it meant more than that. In the morning he would ask for a horse and provisions, so that he might continue on his errantry.

He talked himself round as the night wore into dawn. The fire burned itself to ash. The room grew cold. He slipped into a light and restless sleep, much vexed with dreams; but what they were, as soon as he woke, he could not remember.

*   *   *

The Lady Elen was not at her guest's disposal. Her chamberlain regretted the discourtesy, but she had duties that would not permit delay. When she was done, the maid said, she would summon him.

This was not a man whom Edmund could overawe with haughty manners. He wore the plain white robe that all but the lady seemed to wear here, and no mark of rank, no ornament but a simple silver cross that hung on his breast. The cross did not comfort Edmund. Its bearer had an augustly silver beard and a manner of great dignity, as if he had been a prelate, but something about him— perhaps his eyes, that were amber-brown like a wolf's— was peculiarly un-Christian.

"While you wait upon her," the chamberlain said in his soft voice, "there is a custom of our castle, a request we make of every guest. You will not take it amiss, I trust, if I bid you follow me, and do as I bid."

Edmund stiffened. He did no commoner's bidding. But the yellow wolf-eyes were fixed on him, and the hot words died in his throat. He bowed a fraction, no more but no less. "As you wish," he heard himself say.

The chamberlain inclined his head a fraction more than Edmund had, and led him out of the chamber.

He was, it seemed, conducting the guest throughout the castle, letting him see what was to be seen. It was a castle much like any other, and yet like its lord and its chamberlain it was subtly different. There were women everywhere: in the kitchens, in the hall, laboring in loom-house and stable, even in the forge. Even in the clash of arms he found them, sexless in mail or in boiled leather, but there was no mistaking the shrillness of their voices.

Women in arms, learning the arts of war. "Truly," said Edmund, but softly lest his guide hear, "this is the devil's kingdom."

Two ways only his guide chose not to take. One was

that which led to the outer gate. The other led inward
to the castle's heart.

Edmund took note of every postern gate, and every
cranny that might lead to a secret passage. But he was
too well guided and too well guarded; he could not slip
away.

They circled the castle slowly. Each circle drew closer
to the heart, to the tall white keep in the center of the
wards. There was the hall in which he had awakened.
There also was a passage with a guard of knights in white
armor, their device a silver swan on a blood-red field,
who stood silent across his path and would not let him
enter.

If a castle had walls and a keep, those were constructed in a particular fashion: guardroom below, hall
above, solar behind or above that, and chapel near the
hall and the lord's chambers. This passage then must lead
to the lord's rooms, and to the chapel. There had been
another without, a shrine built into the wall, with an
image of the Lady in her blue gown, and a priest singing
mass for a congregation of white-robed worshippers. It
was an older rite than had become the fashion, but Christian still, from all that Edmund could tell. The priest had
worn a tonsure as was proper, and sang in sweet Latin
with a mingling of foreign words, the same language perhaps in which the harper had sung.

Still, a castle might have a private chapel as well as a
public one; an oratory for its lords, where they might
pray without the distraction of the common crowd.

Edmund strained to peer past the guards. Lord's chamber, private chapel—whatever they guarded, it must contain some great treasure. He heard nothing, nor saw
aught but stone walls untapestried, and a stone floor, and
at the far end a stair.

His guide gripped his arm lightly but with no yielding
whatever. "Come," he said.

Edmund had perforce to follow. The chamberlain led him away from the swan-knights and the high proud hall into darker, smaller passages. These were not ways that he would have chosen to walk, but he was not given to choose.

They came in the end to a second hall, but one much less proud than the first. It was a servants' hall, and crowded with them. His nose wrinkled at the stink of common flesh, common sweat, wool and dogs and ale. No wine or perfumes here. Those were for their betters.

One of the gray throng of servants cried out at the sight of him. There was a flurry, a body that scrambled amid the flocks of commoners and burst forth to fling itself at Edmund's feet. It was Alfgar, weedy and stick-limbed as ever in the white livery of Montsalvat. "My lord! Oh, my lord, I thought you'd died."

Edmund kicked his erring servant in the ribs, and not gently either. "No thanks to you that I lived."

"On the contrary," said the chamberlain, steely gentle. "He came to us out of the wood and showed us the way to you. He was much shattered by the ordeal. He has only now come to his senses."

Edmund was not in the least abashed. "What, is that what he told you? Did he tell you he abandoned me, after failing signally to preserve my belongings from bandits?"

The chamberlain raised a wolf-gray brow. "Every man sees what he best may see." What he meant by that, he did not choose to explain. He said, "It is the custom of our castle that whoever guests here must also know the meaning of humility. Therefore every guest is granted a night of being waited upon, and a day or a week or a fortnight of waiting upon others—how long he does so is the reflection of the purity of his spirit."

"That," said Edmund, "is the most preposterous thing I have ever heard."

"My lord," said Alfgar at his feet, "it is true. Except they told me I should learn how to be haughty, and put me in a bed that was much too soft, and fed me bread that had all the savor of raw flour. Take your fine white bread, I said, and give me the good tough brown loaf I've always had. And then I made them bring me here."

Edmund glowered down at him. "Is this your doing?"

"Saints and angels," said Alfgar, "of course not."

He hardly had cause to lie. Edmund fixed his glare on the chamberlain, who had stood by with seeming endless patience, letting the servant babble on. "Sir," Edmund said to him, "take me back to my proper place."

"This is your proper place," the chamberlain said. "You will remain until the lady summons you."

And having said that, he turned on his heel, not even a word of farewell, and walked away. Edmund sprang to follow. Burly bodies stood in his way: thickset wool-clad men and women with affable, implacable faces. "Come, young cockerel," they said to him. "Isn't humility a Christian virtue? And aren't you a very perfect Christian knight?"

They forced him to nothing. He simply was not given to choose what he would do. First he was set to scouring the hearth with ashes and water, and when he refused he met the wall of them, urging him back and back till he toppled into the ashes. When he was all blackened and fouled, they hauled him up, thrust a brush and a bucket into his hand, and bade him do as he was told. And stood till he did it, a threat the more alarming for that they never quite named it.

They tormented him from morning till far in the night. He was allowed to eat once or twice, bites of hard bread or savorless meat between scouring the hearth and scouring the great cauldrons that hung over the fire. When at last they let him go, there was no bed for him, no rest but on the stones that he had scoured, without blanket or coverlet, only the white robe that now was gray with soot and grease and worse.

Morning came far too soon, with no respite. Someone thrust into his hands a cracked cup full of sour ale and a hard knob of cheese, and barely gave him time to sip the one and gnaw the other before he was set to work again. He had come up in the world: he was set to scouring the servants' hall, and after that the passages that led to and from it.

Alfgar, the traitorous creature, had forsaken him the moment he was relegated to servitude. He saw the long gangling figure here and there, walking free and doing no labor that he could see. His heart burned with the injustice of it.

But the Lady Elen did not summon him. She had forgotten him. He could not approach her: whenever she might have been within his reach, he was prisoned deep in the servants' hall, immersed in as foul a labor as his jailers could conceive of. They took a perverse pleasure in it. What joy it must be, he thought, for commoners to vex a nobleman.

He would have revenge on them all. He swore it to himself, crouching on aching knees, scrubbing stones that had not been cleaned, surely, since the world was new.

He traced every inch of that castle on his knees—nor did he miss the meaning of it, if meaning there was. Anger deepened and went cold; and then he could think, and even plan. He was watched always. He was never alone, even in the garderobe: there was someone outside looking in, neither smiling nor frowning, simply keeping watch.

But they could not stand guard over his thoughts. He hugged them to himself, alone in the nights on the hard hearthstone. He was a knight of God. The Lady had promised him the Grail. He would have it. But first he would raze this castle to the ground.

*   *   *

It was clear that they never meant to let him go. He began to wonder if some of the others were prisoners as he was, men of noble lineage taken into slavery. None admitted to it, nor did any seem aught but common-born.

In scouring the castle's floors, he came often close to the guarded hall and the swan-knights. They who had taken no notice of the knightly guest, took even less notice of the scullion groveling on the floor. There was never anything in the passage behind them, no door open, no lamp lit that had not been there before. Nor did he ever see the Lady Elen.

He suffered servitude for an endless count of days, from winter into spring, though he never measured it till he scoured the guardroom one sun-brilliant day. He heard a sound that made him start: the sound of water running. Ice was melting on the roof and the walls, runneling down, spreading in bright pools in the courtyards. They were cold, those pools, snow-cold. He had to drain them into the gutters lest any passing nobleman be discommoded by wet feet.

At the very end of his patience, when he was within a breath of breaking and running mad, he was set once again to labor near the hidden hall or chapel. This time he was given a broom and bidden sweep the floor and chase the spiders from the vaults. It was lighter labor than scouring stones: perhaps it presaged a rise in his fortunes.

He brooded on that as he swept, working his way through the hall to the passage. There he paused. He knew it, surely; he had seen it often enough. But there were no knights on guard. The corridor was empty, its entrance unguarded.

All the long days of waiting, suffering, biding his time, came to a single sword-keen point. He did not even pause to think. He dropped the broom, heedless of the clatter, and darted down the passage.

It was a simple passage, stone floor under his feet, stone vaulting over his head. Nothing in it breathed of secrets.

And yet there were secrets in it, or why had it been guarded for so long?

Maybe the treasure had been taken away.

He would have heard. That was a peculiarity of the servants' hall, a truth that he had never suspected till it stared him in the face. Servants knew everything. Even the lowest of them all, the scullions in the ashes of the fire, heard every rumor, knew every scandal and scurrility. None of that was spoken of their lady, nor was she known to have gone away, or sent anything away.

Whatever had been there was still there. But the guards were gone. He could take it as an invitation, if he chose.

He set foot on the stair that led upward. It was steep as castle stairs could be, cut narrow and close to the wall. He ascended with care. There were no doors, no side passages. Only the door at the top, heavy dark wood bound with bronze.

It was not barred. With thudding heart he set hand to the latch and lifted it slowly. The hinges were well oiled. The door opened quietly, creaking only a little.

Light poured out, dazzling after the dimness of the stair. And yet it was plain daylight, no more, no less. Sunlight shining in a high tower, its every wall a window, and every window a miracle, glass like myriad jewels, each one shaped to catch and transmute the sun.

Edmund caught his breath. He saw only slowly what lay beneath the glory of the windows: a perfect circle of a room, and a shape that could only be an altar, and a still dark figure before it.

It was dark only in the light. Its robe was the perpetual

white of this place called Montsalvat, its hair ruddy above it. "Lady," he thought or whispered. "Lady Elen." She was fully as beautiful as he remembered, a beauty neither dimmed nor robbed of passion by the garment she wore.

She regarded him gravely, without either alarm or bafflement, as if she had expected him. "So," he said to her. "You test all your guests. Did I fail too miserably? Was I supposed to have found you long before this?"

"No," she said. Her voice was calm. "All who come here, come only in good time."

"I was a slave in your kitchens for a whole season of the moon!"

"Yes," she said, no more perturbed by his shouting than she had been by his rudeness. "It seems you had need of it. Have you learned yet to lay aside your pride?"

"No," said Edmund. He had not meant to answer her so quickly, but his tongue had a will of its own. It insisted on telling the truth.

To his lasting astonishment she smiled. "Look!" she said to the air. "An honest man." She held out her hand. "Come here," she said.

Edmund had had his fill of doing these people's bidding. He dug in his heels. He would not have been startled if her swan-knights had appeared behind him and flung him on his face before her. But no one came. She was alone.

He was unarmed, but she was a woman. Hard labor had made him strong. He could seize her, have his will of her, take all his vengeance in one swift blow.

He could not move. Her beauty was a weapon as keen as any sword. Even the Lady of Heaven was hardly as fair as she.

He crossed himself, appalled. All that he had suffered,

all that her people had done to him, and one sight of her face made him forget the whole of it.

She grew weary of waiting for him to come to her. Rather than resort to temper as a lesser lady might, she simply and devastatingly came to him. Her presence rocked him on his feet. Her touch, he knew, would burn.

She offered none of that. She stood in front of him, forthright as any man, and said, "There was a thing that you prayed for, the night of your knighting. Are you certain that you wished for that above all else?"

Edmund caught his hand before it rose to sign the cross again. "I prayed for the Grail," he said. "No doubt I was callow and a fool."

She did not deny it. "And did you expect that you would find it?"

He could not meet her eyes. "I ... thought nothing of being worthy or unworthy. I had only the plain desire."

"Was that the lesson you learned in my scullery?" she asked.

His back went stiff all over again. "I learned nothing in your scullery but anger and outrage."

"And yet," she said, "you could come here. None comes who is not ready to see what is to be seen. Of course," she mused, "some die or go mad, or go away in despair."

"It is said of the Grail," he said tightly, "that only the worthy may see it. The unworthy are denied the light of its presence."

"Many things are said of the Grail," she said.

She turned from him to the altar. It was a plain shape of stone, unpolished, unadorned. There were no sacred vessels on it, as there was no image in that room, only the living jewels of the windows, and the living woman before him. As she moved to the altar, the light seemed to gather to her in its myriad colors. Her robe was

washed with light, till it seemed the color of heaven, pure
and cloudless blue.

No, thought Edmund. It was illusion. She bore no re-
semblance to his beautiful Lady in her mantle of stars.
This woman was all earth, all flesh. When he looked at
her, he thought nothing of heaven's bliss, only of rutting
in the furrows.

He thought of seizing her and pulling her down and
taking her where she lay, full in front of that altar which
bore no sign of Christian worship. The thought rose till
it nigh possessed him. His body shook; it burned.

"Sweet Mother of God!" he cried aloud.

The Lady Elen looked over her shoulder. Her glance
seemed to him arch, wanton, the glance of a woman who
invites her lover into her chamber. Her voice however
was cool, cool almost to coldness. "Yes. Call on the
Lady. She loves you as she loves all young things, however foolish they may be."

Edmund's knees gave way. Something in the way she
said it, in the way she stood and looked at him, told him
a terrible truth. Her Lady was not the gentle creature
who had borne a son to God. This was another, a
stronger, wilder, far more pagan Lady, not mere handmaiden but goddess herself, and equal to the gods.

Elen had turned away from him yet again. She did not
kneel before the altar as a Christian might. She spread
her arms in her robe that was now white, now heaven-
blue. She sang in the tongue in which she had sung to
the harp, in that same eerie measure.

Had Edmund been a saint or even a decently pious
Christian, he would have countered every word she sang
with a word of Christian sanctity. But he was no saint,
no more than he had been before when she sang in the
hall. He was no more a Christian than lips and tongue
could make him. He had wanted the Grail, but had not

taken care to whom he prayed for it, nor cared, despite all his protestations, for any glory but his own.

A Christian would have made virtue even of servitude. Edmund had only fed his pride, and wallowed in rancor.

The Lady of Montsalvat chanted her pagan hymn before the altar that was consecrated, as far as he could see, to nothing but light. And there was light: brighter than the sun, brighter than the soul that looks toward God. In that light he saw his heart's desire.

A cup. A plain and rather ugly wooden cup, and in it a ghost of indifferent wine. No gold, no jewels, no beauty of splendor. This was a cup that could belong to a carpenter, a poor man, a common laborer: a man who had died the death of a criminal, in the mockery of princes.

Edmund lay on his face, but nothing could blind him to the vision. It was holiness pure, untainted with mercy.

"Come," said the lady's voice, cold and clear as a morning in winter. "Take this cup of your desire. Drink if you will, if your courage suffices. Drink deep in the Lady's name."

He was on his feet with no memory of rising. She stood in front of him. In her hands was the ugly wooden cup. The wine in it was as red as blood.

He gasped, recoiled, but drove himself forward. His fingers never quite brushed hers as she laid the cup in them. It was simple wood, no torment of hellish fire, not even the thrum of sorcery. The wine was wine, and not the best: the wine of a commoner who had never aspired to be lord of anything.

"In Christ's name," he said as he lifted the cup to his lips, "and in the name of his Mother."

The Lady Elen inclined her head. His defiance did not offend her, nor did she shriek and shatter before the force of the holy name. "It is all one," she said. "The Lady and the Son, always, since the world was made."

Edmund shut eyes and ears to her and drank of the

wine. Its taste was faintly bitter, distinctly sour: the taste
of humility. He drank it to the dregs. If he died of it,
then so be it.

It did not kill him at once, if it was going to kill him
at all. Warmth spread through him, a little like the fire
of the soul that had brought him in search of the Grail.
But that fire had been built in pride. This was a quieter
thing, with a heart of truth.

The cup was empty in his hands. There was nothing
beautiful about it. And yet, he thought, that was its own
beauty: the beauty of a living thing, shaped for a purpose
by hands that had never known pride. He laid it gently—
reverently—on the altar that, like the cup, had little in
it of artifice. No lightnings flared. No choirs of angels
sang, nor did devils howl. There was only the silence,
and the jeweled beauty of the light.

"Lady," he said, and perhaps he spoke to his Lady of
Heaven, and perhaps indeed she was the same as the
Lady who was worshiped here. Perhaps they were all
the same, as the living Lady Elen had said. "Lady, I
thank you."

Simple words, inadequate surely, but they were all he
had. He made no extravagant offers of devotion, glory,
service. All that was gone in the light and in the taste of
the wine.

The Lady Elen took his hand. Her touch was warm, a
living human touch. Her smile was heart-stoppingly
sweet. "Now you are free," she said, "of my servitude."

"No," said Edmund. It was as true as all the rest of
it, and as inescapable. "I shall never be free. I am my
Lady's servant, nor will she ever let me go."

"Her servant? Not her knight?"

He flushed, and stiffened with a remnant of pride. "I
was not a worthy knight."

"No?" asked the Lady Elen.

"I lost my horse, my armor. My servant—"

"Your servant has never thought ill of you. Not bad for a lord, he said to me. Stiff in the neck, and not much eyes for anybody but himself, but a good enough young cockerel for that."

Edmund caught himself laughing, brief and painful. "That is Alfgar to the life. But, Lady—"

"You were," she said, "a dreadful scullion and a worse manservant. There is no help for it. A knight you are, and a knight you will always be. Only remember a little of humility. If nothing else, it will astonish anyone who knew you before."

He could be outraged, or he could smile as painfully as he had laughed. "I think," he said after a while, "that that will do. If my Lady wills."

Elen bowed her head to the name and led him away. He glanced back only once. The cup lay on the rough stone altar. The light had changed. It was softer now, the light of evening and not of noon. It washed the cup with gold, studded it with jewels. For a moment he thought he saw it as he had dreamed it, a cup fit for a king. Then it was simple wood again, a carpenter's cup, but filled to the brim with light.

And what was the truth?

"Does it matter?" he asked the air and the light and the cup of the Grail.

He received no answer. He had expected none. The Lady of Montsalvat led him by the hand, out of the shrine of the light, into a world both dim and impossibly splendid: plain mortal earth, that belonged to every man. Even a callow fool.

He found that he was smiling. It was a smile he had not known before: more rueful than glad.

It was enough. The door of the shrine closed behind him. The light of the Grail was gone. But he remembered. He would not forget.

LADY OF AVALON

by Diana L. Paxson

> "At Ilchester, the first English of Somerset consti-
> tuted a garrison. They were needed, for in the
> marshes ten miles to the north Glastonbury is re-
> ported to have remained in British hands for several
> generations to come."
> —JOHN MORRIS, *The Age of Arthur*

The forest echoed to the sound of toppling logs. A moment ago I had been fleeing like a winded doe. I remembered tripping, and then the world had come apart. I
took another breath, listening for the clatter of hoofbeats, but if the Saxons had heard, they had not con-
nected the noise with their quarry. I started to push
myself up and felt a whiplash of pain. Only then did I
realize that when the deadfall came down, it had
trapped me.

I muttered a few of the epithets I would have used to
the maidens under my authority in Avalon. I had learned
how to read the forest for signs of human meddling half
a lifetime ago. Even running for my life I should have
been able to avoid the deadfall. It was rage, not fear that
had distracted me, and now I would never find the royal
maiden I had been sent to save.

I rested my head against the damp ground, striving for
calm. Light dappled last year's dead leaves and glowed
through the petals of the primroses. Doubtless, if I tried
to move again, the dull throbbing I could feel in my thigh
would resolve itself into a very specific pain.

The log that had fallen across my legs looked extremely solid. The desperate hatred of the men who had
built the deadfall still clung to the wood. I should have
led my pursuers into the trap and let it do the work for

which it had been intended. It was a grim twist of the fate that was betraying the last British kingdom in the West Country to the advance of king Ceolwulf's warbands that our defiance should have trapped the Lady of Avalon.

I took a breath and tried to pull free. The resulting agony took consciousness with it.

When I could think again, the log had settled more firmly. The bone must be broken. Grimly I considered my options. If the scavengers did not get me, it would be a race between wound-fever and hunger. Better, I thought, to send my spirit out while I still had the discipline to do so, and abandon my flesh to whatever fate might come.

I settled my cheek against the new spring grass, drawing in the fresh scent of it with an aching sense of loss. Such a miracle, the grass, each blade crafted by the Lady's love. A pity I had never taken the time to enjoy it. It was said in Avalon that a high priestess always knew when her death was upon her. Perhaps this time even Death had been taken by surprise, or perhaps that gift, like so many of our ancient magics, had been lost since the Saxons overran the land.

"Ildierna I have been . . ." I whispered. "It is Ildierna whom I now release. . . ."

I let my breath move in and out, ever more slowly, counting, waiting for the shift into trance. And then, from one moment to the next, the sounds around me became distant. I concentrated my awareness on my hands and feet and then began to draw it slowly inward until I felt only the erratic beating of my heart. Waves of energy rolled through me as I withdrew even further, the crown of my head pulsed painfully, and suddenly I was free.

I looked down on my body, sprawled beneath the tangle of logs and branches, seeing the heavy limbs of a woman no longer young, a woman with silver-streaked russet hair and work-worn hands who had never been beautiful. The blue veil had been lost somewhere in my flight, and in the fading light I could see the crescent tattooed between my brows. For a moment I felt anger that this poor body should be denied the honors it would have received had I died on the Tor. But that was foolish. Let the clean earth receive my bones. I had lived before, in other bodies, and no doubt would do so again.

But before I could depart, one duty remained. Rising further, I sought the network of bright pathways visible to the eyes of the spirit that linked the sacred places of the land. One of the greatest of these leys ran up toward Avalon from the southwestern tip of Kernow. As roads they might appear, but they carried a current strong as any river. Once I touched the ley I was borne swiftly toward my goal.

The sun was going down beyond the marshes that surrounded the Tor. The eight priestesses who remained behind the barrier of mist that separated it from the ordinary world of humankind should be making the sunset salutations now.

"Senara—" I sought the one who had been most like a daughter to me. The clouds thinned, and for a moment I saw her. "Hear me, Senara, for I pass, and you must guard the Mysteries now!"

In her face I could see amazement turn to sorrow. Then the mists swept between us, and another face formed before me, netted with the lines of age and framed in silver hair. But the ornaments of a priestess, the most ancient and sacred of the regalia I wore in the ceremonies, were on her brow.

"My daughter, you have served well. But you must go back to your body now, for your work is not done!"

"That body is dying—" I began.

"Not yet, though there will be great pain. Return, that you may accomplish your task."

I knew the voice that had sent me on this fatal journey a moon ago. The spirit who spoke now had been perhaps the greatest of us all, the founding priestess of Avalon.

"Lady Caillean," I whispered, "forgive me. I failed."

"You have not failed, if you will endure to the end." Blue draperies swirled as she pointed, and the authority in that gesture slammed me all the way back into my body and I knew no more.

When I regained consciousness, every nerve in my body was screaming, but the weight that pinned me had gone.

"The leg looks bad." The words were in Saxon, which I could understand if I tried, and I twitched despite my pain. "Better kill her now and tell the Lady we did not find her in time."

"The Lady Gytha would know we lied," said someone else. "And tell the king, and he would have our ears. There is nothing he will deny her while she is carrying his child."

It was dark, but there was flame around me. I whimpered and tried to open my eyes. I flinched from rough Saxon hands and rough Saxon voices as they pulled the rest of the logs away.

"Best get her onto the litter, then," said the first man. When they touched my legs, I screamed despite my resolve, and then, mercifully, fainted once more.

The Goddess herself could not have kept me conscious for most of the journey that followed. By the time I was brought to shelter, my leg had swollen so that it could not be splinted. They could do little more than lay me out as straight as possible and keep me from thrashing about when the fever came.

For a time I was too exhausted to follow the guttural babble of Saxon around me. But I had always been strong, and gradually, little though I desired it, I began to heal, and those who tended me changed from faceless barbarians to people, as various in character as my own folk.

Listening to their talk, I learned that I lay in the house where Ceolwulf, king of the West Seax, had established his youngest wife, Gytha, while he carried his war into Kernow. There was a constraint in their voices when they spoke of her. I wondered why, for she was little more than a girl, pregnant with her first child and, though he had grown sons by other women, the apple of her husband's eye. The Lady herself I saw rarely. She was one of those women who lost flesh during pregnancy. Her heavy breasts and gentle curve of her ripening belly looked almost grotesque beneath the thin face, too long for classic beauty, but her fall of hair was the same pale gold as the primroses. Her skin was pale, lightly freckled, and her eyes, the one time she had looked directly at me, a luminous gray. There was no reason, of course, why she should trouble herself with a British thrall, but I gradually came to the conclusion that she was avoiding me.

It was high summer and we had moved to another of the king's houses by the time I was on my feet and discovered that my thigh bone had knit crooked and I would never walk without a limp again. That was an evil day, as ill as the day they fitted the thrall ring around my neck. It was hard to keep my tongue from calling down the curse of the Goddess upon them. At first I bit back my wrath because I thought that for some reason She wanted me there. Later, time and toil wore me down until my spirit seemed as enslaved as my body, and Avalon only a dream, wrapped in mists from beyond the world.

Sometimes Ceolwulf came home, filling the steading with warriors who drank and quarrelled and left behind them the smell of spilled beer. I could have brewed a

potion that would send the old king to sleep for good,
but by then I had taken the measure of his heir, Cynegils.

The king was an old wolf, dangerous, but with dimin-
ishing powers. His son was young and deadly, eyeing his
father's high seat and those parts of Kernow yet uncon-
quered with the same greedy glare. I had hated Ceolwulf,
but I trembled to think of what would come to my people
when the wolf cub was in power.

It seemed to me that Gytha feared him also, though
she served him as graciously as she did her lord. And I
served them all, doing as I was bid without protest until
I became as familiar and unremarkable a part of their
lives as the benches in the hall.

At Midsummer my people were accustomed to build
bonfires and carry torches around the fields to encourage
the corn to grow. Though the Summer Country was now
the land of the *Somersaete* and the peasants toiled to
feed new masters, the rite had not changed. I remembered how the priestesses of Avalon used to pass through
the mists to bless the ploughlands around the Tor. Here,
it was the Lady Gytha who went out with her women to
make offerings to the spirits that ruled the fields. The
wind rippled through the grain and the Lady's shining
hair, carrying away the Saxon words. For a moment I
felt as if I were looking at one of my priestesses, and my
eyes filled with tears.

The steading where we were now had been built on
the ruins of an old villa to the west of Lindinis, where a
Saxon war-band laired in the barracks that had once sheltered a Roman garrison. A day's march to the northeast
lay the island of British territory that surrounded the
Tor.

Since the time of Arthur the Isle of Avalon had withdrawn even farther into the Otherworld. The monks who
had raised their church where once the holy Joseph had

dwelt thought it was their prayers that kept the heathen
at bay, unaware of that other reality in which the last
priestesses of Avalon worked their magic. Those few
with the Sight who glimpsed us thought us demons sent
to tempt them, and we kept our secret well. It had been
many centuries since Joseph of Arimathea hailed us as
sisters upon the Path. While the Saxons threatened on
every side, there was no tolerance for any of British
blood who practiced pagan ways.

After the blessing of the fields Gytha seemed white
and strained. Later that night I heard an outcry from her
end of the hall, and women came out, babbling that their
lady was bleeding, that she was going to lose the child.
I sat up in my corner, straw rustling. She had passed the
time when a woman could miscarry without risking herself as well as the babe she bore.

"I have given her a tea of chamomile and leaf of bramble," old Berkta was telling Gytha's maidservant, "and
we are soaking cloths in an infusion of birch and oak
bark to stop the bleeding. It is up to Frija and the
Blessed Mothers now!"

I nodded. Though the names were a little different,
the herblore of the Saxons was not so different from our
own. But there came a time when medicines were of no
more use, even when administered with the proper spells.
I got up, wincing as my stiff leg took the strain, and went
to warm myself at the fire. The women continued to talk
of births and the mishaps of pregnancy.

I turned to Berkta. "The Lady is ill?" Even a thrall
could have figured that out from the uproar. When the
woman had explained, I pushed back my headwrap to
show the crescent on my brow. "Among my own people
I was counted a wisewoman," I said carefully. "Maybe
there is something I can do."

It was a measure of their anxiety that they took me
to where their mistress lay without questioning. The

Lady Gytha had always been pale, but now her face was as white as the bleached linen on which she lay. Her gaze flickered as she saw me, then she sighed.

"You have come," she said in Saxon. "This is my weird, then. *She* told me you would lead me home. . . ." Her eyes closed. The women looked at each other in alarm, but I bent over the bed, stretching out my hands to sense the life-force that flickered so erratically through her thin frame.

Over her womb it pulsed strongly, but Gytha's heart was faltering. I began to move my hands up and down her body, sweeping the power back along the proper channels. She twitched and muttered, but after a time the energy seemed to stabilize and Gytha grew easier.

"Go to the well and soak cloths in the coldest water," I told the women. "Lay them on her womb."

When they had gone I set my hands on Gytha's belly. I could feel the life-energy of the child strongly, and the tremors in the muscles of the womb. The babe was healthy; it was the mother whose body was rebelling at the burden it bore. I bent over the smooth curve and began to whisper a spell of comfort, that drew up power from the earth itself to cradle the life in the womb. I could feel the tension easing as I sang, and presently that song shifted to a song like a lullaby.

Gytha sighed in her sleep and smiled. Her color was a little better now. I paused, looking down at her. "Mama, sing to me," she murmured without opening her eyes. I began again, then stopped, my own heart pounding. She had spoken in the British tongue.

The women came back then with the cold cloths, and Gytha woke as they were applied. I drew Berkta aside.

"Where does the Lady come from?" I asked. "Who were her people?"

"Her father was a chieftain of the Hwicce up north, who are oathbound to the Mercian kings."

"And her mother?"

The woman shrugged. "Who knows?"

My heart pounded heavily. The Saxons who had settled above the Sabrina had come as allies, buffers against
their countrymen, not conquerors. Though it sounded
like a lullabye, I had sung a teaching song of Avalon.
Had this child's mother been one of the royal maidens
of Gwent who were sent to us to study for a time?

As the night wore on, I realized that when I came
forward to nurse the Lady I had uncovered more than
the crescent on my brow. With the use of my skills my
old habit of command had returned to me. The other
women seemed to sense it, and by morning my authority
to rule the sickroom was accepted.

It was just as well, for near dawn, when Gytha stirred,
I noticed that a different woman brought in the herbal
tea for which I had asked. I took the beaker and bent
to set it to Gytha's lips. But as I leaned over, the scent
came to me. Pulling back, I took a sip of the tea.

Rolling the liquid over my tongue I sorted through my
herblore. There was a bitterness here that did not belong
to the bramble leaf, and something minty, imperfectly
covered by the sweetness of the honey that had been
mixed in.

"Is it not warm enough?" asked the girl who had
brought the tea. "I can take it back to the fire." She
spoke boldly but her gaze flicked away.

"No doubt," I said dryly. "And then somehow you
would stumble and toss it in." I turned to Gytha's maid.
"Wake Osric and bring him here. Hold her—" I snapped
as the girl started to slip away. And old Berkta, who was
twice my size and strong as a warrior, gripped her arm.
I looked at our captive carefully, and realized she was
one of the girls young Cynegils had taken to his bed
most often when he was here.

"What is it?" Berkta asked without letting the slut go.

"Taste this and tell me." I held out the beaker. For a moment she held it in her mouth as I had done, then with an oath she spat the liquid onto the straw.

"Is it poison?" cried the maid.

"Dragontongue!" Berta exclaimed, "and something else, flea-mint most likely, as well. 'Tis not poison. I've given such a mixture often to help when a girl's courses will not come. But given to a breeding woman it would certainly bring the child untimely, and weak as our Lady is, likely kill her as well!"

By this time the leader of the houseguard had come. I stood with eyes downcast as Berkta repeated the accusation and the weeping girl was dragged away. I had thought Gytha too exhausted to note what was passing, but when Osric left, her eyes opened.

"You saved me," she whispered. "I thought . . . you were my death. . . ."

"I will give you life," I answered in her own tongue, and kissed her on the brow.

Several days passed before I judged Gytha to be out of danger, and during that time I was with her constantly. Often in the deeps of the night she would lie wakeful, and I, trained from my youth to such vigils, would watch beside her.

"The men who found me said it was your word that had sent them," I said once. "But then you seemed to fear me. Why?"

Gytha's gaze flicked to mine and then away. "Since my childhood," she whispered, "I have *seen* things— sometimes what was happening afar off, and sometimes things that were yet to be. When I was little my visions terrified me, for they were so often of blood and fire. In the old days, when our people lived across the sea, they would have sent me to be trained as a seeress like Walada, who made the Romans fear. But there is no one with that wisdom in this land—"

Something in my face halted her, and she gazed at me with widening eyes. "You know!" she exclaimed. "You understand!"

"More than you can imagine!" My heart was pounding. I leaned forward. "I could not have imagined there was any way in which our people were the same—but I am just such a one as Walada was, among my own kind!"

"I thought all of the British folk were Christian now. Are you the last, and alone?" Gytha cried.

I started to answer, then grasped her hand. I had the right to reveal myself, but until I understood where this might lead, I dared not speak to her of Avalon.

"Was it I whom you saw, in the vision that frightened you so?" I asked then.

"I was dozing," Gytha said dreamily, "as I did often in the afternoons when I was first carrying the child. It seemed to me that I was floating above the world. I recognize Lindinis, and the river, and the wooded lands beyond. And then I was drawn downward and saw you lying beneath the fallen trees. I pitied you, but I did not know what to do, and I was trying to wake up when a cool mist swirled around me, and I saw—" She coughed and then took a sip of tea.

"You saw a woman draped in blue with an ornament of silver set with river pearls upon her brow ..." said I. The clear gaze flew back to me.

"I thought she was one of the Norns," Gytha said simply. "She told me that I must send men to find you. She said you were my doom."

"And thinking that, you obeyed her?" I stared as she shrugged with a purely Saxon fatalism. My own people, when they grow fey, run upon disaster like lovers.

"No one can escape his weird. But then I saw you in the flesh, and I was afraid."

"I cannot tell you what will come of this," I said honestly, "but the one who spoke to you was among the greatest of our priestesses. I do not know why we have been brought together, but whatever happens, I tell you now that the Great Mother, whom both our peoples honor, though by different names, holds us in Her hand!"

There had been an herb garden in the Roman villa, and even after years of neglect some of the plants survived. It reminded me of our garden in Avalon, and since we came here I had spent what free time I was allowed in weeding and pruning and bringing it into order again. On sunny days Gytha and her women liked to sit there and sew or spin. Gytha had recovered so well that I concluded Cynegils' leman must have given her herbs to start the trouble in the first place, and she laughed and chattered with the others. It was on such a day, near the beginning of harvest, that we heard the sound of a horse being ridden hard along the track that led to the hall. I pulled myself to my feet, brushing earth from my hands.

I told myself this news was of some battle, or perhaps to say the king was on his way here, and we should begin preparing food for his men. But even then, I suppose, I knew better. Gytha had covered her eyes with her hands, and behind her fingers her skin had no color at all. And yet when Osric came to tell her that Ceolwulf had been wounded, she was able to greet him with composure and give orders to prepare a packet of herbs and dressings to go with Berkta, who was being sent to nurse him, and her prayers that he might soon be well.

It was only when we were alone that she wept in my arms. "Ceolwulf is dead, Ildierna," she whispered. "I have seen it. By the time Berkta gets there, they will have sent him to Wodan and his heirs will be drinking the funeral ale."

"His heirs—" I repeated, as she set her hands protectively across her belly. "There were three sons, were there not, besides your child? Which of them do you think will be chosen king?"

"Cynegils is the strongest," she said softly. "Even while my lord was alive he challenged him. He has been building a following among the younger men."

"But why should that matter?" I asked, not daring, yet, to speak the idea that had come to me. "Will they not send you back to your kin?"

"Not until my child is born," Gytha said softly. "And if it is a son—" I put my arm around her and felt her trembling. "Ildierna, I am afraid!"

The noise of half a hundred feasting warriors was like a physical assault on the senses, echoing between the bones of the skull. Barely a moon had passed since the old king was laid in his howe with his favorite hound, his armor and his jewels and grave furnishings, and the chieftains of the West Seax had concluded they would be wise to recognize the claims of his eldest son. Cynegils had lost no time in taking possession. Some said that the manor where we were living ought to belong to Gytha by dower right, but Cynegils seemed to consider both the holding and its mistress part of his inheritance.

I watched, frowning, as she bore the ceremonial drinking horn across the hall. It wanted little more than a moon until she should be delivered, and the great bulge of her belly rendered even Gytha's grace ungainly now. She had knotted up her fair hair and secured it with jeweled pins beneath a light veil, and heavy earrings of chip-carved gold set with garnets swung from her ears. Everything about her proclaimed her royalty, and whatever comments men might make stilled as she passed.

Only Cynegils was unaffected by her dignity. I could not hear her words as she offered him the horn, but his laughter was clearly audible. He reached up beneath the folds of her mantle and squeezed her breast, and I saw the angry color flame beneath her fair skin. Then he drank deeply from the horn.

"Let these good fellows here have a taste of your sweetness—none of your black looks," he added as she flushed again. "Give them something to drink, woman. What did you think I meant? You can retire when they've emptied the horn. D'ye think I'd take you now?" He poked her belly and grinned. "Until you've whelped you're safe enough from me!"

Gytha was shaking by the time she finally reached the door. I took the horn from her and sent the rest of the younger women to escort her back to the smaller building where the women slept when the king and his hird were feasting in the hall. Berkta was big enough to repel unwelcome advances, and I knew a spell or two that would make a man think me even older and more ill-favored than I am.

That night the drink flowed freely. Cynegils was young and ambitious, and I winced as he boasted how he would drive the British of Kernow into the sea. The sorrow of it was that he could well succeed—he had the crafty mind and the force of will that makes a conqueror.

I moved among the men with my pitcher of ale, my back bent submissively, my headwrap covering the blue crescent on my brow, gradually working my way toward the high seat.

"Will you marry the woman?" asked one of the men who lounged at Cynegils' side. No one paid any heed to me.

"What need?" he replied. "The dowry is paid, and her kin too diminished to enforce the contract. She'll do well enough for a concubine."

"And the child?"

"Is nothing, unless the head of the house acknowledge

it," Cynegils grinned sardonically, "and I am already too well supplied with kin!"

At least the Christians did not allow a father to reject and expose a newborn child. In times of famine there might be some reason for it, but this was pure political expediency. I thought longingly of the bright mushrooms I had seen last time I walked in the woods beside the field, but if I poisoned Cynegils, Gytha might well be blamed for it, and what if his brothers were no better than he?

Though my pulse was pounding, I did not allow myself to hurry. When I had emptied the pitcher, I moved off as if to refill it, but I did not return. At this stage in her pregnancy Gytha slept often, but not deeply. A touch was enough to bring her awake, while a murmured sleepspell kept the others snoring. Softly I repeated what I had heard.

"I feared this," she replied. "When my child is born, you must tell them it died and carry it to safety."

I shook my head. "Cynegils is a careful man. He will appoint witnesses. I have thought on this as well. Come away with me, Lady, for I tell you now that I am not the last of the priestesses. Beyond the mists that hide our refuge even Cynegils cannot pursue you. Come with me to Avalon!"

For a long moment Gytha stared at me. "Are you mad, or am I?"

I stood up, pushing the cloth back from my brow, and with it, all appearance of servility. "I am the Lady of Avalon, and I speak in the Great Mother's name!"

The flicker of the oil lamp showed me how her face changed. I could feel the power I had invoked pulsing around me. What did she see in mine?

"Ildierna!" she whispered, "You are wearing the ornaments that *she* wore—the Lady in my vision!"

"They are mine by right," I said softly. "I am the heir

to her power. In the name of the Goddess, I bid you
come with me!"

By the time the sun rose, we were well away from the
hall. I had put Gytha on an old horse—easy to track,
but what we needed was to gain distance without using
up her strength right now. I could have wished we had
fled sooner, but Gytha would not have believed in the
danger. The men always drank most deeply their first
night of feasting. If Cynegils meant to leave guards with
the Lady, our best chance to get away was while they
were still sleeping off their ale.

I moved as slowly as the horse, for I had used up my
own strength in spells—a glamour on the pillows stuffed
in Gytha's bed that would encourage the illusion she was
still sleeping there, a charm of confusion around the
gates that would make it hard for them to pick up our
trail, and whenever our road forked, a sign sketched in
the dust to draw any pursuers the wrong way. It helped
that we were traveling toward the rising sun. Once Cynegils realized that Gytha was gone, he would expect her
to flee north towards the Sabrina and her own tribe, not
eastward into British lands.

By noon we had come nearly to the end of Saxon
territory without, as far as I could tell, being seen. Gytha
was swaying in the saddle. I pulled the horse into the
shelter of a hazel copse, weaving the branches together
behind us. Gytha was almost too tired to eat, but I
coaxed her to take a few bites of oatcake, and cut
branches to make her a more comfortable bed. In moments she was asleep.

I leaned back against a tree, hoping that the aches she
had complained of were no more than the strain of riding, and not early labor. Strenuous activity could easily
bring it on, but if the babe could only wait until we
reached our goal, it would be welcome.

Thinking about it, I found myself smiling. It had been a long time since a child had been born on Avalon. Beyond the screen of leaves the patterned stubble of the harvested field glistened in the sun, and a lark was singing, somewhere too high to see. I, too, must have been exhausted, for without my knowing, my musings passed into sleep.

Gytha's cry woke me. "He is coming!" She clutched at my arm, her eyes dark with fear. And then, while I still was blinking, I saw the queenly self-control reasserted. "I *saw* Cynegils on the road. You must leave me, Ildierna. If he catches us, he will do no more than take me back, but you he will kill."

I shook my head. "Do you think this surprises me? I expected no more than to delay him. We will have to let the horse go now and hope he will follow it."

For a moment she was silent. "What is it?" I said then. "Are you beginning your pains?"

Gytha sighed, then smiled. "I am well enough. Let us go on."

As the shadows lengthened toward sundown, we moved as quickly as we dared, keeping to the tangled bits of woodland that divided the tilled lands. Our pursuers could come straight across the fields, but only if they knew which fields to cross. To search the land closely would take time. We were in British territory now, and the Saxons would be far more visible than we were. If Lord Uethen heard of their presence, he could raise more men than Cynegils had brought along. Gytha had thought me mad, but though her steps slowed, as we went on, I could see hope growing in her eyes.

Though I tried to keep to cover, there were times when we had to cross a track. Reaching one of them, I halted suddenly and took Gytha's arm.

"What is it?"

"It is all right." I pointed up the road which ran straight toward a little hill below which some Christian holy man had built a hermitage. "Look beyond the chapel. What do you see?"

She peered beneath her hand. "There is another hill, in a line with this one. It is pointed, and ... it *glows!* Is it the Tor?" She turned to me in excitement. "So near!" The hill was crowned with oak trees. Behind it the land fell away into a purple haze. Clouds were massing on the northern horizon, but the Tor shone with rosy light.

"You see, I have not led you astray. By the time night falls, we will be there." I laughed and started to cross, and as I did so, heard the clatter of hoofbeats on the road.

Swiftly I thrust Gytha back beneath the sheltering branches and drew my earth-colored mantle over us. There was no time for more than a swift spell of warding before the horsemen swept past.

When they had gone, we lay for a long time where we were, listening to the rising wind stir the treetops and waiting for our heartbeats to slow. I had underestimated Cynegils's intelligence. Once he realized we were not heading northward, he must have assumed that Gytha would seek refuge with the British. All our skulking through brush and briar had been a waste of time and energy. The Seax-king had no need to track us—he had only to block the one road that led through the marshes before we got there, even though we wished to go not to Lord Uethen, but to Avalon.

"Will you mind a night in the woods?" I asked. "We must hide until he is forced to go home again."

She shook her head, smiling, but as she began to pull herself up, she stopped short, frowning. "Was the grass wet?" she asked, turning around. I frowned in consternation as I saw the damp stain on her gown, but I kept my voice even as I replied.

"The seal that closes the womb has broken," I replied. "That is the water in which your child has been cradled, and soon it will be born."

"Not here! Don't let the baby come now!" She looked around her at a forest which suddenly seemed much darker.

"My dear, not even the greatest of priestesses can hold back the tide when it is coming in or a babe ready to be born! Are you having pains?"

"Only an aching back, from walking so far." She tried to smile.

I was not so sure, but at least she was not in active labor. "We have some time, then." I said bracingly. "But I think we must try to reach Avalon tonight after all."

We moved on as swiftly as Gytha could go. I had meant to follow the causeway to the landing where I had left the skiff when I set out on my journey. But the folk who lived at the edge of the marshes also kept such craft, and remembered their ancient ties with Avalon.

It was growing dark faster than I had expected. As oaks and hazels gave way to clumps of reed and stands of alder and I glimpsed the hut I was seeking, I saw why. It was not night but the storm that was closing upon us. The treetops bent to a damp wind. Gytha leaned against a tree, rubbing the small of her back, though she had not complained.

The woman who came out of the reed hut was dark-haired and fine of bone and shy as a wild thing until she saw the crescent on my brow. Faery blood there, I thought. Perhaps some of her forebears had rowed the Lady Morgaine's barge. The craft she offered me was little more than a raft, but it would get us where we needed to go.

I settled Gytha into the bow, noting how she stilled, lips tightening, then sank back again. Then I pushed off, balancing in the stern with the ease of long practice and leaning my full weight against the pole. The water had gone slate gray as the clouds gathered; Gytha shivered as she looked around her, then another pain came upon her, and she closed her eyes.

Grimly I eased the boat through the narrow channel between the reed-beds, watching for the subtle signs on branches and the knotted reeds that marked the way. The wind blew more strongly; we had almost reached open water. Then someone shouted. The pole slid on the soft bottom as I turned.

Certain of my ability to read the secret markings by which the marsh-folk marked their ways, I had not thought to ask exactly where on the lake we would emerge. The water stretched before me with the hill beyond it, crowned with St. Michael's tower, but the final leg of the channel was in the lee of the causeway. And there, waiting like wolves at a river-crossing, were Cynegils and his men.

Something flickered through the dusk and splashed into the dark water. I flinched instinctively and only realized it had been an arrow when it bobbed back to the surface.

"Halt, or be spitted!" cried one of the warriors. Two of the riders had already jumped their horses down from the causeway and were crashing through the reeds.

Gytha sat up, her face white in the gloom. "How dare you!" Her voice shook with anger. "Put your weapons down!" A thrown lance sang past and I rammed the pole into the mud, propelling us another boat's-length away.

"A fit mother for heroes!" Cynegils laughed. "Perhaps I will marry you after all! Tell your slave to stop if you want her to live!"

"Ildierna, it is no use. The monks could not defend us even if we reached the farther shore—" Gytha cried, but I shook my head and thrust once more with the pole. Above the shouting came a rumble of thunder, and the first splattering of rain. One horse had bogged down among the reeds, but the other was in the water now, thrashing as the rider tried to head it our way.

I dodged another arrow and took a deep breath. To summon the mists was difficult even when all was still, and each year it seemed to grow harder. Could I do it after so long?

A last heave with the pole sent us skimming across the dim waters. Then I let it fall and lifted my arms, eyes tight shut and soul straining, putting all that remained of my strength into the Call. My body arched like a swan taking the sky, and if a spear had transfixed me I would not have known. In that moment, my soul, ascending, touched that other reality in which the holy isle survived, and I reached out and brought it down around us with one mighty sweep of my wings.

There was a flare of light as if the sky had opened, and then a flood of rain, but the crash of thunder that followed was curiously muted, and in moments the rain turned to mist as we left the world's weather behind us and entered that of Avalon. I collapsed in the stern, panting, letting the magic carry us the rest of the way. It was only when I heard a woman's joyful calling that I roused myself to creep forward and take Gytha in my arms.

"Look—" I whispered. "Lift up your head, my dear, and see! You have come home. . . ."

Overhead the sky was grim with stormclouds, for Avalon was not yet completely out of step with the world of men. But to the west the clouds had not yet closed in, and the last of the sunset limned the pointed hill before us, with its rock-walled houses and the spiraling path that led to the standing stones, in living gold.

For a moment Gytha gazed, and her eyes grew luminous. Then I felt her body convulse and she cried out as the birthpangs she had fought so long overwhelmed her at last.

*   *   *

Exhausted as she was, Gytha had little strength left for the birthing, but her courage never faltered. And when her daughter slid squalling into the world, she laughed triumphantly. The storm had blown itself out, and the last of the clouds blazed golden in the first light. When the cord had been cut and the babe swaddled, I held her up to face the day.

The priestesses began to sing the hymn to the dawn, but the words I was hearing were in the voice of She who had sent me out to search for a royal lady, it seemed so long ago.

"Ildierna, my daughter, the task I gave you has been well done. Once more the old blood and the new have mingled, and the child you hold will one day be Lady of this isle. Be not afraid, though change engulf you. So long as there are even a few to serve the Goddess, the power of Avalon will not be withdrawn entirely from the world."

WITH GOD TO GUARD HER

by Kate Elliott

Preface

Now in those days it was not unknown for a man of high birth to put aside one wife, with whom he had become dissatisfied, and marry another. Indeed, when kings indulged in such behavior, then dukes and counts might choose to emulate them. But what seems permissible in the world, God may well judge more harshly, as I shall relate.

One

At this time a man of free birth worked fields adjoining the estate of Duke Amalo, near the River Marne. With him in his house lived his mother, Theudichild, his wife Ingund, his two young sons and a daughter, and a few servants. The daughter was called Merofled.

It so happened that the duty of paying the tax to the church fell one month to Merofled.

She was a girl of good stature, having always been granted good health, and was now old enough to marry. Her family bore a respectable name and they had nothing to be ashamed of in their ancestors. Her mother's father was a canon at Vitry and it was said that his great-grandfather was dedicated in martyrdom in Lyons.

But she had not yet married, nor had her father betrothed her to any man. Some said her father and mother favored her excessively, making her too proud to wish to submit to another man's lordship, others that she was too pious to wish to marry. A few had been heard to whisper that her grandmother, Theudichild, an irascible old tyrant, preferred Merofled's sewing to that of any of her servants or even to that of her daughter-in-law's, and would not allow the girl to leave her father's house so that the vain old woman would not have to do without the luxury of finely-sewn garments.

On this day, Merofled received the pot of candle wax from one of the servants and with only a young serving girl as attendant walked down the road to deliver the wax to the church. In this way, with each household paying its portion of the tax, candles always burned at the altar.

The two young women were forced to move off the road when a great entourage rode by. The serving girl bent her head and knelt at once, but Merofled neither knelt nor looked down.

First walked clerics in their vestments, and after them the kinsmen, friends, and vassals of the Duke, for Merofled realized that this must be the retinue of Duke Amalo. They came in a crowd, kicking up a wide swathe of dust.

She had never seen the Duke except at a distance and so did not recognize him at once when suddenly a rider pulled to a halt and stared straight at her. He was tall, finely dressed, and rode a horse with silver harness and a saddle trimmed with gold. The rest of the column pulled up beside and behind him.

"Who is this girl?" the Duke asked one of his attendants, a certain Count Leudast.

"I do not know," said Leudast, and he turned to another man and ordered him to speak to Merofled.

The servant asked her name and she answered, boldly and not without pride. "I am called Merofled, daughter of Berulf and Ingund."

Having had her words repeated to him, the Duke rode on.

Two

Duke Amalo was a man of sudden passions, the sort who most wishes to have what he does not yet possess, and being unused in any case to having anything denied him.

This is what he had seen: a handsome girl, in the bloom of youth, and wearing dress that was simple yet clean and well-made, which is one of the marks of good family. As well, she had spoken clearly and without flinching.

"Find out about this girl," he ordered his servants.

One of his clerics inquired in the village and returned to him with these facts: That the girl was of free birth and that she came of good family on both sides, including, as I have mentioned before, the grandfather's grandfather who had been granted the glory of martyrdom on this earth. That her father, Berulf, paid his taxes regularly to the church, attended services without fail, and was altogether a man of good character whom God had rewarded with prosperity. That Berulf and his wife gave alms to the poor and had endowed the church in the village with a silver chalice and two finely-woven tapestries, one depicting Judith and Holofernes and the other showing St. Martin giving half his cloak to a poor man.

Duke Amalo mentioned nothing of these inquiries to his wife, by whom he had by this time five children, two of which had died in infancy.

Three

For some days after first seeing Merofled by the roadside Duke Amalo went about his business in the usual fashion, hawking, hunting, seeing to his estate. But more than once he led his retinue along the road that led through the village. Finally, when no more than three Sabbaths had passed, he took his clerics and the rest of his entourage and attended mass in the village church. There he tended to his prayer assiduously, kneeling in the front rank of benches with his hands covering his face as befits a pious man. However, rather than praying, he used his hands as a screen so that he might stare at the young woman Merofled without betraying his interest to all and sundry.

When mass ended, he lavished silver and gold vessels on the church and donated a great deal of money to the support of the clergy, so that all spoke well of him when he left and returned to his estates.

Four

By this time, however, Duke Amalo had been seized with a consuming desire for Merofled.

The next day, therefore, he summoned his wife to him. "It is time," he said to her, "that you travel to your estate near Andelot so that you might put your affairs in order there."

By this means he intended to be rid of her.

Now, as her estate in Andelot came to her as part of her inheritance from her father, and as it lay near her relations, she was not averse to going, although the journey was a long one. So, suspecting nothing, she agreed. She took their elder sons with her, leaving the youngest son behind.

Five

From the shelter of an oak grove, Merofled watched the entourage pass, Duke Amalo's wife and all her retinue, her women and servants, her priest and deacons, horses, wagons, and a few dogs. Then she walked quickly home, to her father's hall.

Now Merofled was not a fool, and if she was proud, it was in part because she had a sharp mind and could see what other people sometimes failed to notice.

For this reason she found one excuse and then another to stay near her father's house, never venturing outside the fenced yard that confined the livestock.

Six

Meanwhile, Duke Amalo called his steward to him. He carefully wrote up a deed which would transfer the ownership of one of his estates, near Chalon, to Merofled, upon the consummation of their marriage, as was the custom at that time.

He then sent his servants to the house of her father, where they delivered themselves of this message:

"With these words Duke Amalo addresses you: 'I have recently sent away the woman who was my wife, and am now inclined to take a new wife. If this is satisfactory to you, then your daughter Merofled may accompany my servants back to my hall with whatever possessions you choose to settle on her.' "

Seven

Berulf was a man of great piety and virtue, but while his good deeds were legion, he was not known for looking over the wall to covet his neighbor's possessions. Thus he was taken aback by this salutation.

He retired at once to his bedchamber and sent for his daughter Merofled. "Is this what you wish?" he asked her, not hiding his surprise.

"Why should I wish to be married to a man who sends

his wife away as soon as he sees a woman who appears more comely to him?" she replied. "I would rather be married to a man of my own rank, whom I would not fear. If Duke Amalo should beat me, we would have no recourse, for his relations are more powerful than ours."

Her father saw the wisdom in her words and he returned straightaway to the Duke's envoys and sent them away with his refusal.

Eight

Anyone might imagine that this answer did not please Duke Amalo.

He raged for several days, whipped his hounds, and beat several servants who were slow in obeying his commands.

Then he threw himself on his knees in front of the altar at the chapel on his estate and prayed. His father had placed in this chapel some relics of Saint Sergius, and Duke Amalo set a copy of the Psalter atop the reliquary. He spent one whole night in prayer and another two days in fasting and vigil.

After this he opened the Psalter and read from the first verse at the top of the page. It said: "They are utterly consumed because of their iniquities."

These words dismayed him, and he wept.

After this, he did not mention the girl Merofled for ten days.

Nine

As the days passed and nothing happened, Merofled began to believe that she had misjudged Duke Amalo's intent. With a lighter heart, she went about her duties. After some days her father approached her and said these words:

"My child, it is, alas, time that we thought of a worthy alliance for you."

"My lord," she replied, "we must trust to God to provide what is necessary. If a good match presents itself, I will accept it. If it does not, then I am content to devote myself to good deeds and to God's work, and to remain a handmaiden of Christ."

Berulf accepted this answer gladly, since he was in no hurry to lose his daughter.

Ten

One night soon after this it happened that Duke Amalo drank too much at dinner. When he thought of going to bed, he thought at that same moment of the young woman whom he desired. By this time he was completely drunk.

"Go to her house," he said to his servants, "seize her, if she will not come willingly, and bring her to my bed." He went to his bedchamber to await her.

When the servants came, more than ten of them, to Berulf's house, they made their demand.

Merofled stood up proudly and faced them. "I and my father have already given our reply. Now begone from this house, where you are not welcome."

At this, the servants swarmed forward and grabbed hold of her. Her father sent his elder son running to fetch his sword, and even old Theudichild laid about her with her walking stick, but the servants were better armed. Merofled fought against them, overturning tables and chairs, but at last they pinned her arms behind her, tied them, and carried her off like a sack of grain.

No one in the house dared follow, because of Duke Amalo's rank and family.

Eleven

In this way Merofled was brought to Duke Amalo's house. Once in the house they set her down and untied her, thinking that now she would accept the honor of the duke's attention, but at once she struck about her with her fists and ran for the door.

It took three men at arms to subdue her. They hit her in the face until her nose bled and dragged her upstairs to the bedchamber, where, still fighting, she bled all over the bed, staining the covers red.

Duke Amalo had not waited in tranquil silence while this kidnapping took place. He had taken off his sword and belt and most of his clothing, in anticipation of her arrival. He also had at hand more wine, and when his men dragged Merofled in, he poured a new cup.

"Leave us!" he shouted, and they hurried out, so that Amalo and Merofled were left alone in the chamber.

Stanching the blood from her nose, she climbed off the bed and stared defiantly at him.

"Here is wine," he said, offering her the second cup, "with which we will drink to the consummation of our marriage."

"I refuse it, just as I refuse your offer of marriage, just as I refuse to inhabit your bed."

This was too much for the duke's uncertain temper. He threw the cup down and it shattered into pieces, the wine staining the carpet a red as deep as the blood that stained the bedcovers. He grabbed hold of Merofled and struck and slapped her. Now he was a man made strong by years of riding and hunting and war, and though Merofled resisted, she was by this time dizzy with the blows she had taken rather than give in to his blandishments, high rank, and threats. Her heart was still strong, but her flesh was weakening from the abuse it had taken, and suddenly she went limp despite her efforts to continue resisting.

As if this was encouragement, he took her in his arms and laid her down on the bed beside him, ready to make her his wife. So overcome was he by her closeness, by the expectation that his desire would now be fulfilled, and by the great amount of wine he had drunk, that he shut his eyes.

Merofled had given herself up to prayer and to her belief in God's judgment. She felt Amalo's grasp slacken just a bit, and taking this as a sign from God she summoned up every last portion of strength that God had granted her. She caught sight of Amalo's sword where he had placed it on the chest at the head of the bed.

Stretching out her hand, she took hold of the hilt and drew the blade from its scabbard. Aroused by her movement, Amalo opened his eyes and began to roll on top of her.

Needing no further encouragement, she struck him as hard as she could with his sword. The blow took him in his naked chest, and he howled in pain.

At once, servants ran into the room. They broke into great clamor while Amalo screamed and moaned. His soldiers grabbed Merofled, disarmed her, and pulled their own knives and swords in order to kill her immediately.

But Amalo, seeing this, took hold of himself. Weeping, he cried out to them.

"Stop! The sin is mine, not hers, for I tried to rape her. She only did this to preserve her honor. Do not hurt her."

As soon as these words left his lips, his eyes rolled up in his head, blood poured from his mouth, and he stopped breathing.

By this time others of his family, relations and servants, had come rushing into the chamber to see what the commotion was about. When he died, a cry of grief and disbelief rose from them all and they were filled with consternation.

Twelve

While servants and family alike stood in the room lamenting, Merofled struggled to her feet and, still dizzy, crept out from the midst of that host. They were all so consumed by grief and astonishment that they did not at first notice her escape.

But with God's help she made her way out of his house and ran home.

Now you may imagine the consternation, of a different kind, that erupted in her father's house when she came in, her clothes torn, her face bloody, her body covered with bruises.

At first her family covered her with kisses, thanking God for her safe return, but when she told her story, they barred the doors and windows and her old grandmother, Theudichild, began to keen with a new grief.

"Ah, child, you have brought ill luck on us. Now Duke Amalo's relatives will ride here and avenge themselves on our house. They will kill my sole remaining son, my grandsons, and no doubt burn down the only house I have ever known. If you had only given in to him, knowing that his power ranks far above ours, you should have had a good marriage gift from him, and we should have had peace."

"It is not I who have sinned!" said Merofled. "I have only protected my virginity and the honor of this house."

"That may be," said her father, "but his kinsmen will avenge themselves on you and your family nevertheless."

"Then I will go to the King himself and plead my case!"

Her family protested at once that she could do no such thing, for she was weak from loss of blood and from

the beatings she had sustained, and the roads were not
always safe.

"God will guard me," she said. She washed her face
and limbs and she put on clean clothes.

Thirteen

At dawn, she took her father's gelding and two servants and without fear set out on the road to Chalon,
where it was said that King Guntram was now staying,
for in the month of September he liked to celebrate the
feast day of Saint Marcellus in the church dedicated to
the saint.

A full thirty-five miles she rode, and when she came
to the city of Chalon, she went directly to the church.
The King and his entire retinue were worshiping in the
church, but Merofled walked into the church without hesitation. She begged to be brought before the King. When
his guards admitted her to his presence, she threw herself
at King Guntram's feet and in plain language told him
everything that had happened to her.

Because he was a God-fearing man, King Guntram was
filled with compassion for the young woman. He rose.
Every person in the church quieted in order to hear him
pass judgment.

"God has already passed judgment in this case," he
said. "I would not challenge what he has allowed to come
to pass. For this reason, I grant you, Merofled, daughter
of Berulf and Ingund, your life, for you have lawfully
protected yourself against theft."

"What of Duke Amalo's relations, King Guntram?"
she asked boldly. "I am of free birth, and my family is
a good one, but we cannot protect ourselves against any
revenge they might intend, for they are more powerful
than we are."

He nodded, for this was indeed a reasonable concern.

"Then I place you under my protection, and I prohibit any of the dead man's relations from exacting vengeance on you or your family."

So it was done.

Fourteen

With this royal edict in hand, Merofled rode home, having protected herself from Duke Amalo's brutal attentions and her family from the vengeance of his kinsmen.

Nor have I heard that any other incident disturbed her life, which, with God to guard her, proved both long and prosperous.

APPRECIATION

by C.J. Cherryh

One of the things that struck me first and most forcefully when, without any contact with writers or the science fiction field, I became a professional writer back in 1975—was the lack of jealousy or turf-defending on the part of senior professionals.

My first convention was the WorldCon in Kansas City. I was *so* out of touch with the science fiction field I showed up in heels, frock, and never, ever attended a panel, first because I was (thanks to the heels) generally late, and second, being straight from academe, I didn't think it proper to enter the hall late. I should have perhaps noticed that other people were not in my uniform— but I was a little overwhelmed.

And the night of the Hugo Awards, hearing that other writers were wearing tuxes and formals, I decided my dress wasn't nice enough to go, so I sat out the Awards in the coffee shop.

Marion was sitting out the Awards, too, being a little under the weather that night—she graciously said, well, she didn't think her outfit was very formal either, and we sat, soaked up whatever we were having, I forget, for a long time, and discovered common interests, common studies—we talked later, in a hotel room, and she was generous enough to compliment my work.

Marion is one of the reasons *why* my initial introduction to the field was so positive—she's a force of nature, a generous, energetic breeze through the field who's had an immense influence on its images and its young writers.

And continues to have. Good for you, Marion.

SING TO ME OF
LOVE AND SHADOWS

by Deborah Wheeler

On a honey-scented spring morning, the young widow
Solange sat spinning the wool from her own sheep and
patiently repeating the melody of her newest song while
Gaétan the minstrel struggled to set chords to it. The
sun cast a narrow strip of shadow from her house, one
of a half-circle that made up the tiny village. A breeze
carried the mingled smells of hot earth, leeks and thyme.
A short distance beyond lay the manor house of Val-
Joli, whose ancient, battered stones had been pried from
the last remnants of the Roman road.

Blowing out his breath, Gaétan set the lute across his
knees and stretched his fingers. He was only a few years
younger than Solange and almost as homely.

"Don't give up," Solange said, tucking a tendril of
russet hair under her linen coif. "You sing so well."

"Yes, I can sing. But nobody wants to hear my *chansons de geste* anymore. They're bored with tales of high
valor; today it's all love and ladies' favors, and I'm no
good at that." He sighed again and stroked the feather
he used to pluck the paired catgut strings.

"*Maman* sings pretty songs," said Jeannette, Solange's
stepdaughter, as she wound the spun thread on a frame.
Although she was twelve, she wore an outgrown child's
smock.

A smile curved the edges of Solange's mouth. She'd started making songs when she was a new widow, left to care for her husband's halfwit sister. Some said Jeannette ought to have died of the same fever, too, but whether it was by the Virgin's blessing or some other power, the child lived.

The minstrel picked up his lute again. Solange began humming and gradually a melody unfolded.

"A sky so pure," she sang, "a sun so bright.
Love brings hope to darkest night.
A man of feathers longs for his promised bride,
A golden pipe moves the hardest heart to stone,
Through fire and water—"

"Hark!" Gaétan rose to his feet. "There, on the north road!"

The distaff stuttered and bumped against the ground. Solange followed where Gaétan pointed, squinting against the patchwork brightness of the fields, some green with new-sprouted wheat, others fallow this season. Along the road, dust billowed into the air, blurring the shape of galloping horsemen.

Solange frowned. Who rode at such a speed on a day like this?

"Jeannette, you must go out with the sheep," she said. "Quickly now! No questions!" As the girl scrambled to obey, Solange uttered a silent prayer to the Virgin to keep her from running to see the strangers. They wouldn't understand her desire to please, her simple innocence. Earlier this spring, Jeannette had stolen the entire week's baking of sacred host from the chapel and crumbled it over the cabbages as a charm against caterpillars. Whoever drove their horses like that would not be as forgiving as the priest.

*   *   *

Solange was summoned to the manor house to help air linens, make beds, replace sodden floor rushes, carry water, pluck chickens, and scrub pots. The kitchen servants supplied the details—it was the Duke's own nephew, François, whom they guested tonight.

The central hall rang with men's voices, the clashing of ale-mugs, the snarls of the hounds as they fought over the bones from the suckling pig, the beating of tambours and trilling of pipes from the corner. Old Sir Alain sat at his table, flanked by his bailiff and three young strangers. Solange caught a glimpse of them now and again as she threaded her way between the trestle tables, a full beaker of ale in each hand, dodging an occasional pat on the buttocks. They wore sparkling rings, tunics trimmed with marten and, most curiously, rows of golden buttons. She'd heard of this latest fashion, but had never seen any before.

The feast went on for hours, it seemed, with always more to carry or something to be done faster. Solange, though she had been married for three years before the fever carried off her husband, had not realized that men could eat and drink so much.

Gaétan began his performance with a lively tune, then shifted one of Solange's own songs. The chatter died down as one after the other of the guests stopped to listen.

"Since you ask me to sing, my lords, I will," Gaétan sang again, this time the words of Bernart de Ventadorn,

"Yet I weep when I try;
My heart fills with tears . . ."

Standing in the corner, clutching an empty ale beaker, Solange felt an unbearable sadness sweep through her, a longing beyond words. Gaétan's voice blended with the rippling notes of his lute, sweet and grief-stricken all at once. Even the Duke's nephew fell silent.

She sang the same melody as she made her way home that night. As she trudged along the moonlit path, the song changed. Her voice no longer seemed to be her own; it built and soared, weaving shadowy images. Her heart beat faster and a frenzied strength surged through her. She raced around the final curve. Something was wrong, terribly wrong. . . .

"Jeannette!" The house lay still, the air faintly musty with the night-dampened thatch. As she scrambled up the ladder to the sleeping loft, she was certain she would find the pallets empty. But there was Jeannette, blinking and sleepy-eyed.

"*Maman* comes so late."

Solange sobbed with relief. "I was at the manor house, *chérie,* serving the *seigneur*'s guests."

"Oh! I wish I see them, too."

"Hush, child. Go back to sleep." Solange cradled Jeannette in her arms. *She is no longer a child. I must find a husband for her, or a dowry so that the nuns at Rocamadour will care for her after I am gone.*

A whisper, sweet in the darkness: "Sing to me, *Maman.* Sing to me of love and shadows."

Solange began the song she'd made during Jeannette's illness. Over the years, more of the story had come to her—how the knight had pined for his dead lady, how he sought her even in the gates of death, how he poured his love, his very soul into his song and won her life back again. Jeannette's body softened.

As Solange drifted off to sleep, the melody twined through her thoughts; the images shifted, but she could never see them quite clearly. Ghostly voices drifted through her mind as she fell into fitful slumber.

* * *

The Duke's nephew and his companions stayed for a fortnight, drinking and feasting late into the night. Despite Solange's protests, Jeannette was pressed into service at the manor house. One night Solange could not find her when it was time to go home, nor did Jeannette return later. The stableman found her body behind the watering trough the next morning; the horses, scenting blood, refused to drink.

The bailiff's buxom wife led Solange to the chapel and helped her prepare the body. In this heat, burial must be quick. Solange washed Jeannette as tenderly as if she were a sleeping babe and wrapped her in a shroud of her own weaving.

Later in the afternoon, one of the bailiff's young sons came running up to Solange's house with the news that the murderer had been found and the Duke's nephew was going to hang him.

Solange lowered herself to the bench beside the hallowed tree which stood in the center of the village. An icy calm settled over her like a second widow's veil. Her eyes were fixed straight ahead, taking in the Duke's nephew sitting in Sir Alain's great chair, a scowl on his beardless face. This morning, he wore a mantle of solid blue. His companions stood behind him, one fair and the other ruddy. Sir Alain, standing on the other side, looked grim.

The Duke's nephew straightened in the chair. His voice was unexpectedly tinny, Solange thought, with no music running through it. "Inasmuch as this manor is held in fief to my uncle the most puissant and noble Duke of Pontdebois, I will try this crime in his name."

The shepherd boy was brought forth, trembling between two guardsmen. Cries of protest broke out from the villagers. They all knew the boy; he was rough-tempered but young, and he'd been Jeannette's playmate when they were children.

One of the nephew's companions, the fair one in blue, suggested they put the boy to the ordeal, perhaps drawing a stone from a cauldron of boiling water without burning his hand. The Duke's nephew waved aside the suggestion; he made no secret that he'd wanted to leave that morning.

The voices of the men, the boy's sobbing denials, swept over Solange. Her breath came light and fast. She swayed as if she would faint.

The bailiff's wife, at her side, motioned for her to hush, for the Duke's nephew had pronounced sentence. The guardsmen led the frantically struggling boy toward the road, where a rope slung over a sturdy branch served as a gallows. At least, the wife murmured as she crossed herself, they weren't going to hang him right there from the sacred tree.

Solange moved slowly through the days, as if her body did not belong to her anymore. She wept until her eyes were dried out. Her head filled with a sonorous, rhythmic melody, music the color of endless night. She tried once or twice to sing it, but found that a noose had been drawn around her own throat, that no sound might pass.

She sat for a long time with Jeannette's few possessions on her lap—the worn smock, smelling of sheep and flowers, the heavy wooden sabots, the chemise of tow linen, stained with blood and grass. She traced the pattern of embroidery on the neckline and pocket, the stitches Jeannette had shown her with such pride. She felt a lump, something hard and rounded, caught in the folded edge of the pocket. Puzzled now, she drew it out, and gazed with amazement at a golden button.

She stared at it, at first unable to understand how Jeannette could have come by such a thing. But no, it had not been carefully placed in the safest depths of the pocket, as she usually carried a feather or a pretty pebble. It had caught, as if by accident, in the pocket edge.

Music rose up within her, insistent and dark. She saw a tomb in a great cathedral gaping open and a hideous figure bursting forth, then a man in scholar's robes crying out in torment as he held up his bloody hands.

She gathered herself and went up to the manor house; it was late morning and Sir Alain had not yet dined. The hall echoed now that the Duke's nephew and his party had departed. From the piles of ledgers and the expression on the bailiff's face, Solange guessed they had been summing up the wheat and ale consumed, the beef slaughtered, the furniture broken, the precious beeswax candles burned during the brief stay. Unless the harvest were exceptional, they might all go hungry next winter.

"Mon seigneur," Solange began, "I seek justice for the death of my stepdaughter. I have found proof—"

Sir Alain silenced her with a bleak eye under a jutting gray brow. "Justice?" His gaze flickered over the ruin of his hall. "We've had the Duke's own justice here. The thing's over and done with, I say." He thrust out a hand and a page handed him a full tankard. He drained it.

"As for you, you've been unmarried too long, that's what's wrong with you. You need a husband and babies of your own."

Solange blinked in surprise. "I—I—" she stammered. "I've had a vision, yes, that's it, summoning me to pilgrimage."

Sir Alain blinked, as if considering one less mouth to feed balanced against one more pair of skillful hands. Yet he was a devout man, a pilgrim himself in his own time. "When the holy saints speak, we must obey," he said. "You have my blessing to go."

*   *   *

It was an easy matter to convince Gaétan to leave Val-Joli. Ever since Jeannette's death and the boy's execution, he'd complained about how dreary the hall had become. With Solange as his accompanist and songwriter, he said, he could make a place for himself at the Duke's own court. Solange thought this an excellent idea. Women sometimes performed with troupes of *jongleurs*. She made arrangements for the neighbors to tend her sheep and strip of field, and made a will leaving everything to the Church should she not return.

Familiar sights and sounds soon fell away, to be replaced by strange crossroads, castles with mighty walls and towns where houses crowded together like pigs at a trough and with as foul a stench. Solange already knew Gaétan's favorite *chansons;* now he taught her to play the lute and rebec.

One seigneur, hearing them sing at his hall, hinted he might be glad to have them stay longer, but not even Gaétan was tempted; the manor was even poorer than Sir Alain's.

They arrived at Chavrinet in the middle of a downpour. The baron, delighted at the diversion, insisted they stay. But the next morning, Gaétan was afflicted with a flux and a fever. The baron was known as a man of little tolerance; Gaétan was terrified they'd both be thrown out. He lay on his pallet, unable to get up, and insisted he could sing.

Solange pulled on Gaétan's loose *bliaut* and tucked her hair under his feathered cap. She picked up his lute. Gaétan roused enough to realize what she meant to do. "You'll be found out and burned as a witch!"

"And you'll die out there in the storm," she retorted. "See, I have no more beard than you do and the hall's so dark that no one, least of all the baron in his cups, will get a good look at me. They'll hear a minstrel, so that's what they'll see."

Eventually Gaétan gave in. Solange was right, if any at the baron's table took her for other than a beardless youth, he said nothing of it. Three nights she sang alone, Gaétan's *chansons* as well as a few peasant songs, a *dit* or two, and some of her own. By then, Gaétan was well enough to move on. The baron was so pleased he paid them in coin and presented Solange with a lute, old but still serviceable, perhaps left behind by some less fortunate troubadour.

After that, Solange cut her hair and traveled as a man. They met up with a small troupe of *jongleurs,* who welcomed the addition of a skilled singer and accompanist. The troupe was headed for Poitiers in Aquitaine. When their paths diverged, Gaétan begged Solange to join them.

"Poitiers is a much larger court; we can sing for the ladies, teach as well as perform."

She shook her head. "I must to Sainte-Foye."

"For the love of Mary, why? The two of us can make a great fortune."

Solange kissed him on each cheek as a brother would. "Then I wish such a fortune to you, my friend, and if it is the will of the good God, we will meet again."

Solange made her way along a river cut through a ravine, past a ruined castle that seemed to spring from the substance of the rock itself, and into a forest. The pungent smell of decaying wood tinged the air. Deer eyed her from the inky shadows and squirrels scampered across her path, chittering. Once she heard a boar in the distance. More than twice, she thought of turning back.

Toward the end of the day, she forced her tired feet onward. The forest roof cut off the sun long before dusk; she startled at the rustling in the undergrowth or the sudden snap of a twig. She unslung the lute and tuned it as she walked. To lift her spirits, she chose one of

Gaétan's *chansons de geste,* a complicated tale of carnage and heroism. But the tune kept wandering, as if the lute had developed a will of its own. She found herself singing about a lady in a torn white gown, hair streaming down her back, bloody sword in hand—

And then suddenly she became aware she was not alone in the forest. The stars cast a pale, milky light; she could not see more than a few paces. She stopped, hands motionless over the strings, breath held.

A man's coarse laugh sounded in front of her. "Ho! We've netted us a minstrel!"

The next moment, torches flared into brilliance from behind tree trunks. Solange found herself surrounded by dark-bearded faces, four or five of them, she thought.

The one who appeared to be their leader held out a hand. "Your money, fair sir," he said.

Solange had given Gaétan most of the baron's purse. She handed over the few coins she had.

"Pah! Nothing!" One of the men eyed the lute in her hands.

She trembled with the thought they might take it from her. She had no fear for her life, only that without the instrument, she would have no way of gaining entry into the Duke's palace.

Solange caught a glimpse of the leader's horny palm, the broken nails, the dirt worked deep beneath the skin. It took a lifetime of labor to grow calluses like that. Outlaws they must be, free men or villeins forced from their lands. The shepherd boy might have been one of them, had he escaped.

"I am accustomed to singing for my supper," she said. "My lords of the woodland, shall I not do so for you?"

"Why not?" the leader said. "If we've empty bellies, at least we'll have full ears."

They led her to their camp, only a few paces away and sheltered from the path by dense brush. She might have passed right by them, had they wished it. While they sat on the ground, she lifted the lute and burst into a drinking song, then one of Gaétan's tales of Eustace the Monk, who outwitted the greedy Duke of Boulogne. The men held their sides laughing at the adventures of the wily monk, an outlaw like themselves.

But, as had happened before, the melody would not hold. Something new pressed to the surface. Her voice grew husky. She sang about a ship with blood-red sails, a ship voyaging for years without end as eerie blue light played across its deck and the crew faded to a ghostly chorus. The outlaws' mouths hung open. When she sang of the lady who loved the captain, throwing herself over a cliff for his sake, their eyes glistened.

"No other ears have yet heard that song," she told them in the breathless silence that followed. "I sang it for you alone."

The next morning they sent her on her way with her lute.

Solange came out of the woodland and into a broad fertile plain. Here the river grew wide and lazy. Crops simmered in the heavy sunshine. From afar, she spied a castle, larger and more complicated than she'd dreamed possible. A moat encircled it, bright as a mirror. It made Sir Alain's manor house, which she had once thought so grand, seem like a cottar's shed. The peasant houses looked well-kept, the sheep fat. A stone bridge, still half covered with wooden scaffolding, arched across the river, joining the town to the ramshackle village on the far bank.

As she drew nearer the castle, peasants straightened up from the fields to stare at her, but not in an unfriendly manner, she thought. A few children, wearing smocks that reminded her of Jeannette's, ran laughing toward her.

The closer she drew to the castle, the more traffic she met on the road, carts, flocks of sheep and chickens, traders with laden asses, beggars, even a Jew in his pointed yellow hat. She marched up to the barbican gates.

"Another singer, eh?" said the guard. "Why does every warbler in Pontdebois think he's good enough to sing for our Duke?"

Solange retorted, "Why does every tin-eared untaught varlet think he knows more about music than a trained minstrel?"

For an instant, she thought he'd cuff her for her insolence, then he threw back his head and laughed. "By Our Lady, lad, if you sing so boldly as you speak, you'll earn yourself a pretty dinner tonight. Go on in!"

By the time Solange wound through the maze of drawbridge, portcullis, gates and more gates and across a vast courtyard, she was thoroughly bewildered. She'd never seen such a profusion of people, enough to fill Val-Joli several times over, all rushing in different directions—knights tilting at quintains, stablemen leading prancing warhorses, pages in livery, kitchen drudges with buckets of water or steaming platters, men unloading carts and stacking barrels, canvas sacks and earthenware jugs, farmers with fat geese under each arm, pigs squealing.

Within the great hall, things were no less busy, although there were fewer animals. The ceiling arched halfway to heaven. The steward's assistant, a man with thinning yellow hair and a harried expression, waved her to a corner. He told her she could play tonight with the other performers and while the Duke was generous enough with the first night's dinner, if he wasn't pleased, she'd be on her way on the morrow.

Solange followed maidservants across a narrow courtyard to the cookhouse. She'd never dreamed of such a kitchen, the gigantic cauldrons, the spits and chopping blocks or the huge, freestanding ovens. The cooks were glad to hear a jolly song as they worked. They plied her with ale and cold bacon. She asked about the Duke, his sons, his heirs, what sort of men they were, what sort of song they liked.

"Our Duke's a fine one," said the assistant baker, rolling out pastry dough for the pigeon pies. "A fair man, aye, and a grand fighter."

"Look to his sons, though, and that nephew of his," the under-cook said, pausing to carefully inspect the peppercorns before grinding them in a mortar and pestle and adding them to a rich sauce. His eyebrows twitched and he sniffed appreciatively. "Nothing to fight against, no crusades to go on, nothing but tourneys and trouble. The younger generation doesn't understand the meaning of discipline!"

By the time the Duke and his court had gathered for the evening meal and festivities, Solange knew all about him, each member of his family, his vassals and their kin, the steward, marshal, and senior staff, their dress, habits and preferences in ladies. She knew that the nephew's two companions were Guisbert des Rivages and Olivier de Foretvert, and how each happened to be at Sainte-Foye, Guisbert a third son by fosterage and Olivier initially a hostage for his rebellious father and then by choice as François's bosom friend.

There they were, sitting at the Duke's own table, not too near, but well above the salt. They wore different colors than they had in Val-Joli. Different colors . . . but the same golden buttons.

She listened while the other entertainers sang or danced or performed tumbling stunts, first a group of musicians from Poitiers in Aquitaine and then a *trouvère* from the north.

As she stepped forward to take her turn, the Duke had glanced away and begun talking to the lady at his side.

"Ho-jo!" she sent her voice heavenward, "Ho-jo-to-ho!" The lute joined her hunting cry, a driving rhythm like the galloping of horses' hooves. "We are the Sky Maidens, come to gather up the knights fallen in glorious battle!"

The Duke looked up, as did the lady. He was so bejeweled, Solange could scarcely make out his face. His mantle was red like a flame, trimmed with snowy ermine, and his rings sparkled in a dozen hues. Even his beard was interwoven with threads of gold.

Solange gave herself over to the song, let it lead her through a tale of dragon's treasure, a lady lying in enchanted slumber, a hero's mighty deeds. At times, the Duke pounded on the table with his goblet, keeping time, at others the room grew hushed. After the last rippling chord died away, she paused, then bowed to the applause. The Duke gestured her to his table.

"I've not heard such a fine tale in years, not since that fellow from Provence gave us the *Chanson de Roland*. What was his name?" He turned to his wife.

"Conon, dear. And he was from Dordogne."

Solange stole more glances toward the nephew and his companions. No buttons were missing from any of them. Not even men as rich as the Duke's own family could own more than one set of golden buttons.

"You'll stay and sing for us again!" the Duke said.

Solange bowed again. As the angle of her vision shifted, she caught the gleam of a subtly different metal on one of the buttons adorning the nephew's friend, Olivier de Foretvert.

Solange played the next day for the Duke's wife and her ladies-in-waiting as she sat in her bower, embroidering and gossiping. Solange could not help comparing the airy chamber to her own front step, where she had wielded the distaff and sung her songs for her friend

Gaétan. For the ladies she performed the tale of the birdman and the golden pipe, then a melody about a lover presenting his lady with a silver rose. The ladies cooed like doves and the Duke's wife said that if she had been the lady in the song, the knight would have left far more than a flower in her lap.

The day passed pleasantly, with plenty of time during the afternoon, under the guise of courting a pair of maid-servants, to learn where the bedrooms for the Duke's important guests were. At Val-Joli, only Sir Alain and his lady had their own separate chamber. Solange slept on a pallet in the great hall, along with the other servants, lesser guests, pilgrims, and entertainers.

The castle lay dark and quiet as Solange crept to the door of Olivier's chamber. At the end of the curving passageway, a lone torch burned low in its holder. The dagger felt like burning ice when she drew it. Her palms were wet, her tongue dry. With a prayer to the Virgin, she tried the latch of the door. It rose with a faint *snick!* She froze, heart pounding, ears straining, but there was no alarm.

The door swung an arm's length open before the hinges creaked. Carefully she slipped through. Inside, the room was almost as dark as the corridor. She tried to breathe silently as her eyes adjusted and she made out the bed, the wooden clothes pole by the far wall, the massive chest at its feet. She tightened her grasp on her dagger.

Step by step she drew closer to the bed. Moonlight cast a barred pattern across the covers. Olivier slept on his belly, one arm hanging carelessly over the edge. Through the pounding of her heart, she heard his breath, the faintest wheeze of air. Jeannette had sometimes made a sound like that.

He looked so innocent lying there, so like a child. As

if the thought had softened her heart for the merest moment, doubt now crept in. What if she'd seen wrongly? Or what if there were some other, innocent reason for the change in the button?

The dagger trembled in her hand. Soft as a shadow, she backed up out of the room.

"Minstrel, give us a song, a tale of love and adventure!" the Duke's voice boomed out from his table.

Solange had been preparing for this moment all day, pondering what she could sing, what might provoke some reaction in Olivier to reveal his guilt. Yet all day, too, the familiar dark music had been building in her. She heard only the merest snatches of melody, no clear images yet, but she knew that she could not hold it at bay for long. She began with the words of the monk Abelard:

"Peace, oh my stricken lute!
Thy strings are sleeping.
Would that my heart could still
Its bitter weeping."

"How now?" the Duke's nephew cried. "Why so downcast? What sorrow has come to you? The love of a noble lady or the emptiness of your purse?"

Solange strolled along the length of the Duke's table. "My lords, it is a most unchivalric deed that weighs my heart, a murder so foul it is not fit for your noble ears."

To the clamor of requests, she told the story of a simple peasant girl, ravished and slain by a passing noble, of how the shepherd who had loved her was wrongfully hanged for the deed, how the killer had gone free.

"I have heard that if, on a certain night of the year, the felon hears a certain song, it will enter into his mind so that he will never be free of it until he confesses his deed."

A moment of silence passed along the table, Olivier broke into laughter, as did the nephew and Guisbert, his other companion.

The Duke's wife clapped her hands. "What a pretty tale!"

"Yet I have heard stranger tales come true," the Duke said soberly. He of all the nobles had not made merry at Solange's tale. His eyes glinted. "And would you sing that song in my hall?"

"My lord, I charge no knight here with such dishonor," Solange replied. "I told the tale but to amuse." As she began her first song, one of Gaétan's *chansons,* she noticed that the Duke's expression did not lighten.

Soon, however, she was lost in the music. A tide of images pressed at her, filled her. She sang of a princess crying out for revenge for her slain father, of the voice of a dead child crying out for its mother, of a gigantic sword hanging aloft, of a wound that would not be healed. Each note, each phrase, seemed to draw her even deeper into a world of splendor, of passionate, haunting melodies and incandescent yearning.

Over and over she returned to one theme. Insistent and passionate, it thundered through her head. Her fingers danced over the strings; the lute quivered as if it were alive. She heard the words ringing out in her own voice, the tale of a man locked away from the sun, a pale phantasm, forever longing, forever bereft of hope. His soul cried out in her music, pleading, agonized. . . .

How long she went on singing, Solange could not tell. A madness had infected her. Her voice seemed no longer her own, but possessed of preternatural force and clarity. She had not known a human throat could produce such beauty. Her eyes saw beyond the hall, to a palace lit with heavenly lights and garlanded with hangings in gemstone hues. She heard faint spectral music, pipes and viols and horns which tore at her heart, sweet beyond imagining.

Her song soared on this new music, carried ever higher and stronger. At one moment, she caught tears in the eyes of the stern Duke, at another, Olivier's pale face, at still another, the rapt gaze of the steward.

Slowly the music crested and slowly died. Its magic had left her wrung out, dry. Her fingers lurched across the strings. Her throat felt raw; her legs trembled so fiercely she could hardly stand. She bit her lower lip to steady herself.

The Duke blinked and shook his head, as if to clear his eyes. Beside him, his lady dabbed at her eyes. For a long moment, no one spoke, not even from the depths of the hall, where the common folk and servants had stood listening. The Duke drew a breath to speak.

Suddenly the hall was pierced by a shriek of raw anguish. The Duke's nephew jumped to his feet. The goblet at his elbow clattered to the floor. He clapped his hands to either side of his head. His eyes stared, wide and white, while his mouth drew into an inhuman grimace.

"Stop it!" he screamed at Solange. "Make it stop!"

"The minstrel sings no longer," said the Duke. "His song is finished."

"No! No! The music goes on and on! It's in—my—mind!" With a horrible cry, the nephew bolted from the room toward the outer gates.

The Duke motioned for men-at-arms to go after him. A great whispering and murmuring burst out in the hall. The Duke motioned Solange forward. Praying she would not collapse in a heap, she approached.

Her hand moved, seeking the pocket deep in the folds of her *bliaut*. She drew out the golden button and placed it in the Duke's outstretched palm. Her heart felt suddenly bright, as if charmed by the magic pipe of her song. She blinked back tears. When her vision cleared, the button was gone and the Duke nodded gravely.

"When you return to Val-Joli, I will give you a letter for Sir Alain," he said. "A relief from taxes for a year."

Solange had not told him where she came from, but she did not think much could remain hidden from this Duke. Young Olivier might have some explaining to do, as to how the buttons came to be exchanged. But she had seen the madness in the nephew's eyes. No holy waters or saint's relic could grant him ease. Death would have been kinder.

"As for you," the Duke went on, "I will send a horse and a guard. It is not safe for a ... person to travel alone, even one armed with so powerful a weapon."

She bowed her head, preparing to take her leave. They both knew she could never sing again at Sainte-Foye. The road called to her, and the comfort of her own house, a distaff humming to life between her hands, a sunny morning. And perhaps a friend to sing with.

She wondered what new songs would come.

THE WELLSPRING

by Katharine Kerr

Down in the thicket the shade fell dappled, cool in the
windless summer day. Among aspens the spring welled
up clear, a noiseless bubble of water through white sand.
When Gwanwyn knelt, she felt the Presence. The priests
said an evil spirit lived in the spring, but she was con-
vinced that the spirit was holy. Either way, at times the
Presence did deign to show her visions. Gwanwyn
opened the leather pouch hanging from her kirtle and
took out a piece of honeycomb, wrapped in green leaves.
When she laid it down upon the grass, the Presence
grew stronger.

Gwanwyn stared into the still waters and the rippling
image of her own face, roundish and pale under blonde
hair, pretty without being beautiful. *Owain, O Holy Virgin, please, show me Owain!*

As she chanted his name over and over, the dappled
shadows blended to a darkness, then welled until the
dark at the heart of the spring filled her mind. In the
midst of the darkness, bright-lit in a ray of sun, Owain
stood with his sword in his hand, his helm tucked under
one arm. Gwanwyn saw her father standing nearby and
laughing, his head thrown back. *So. They're both safe,
and the battle over.* Gwanwyn smiled as if they could see
her in return. Then the ray of light turned bloody, picked
Owain out, and washed him in gore.

Screaming, Gwanwyn leaped to her feet. The spring

was only a spring again, but the thicket seemed to shiver with the memory of her scream. She clasped her hands over her mouth and stood shaking, deathly cold in the summer air.

"What's so wrong?" The voice came from behind her. "Did you see somewhat in the water?"

Gwanwyn spun around. Standing among the trees was a stranger, an old woman. Tall and spare, she wore shabby traveling clothes, a blue cloak thrown over a much-mended dress that once had been green, but her lined face was so strong that her white braids, wrapped round her head, seemed a queen's crown. Just beyond stood a gray palfrey and a large gray dog lying patiently beside it.

"Who are you? I thought I was alone."

"My horse smelled the water, and he's thirsty. May a traveler drink at this spring?"

"If the Holy Virgin allows it, you may."

The old woman nodded, as if tucking this bit of lore away, then went to fetch her horse. When the dog sprang up and followed, Gwanwyn leaped back. It was, in truth, a great gray wolf from the far highlands, with a black roach down his back and narrow yellow eyes.

"He won't hurt you, lass. I've had him since he was a cub, and I raised his mother, too." The old woman busied herself with slacking her horse's bit. "My name is Rosmarta, and I'm on my way to the village. Who are you?"

"Gwanwyn of Dun Pennog. My apologies! I've quite forgotten my courtesies, haven't I? How does your journey fare? Will you seek shelter in my father's dun?"

"My thanks, but I won't. I have a cousin in your village, old Mab the herbwoman." She hesitated, looking Gwanwyn over with calm, gray eyes. "You know, lass, sometimes roads cross for a reason."

Gwanwyn smiled politely, tried to think of an answer,

then decided that Rosmarta didn't truly expect one. When the horse and wolf had drunk their fill, Gwanwyn showed her the way to the village by her usual shortcut, a narrow track that wound across the meadows. Mile after mile, the rolling hills of southern Rheged stretched round them, a long green view crested with trees. Here and there in meadows grazed white cattle, switching flies.

"You'll pardon my asking," Rosmarta said. "But what's a high-born lass like you doing out without an escort?"

"I like to be alone, and besides, all the men are off with Father. The Irish have been raiding again, you see."

"Well, that's ill news!"

"It is, truly. They burned a church, you see, and a monastery, too. They killed the monks, all of them."

"How dreadful." Yet her voice had no mourning in it. "A terrible thing."

"Well, the monks were all good Christian men."

"No doubt."

Gwanwyn hesitated, waiting. Rosmarta never crossed herself.

"And what about you, my lady?" Gwanwyn took refuge in courtesy. "Have you traveled far alone?"

"I have, but who's going to bother one poor old woman? Besides, there'd be pity in my heart for the man who dared attack me in front of Giff here."

The wolf stretched back lips over strong white fangs and waved his tail.

About two miles from the spring, an untidy clutter of round thatched huts spread out around the crossroads. At the common well in the center of the village, a gaggle of old women in black and gray dresses were sitting and gossiping. A couple of small boys kicked a leather ball back and forth and raised little puffs of dust in the road. As Gwanwyn and Rosmarta walked by, everyone curtsied, but in a rather absentminded way. Old Mab's house stood off by itself in the middle of an untidy garden, scented with the bitter and the sweet of fifty different herbs. When they opened the gate to the jingle of tiny brass bells, Mab came waddling out, her smile vast among her many chins.

"And there you are, my sweet cousin! And the Lady Gwanwyn, too, by the Holy Mother herself!" Mab made a surprisingly graceful curtsy. "How fares your father, my lady? Any news?"

"I saw—I mean, none yet, good dame. But I pray every night he'll come home safe."

"As well you might." Mab glanced at Rosmarta. "It's the Irish again, you see, coming up the creeks and stealing everything they lay their foul paws on and burning what they leave behind."

"So our young lady told me. I heard about the monastery."

Mab and Rosmarta exchanged the barest trace of a smile.

"But now, we're all in danger, like," Mab went on, and now her voice trembled. "They kill anyone who won't make fit slaves. A terrible thing it is."

"It is, it is at that," Gwanwyn said. "And we've lost ever so many good men, fighting them. I only pray I won't lose my betrothed, too. I worry so about him."

"As well you might." Mab gave a firm nod. "And will you take my hospitality, my lady?"

"All my thanks, but your cousin must be tired, and I'd best get back to my duties."

Lord Cadvaennan's dun lay half a mile from the village, close enough for his folk to run for shelter when raiding parties came marauding, on the top of an artificial mound surrounded by a double ring of earthworks. At the crest of the mound stood a wooden palisade, enclosing a stretch of bare dirt, a row of stables, a scatter of sheds, and the wooden longhouse of Dun Pennog, where

Gwanwyn had presided, mistress of the house, ever since her mother's death three years before. Over the brass-bound doors hung a row of severed heads, roughly dried in sun and sand, then nailed up for all to mock, the blond and bearded heads of Irish raiders. Alone among all the lords who swore allegiance to Urien, the king of Rheged, Gwanwyn's father had won the name of Scotbane. Everyone swore that Lord Jesu himself must be helping Cadvaennan find the murdering scum, and great honors had come his way for it, too. But Gwanwyn knew that the luck came from a man named Vortin, who joined her father's warband the summer before. He tracked the marauders down as easily as if he could see them from far away.

All that afternoon, while Gwanwyn and her women sat spinning wool and singing to one another, she found her mind drifting from the songs to Rosmarta. Visitors of any sort were rare, up here in the hills, but for one of the commonfolk to have a visitor was unheard of. Toward evening, when the poor light forced the women to tidy the spinning away, Gwanwyn asked the eldest of her women, Anghariad, if she knew of Mab's cousin.

"I don't, at that, but Mab herself's a strange one." Anghariad raised a significant eyebrow. "She wasn't born round here, you know. I remember when her husband brought her home, a long long time it was. All the way from Tŷ Gwin, it was."

"As far as that? Why, that's two days' ride!"

Anghariad nodded and laid her finger up along her nose, as if in warning of strangers.

All the warning did, though, was prod Gwanwyn's curiosity. In the morning she set some of her women to spinning and others to baking bread out in the kitchen hut, and on the excuse of moving from one group to the other she could slip away and go down to the village. She found Mab and Rosmarta working out in Mab's kitchen garden, plucking snails and green worms from Mab's cabbages and drowning them in a leather bucket of salted water. At the sight of her they wiped their hands on their dresses and curtsied.

"And what may I do for you, my lady?" Mab said.

All at once Gwanwyn realized that she'd never thought of excuse or reason. Both women laughed, but in a kindly way.

"Drawn by your curiosity, I'll wager," Rosmarta said. "Well, come sit down while we work."

Stammering apologies, blushing, Gwanwyn sat down on an old stump for want of a stool.

"Tell me somewhat, lass," Rosmarta said. "Has the Holy Virgin ever appeared to you at that spring?"

"How did you know?" Gwanwyn blurted, then blushed scarlet. "I mean, oh, please, don't tell the priests. I don't want to be shut up in a nunnery all my life."

"No doubt," Mab put in. "Though you'd have a quieter life there than you will as Lord Owain's wife."

"I don't care. I don't want a quiet life."

"No doubt on that, either," Rosmarta said, smiling. "But I knew because you said I could water my horse if the Blessed Virgin let me."

"Oh! Of course! Well, I've never had a true vision of her. I mean, she's appeared to me, but she doesn't look like the priests say she should. She comes in a green dress with flowers in her hair, but I know she's not an evil spirit, I just know it, and so she must be the Virgin. Who else is there?"

"Who, indeed?" Rosmarta sounded suddenly weary. "Who else is left to give women their visions?"

Both Mab and her cousin were looking at her, watching in friendly concern like a pair of nursemaids watching their charge toddle to its feet and take a first step or two.

"Well, no one," Gwanwyn said, puzzled. "What do

you mean, left? You don't mean the horrid old demons, do you? The ones people used to think were like God?"

"You're the one who said your lady couldn't be evil, not me," Rosmarta said. "And you're the one who's seen her, not the wretched priests."

Gwanwyn got to her feet. She shouldn't be sitting here, listening to heretical things!

"If she's not the Holy Virgin, who is she?"

The sinful question seemed to have asked itself. Gwanwyn clapped a hand over her mouth in horror, but the two women merely smiled.

"A holy virgin," Rosmarta said. "That bit's right enough."

Gwanwyn hesitated, on the edge of asking more.

"I've got to get back," she said instead. "The spinning's near done, and I've got to parcel out the threads."

"Come again if you'd like," Mab said. "You're always welcome here, my lady."

And on the morrow Gwanwyn did come again. This time she found Mab spinning up the clumps of gleaned wool, her widow's right to gather. The old woman sat on a high stool and let the spindle drop, over and over, while she fed the carded fibers in to the growing thread.

"My cousin's gone a-gathering herbs, my lady," Mab said.

"No doubt. She's a wisewoman, isn't she, Mab?"

"There's wise and wise, my lady."

"Well, so there is. But does she know grammarie?"

"What?" Mab laughed, as merry as a lass. "How could a woman possibly know such things, and them as dark as dark?"

"She knew I'd seen the lady of the spring."

"Well, you as good as told her yourself."

"Maybe so."

"She's a good woman, my cousin," Mab went on. "As nice as you please."

Yet Gwanwyn was remembering the way that Rosmarta said, "sometimes roads cross for a reason." There'd been naught of the goodwife in her voice then. She walked back to the dun, wondering and in spite of her own strictures, hoping that Rosmarta knew forbidden lore.

Close to sunset, Gwanwyn knew with a sharp urgency that her father was riding home. She climbed the catwalk on top of the palisade and stood looking down at the road. After some minutes she saw a cloud of dust coming fast: the warband sweeping through the village at a trot. Her father and Owain both were safe and riding at the head. Whooping with joy, she turned and yelled orders at the servants. One ran to open the gates, another to warn the cook. Just as Gwanwyn was about to climb down, she noticed Rosmarta, standing at the bottom of the hill with her wolf beside her, watching as the warband hurried by. It was a reasonable curiosity, no doubt, on the part of a stranger, but the old woman stood so straight and still that Gwanwyn wondered just what she was doing there.

With shouts and the thudding of hooves on hard ground, the warband swept in through the gates, twenty men home safe, five men wrapped in blankets and slung over saddles. As the servant came running to take the horses away, Gwanwyn climbed down and shoved her way through the mob to her father's side. Cadvaennan was lifting a leather sack down from his saddle-peak.

"Boy!" he yelled at the nearest servant. "Run and get me a pike."

As Gwanwyn curtsied, she saw blood seeping through the seam.

"Father, thanks be to the Holy Virgin for bringing you home safe."

"Safe?" Cadvaennan grinned through his filthy beard. "Thank her for the victory, lass."

Gwanwyn turned to find Owain right behind her. She threw herself into his arms and clung to him while he laughed and stroked her hair and told her she'd been silly to worry over him. He reeked of sweat, his horse's and his own, but over it all hung the smell of other men's blood. Gently he pushed her free and gave her an affectionate slap on the behind.

"Run and set the servants working, will you? I could drink enough ale to drown a horse."

"You shall have it, my love. Father, shall I have them lay out a meal, too?"

Cadvaennan was paying her no attention. A page was kneeling before him and bracing a long spear against the dirt while his lord took a man's head out of the sack, its dark beard stiff with blood. He flipped it neatly round and ran the severed stump of the neck onto the spear with a sucking, squelching sound. The warband broke out cheering.

"Another Irish captain sails to hell tonight!" Cadvaennan called out. "Set it by the fire to dry, lad. I'll be making a drinking cup of his skull soon enough."

When the men burst out laughing, Gwanwyn turned and ran for the longhouse. At the door she collided with someone coming out.

"Oh, my pardons!"

"No matter," Vortin said.

When he laid a hand on her shoulder to steady her, Gwanwyn shrank back. Tall, stoop-shouldered, Vortin smiled down at her, a thin smile tight on a thin, scarred face. For all that he rode with the warband, Gwanwyn had never heard the bard give him credit for a single kill, but her father swore that a scout like him could earn his mead without swinging a sword. The warband whispered about it, just as the servants did: grammarie, they muttered, he has dark magic and strange grammarie in his soul.

"I'll come inside with you," Vortin went on. "I've a question to ask you."

Since she couldn't be rude to a man her father favored, Gwanwyn forced herself to walk beside him into the great hall, an enormous room set with wooden tables on the straw-strewn floor and two stone hearths at either end. While she gave the servants their orders, he watched her with his ice-blue eyes all narrowed and calculating, then caught her elbow and steered her into a corner.

"When we were riding up the hill, I saw an old woman, a stranger, with white braids round her head. Do you know who she is?"

Gwanwyn hesitated, utterly unwilling to tell him, but she couldn't give a reason why.

"You answer me, lass. I know cursed well you know."

"Her name's Rosmarta. She's a cousin of Old Mab's."

"Oh, is she now? Oh. Is she now!" He turned and walked away.

Gwanwyn shuddered and plucked at her sleeve where he'd touched it. If there'd been time, she would have changed her dress.

That night saw a victory feast in the great hall, lit by both torch and firelight for the celebration. The warband crowded round the tables and chivvied the servant girls as they hurried from man to man with pitchers of ale and plates of meat. At the table of honor up by the hearth, Cadvaennan put Owain and Vortin beside him, one at either hand, and Gwanwyn, of course, sat next to her betrothed.

While they ate, Cadvaennan and Owain took turns telling her about the raid, boasting of their kills and praising those of their men. Vortin picked at his food and said little, but every now and then he would look Gwanwyn's way and give her a smile like the grasp of a sweaty hand. Eventually Gwanwyn make a pretense of having to see to the servants and fled the table. The warband had broken out singing, leaning together and laughing their way through a song about a mythical wench who liked her men five at a time. Gwanwyn circled round the edge and went to the doorway, where two of the boys were rolling a barrel of ale into the hall. Seren, the cook, was hovering round and snapping our orders.

"The ale's running low, my lady, and we don't dare stint this lot with the mood they're in tonight."

"True spoken, but let that barrel settle before you dip from it. They're too drunk to know dregs from drink, so just finish the other up."

"I will, then, my lady. And the bread's gone, too, I—" Seren paused, looking doubtfully over Gwanwyn's shoulder.

"It's hot in here," Vortin said, and he was smiling, as sly as a stoat. "Come walk with me outside, my lady. We'll catch a breath of air."

"I won't. My place is beside my betrothed."

"Oh, is it now?"

Seren was staring down at the floor, her mouth slack, her eyes unfocused, as if she slept where she stood. All at once Gwanwyn felt Vortin's mind circle hers like a physical rope, catching her, pulling her, dragging her to do his will. When he laid his hand along her cheek, she wrenched away in blind panic.

"Stop it! Don't you dare touch me!"

Vortin swore under his breath and stepped back just as Seren woke from the spell and screamed, a reflexive echo of terror. Men rose, men turned, the hall burst out with shouting. Gwanwyn raced down its length and threw herself at Cadvaennan's feet.

"Father! He would have dishonored me."

With an oath Owain sprang up and ran for Vortin, but the warband got there ahead of him. They swirled around the sorcerer, grabbed him, shoved him back and forth between them and cursed him with hatred too long hidden as they hauled him down to face the lord. Vortin was perfectly calm, even smiling as he ignored the shoves and oaths.

"You black dog!" Owain snarled. "I've seen you sniffing around my lass for too long now. So it's come to this, has it?"

Owain gave him one last shove that sent him face-to-face with Cadvaennan. Vortin shook himself, dusted off his tunic with fastidious fingers, then shot the men a look that made them fall back.

"My lord," Vortin said. "I swear by every god that I had no intention of dishonoring your daughter. I only wished to talk with her." He shot Owain the blackest look of all. "I most humbly submit, Lord Cadvaennan, that I'd make her a better husband than this bull-faced lout with the brains of a wallowing hog."

His sword half out of the scabbard, Owain started for him, but three men caught him and held him back.

"Wait! here! Let's have a fair fight of it, lad."

Although Owain shook their hands off, he stepped back.

"Vortin's served me well," Cadvaennan said. "But the lass has been sworn to Owain, who's also served me well. So. Vortin, will you face him in single combat?"

All the men snickered, grinning Vortin's way and elbowing each other. As Gwanwyn got to her feet, she felt her pounding heart begin to calm.

"I will," Vortin said. "Whoever lives shall have her."

"Done, then," Cadvaennan said. "Lad! You! Leave that ale alone and go round up some torches."

Even the serving maids trailed along to watch when everyone trooped out to the ward. Four boys with torches took their places to mark out the corners of a rough square while the warband lined up round the sides. In the torch-thrown shadows up above, Irish heads seemed to be grinning. Owain and Vortin strode into the middle of the square. They drew their swords and held them straight up in front of them for the pledge.

"May the gods favor the stronger and the better," Cadvaennan said. "Now!"

Owain stepped forward and flung up his blade for a feint, but Vortin refused to move, merely stared him full in the face. Owain hesitated, started to step forward, then caught himself with a drunken shake of his head. Their jeers dying away, the warband pressed closer until the torches flared up with a sudden smoky burst, driving them back. Owain began to lurch and stagger as if he had a fever while Vortin watched with a thin smile. All at once, Gwanwyn remembered her vision at the well-spring. She wanted to scream a warning, but no words would come. Owain turned his sword point his own way and took another step, stood swaying, the point of the sword glinting as it bobbed just below his ribs. Then he lurched forward and fell, the sword biting deep into his chest, to lie in a crumpled heap. Blood oozed round him and sank into the dirt. A servant boy dropped his torch and screamed.

The men broke, shouting, milling forward to mob Vortin. Swinging the flat of his blade and calling them off, Cadvaennan pushed his way through to the sorcerer's side.

"A pledge is a pledge. The lass is yours."

The warband howled in rage, and Gwanwyn howled with them.

"How could you, Father? He didn't even fight with a true man's weapons!"

When the men shouted their agreement, Cadvaennan swung round and slapped her across the face.

"You do as I say!"

Yelling and demanding answers, the warband surged forward, hands on sword-hilts, and surrounded Cadvaen-

nan and Vortin. In the cover of the confusion Gwanwyn
slipped away from her father's side, worked her way
round the edge of the mob, then ran for the gates. She
had no idea of where she was going, no hope of a real
escape, but she kept running, stumbling down the dark
hillside. From behind her, she heard the angry shouts of
the men and her father's booming voice, demanding silence and order. At the bottom of the hill she paused,
weeping blindly, gasping for breath.

The wellspring. Rosmarta's voice hissed in her mind.
Gwanwyn, go to the wellspring.

Gwanwyn threw up her head like a startled horse:
there was no one in sight. Yet she hesitated only the
briefest of moments before she took out running, racing
across the meadows in the moonless night. The tall grass
caught at her ankles and dress; once she fell, but she
picked herself up and ran, her chest aching for breath.
Far, far ahead of her in the dark she saw a dim shape
that promised trees—but too many trees. She'd taken a
wrong turning. She paused, looking wildly around her,
the tears coming again, hot, unbidden, blinding. Through
the clear still air came the sound of horses, the jingling
of bridles and the shouting of the warband. They were
on her trail, hunting her down like a doe.

Something was moving through the grass. Gwanwyn
choked back a scream just as Rosmarta's wolf trotted up
to her, its tail wagging like a dog's. It whined, an impor-
tunate chirp, then turned to trot off again. When she
followed, it whined in satisfaction and led her off at an
angle. In a few minutes she saw the familiar silhouette
of the aspen thicket just ahead, but too far—she glanced
back to see the distant shapes of men on horseback coming fast after her with torches held high. The wolf howled
once, then darted past her straight toward the warband.
Gwanwyn summoned up the last of her strength and
raced across the meadow. Behind her she could hear

horses screaming, men shouting and cursing, as the wolf ran among them and sent the horses into a frenzy of fear. She dodged into the trees, tripped over a thick root, and fell headlong, her outflung hands splashing into the cool water of the spring. Sobbing, choking for breath, she hauled herself up to her knees. She could run no farther, but Rosmarta was standing on the far side of the pool and smiling at her.

"Well and good. No man can touch you where the Goddess gives me power."

Gwanwyn's tears stopped in sheer surprise as she realized why she could see the old woman. The thicket was glowing with strands and shreds of pale blue light as thick and palpable as sheep's wool, caught all tufted on twig and branch. Rosmarta held out her hand.

"Get up, child. Come round and stand next to me."

When Gwanwyn scrambled up, she looked back to see the warband riding this way and that across the meadow. No one headed toward the thicket, as if the light hanging there blinded men's eyes.

"I've been tracking this Vortin down," Rosmarta said, as calmly as if she were remarking on the weather. "Tonight, he'll come to me. I've hung my bait out on the trees."

"My lady, does he truly know grammarie?"

"How could you doubt it, after what you've seen? Think, lass! Oh, here, you don't need me biting your head off, do you now? Forgive me. I wanted so badly to save your betrothed's life, but I got to the dun far too late. But he'll be avenged."

"You were there? I didn't see you."

"Of course not! It wasn't magic; I was standing in the gate, and you had other things to watch. I—" She stopped, pointing to the meadow where a single torch bobbed and dipped as its bearer rode steadily toward them.

At length Gwanwyn could make out Vortin riding in the pool of yellow light. About thirty feet away he dismounted, awkwardly holding the torch up away from his horse's head.

"Who are you?" he called out. "Meddling old woman!"

Rosmarta merely laughed. When Vortin strode into the thicket, the torchlight sparkled on the water of the spring.

"Give me that lass! She's my betrothed."

"Oh, is she now? Your master Emrys might have a thing or two to say about that."

Vortin froze, the color draining from his face.

"So," Rosmarta went on. "His name means somewhat to you still, does it? Here, did you truly think an oathbreaker like you could ride away and do whatever he liked? Didn't you realize that someone would be coming after you?"

With an animal howl, Vortin hurled his torch straight for her head, but it fell short into the pool with a great gush and roil of hissing steam. Gwanwyn felt the Presence rise up, furious at his defilement.

"You dolt, Vortin," Rosmarta said.

Vortin lunged forward, staring at her in a way that Gwanwyn could recognize now; he was trying to bend her will to his own. When Rosmarta laughed, as merry as a lass at a market-fair, Vortin's face darkened and the veins began to throb at his temples. He drew his sword and strode round the edge of the spring. From across the clearing the wolf broke cover and flew for him like a thrown spear. With a yell Vortin twisted round to meet the attack, his sword half-raised. And stood, merely stood, caught, frozen as stone-still as Owain had been forced to stand in front of him. The wolf struck with a growl. Gwanwyn spun round and clapped her hands over her eyes. There was one bubbling scream, then silence.

"It's over. You can look now, child. Come now, it's not like you haven't seen dead men before."

Gwanwyn turned to see the wolf drinking from the spring and Vortin lying facedown in the grass. The Presence was dancing beside him, so corporeal that Gwanwyn could see her, like a beam of moonlight through mist. Gwanwyn raised her hands in worship, but she found she couldn't speak. When Rosmarta laid a comforting hand on her shoulder, Gwanwyn suddenly felt like a sleeper, awakening from a nightmare only to realize that all those terrors she dismissed as dream still have truth in the day.

"But, my lady," she stammered. "Who are you?"

"One who follows the dweomer road, but I pick my way a bit more carefully than this fool ever did. Here, if someone wants to study grammarie, they join what you might call a guild, much like someone who wants to be a weaver or a potter would prentice themselves out— except this guild must keep itself secret and hide from meddling priests. Vortin once served the master who taught me, but he broke his oaths. Off he went to use the secrets for his own gain, like a stupid magpie, gathering shiny stones and thinking them treasures. Well, you see what kind of reward he had."

All at once Gwanwyn had to sit down; her legs simply refused to stay straight. As gracefully as she could manage, she sank down on the grass while Rosmarta hunkered down nearby. With a long whine of a sigh, Giff flopped next to her, by all appearances just an ordinary animal again.

"Can you walk?" Rosmarta said. "Your father will be bound to stumble across us eventually if we stay here."

"Oh, ye gods! But I've got to rest, just for a little bit if naught else."

"Very well, then. And, truly, you need to think. What will you do now, child? If you go back to your father in the morning, when his rage has had a chance to cool, he probably won't even beat you.''

"Probably not, but if I had anywhere else to go, I'd never set foot in his hall again.''

"Why?"

"He would have handed me over to a dishonorable man, that's why! I'd rather beg along the roads and starve than eat at his table again.''

"Would you come with me and join my guild?"

Gwanwyn shoved the back of her hand against her mouth to keep from squealing like a child.

"I marked you the moment I saw you, child. If you can scry in this spring, then you can follow the paths of grammarie. But you have to choose and quickly. Your father will forgive you, but I don't want him asking me awkward questions. If you ride with me, you ride tonight. We'll take Vortin's horse as part of your betrothed's blood price.''

"Owain's dead.'' She said it softly, with wonder, because until that moment she hadn't believed the truth of it. "Why don't I weep?"

"Because you're drained half-dead and exhausted. The tears will come later. Answer me somewhat. Would you have been happy as Lord Owain's wife?"

"Happy? My lady, I never allowed myself such a thought. He was the man my father chose, and he was the best warrior in Rheged. Everyone said so, and I was proud to marry him." Her voice broke. "Now he's dead, and I have naught.''

"Naught? Only your own road? That looks like somewhat to me.''

The light in the trees glowed like lace before a candle flame. The Presence of the Spring hovered close, slender and pale, more solid than Gwanwyn had ever seen her and smiling as if she was urging her to go take this unexpected boon. Gwanwyn remembered all the times that she'd come to the spring, all the hours she'd spent with the Presence, her one true friend. And as she remembered, her life came clear, just as if she'd stepped out of a smoky and airless room to see the sun for the first time.

"True spoken. I have the road."

Rosmarta clapped her hands together three times. The light vanished from the trees.

With Giff coursing ahead, keeping watch and leading the way, they left Vortin's body for Lord Cadvaennan's men to find and hurried across the night-dark meadow. When they reached Old Mab's hut, they found her awake, feeding a few sticks into her tiny fire.

"There you are!" Mab burst out. "My lady, your father rode in and woke up every man in the village to go hunt for you. He was yelling and blustering, but I think me he's frightened half out of his wits, thinking some harm's come to you."

"Well, he won't find me, will he, now? I'm riding with Rosmarta."

"And we're riding tonight," Rosmarta said.

"Ah. He was the right one, then, was he?" Mab nodded in a wobble of chins. "Is he dead?"

"He was and he is," Rosmarta said. "A thousand thanks for your message."

Suddenly Gwanwyn realized why Mab called Rosmarta cousin, as if they came from the same clan—no! the same guild. Mab grinned as if she'd read her mind.

"I always thought you were one of us, my lady."

"Did you, Mab? Did you truly?"

"I did. Your mother had the sight, may the Goddess rest her soul, but all your father ever did was beat her for it, and so I held my tongue when I saw your eyes seeing things beyond what most may see."

"And now she'll learn to use the gifts the Goddess gave her," Rosmarta said, smiling. "And those from the new god as well. Priests! They're like men who find a

chest of Rhivannon gold and use them to stop chinks in
a wall!"

"No doubt," Mab said. "But you can preach against
them later. What counts now is getting the lady away."

"True enough. Can you spare us some food and a
cloak for the lady?"

"Food I have, but a second cloak, no."

"I'll be warm enough," Gwanwyn said. "And I'll pray
to our Lady to keep us safe."

And whether it was the Lady that hid them or not, I
cannot say, but they rode safely through the hills all that
day, and on the day after that, until safe they were in
Tŷ Gwin, the city that once the Rhivannon called Can-
dida Casa, and the Saison dogs, Whithorne. And never,
so they say, did any woman learn grammarie as easily as
the Lady Gwanwyn of Dun Pennog, but as to the truth
of that, I cannot tell you.

KNIVES

by Dave Smeds

Ledda was tending her garden when she heard familiar voices calling her. She rose, a cluster of weeds in her hand, and stared across fields of barley and flax. Bello the Bald and his son were leading their hay cart down the lane that led to her cottage.

She waved to them and shaded her eyes, catching sight of the man in the cart. He was clinging desperately to the slats, obviously unable to sit upright, though the ride was not rough: A stranger.

Now she knew what it had meant to find the sprig of rowan on her great-grandmother's tree that morning, blooming despite the approach of autumn. She went inside, filled her basin, and washed her hands. She would need to perform a Touching.

She emerged as Bello and his son were setting down the yokes. They started to wipe the sweat from their brows, then sprang to action as Ledda cried out. Their passenger was falling off the open end of the cart. They caught him and lowered him to the packed earth.

Ledda had never seen a man display such pain. The stranger's lips were pulled back in a rictus, teeth bared. No sooner had the other men laid him out flat than he folded up, rolling onto his side. Drool stained the dirt.

He was a Roman. A soldier, judging by the armor and greaves. He was tall, with curly dark hair and hints of a muscular build, though he fit his garments poorly. Hol-

lows pocked his cheeks and his movements spoke of bulk
suddenly lost. His eyes contained a wounded-animal
glassiness.

"Julia Ledicca?" the man croaked, peering up at her.

Bello answered. Ledda supposed he was saying, "Yes,
this is she, the healer," but her command of Latin was
meager at best. The stranger turned to her, his expression
filled with pleading, his mouth opening and closing as if
ready to pour out an epic if only he had the gift of
her language.

"Bring him inside," she said. She held up the flap while
the village men deposited the Roman on the pallet re-
served for the ill. She brought her new patient a dipper
of water, which he gulped down eagerly.

"The legion physicians don't know what to do for
him," Bello explained. "He says it is the curse of the
forest folk."

"Mother preserve us," Ledda whispered. Aloud, she
added, "Tell him I'm going to lay hands upon him. He
should lie as still as he can."

Ledda had heard tales that Roman soldiers shied away
from the touches of wisewomen, or any woman at all
save those they took to their beds, but the stranger com-
plied meekly, gratefully. Ledda loosened his armor and
let her palms roam. In less time than it would take to
recite the healer's oath, she had located five areas where
his flesh quivered unnaturally. They were hot, like
wounds. Yet he had no fever. Elsewhere his skin was
cool.

No snakebite marks. No insect stings. No gathered pus
beneath the skin. He had scars here and there, and one
knee was swollen, but the injuries were old and did not
seem related to his main affliction. It was only at the five
mysterious spots that his muscles did not loosen as she
massaged them. On occasion the mere rubbing and ma-
nipulation involved in a Touching was enough to relieve

symptoms. Not this time. She had hoped Bello's reference to the curse might be a figure of speech—every sickness, some said, could be blamed on the fairy folk. But there was no doubt. This was indeed the product of elven magic.

She paused over his left ribs, holding her hands beside one of the loci of his agony. She stared and stared. As the details of her hut dimmed and the aura of the legionnaire revealed itself to her, she perceived a shape woven of the fabric of spirit: A knife.

Its bone hilt ornately carved, its flint blade sharper than steel, the weapon hovered above the ribs, point almost nicking the skin. As if eager to perform for Ledda, it plunged inward. The soldier screamed and clutched his side. Ledda jerked back, losing the Sight.

No visible cut appeared on the man's body. No blood flowed. But Ledda knew he was feeling the blade as if it physically existed.

The soldier gasped. Ledda guessed the phantom flint had withdrawn, leaving the slightly less agonizing discomfort of a fresh wound.

"How often do they stab you?" Ledda asked via Bello.

It varied. At least once a day for each of the five spots, usually just as he was beginning to gain control of the suffering, often when he had just managed to fall asleep. The dark rings beneath the soldier's eyes hinted at many nights when he had not managed to sleep at all.

Ledda rose and paced the room, rubbing her palms and fingers. A Touching often numbed her hands, but never more than this time. "He should stay here until tomorrow," Ledda told the two village men. To the farmer's son she added, "Go fetch my brother from the mill."

The youth departed, nodding respectfully. Ledda uncovered the embers of her cookfire and added two logs. She filled her teakettle from the stream that cut across the corner of her main room—the healer's houses of her people were always built over water—and set it to heat.

Ledda sat beside the pallet again and indicated that Bello resume duty as translator. "Have him tell me his story."

He was Lucius Arpagius, a cavalryman until recently with Agricola, governor of Britain, helping to pacify the Brigantes and other tribes of the north. As a reward for good service and because his knee was healing poorly after a horse had fallen upon him, he had been sent south to areas long since brought under Roman jurisdiction. He was to report to the commander of the garrison at the *civitas* in Canterbury to be assigned to some duty in which his leg would not be an undue handicap.

Well short of his destination, riding alone through the extended twilight of midsummer night, he was drawn from the road by the sound of boisterous laughter and the music of reed pipes and some sort of harp. It seemed to be a mere stone's throw away, but he journeyed nearly half a league, oddly giving no thought to turning back, before he gazed between two remarkably large rowan trees at a fantastical banquet.

A group of some fifty men and women feasted around a sprawling table carved from a fallen oak. The wood was lovingly polished, the pedestals graven with laughing faces and the exposed roots hung with skins of wine. High stanchions held candles that smelled of bayberry and beeswax, but their flames were cold and blue, lacking any of the normal warm golds and oranges. It reminded Lucius of moonlight, somehow captured until the burning wicks released it.

By this spectral light, he saw that these were no ordinary folk. Their faces were abnormally lean and angular, their skin as pale as milk, and their joints seemed to bend in either direction.

That should have been enough to make him turn and speed away. Instead, he dismounted and limped forward, and only the stiffness of his knee reminded him of where he was. He paused at the line between the rowans, thinking that he should tether his horse, then suddenly he was across the threshold.

The diners caught sight of him and waved, holding up strips of venison and portions of bread. They guided him to a seat and placed in his hands an earthenware cup filled with mead. He lifted the fermented honey to his lips, uncertain that he should drink, but then the harpist resumed playing. Without a conscious decision, Lucius poured the brew down his gullet.

A warmth greater than that of alcohol radiated outward from his stomach. His companions laughed at him, jabbering in a lyrical tongue only faintly similar to the Celtic dialects of the great island. They hovered about him, peering at the mole on his cheek—they seemed to have no such blemishes—at the hirsuteness of his arms. They leaned nearer than was polite, yet inexplicably he did not push them back. Simply keeping his balance on his stool seemed labor enough.

His hosts avoided his sword, knife, and anything else on his person made of metal. Their own lack of metalware became blatantly obvious. Their clothes were fastened with laces or cords. Their jewelry consisted of stones or crystals hung on leather thongs. Their weapons were without so much as an inlaid filigree.

The sudden urge to be accommodating overwhelmed him. He stood and removed his weapons, his belt. In due course he was completely naked, yet this did not disturb him, despite the many close examinations of his body. He willingly let himself be led away from the small pile of his possessions.

A figure in long flowing hair and ankle-length robes came forward. Lucius assumed at first glance that it was

one of the women, but the more he looked, the less sure
he was of the person's gender. For that matter, all these
sylvan folk had smooth skin, hairless faces, narrow
limbs—they possessed the androgynousness of children,
though they were adult-sized, with mature calculation in
their eyes.

The elf's face grew larger and larger until it totally
blurred Lucius's vision. Something stirred inside his head,
unleashing a torrent of scenes of his life, his past. He felt
the elf smile. . . .

As the soldier was finishing his account, Ledda rose
and strained the leaves from the mug of tea she had
brewed.

"He cannot remember the visions clearly," Bello re-
layed. "He does not think he fell asleep while he was
there, but the rest of his memory of the night is gone,
save one thing: Every image contained a knife, and after
a time, knives seemed to float about him like gnats. The
next he knew, he woke in the forest with his clothes and
articles beside him. It was morning. No sign remained of
the forest folk or their banquet, though the rowan trees
were only a few paces away."

"How many days had passed?" Ledda asked.

When Bello repeated the question in Latin, the Roman
blinked, clearly impressed. "Three. But he didn't know
that until he found his horse and reached the nearest
village," Bello said. "By then, all he could think about
were the knives."

Lucius added that he had once been stabbed in a battle, and cut on other occasions. He knew what knife
wounds felt like. The first of the elven blades attacked
before he returned to the road. It struck the spot between his ribs, and the shock left him barely able to stay
on his horse. Since then, the torment had not ceased. He
reached an outpost where a physician examined him, but

neither that man nor any other Roman healer could help him. After two months Lucius had leaped at word of a native wisewoman who might know how to lift an elven curse. And here he was.

"And here I am." Ledda pressed his hand soothingly and held the tea to his lips. "Drink this. You will sleep."

Lucius did not even wait for the translation. He gulped, pausing only to draw in enough air to keep the brew from scalding his throat.

The soporific acted quickly, aided by his deep exhaustion. Yet even after he had fallen unconscious, he twitched. Soft moans often escaped his lips.

"Nothing is as cruel as what the forest folk can do," Bello muttered.

Ledda nodded. Lucius had been their plaything, and as the legends said, they relished exploring ways to make people suffer. How different their world must be, and thanks be that it overlapped human Britain in only a few spots, usually only on nights of power, and did so less often as the centuries passed. "Any native would have known not to be abroad on such a night," she said, "and would have recognized the warnings."

The door flap lifted and in stepped Bello's son, followed by Votto, Ledda's brother. The latter nodded at Bello, blinked a few times at the soldier, and began to hone his hatchet to split kindling. Votto had been a half-wit ever since a milk cow had kicked him in the head as a child. He never spoke in sentences. Whenever he was unsettled, he would retreat to some mundane task, such as sharpening his tools or tending the livestock. Ledda could tell he was full of questions about the Roman he could not manage to give form.

"You have fields to tend," Ledda gently reminded her neighbor. "Thank you for your help. Come again in the morning. I will need you to speak with our visitor again."

Bello tipped his head. "At your service. I don't envy you your choices, Ledicca."

"I would not wish them on an enemy," Ledda confirmed. She watched father and son rattle away with their cart, then pensively remained standing beneath the lintel of her home.

Votto's presence soothed her. He might be a poor conversationalist, but he was fiercely loyal and his size intimidated even the boldest of men. Not that the legionnaire was a threat in his condition, but Ledda would have been troubled to be left alone with him. She lived opposite the tilled areas from the rest of her village, first so that her cottage could straddle the creek, but also to be within easy access of the medicinal plants of the wild wood and out where others would not have to breathe the fumes when she made potions. At times such as this, the isolation did not suit her nature.

"Stay with him," Ledda told her brother.

She slipped outside, passed through the rows of herbs she had been tending that day, and followed the stream into the wood. The third tree she passed was her ancestor's rowan, from which she took the rogue sprig of blossoms. The twitter of finches and rustle of shrews among the leaves above and below calmed her with their familiarity, assisting her to meditate.

The Roman presented her with a problem beyond any she had known in her thirty years of life. He had done the right thing to come to her, however. Assuming the mother goddess extended her blessing, she was one of the few people in the province who might be able to help him.

The question was, should she try? He was not of her people. She owed him no debt. If anything, he verged on being an enemy. His nation had subjugated hers.

She pressed her fingers to her temples. How could she even think such thoughts? Her duty was plain. She could not pretend enmity where there was none. The conquest had occurred well before her birth. Even the revolt of Boudicca was no more than a faint childhood memory. A few of the village men had participated, and two had died, but the conflict had never touched Ledda and her family directly. To her, the Roman presence meant no raids by other tribes, new trade goods at market fairs, better roads between the major towns. Lucius was a human being in need. If she did not try to help him, she did not deserve to call herself a healer.

Yet what he asked of her made her legs shake. She inhaled the aroma of the blossoms and dropped the sprig carefully into the pocket of her apron. Unsteady, she bent to a stream and splashed her face. She shivered, but it was not from the chill of the water. To deal with the creatures of faery, she would need to find a new source of courage. She knew the rituals that her task required, but that did not mean that she had ever expected to put them into practice.

She knelt upon the yellow leaves, the first debris of the season, and bowed her head in prayer.

"I will help you," Ledda told the soldier. She said it directly, having been coached by Bello in the Latin. That way the oath became real, less subject to vacillation. Then, via translation, she explained her plan.

Lucius, wincing and breathing thinly, listened with total fidelity and agreed immediately to his part. He pointed to the saddlebags that Bello had delivered with him, and had her remove a small purse.

For the rest of the morning, Ledda ventured from house to house, speaking with neighbors. Some refused her request. Most said yes, and were rewarded with coins from the soldier's purse. When she had as many permissions as she felt she needed, she returned to her cottage, went to the far end of her garden, and dug up patches of soil marked by tiny circles of cobblestones.

To visit elves with any hope of safe passage, she needed an offering. The dirt contained the decomposed remains of human afterbirths. All came from children who had been stillborn—the afterbirths of live, healthy babies were kept by the families to bury near their houses, to add vigor to saplings planted in honor of the newborns. As midwife, one of Ledda's less pleasant duties was to till this soil of sorrow, so that perhaps the gods would not curse the same mother twice.

She sighed as she finished filling a pair of bags, carefully tying the laces. She did not like making use of such sacred material, but it contained the most powerful magic she knew, and the elves craved it—so much so that they were known to steal the babies from women's wombs to have it. They would pay attention to such a bribe.

She wished there were some way to avoid negotiating with the fairy folk. They were not to be trusted. They might blight her for her trouble, or steal her away for a decade, or simply refuse to give her audience. They were capricious and seldom merciful. But visit them she must. They had laid the curse. They alone could remove it.

That afternoon, as Votto gathered provisions and arranged riding mounts for Ledda and himself, the healer sat down and with Bello's help had the legionnaire repeat over and over directions to the site of the elven banquet. Ledda worked the turns and distances into a rhyme to aid her memory.

There was little time for false trails. If the legends were true, the portal between worlds would open next on the autumnal equinox. Getting to the site in time would be a challenge, but she would have to make the attempt. "We can't wait as late as samhain," she explained to Lucius. "I don't know if you will survive the additional weeks." And by samhain, the winter storms would be rolling through, not only making travel difficult, but prompting seasonal illnesses among the villagers which were her duty to treat.

The soldier did not try to refute her assessment. The distant look in his eyes showed that he understood how few reserves he had left. Meekly, he let Bello load him onto the cart. He would stay within the household of Ledda's sister, who would continue to administer herbs to help him sleep and to deaden the pain.

"Try to eat as much as you can," Ledda commanded. He had vomited his porridge that morning.

As the cart bounced over the ruts toward the village, Votto arrived with the horses and provisions. The sun was dipping into the foliage of the oaks to the west, but the pair set out anyway, riding until the dusk grew too deep to continue.

Votto, like most villagers, had never been farther than a day's walk from his birthplace. His gaze was full of wonder at the new hills and dells, at towns twice or thrice the size of the village. He marveled at the width of the first river they came to, and at the ferry barge required to cross it. When learning her healing crafts, Ledda had traveled throughout the south and east of Britain, and still made treks to gather rare plants, but her brother's childlike presence allowed her to see the land in a new, radiant light. That was a much-needed balm, because more often than not she was lost in thought, brooding about her quest.

Once, a pair of men appeared from the woods between villages. One had a scar running down his cheek. Both were muscular and quite dirty. But they took one hard look at Votto's broad shoulders and simply waved and turned back, as if they were respectable locals hunting deer. Ledda rode with eyes in the back of her head the rest of that day, but there were no other incidents. She found herself imagining that they had been ambushed and robbed and that it would be impossible to reach their destination in time—a daydream that held a certain degree of appeal.

But reach it they did, at noon on the day of the equinox. The rowan trees that the soldier had described stood in front of them, separated by perhaps twenty paces. They were indeed peculiarly large. Rowans were typically slender and willowy. Nor did they grow in this region naturally. They could be found only where deliberately planted, as Ledda's great-grandmother's tree had been. These trees were guardians. Not only did they mark the threshold into faery, but legend hinted they might actually prevent the inhabitants from crossing into the world of humankind. Ledda was not sure she believed it, but she saw no point in ignoring the old tales. She carried a staff of rowan, and before nightfall she would don a cloak stained red with the juice of rowan berries. In addition, she wore a necklace of iron links, iron bracelets, iron anklets. Votto was arrayed with his own accoutrements of red cloth and iron.

Such precautions would probably be enough to save Votto from the elven glamour, for he would remain on this side of the gateway. Ledda doubted it would fully protect anyone so foolish as to cross of their own volition.

Nothing else about the spot seemed out of the ordinary, though the overcast sky lent the forest an air of brooding. She ordered her brother to retreat and make camp well out of sight, warning him not to come after her. He was to wait for her until the food supplies ran low, and if she did not return, he was to go home alone. She knew that his concern for her would prompt him to disobey, but he would not think to do so for at least a night or two, and by then he would be safe. At times such as these, his half-wittedness was a comfort.

As the hours dwindled, the creatures of the forest grew unusually silent. An owl, awake far earlier than usual, took up a perch on a high branch and surveyed the area intently. Ledda was able to determine the exact moment of sunset in spite of the cloud blanket: The gap between the guardian trees flickered, and as the gloam deepened, the trees of the true forest grew indistinct. In their place new trees, some of species Ledda did not recognize, gained substance and depth. The foreground was dominated by a banquet table carved of a fallen oak.

True night fell before the elves appeared. One moment they were absent, the next they sat at the table, eating, drinking, and laughing, as if they had been there all along, but invisible to Ledda's eyes.

Deciding that waiting would only make the task more fearsome, Ledda drew in a deep breath and stepped across the threshold.

The fairies turned as one, greeting her boisterously. They held up fruit, bread, venison, cups of mead, skins of wine. She shook her head, and with that refusal she thought she detected glints of anger, of surprise, of intrigue in their glances. They were wondering why she was not yielding to their spell.

All pretense of revelry vanished. Four of the handsomest elves shifted to the forefront, each seeming tall and stately, in clothes finer than any seamstress of the Roman Empire could hope to copy. The four were, in fact, as short as she, and before she could be lured to think otherwise, she cast her gaze downward, denying them the potency of their stares.

"I have a boon to ask," she stated quickly, before they tempted her toward some other course. "I offer this as my token." She set the bags of soil on the table and backed away.

They seemed more interested in her than in the bags, but they remained an arm's length from her, frowning at

her iron ornamentation. She began to worry they could
not understand her language. She did not understand
theirs.

The slimmest elf, oddly the one who seemed most im-
posing, tugged open the sack and idly dipped his fingers
within. He raised a few particles to his nostrils. He smiled
and at a single chirped command, a gnarled, wizened
man leaped from beneath the table and disappeared with
the offering. Ledda gasped—the servant had unquestion-
ably been human; he bore tattoos of the Iceni.

The fairy leader—Ledda thought of him as a lord,
though lady was a possibility—waved his arm toward her,
and though he seemed not to speak, his meaning formed
inside her head: *Ask your boon, and we will consider it.*

She began to shiver. The fact that she heard the
"voice" proved that her body and mind were not im-
mune to intrusion. As if she were Touching, she could
feel the hearts of the fairies, and they were cold. To
make contact with them was like plunging into a pond
at midwinter.

She described the Roman legionnaire and his affliction.
She asked them to remove the curse.

The four elven nobles murmured among themselves.
The leader gave a high, cackling laugh. He gestured
Ledda forward insistently, making it obvious that he
would brook no disobedience. Nervously rubbing her
bracelets, she inched forward until she stood in the center of the quartet. Suddenly they shifted, and she was
face-to-face with an elf with long, flaxen tresses—the
most masculine of all, save for that hair. He reached out,
not quite grasping her head.

Ledda gasped. She was barely aware of the grove, the
banquet, the elves. She was suddenly elsewhere. Around
her were the walls of the mill house near her home. But
not the mill house of the present day. It was the old one,
the one that had burned down a few seasons ago. Naked,

she was sprawled indulgently atop a blanket behind sacks of newly ground flour. Sarro, the miller's son, was lowering his body between her legs, which she was spreading in welcome.

Disoriented, Ledda cried out. To no effect. Her mouth emitted only sighs. Sarro breached her, was engulfed by her wet warmth, and began to rhythmically move his hips.

Ledda knew this scene. She had been fifteen, and Sarro had evolved from childhood companion to likely husband, though they imagined this was a secret known only to them. Two months before they had given each other their virginity. By now they had passed the awkwardness and discomfort of the first few times. Their bodies knew each other. The younger Ledda smiled, limbs taut, wondering how anything could be so good. She was almost afraid of the emotions claiming her—ashamed that her body would rule her faculties so profoundly. She would have done anything for Sarro.

But Sarro died that winter of the pox. That tryst in the mill house had been the pinnacle of their time together. It was the older Ledda's most cherished memory.

And now the elf had taken it, gutted it, laid it out on the table for all to see. As the vision faded, the healer collapsed to the ground, weeping.

The elf stroked its chin, considering her, as if measuring her by the nature of what she considered most private. She realized she was not the first human he had evaluated this way. It was said that his kind were immortal. Lucius had been only the latest victim of dozens, perhaps hundreds.

The process . . . amused them.

A second elf, this one with braided hair and green, catlike eyes, loomed over her. She/he extended hands, and Ledda grew dizzy. Images floated to her mind like the hypnagogic stream seen each night as she drifted to

sleep. The elf murmured, debating which memory to
investigate.

Ledda had no clue how to resist. They would open
her. The iron and the rowan protected her body, but
now that she had let herself venture within their circle,
her inner self was theirs to toy with. She retained control
in only one respect—she was aware of every facet of
the violation, and knew her recollection would not fade,
whereas Lucius, like most humans the fairy folk played
with, had enjoyed the blessing of forgetfulness.

"No," she said abruptly. She could not simply submit.
If her magicks had proven feeble, her great-grandmother
had spoken of one other way to spar with elves, though
it was the least dependable method: she had to appeal
to their principles.

"You dishonor me," she stated forcefully. "I remain
on this spot of my own will." And this, she realized suddenly, was true. If she were willing to forsake the boon,
she could crawl back across the threshold, out of their
reach, leaving them hissing and impotent as they tried to
tug at her metal-laden body. "I brought you tribute. You
will give me what I ask, and leave my soul to me."

The elf with braided hair stepped back, turning to the
leader. They spoke. The other pair of nobles joined in,
provoking a sharp, four-way argument. Finally the leader
raised a hand. He knelt beside Ledda.

Very well, he said. *We will show you what we did.* And
he held up a knife of bone and flint.

Birds, celebrating an unusually warm autumn morning,
twittered in the branches as Ledda staggered through the
trees to Votto's camp. Her brother rushed to her side
and steadied her as she sat on a log.

She had never before realized how intense the colors
of her world were. Especially red, she thought, clasping

at the edges of her cloak. She opened her eyes wider, trying to take the scenery in, claim it.

Votto stared at her with narrowed brows. She patted his hand. "I am well," she said. "Well enough. How long was I gone?"

He held up three fingers.

Three days. Like the soldier. There was still ample food in the saddlebags. The hint of guilt in Votto's posture indicated that he had indeed come looking for her, and was still distressed that he had not found her where she should have been.

"Worry not," she told him. She lifted her fist and opened it, revealing a silvery-gray acorn. "We have only to take this to the soldier, and our task will be done."

Votto grunted, and they headed back to the road.

It seemed every man, woman, and older child of the village was out in the fields as Ledda and her brother returned. The harvest was abundant, making up for the poor crops of the past two years. Ledda acknowledged greetings, but she did not stop to talk.

Her sister greeted her at the door of her home. Ledda ordered a nephew to fetch Bello, then she knelt down beside the pallet where Lucius lay.

He was shaking and sweating. His body was almost skeletal in its gauntness, his face drawn and haggard. The herbal remedies had left his eyes a little less rheumy, but clearly he was wasting away.

She knew what he was experiencing. The elves had shown her with deliberate vividness. Ethereal knives had prodded her, cut her, sliced parts away, until she could not contain it all, could think of nothing but pain. But then it had ended. Lucius, however, had been allowed no escape. The knives had been with him for three months. She was certain that by now, on many levels, he had already gone insane, kept from total dissolution only by a stubborn faith in a cure. As a Roman, perhaps part of him refused to acknowledge the reality of faery and its denizens, nor their power to affect him.

Her arrival helped him rally. He sat up abruptly, calling to her in Latin. She showed him the acorn. He caressed it timidly, obviously unsure exactly how it might help him, but certain that it would. Then he clutched his leg, groaning as a knife pierced him.

Ledda located a small mortar and pestle. She hulled the acorn, placed the meat in the bowl, and began to grind it. Meanwhile, per her instructions, her sister brought fresh water from the well and set it to boil. Bello arrived as Ledda poured the acorn flour onto a cutting board, dribbled hot water, and formed a tiny morsel of dough.

With Bello translating, Ledda explained, "I will cook this into a biscuit. It has not been leached, so it will be bitter."

He nodded.

"He says to hurry," Bello said.

She removed the flatstone from the fire's edge, anointed it with a smear of butter, and placed the disk of dough upon it. The biscuit gradually stiffened and began to steam. She flipped it onto a cloth and held it toward him.

"Eat it as soon as it is cool enough not to burn your tongue."

The soldier blew air to speed the cooling, nibbled first along the edges, then as the steam dissipated, he wolfed down the remainder.

Ledda folded her hands in her lap, and seemed to lapse into meditation.

Suddenly the Roman fell to the floor, spasming. "No!" he cried and burst out with a torrent of Latin.

"He says there is another knife, cutting him behind the knee!" repeated Bello, eyes wide.

"One for the Brigante child he hamstrung because the boy would not lick his saddle clean," she intoned.

Bello hesitated. "Tell him!" Ledda hissed.

Hardly had the farmer done so than the soldier screamed and clutched his face, as if an eye was being gouged out.

"One for the old warrior you blinded when he looked at you defiantly with his one good eye," Ledda said, this time speaking directly at Lucius, who surely understood all too well. He screamed again and cupped his groin.

"And that for the black-haired girl you raped, and for forcing her mother to watch."

The soldier writhed on the floor, tongue rolling over the packed earth, joints straining to their limits, sweat exploding from every pore. Votto, Bello, and the others cringed back. They cast nervous glances at Ledda. Her sister still had hands over her ears, as if she could not believe the words that had come from the throat of her own kin.

Ledda opened her mouth to announce the crimes behind the original five knives, but all at once, the ice inside her broke. She sobbed and lowered her forehead to her palm. "A pox upon all elves!" she choked, shaking with the knowledge of what she had done. The fairies had known she was too compassionate to levy such a sentence of her own will, however much she might agree that the legionnaire deserved it. They had laid a compulsion upon her.

She flung the empty acorn hull into the fire, spitting on the coals. "Send him back to his people," she whimpered. To her relief, her brother and Bello, their faces black with outrage at what she had been forced to endure for so unworthy a person, had already begun to drag the Roman away.

Whimsical were the elves, and seldom merciful. But never would she accuse them of lacking a sense of justice.

A REFUGE OF FIREDRAKES

by Susan Shwartz

Thunder pealed out. Once again the fortress walls of Dinas Emrys crumbled, their foundations cracking apart in the mud.

They may kill us, but they cannot build on our sacred hill! Tangwen thought, with a triumph she was careful not to let show on her downcast face. This was the third time Vortigern's engineers had failed, and his Saxon masters were not pleased at all.

Even the hillside itself shook, just as if some dragon dwelling beneath it shifted and began to wake into rage. Builders, wizards, and warriors cursed. The Queen's women shrieked at each other in Saxon too fast for Tangwen to understand.

For this instant, she was out of their immediate grasp. Seizing the chance, she took to her heels, as fast as she dared on the trembling ground. She had about as much chance of escaping Dinas Emrys and slavery as she had of seeing the Resurrection, but she had to try.

"Wynna!"

The voice that murdered her name pierced even the heavy downpour.

Tangwen glanced over her shoulder, then flinched at the lightning and the heavy roll of thunder, echoing off the peaks of Eryri. Now they looked more like waterfalls than mountains, so hard was the rain, and Dinas Emrys, in the heart of Britain's mountains, looked more like a swamp than a fortress.

Let it suck them all under. That would be freedom of a sort. . . .

"Wynna!"

Tangwen cursed, then breathed a quick Latin prayer for escape. *God, let lightning strike Unferth.* Ill-luck to death-wish a man, but she thought God would understand and His Blessed Mother pity her. Unferth was kin to Hengist and Horsa, and the witch-queen Rowan, who had trapped Vortigern the King and turned him traitor. That alone made him enemy enough. But Unferth had also led the last assault on her family's maenol, the walled stockade that had been her home. And he had caught her as she tried to flee into the hills.

Not all my family. Please, God, let some of them have escaped!

She had tried to die in his filthy clasp and then later, yet she had never succeeded in finding a moment's solitude to try. Until now.

She wriggled through the dense, sodden underbrush. The rain dripped down her neck, and she shivered.

"Wynna!"

Tangwen, she reminded herself. She was *Tangwen*, not Wynna. The Saxon invaders were great name changers. They had changed King to Traitor, Eryri to Snowdon. They had called the British *Wealas*, or foreigners in their own lands. So why shouldn't they change Tangwen to Wynna because it was a sound their rough tongues could say more easily?

Vae victis, which meant "woe to the conquered." Hard to believe she had studied Livy in peace before the Saxons and the Danes and the rest of the pirates had come. She remembered the words of the gentle old priest who had taught her Latin and the history of the British Isles.

"What we need," he had said, "is another Macsen,

come to heal Britain and drive out the heathen. Then Rome will come again."

His blood had stained the hearth before Unferth had dragged her from the wreckage of her home.

Ever since, she had hidden from him as best she could. Many of Queen Rowan's women had called her a fool, told her she was lucky that Unferth would offer a morning gift and honorable marriage, fit recompense for the maidenhead he had stolen from her; but Tangwen had shuddered, remembering her home in flames, her family killed, the way Unferth had laughed.

Who did she think she was to be different? Many women had already taken that way into safety . . . yes, and when Macsen came again, their own blood would spit at them.

If she were caught, the Queen's women, those tyrants with their heavy flails of golden braids, had told her, she might be glad of Unferth's protection. Personally, Tangwen thought she might prefer some of the punishments they'd tried to scare her with. Not even the blood eagle could be worse than having to rejoice that her mother and father were finally out of their pain, or reliving in her nightmares her useless struggles, the painful invasion of her flesh, and the laughter of the man who violated her.

Her breath came fast, and she felt dizzy and sick.

A shout and more lightning sent her crawling farther into the underbrush. Suddenly, the ground was clear. A stubborn briar tugged at the sodden wool of her cloak, and she sprawled into a clearing. One rough shoe went flying, almost into the spring that ran in its bed of red earth through the clearing and around the gently rising mound that dominated the clearing.

She groped with a chilled, bare foot for the lost shoe—

And almost kicked off the other. She knew this place. But she had not known that she was going to seek it, as a fugitive might seek asylum in one of the churches that the Saxons had not yet gutted.

Put off thy shoes from off thy feet, for the place whereon thou standest is holy ground. If Dinas Emrys was Britain's heart, hewn from the flint of Eryri, this clearing had been its soul from heathen times. Before her rose the *gorsedd* where, she had heard, bards sang, Druids had prophesied, and true kings had gone to receive visions.

By the waters of Babylon, we sat, remembering Zion ... the ancient lamentation poured into her mind, and tears poured down her face. Here, for all the lush greens of moss and leaf, cradled in flint cliffs, lay Britain's heart, cleft to the foundations of the rock itself.

She stared into the water. *Not one small vision left for me? Please?* She hardly knew what she was asking. Any visions left her would be of fire and blood. This was foolishness. She had no chance of escape, ill-clad, unsupplied, and unarmed as she was.

"Wynna, you must come quickly!" The voice was too high to be Unferth's. Could Tangwen fight off a healthy Saxon girl? Even Saxon children of ten summers were taller than she.

Something red and golden darted across the swollen water. Let the earth engulf them. Let a dragon come and consume them. There was magic in this hill. Why not a dragon? And why should she not summon it?

She groped for her lost shoe. Pain nipped at her hand, and Tangwen drew a sharp breath in a hiss of pure panic. Please, not a snake! She forced herself to turn to see. *If a serpent bit you, you would swiftly die. And you do not want that, do you?*

Of course, it was no serpent that had stung her; any such creature would be coiled in on itself, safely away from the rain. What glinted on the ground was neither serpent nor pebble, but a flint knife, the rock flaked skillfully away from the core to create a blade that was sharp after—how many years? It might have been chipped before the Flood, even, and concealed until this new Flood washed it up before her.

Or maybe it was not so old. Such blades had been made by the *Picti,* who had withdrawn into the hills when the British came.

Did their survivors rejoice now to see their conquerors overthrown?

The Queen's woman had kept knives from her. Now she had one. She might not have to summon the dragon just to protect herself. But for her people ... to free them if she could, to avenge them if she dared ... here in this sacred clearing, how would one summon the firedrake?

"Tangwen!"

Her name called again. Not "Wynna," this time, but actually a fairly close attempt at "Tangwen." She muttered something she had heard when serving mead to Rowan's kinsmen. In her lost home, no warrior was ever permitted to curse at a female server, much less a daughter of the house. She had flinched, but Rowan had only laughed.

Whoever had sent Aelflaed in search of her had been terribly clever. Tangwen could never outrun the Saxon girl or outfight her. Or maybe Aelflaed had come on her own. Conquered and conqueror could never be friends, but she had to admit that Aelflaed had tried to treat her kindly.

Aelflaed would leave her no time for visions, no time for curses, no time to summon any power that lay in Dinas Emrys.

Quickly, she tucked the ancient, deadly little blade into her gown. She had time enough for that, just as Aelflaed, muttering to herself and breathing in heavy gusts, broke through the underbrush.

"There you are, Tangwen!" She set her sturdy arms on her hips. "Do you *want* us both to get a beating?"

"Why should you get one?" Tangwen asked.

"I came after you without leave," she said. "Look at you. Clothes half ripped off your back, and one shoe lost. You wouldn't last a night in these hills all by yourself. If the wolves didn't get you, the lung rot would."

Kindly meant, if crudely said. Aelflaed started toward her, and the British girl gestured furiously. Here was no place for heavy Saxon trampings and stampings about, for Saxon scoldings and Saxon names. She was surprised when Aelflaed stayed where she was and looked curiously about her.

"Eald enta geweorc," she said. "The old work of giants, like the standing stones. Bad place to freeze to death or drown."

"Better that than Unferth." Tangwen shuddered.

Aelflaed grimaced. "I thought I'd get you back, and then I'd ask my father what we could do about Unferth."

Why "we?" She had asked Aelflaed that just once. Why did she bother to care? *We would live here forever,* the Saxon girl had told her, her broad face somber for once, *and we would be good neighbors.*

It hurt to be grateful to one of the conquering race, but what safety Tangwen had at the half-Saxon court, she owed Aelflaed. She had picked out Tangwen in the crowd of captives and smiled at her, God only knew why. God only knew why, too, Tangwen had let herself ... well, not precisely smile, but respond to that gesture. Whereupon Aelflaed had appealed to her father who had spoken to Rowan. And that discussion had made the Queen decide it would be to her credit if she were served by a Welsh girl of noble breeding.

Aelflaed had told Tangwen that she was not a slave but a hostage. That was, from ancient times—so she said—a rank of honor among the Saxons. When Tangwen had nightmares, Aelflaed had waked her almost gently, and, in an attempt to comfort her, had taught her many of the gloomy Saxon songs. There was one about a woman awaiting her lost mate that always made Aelflaed cry; Tangwen preferred the one about the bard who closed each verse with "That passed; this may, too."

Aelflaed meant to be a friend, but at this moment, Tangwen could have launched herself at her throat. Now she would have to go back, have to lie and smile and obey—and go on dodging Unferth as long as she could.

The Saxon girl came closer to Tangwen, had her by one arm and was shaking her. Tangwen pulled free.

"Please, don't say that you are seeing visions, too!" she demanded. "The hall is buzzing like a hive whacked with a sword. The Queen has slapped three of us already, and King Vortigern shouted at the masons that if they couldn't build a wall that stayed up, he'd send them to the tin mines. And Maugantius—" she spat and made a warding-off sign,—"has been prophesying twenty to the dozen while all his little mages have been scuttling around behind their master."

"Ugh," Tangwen said. Rowan's wizards weren't just pagan; they literally turned her blood cold.

The red and gold streak she had seen in the water in the old shrine flashed across her memory like a comet. "I wish I could summon the dragon."

She was not aware she had spoken that aloud until Aelflaed shook her. "And what good would that do? Maugantius would only wrest it from you. His will is strong and fell, and it is even stronger now. . . ."

The lightning flashed again. For a moment, Aelflaed's pale eyes glinted blue, then hollow with shadow as the lightning faded, like the polished eyesockets of a skull used as a drinking-cup.

"Well, just when Vortigern—" The casual contempt of many Saxons for the traitor who brought them here rang in the girl's voice, "—was threatening his builders, in came Maugantius's slave and said they'd caught the boy without a father and were bringing him here!"

Last time Maugantius had a fit of prophecy, he had raved of a boy without a father. When he had recovered (and was done soiling himself), he had demanded that the king send out watchers to catch the boy and bring him to Dinas Emrys so his blood could be mixed with mortar and the king's fortress would stand. That one had given her the worst nightmare yet.

So many men had been slain in the wars that many boys—and girls, too, like Tangwen herself—didn't have fathers these days. But that wasn't what the wizard meant, and you didn't have to be a pagan to understand. Perhaps his meaning was even more fearsome to Christians. For Maugantius spoke of a child demon-born, perhaps with a demon's powers.

"I knew no one would ever notice if I came after you," Aelflaed rattled on, blind and deaf to Tangwen's shudders of horror.

To Tangwen's absolute horror, she began to cry. Here she was, plotting to summon—oh, heaven or hell only knew what, and Aelflaed was kind to her. How could she bear to see this hillside or even this enemy girl charred to ash?

Aelflaed's blue eyes widened in dismay, and she hugged Tangwen close.

Now would be a time to use the little knife and make her escape, but she knew that only a worse traitor than any Saxon would do that to another girl, and one who had treated her fairly. Doubtless, in time, there would be other such Saxons, and she would never get free, never have her revenge. She sobbed harder.

"Not the wanhope, Wynna," Aelflaed pleaded, losing control of Tangwen's name. "Please, not that."

Wanhope was something akin to despair; and despair

was deadly sin. Her own impulse to comfort Aelflaed,
even to lie, shocked her. Instead, she made herself sneeze
to distract her so she would not ask the surprisingly
shrewd questions she could come up with on occasion or
offer the sympathy that it was so tempting to accept.

"We have to get you back before you catch your
death!" she said, and began to pull her toward the
Queen's bower.

Dripping and miserable, Tangwen stumbled along in
the other girl's wake, scarcely heeding her plots about
the best way to filch a dry gown and cloak.

Tangwen might have been able to talk Aelflaed into
letting her go, but, clearly, the Saxon girl had come to a
decision. That meant Tangwen knew she could never
wrestle free or change her mind. She would have to go
back and see this "boy without a father" who would
probably turn out to be a freak or a fraud, and definitely
some countryman of hers; if things went as badly as
they'd been going for months, she would probably have
to watch one more British man slain before his time.

Wrapped in a borrowed cloak and wearing Aelflaed's
second-best gown, kilted up over her belt because the
skirt was a foot too long for her, Tangwen stood in the
shadows behind Queen Rowan. What a shame they were
not deeper or that the ground would not just shake, but
yawn open and engulf her.

Smoke rose from the firepit in Vortigern's hall, rebuilt
now Saxon-style for his bitch-wife. It clung sullenly in
the dampness to the pillars and dulled the crimson and
gold splendor of arms and the jewels of garnet and gold
that men and women alike had donned, waiting for Maugantius and his twelve wizards to bring the boy without
a father before the King and Queen.

Rowan licked her lips, stained the color of poison berries, like her name, and twitched with chapped hands at

her richly dyed cloak. Behind her, the other women shifted; one laughed too shrilly at a whispered comment, then broke off her laughter a little too fast.

King Vortigern, who should have been a shield to the British, sat on the high seat wearing British plaids and Saxon gold. The heavy torque about his neck looked like a slave's collar, not a king's ornament. The renegade who had been High King shifted uneasily, as if wishing himself sacking a city, studying the ruins of Dinas Emrys' walls, or anyplace but here.

Maugantius, wearing robes stitched with signs that Tangwen did not care to look at, strode forward. Tangwen clasped one hand at her breast, where the flint knife rested. Touching it seemed to calm her. *That passed; this will, too,* she repeated in Saxon. To her surprise, the words reassured her.

"O King," said Maugantius, a Saxon bowing before the British king too deeply for true respect, "you asked what must be done that the walls of this fortress stand. And my brothers and I held council and asked the gods. Thus we were told: 'If the blood of a son who had no father could be had and mixed with the mortar, the work would stand.' And thus you sent throughout the kingdom to find the son who had no father. Behold!"

The wizard clapped bony hands, and one of Hengist's chief thanes—*Unferth, wouldn't you just know it!*—came forward, clearly guarding a minor British chieftain.

"Tell us what you saw," Maugantius commanded, as if the British noble were a slave. He swooped to stand over the shorter, darker man, whose fingers, almost concealed against his side, made a warding-off sign.

"In Caer Myrddin," began the chieftain, "boys were playing ball. Whereupon two of them began to wrangle. 'Be silent,' said one to the other, 'and do not compare yourself to me; for I am noble by my father and mother both, and as for you, you have no father.'"

He fell silent, and Unferth prodded him, grinning.

"Straightaway, your men laid hold upon the boy and brought him to me, with orders to send him and his mother before the king."

Again, Maugantius clapped his hands. His attendant wizards paced in, escorting a woman in nun's garb and a young man.

Aelflaed murmured sorrow. "He's just a boy."

How many men and boys have already died for Britain? Tangwen would have liked to have asked. Starting with her own father and brothers.

Queen Rowan leaned forward, gaudy in her jewels and brightly dyed robes. Her heavy braids fell over her plump shoulders, and Tangwen could see where their gold was tarnishing. It was time to reapply the smelly herbs and dyes. Compared with the dignity of the nun, who had the dark hair and poise of the old British nobility, she looked even cheaper and more awkward than usual.

King Vortigern gestured, and the nun made him her reverence. Traitor though he was, he remained High King of Britain. As if her bow reminded him, his voice rang out clear and royal.

"You are the Lady Niniane?"

The nun inclined her head.

"And—your son?"

Another half-bow. "He is named Myrddin, and he is about to enter holy orders."

Tangwen raised an eyebrow. This Myrddin-without-a-father looked more like a boy than a man of at least fourteen—her own age. And she would have been surprised if he had ever seen the inside of a church. He seemed like some fledgling from the hollow hills, a servant, perhaps, of the pool within the glade here at Dinas Emrys.

And on his brow he bore a pale scar that meant he might even follow Mithras, the ancient patron of Old

Rome's legions, rather than Christ. If so, the warrior's god had been defeated. Defeated long ago: this monk-to-be looked like a clerk and no warrior at all.

Vortigern seemed to miss all of that. But then, he had never been much for noticing people, until he cast eyes on Rowan and she had bespelled him.

Now he summoned up the remnants of his courtesy. "On your honor, lady," he asked the woman who must once have been his loyal subject, "and by your faith, who is the father of your son?"

The woman did not flinch.

"By my faith," she said, her voice carrying into the farthest and smokiest corner of the great hall, "I do not know. I was the only daughter of the king of Dyfed. When still young, I entered the convent at Caer Myrddin. And as I slept among my sisters, in my sleep, I saw a young man who kissed me; but when I awoke, there was no one but my sisters and myself."

Queen Rowan licked her lips, and Tangwen felt herself flush. The nun's smooth face remained pale, chaste now after so many years.

"After this," said the nun, "this boy was born to me. And on my faith in God, more than that has never been between any man and myself."

The High King cleared his throat. "Could this be true?" he asked Maugantius, as if he hated the question.

"Aye," said Maugantius. "For it is known that there are spirits that live between sky and land, able to bring forth live young. This lad, as I suppose, is one such."

"And is there no other way?"

"Not if you want your fortress to stand." Contempt was in the wizard's voice.

"Call the boy before me," the King ordered reluctantly. "Lady," he turned to the Lady Niniane, "I thank you for your obedience. Your son shall be honored as one of my warriors. See that this lady is richly housed," he told the Queen. "Now!"

Rowan gestured, and a woman led the nun away before the King beckoned Myrddin to stand before him.

"Lad," he said, "young Myrddin, you are a clerk and no warrior, yet to defend Britain, it is necessary that you spill your blood. For we have been told," his voice grew thicker, and he gulped at a horn of mead, "that your blood must be mixed with mortar that the stones of Dinas Emrys be strong and Britain be safe."

"Why?" the boy asked. "What makes my blood of use more than other blood?" Oh, he was a cool one. Tangwen could feel Aelflaed's hand grasping her arm, and it was trembling.

"Because of what the Mage Maugantius and his twelve fellows have told me."

"Bring them before me," the boy said, with a gesture more royal that anything that Vortigern could manage. Before the king could do so, or their leader could stop them, the wizards filed toward the throne.

"Why have you told the king that my blood will make the work stand?"

"The rain has made the walls topple."

The boy raised a slender, dark eyebrow. Almost instantly, as Tangwen thought, the darkness in the hall seemed to dissipate and the smoke fly up through the vents in the roof. High overhead, the sun broke through the clouds, and Tangwen sighed as if a great burden had been lifted from her back.

"Let us see these ruins of yours," the boy said. His tone was a little sharp, and more than one mason—and at least two wizards—flinched. Not bothering to wait for his armed escort, he strode from the king's hall as if he knew the way. King, queen, court, and all followed like kitchen staff called for in haste.

*   *   *

Tripping over Aelflaed's gown, Tangwen followed the rest of the court to the ruined walls. Beneath the hill fort of Dinas Emrys itself, the valley spread out, a hundred different greens of field and forest, with the silver-grays of a river running through it and clouds high above.

Tangwen shivered as she saw who followed the boy Myrddin: not the High King's troop, but several of Hengist's most feared men, Unferth among them. Red anger lurked in his eyes, and she shrank back so he would not see her.

But if she were afraid, the boy without a father seemed as calm as if he stood in the midst of friends. He pointed to a pile of rushes below the scaffolding, probably tossed there to provide a dry path.

"What lies beneath those rushes?" he asked Maugantius as he might ask a servant to shift a chest or bring a bench.

The wizard bristled, his beard quivering with outrage that his victim should question him as though he had a perfect right.

You don't know, Tangwen thought. And indeed, Maugantius had to admit that. To her surprise, the boy flicked an amused eyebrow at her.

"Let men dig beneath those rushes!" Myrddin ordered. Even the senior warriors leaped to obey him.

When quantities of earth and mud had been overturned—the Queen had not ceased to complain of stained robes—a large pool of water was revealed. The water quivered, much like the water in the forest shrine to which Tangwen had fled. It was impossible to see what lay beneath its surface.

"What is in that pond?" asked Myrddin.

Again, the wizards had to confess ignorance; and again, Myrddin gave orders—this time that the pond be drained. Anxious to spare themselves a short lifetime

laboring in the tin mines, Vortigern's engineers leaped
to the task.

The labor took hours, yet no one moved—except girls
like Tangwen and Aelflaed who might not stand idle
while their elders hungered and thirsted. Vastly daring,
Tangwen brought ale, apples, and cheese to Myrddin's
mother, who laid a long hand on her brow, blessed her,
and would accept only fruit and water.

"What shall we see when the water is drained?" King
Vortigern asked halfway during the process.

"You shall find in the pool a stone chest. In that chest,
sleep two dragons. When they wake, they fight. It is that
struggle that topples your walls."

Dragons! She had but dreamed of loosing a firedrake,
yet this boy without a father had come as timely if she
had called for a servant to aid her and been obeyed.

A muttering showed that the court listened as if bespelled. Only the masons and builders muttered. They
seemed unable to drain the entire pond.

"So mighty you are, and yet you require my help?"
Myrddin raised his dark brows. He muttered, gestured,
and water ran from the pool in five running streams.

As the pool drained, the stone chest that Myrddin had
spoken of appeared. A muttering went up around the
court.

"Open the chest," said Vortigern, his voice hoarse.

No one moved.

"I said, 'open it!' " he shouted. "You, wizard! Let me
see you open it yourself! Put your back into it."

Tangwen had her hand over her mouth. Aelflaed's
shoulders shook. How could they laugh at a moment
like this?

Easily, since Maugantius was obviously so angry.

She felt eyes on her and pinched Aelflaed's hand.
Rowan's eyes glared at them both. *We're not elf-shot yet,
Wynna,* mouthed the Saxon girl, and her shoulders shook

even more. Rowan's lips tightened, and her glare promised that life would be unlivable for the next long while.

Water still dripped from the rough lid when Maugantius reluctantly approached the stone chest. It had no
lock. Muttering and gesturing in the sign to ward off evil,
he threw open the lid.

Two immense dragons—one red, one white—struggled
out of the chest. They stretched as if they were stiff after
long imprisonment, mantling their wings and belling
shrill warcries. Gouts of smoke belched from their
mighty jaws as they rose into the air and tore at each
other.

There flew the Red Dragon of Britain, Tangwen
thought. How swift it was, how splendid, and how fierce!
Her eyes filled with tears. If the red dragon flew, could
it be long till the Emperor came again? Oh, Aelflaed
had been right. The firedrake was not for the likes of a
girl too silly to preserve freedom and maidenhead to
summon. God was merciful and sent this lad, so soon to
be a monk, to summon it in her place.

But if the red dragon were swift and fierce, the white
firedrake was stubborn and strong, just like the Saxon
invaders. Even as the red dragon rose, the white dragon
darted forward and gashed it with its fangs right where
wing joined shoulder. Tangwen caught her breath in a
gasp that was almost a cry of pain itself. That was *her*
dragon!

Screaming, the red dragon swooped down on the white
and drove it back to the middle of the pool where it lay,
poised as if to spring.

"What does this mean?"

Maugantius had struggled back to his feet. His robe
was smeared with filth, his mouth was open in a square
as he screamed something that might have been curses,
or commands, or a banishing spell, and his hands cast
clawlike shadows on the ground. Compared with the

composure of the boy without a father, he looked more ludicrous than fearsome.

Tangwen shivered.

Myrddin stood like someone staring into the distance, looking for a messenger. He leaned forward, expectant. Then, visibly, he trembled. His eyes widened and rolled up in his head.

Tangwen knew the instant that the vision struck and took possession of him. The boy without a father flung out his hands and wailed. Then he straightened, and nothing remotely human shone from his eyes as he cried out, "Woe to the red dragon, for her danger hastens, and the white dragon shall seize her caves. The white dragon means the Saxons, and the red dragon, which shall be conquered by the white one, signifies the British. For this, shall the mountains be leveled like the valleys, and in the valleys the rivers shall flow like blood."

He sobbed, and tears poured down his face. Then, as the prophecy gripped him yet harder, he screamed like a starving eagle.

All about Tangwen, people swayed, as enthralled as Myrddin himself. She, too, fancied she could see the dire battles between red and white dragons, villages consumed, towns on fire, cities torn apart while eagles screamed from the crags and the creatures of the zodiac itself tumbled from their places and turned to scratch and bite.

It was *her* dragon, too, she thought. Hers and Britain's, come at their moment of greatest need. This boy of no one's blood should not rule it wholly, should not be the only one to speak for it. She clenched her hands in her sleeves, angry that should be the case. The hand that the stone blade had nicked twinged again.

In that moment, only the flint knife she kept concealed in her clothing saved her from being drawn in. As Myrddin's prophecies shrieked to a climax, she pressed her finger once again against the chipped blade. The slight pain brought her back to here and now: where a boy spoke with the tongues of madmen and angels, and where men and women listened in awe and more than a little terror.

From nowhere clouds surged to cover the sky. Once again, the thunder rumbled. And then the lightning leaped from the dark clouds, tearing and searing the sky. With a last scream of "there runs the firedrake!" the boy Myrddin staggered, then steadied himself against the stone chest.

Tangwen sighed. She thought she could see a trail of stars.

"Now, Lord King, you can build your walls!"

He gasped, then fell facedown. His long black hair flowed out into the shallow water.

The dragons, red and white alike, were gone. All that remained was the empty, scorched stone chest.

In that instant, only Queen Rowan moved. She was a witch, Tangwen thought; perhaps only she dared to move. "Pick up the lad before he drowns!" she ordered, and followed that with a rapid stream of commands about baths, warmed furs, and attendants.

"Shall his mother tend him, lady?"

The question came as Tangwen tried to slip back into the shadows.

"I think not," said the queen. She smiled thinly. "I imagine that the boy will sleep now and that the Lady Niniane is eager to return to her convent."

Rowan paced forward to stand over the unconscious Myrddin. Under the mud that streaked him, he was very pale. She reached out to touch his face. Tangwen had seen her reach that way toward a bauble: not care, but pride of possession. Her gaze fell on Tangwen, and the girl realized that none of her small deceptions had escaped the older woman.

"Ice cold," she said. "What better way to warm him than one of his own? You, Wynna. Come here, girl. You are old enough to be properly a woman now, as I have heard. You shall tend him."

And this time, Tangwen could not hide.

Adorned as if for a bridal—if that bridal were in a brothel, not a church!—Tangwen sat beside the sleeping Myrddin. As she knew quite well from having been forced to help bathe him, beneath the mounds of soft furs and woven coverlets, he was bare, and his skin was very pale.

The queen's women had spared her nothing. After tucking the boy without a father into bed, they had laid hands on Tangwen. Laughing mischievously, they had bathed her, too, then stained her lips with berry juice and rubbed sweet oils on her hands and body. The berries tasted bitter, and the smell of the oil threatened to make her sick. She had been silent, frozen during the entire procedure, and that had made the women laugh even louder. *Unferth's hands on her, his body weighing her down, the tearing in her deepest privacy . . .*

This was but a boy, she tried to tell herself.

He is a man! *You saw for yourself; he is no eunuch, but a man; and this is what men do.*

"Why such misery, girl?" Queen Rowan demanded. "If you come away with child, and that child is a son, Maugantius will take him to be a wizard and give you gold. How could you expect better fortune than that?"

"He is one of your own, at least," Aelflaed had whispered, "and quite handsome in his way. They say it helps to drink something. I have left you some wine."

But even Aelflaed's attempt to help had not lifted Tangwen's sick misery. All she could think of was Unferth, reaching for her. Her flesh relived its violation, and she wanted to die.

Reaching into the bosom of her gown—new and garish, like all of Rowan's choices—she fondled the tiny flint knife she had found only that morning. She was glad she had managed to hide it from the queen's women. If the boy woke and proved indeed to be a demon, it would let her escape him.

And if he proved to be merely a boy—what then? She asked herself.

When then, indeed? If Maugantius claimed him, he faced no safe future either. And he was no Christian; he might welcome the release that the blade from the hollow hills could give him.

She pulled the blade out. If Myrddin were a demon, once he waked, she would stand no chance against him.

Best kill him now? she asked herself, staring at the blade. So easy a thing it would be to strike a death-blow. Saxons did it all the time. She hesitated, and she hated herself for her indecision.

"Is that knife for me?" Myrddin's voice was quite steady.

Tangwen jumped as if the blade had been heated in fire. Her hand shook, letting the blade drop onto the furs of his bed. The young wizard made no move to capture it. Instead, he fixed Tangwen with his eyes: wide, the gray of her people, with no hint of evil in them.

"Why are you here?" he asked.

"Why do you think they made me come here? You are their honored guest, and I . . . I am to welcome you."

The blush that spread over Myrddin's pale face surprised them both. "They send me a countrywoman—the Queen's British maid—to warm me?"

She nodded, blushing with shame herself. "Queen Rowan—" she spat out the name, "—is no friend to me."

"Yet sending you here will protect you from what you

hate most," Myrddin told her. If he had raised a hand to pat hers, she would have screamed, snatched the dagger, and tried to strike; but he lay still, and his very defenselessness calmed her.

There would be a feast tonight; that was true. At least, if she were shut up here with a young wizard the entire court feared, Unferth would not dare to seek her out.

She regarded Myrddin with a little less fear. "Is it true what you said at the walls?"

"Lady . . . you have a name?"

"They call me Wynna, but my *name* is Tangwen."

"Lady Tangwen, I don't know what I said. *It*, the power or whatever you call it, comes over me the way inspiration seizes a bard. Things go strange in front of my eyes. All I remember is fear. The King told me, I should die like a warrior, but I . . . I didn't want to." He moistened his lips. "Is there anything to drink?"

"There's wine. Mead, too."

Myrddin shook his head. "No wine. Barley water, if you have it."

Tangwen rose, sniffing at the pitchers. She found barley water, poured it, and held it out to him. He tried to rise, but fell back against the pillows.

"Weak as a kitten," he judged. He licked his lips again, but would not ask, so she held his head to drink. His hair was still damp and very soft.

"Is it true what they say about you?"

"That I see things? Aye. I see them. Like shapes in fire or smoke. Winged things, like souls."

"This time it was dragons," she told him.

"So? The fates of countries, of kings come again—" Myrddin's gray eyes seemed to widen, to fill with smoke, then to clear. Tangwen felt herself drawn to meet them. She saw in them not her own image in cheap finery, but flint, like the knife she had dropped, and buried in the flint, the bright hilt of a Roman sword.

"A blade you bear," he whispered, "yet your power lies not in wielding it, but in holding your hand. . . ."

"Stop that!" she choked.

"Stop what, lady? What did I say? I beg you, tell me!" Myrddin cried, but Tangwen had snatched up the little flint knife and fled. At that moment, she feared this one strange lad worse than Queen Rowan or even an army of Unferths.

How long or where she ran, she never knew. When she finally came to herself, her ribs heaving, her free hand pressed against them as she fought to catch her breath, she found herself halfway down the slope, very near the thicket in which she had tried to hide that morning and found the ancient shrine of her people and the knife she had taken away.

With some vague notion of giving it back, she headed for the *gorsedd*. The moon was full; she would have no trouble finding her path. And she would see the moon twice that night: once in the sky, a second time reflected in the sacred pool.

But the underbrush was trampled now, the privacy of the ancient shrine broken. For a moment, she thought of turning back. She could not bear to see the water fouled, or filth daubed upon the rocks.

Then the air turned strange. Piping seemed to fill the air—high, shrill, and so faint that she could not find its source, in the night sky. A wind rushed by, and she remembered Myrddin's words: the wind was heavy with "winged things, like souls," just as he had said.

She pushed through the broken underbrush and paused outside the clearing. A man knelt before the central mound. Even as she watched, he threw himself upon it. His image, slightly clouded, shimmered in the water, blocking out the roundness of the moon.

"Show me my fate!" King Vortigern commanded air

and earth. Both were silent. Could the king's shoulders be shaking? Could the traitor, the coward, the woman's plaything actually be weeping? Tangwen decided the moonlight was deluding her. She reached for her tiny flint knife. The kiss of its blade would restore her to her right mind. And then ... and then....

She padded closer on slippered feet. A few quick steps, a stealthy blow, and her people—Britain itself—would have vengeance on this traitor. *She* would be the crimson dragon.

And she would be a killer.

Better to be a killer than a victim!

Well, wasn't it?

She hardened her heart and repeated her litany of woes. Vortigern had let in the Saxons. He had married a heathen witch. He had allowed her home, her family to be destroyed.

Sensing her presence, the king turned and slowly rose to his knees.

"I would have killed the boy," he said. "So it is just. And it is a better fate than living as I am, a king whom Saxon and Briton alike despise. Go ahead."

He stripped off the heavy gold torque at his throat and raised his chin.

Was he taunting her? She was just a girl, and no warrior, even though the hero tales of their people sang of women as skilled in arms as any man.

No. The High King of Britain knelt before her as if ready to be sacrificed. Such things had happened before in this place, she suddenly knew, long before the coming of Christ. In the bad times, it was necessary that the king die for his people. If the times called for the death of a good king, how much more would they cry out to heaven for the death of a bad one?

Her hand fell. Sacrifices had been done in days gone

by, but never by the likes of her. *Judith,* she told herself.
But she was no Judith.

"I told you, go ahead!" The king's eyes held torment.
Death for him would indeed be a mercy, but he could
not command her in this.

What had Myrddin said? Her power lay in not
striking?

Coward! she taunted herself, trying to summon up rage
enough to strike. But the rage was gone, replaced by a
coolness of judgment akin to Myrddin's own.

Perhaps the worst vengeance she could take from this
king who had betrayed her and her people was not to
slay him. He knew he had betrayed his people. He knew
that, whatever goals he had once held for Britain, he had
thrown them away. And she was condemning him to life.

"I will not kill you," she said. "Traitor or not, you are
still the king."

Replacing her knife in the bosom of her gown, she
turned her back on him and walked numbly back toward
the hall. Common sense told her that she was just a girl;
it was not her place to determine the fates of kings. But
still the piping thrummed in the sky and grew louder as
she neared the hall. Even the shouts of raucous song and
laughter from within could not drown out its batlike
music. The old priest who had died with her home and
taught her that the Sight was a snare and a delusion; but
she had seen Myrddin's eyes tonight, and she had heard
the piping. The fates walked tonight, and she feared they
walked at her side.

"Wynna! Lonely, little one?" Something else leaped
to her side and snatched her off her feet.

Unferth! He smelled of sweat, of the beer he had
swilled, and the mutton he had devoured all night. And,
his belly sated, his mind turned now to other pleasures.

She tried to scream, but he clapped one huge palm
over her mouth—as he had the night her family died.

She kicked and twisted, trying to reach her flint dagger within her gown.

He followed her gesture and laughed. "Let me help you, sweetheart!"

He ripped at the flimsy cloth. It tore almost to Tangwen's waist. The flint knife went flying into the night shadows. Horror made her strong, and she pulled free, to scream once and with all her heart.

"Leave her alone," ordered a voice from the darkness.

"Who's to make me?" Unferth demanded hoarsely. He was stalking Tangwen, enjoying the game, which, as he was perfectly assured, could only end one way.

"I will." It was the King. Vortigern emerged from the shadows. "Leave the girl alone."

Unferth laughed and spat. "You? A puppet king, tied to your queen's skirts! You cowardly Welsh dog!"

"Get back, child," Vortigern said. Tangwen began to back up. But Unferth kicked at her, and she went sprawling toward the king. In that moment, Unferth leaped. He had the knife with which he had cut his meat at the feast, and it glistened in the moonlight as he swept it at the King.

Vortigern drew his belt knife also, and Tangwen tried desperately to roll out of the way.

She gasped as her hand hit something sharp—once again, it was her flint blade! She snatched it up as the two men hurled themselves at each other. They clung and grappled. Unferth, younger and bigger, soon had the advantage. His big hand grasped King Vortigern's wrist and squeezed till his knife dropped onto the churned-up earth. The king's left hand struggled to push Unferth's chin back until his neck cracked.

The attempt was useless. Unferth laughed, looking into Vortigern's eyes as he savored the moment before he delivered the final blow.

"Run!" gasped the king, but Tangwen held her

ground. She might run now, but she could not run forever. Sooner or later, Unferth would catch her. Unless
he were stopped.

"Take this, lord!" She leaped forward and pushed the
knife into the king's left hand.

His fingers closed around it, drove it with desperate
force into the big Saxon's back. Blood sprayed out, almost on Tangwen's ragged gown, and she jumped back.
Vortigern shoved himself free of the dead man and rose
to his feet.

He pulled the knife free and cleaned it in the earth,
then held it out to Tangwen.

"Your hand is bleeding, child," he said.

She let it drip an instant longer upon the earth. Let
this place have its sacrifices, innocent and guilty alike.
Then she took her knife back.

"I believe there is someplace else you should be," he
remarked. "I suggest you go there—and speedily. I could
defend you against that filth ... but against the queen
when she has blood in her eye ..." he broke off. "So,
let us say I have not seen you, this night. And you have
not seen me. My fire may be put out, but I have saved
one brand from the burning. May heaven lay that to
my account."

"May it do so indeed. I shall tell no one. But I tell
you. I saw a king tonight." In voice and an even deeper
bow, Tangwen gave him the tribute he had earned.

"Did you, indeed?" Vortigern laughed, a sad, bitter
sound. "Then it must have been the moonlight, and not
poor Vortigern. Good night, lady. Remember me with
charity in your prayers."

He walked into the hall before she could reply and
left her standing over the body of her enemy. It would
be easy enough to explain his death; men had died in
drunken brawls before this, and Unferth was known to
like a quarrel.

A cloud blew before the moon. The light in the water died, and the piping in the night air died away. The silence drew itself out.

Before they find you.

Tangwen fled back to the known terrors of Myrddin's room.

Somehow, Myrddin had managed to sit up and even dress himself. A goblet cupped between his palms, he seemed to be waiting for her. Those bafflingly clear gray eyes went straight to her bleeding hand.

"That will fester if you got grit in it." No mention of her torn clothing, of the way it revealed her body. Wedded to power, he seemed indifferent to the flesh. "I'll need wine to clean this," he ordered.

She brought the wine and braced herself. When he judged her to be as steady as she might, he grasped her hand and poured the wine over it. She gasped as the wine cleansed the cut and dripped into the goblet.

She stared into its troubled surface. "We are close now," Myrddin whispered. "And you have seen visions. Tell me what you see."

Patterns formed and reformed in the cup. A man with bright hair, bringing brighter fire and sword to slay the king who had saved her; a ring of standing stones; Myrddin himself, much older, kneeling before a king whose face she had never seen, and finally . .

"My sister! And my younger brother." They were her kin, all right, older, paler, likely to glance over their shoulders in remembrance of old fears. Her older sister went girded with a sword. Her younger brother walked with a limp that he had never had before. But they were family; and they had found a new home, its timbers still rough-hewn; a life.

The image of her life to come blurred. Blood and wine dripped from her hand into the goblet, and more patterns and faces formed within it—a hawk tethered, an aging king who cried for help, a man trapped in the hollow hills, a man with the face and eyes of . . .

Myrddin's hand jerked convulsively, causing the goblet to spill. His face was bleak.

"You saw it, too," he stated. They had been so close in that moment that Tangwen had seen his fate as well as hers—and hers was far, far kinder.

Since losing her home, Tangwen had refused to weep before anyone, but now she cried bitterly. Not just for the joy of knowing that people she had mourned as dead lived and would welcome her, but for the king who had saved her, yet must die, and for the young man beside her who dreaded the trap that awaited him, yet must not turn aside.

He did not turn aside from Tangwen either, but bandaged her hand with a physician's skill. Then he held her as she wept herself out, and they fell asleep on the one bed, goblet and flint blade between them.

When she woke, the boy without a father was watching her. She was almost sorry . . . no, best not think that. He had powers—who knew if he could read her thoughts?

He smiled, and her cheeks flared the crimson of the firedrake.

"I have dreamed true," Myrddin said without other greeting. "The king will free me, and the wizards will not stand in my way. So I have been wondering what you should do."

She shook her head. "We know what I will do," she reminded him. "I shall find my family, and we shall found a great house."

"And for now?" he asked. "Do you recall, my mother blessed you? Would you go to her? King Vortigern favors you and would release you to such service."

Then knowledge of what she must do before her true

future began came to her, as surely as if she, and not Myrddin, were the prophet.

"Your king will come," she said. "And I know now, I will live to see him. I shall wait here, for it is truly said that they also serve who only stand and wait. Vortigern called me a brand saved from the burning. It may be I can pull other such brands from the flames to come."

She thought of Aelflaed, perhaps her father, and those others who had shown her kindness—British folk, yes, and those Saxons who had come to live, not loot, in Britain. *We would be good neighbors,* Aelflaed had told her. Possibly, they would.

"But will I see you again?" she asked.

The young wizard's face went somber. "In every creature that has wings." He took her wounded hand and kissed it. In that moment he was all man, not mage.

"But it is a kingdom I must found, not a family alone. Seeing you, I could wish it otherwise."

"I suppose you could not change us into hawks and let us fly away, could you?"

Sadly, he shook his head. They both smiled.

"Then accept this in remembrance." She handed him the flint blade, then turned away to hide her tears. To think that once she planned to strike him with it! The idea made her smile, and that was good; she wanted him to remember her smiling as they said farewell.

Myrddin rose and reached for his cloak. Soon they would come for him, and he would go—to whatever glory and whatever harder fate awaited him. As he fastened the brooch—a bronze dragon, Tangwen noticed—at his throat, a knock came at the door.

He bent and laid his hands against her face. The touch made her think of cool water, a spring breeze, leaves brushed with rain. It was a man's touch, yet she did not flinch from it. Not all men were Unferth, she knew that now. Some were Myrddin. Some were Aelflaed's father.

And some were even like Vortigern, God forgive him more than he deserved.

"What I can, I give you," he told her. "Tangwen, who was Wynna, you shall live; you shall thrive; and you and your daughter shall serve my king. She will be as wise as you and even more brave. Take still another name for yourself and bestow it upon her when you first hold her in your arms."

He bent and kissed her brow.

"Be Linnet hereafter," he breathed. "Fly free and rejoice. When you meet my king, speak well of me. And may the gods reckon it to my account."

The door swung wide. Guards waited to lead Myrddin from his room. She pulled her gown together as best she could: it was not in her clothes that she kept her dignity, in any case, but in her spirit. She walked at Myrddin's side into the hall.

Vortigern the King nodded. In another man, it might have been a wink.

Demurely, she bowed to Rowan, turning a bland face to her avid gaze, then going to her place among the Saxon Queen's other maids. It was only for a time, she knew that now.

Light poured down, and her eyes welled up with tears. When the dazzling subsided, the boy without a father had gone. Smiling at Aelflaed, Tangwen—no, Linnet—set about her tasks.

When the red dragon returned, he must not find her idle.

APPRECIATION

by Charles de Lint

I have a warm spot in my heart for Marion—not just because of the many fine novels and stories of hers I've enjoyed over the years, though Lord knows, that would be reason enough. When I think of the hours of pleasure I've had from books such as *The Mists of Avalon, The House Between Worlds,* and, of course, the Darkover series, I can only be grateful that she decided to take pen in hand and tell these stories to us instead of becoming, say, a nuclear physicist.

But the books aside, Marion was also very supportive to me when I was beginning my career, finding homes for some of my earlier stories in her anthologies and always ready to offer a bit of constructive criticism to make those same stories read so much better. That kind of support is invaluable to a beginning writer, and now that I've been writing full-time for over a decade myself, I can only marvel at how she found the time to help me and so many others over the years. Whatever Marion herself got out of the field, she's repaid that debt many times over by now.

I'm not sure that my own work has been influenced by Marion's (except, of course, in that way that, through the creative process, everything we experience comes out again in one form or another), but there was one concept of hers that I've always delighted in: the idea of a series being based on the background of the stories, rather than on continuing characters. One gets to enjoy the familiarity of the setting, and also knows something of its overall history—sufficient touchstones in a field that increasingly needs trilogies, series, *et al,* for marketing purposes—but the stories can still deal with individual characters. Because these characters don't need to carry on from book to book, anything can happen to them. They can be changed so much as to remain unrecognizable by the end of the story. In short, their lives are like those of real people, instead of being dictated by the marketplace.

The idea of a series being based on a continuing background is a wonderful conceit and while it might not have been original to Marion, I first ran across it in her work and still feel today that there are few who have done a better job of it than she.

Here's to many more stories from her, be they set on Darkover or wherever she cares to turn her discerning artist's eye.

THE HAG

by Lawrence Schimel

The witch's fork fell to the floor during dinner.

"Man coming," Avery told her.

The witch did not doubt her familiar. He had always been better than she at reading omens.

"I wonder what he wants," she said, wiping the fork against her skirt and knowing Avery would know. She stared at the cat, who would not open his yellow eyes to look at her. His tail swished back and forth over the edge of the table.

"Love potion. It fell facing East."

Instinctively, the witch looked to the window, where she could see the forest to the East of her cottage. She wondered if he would be coming from that direction, a traveler. She would ask him . . . But, no, he would likely be just another townsperson from the South. She almost asked Avery, but held her tongue. The cat silently swished his tail and did not open his eyes.

After dinner, the witch carefully arranged her cottage while waiting for the stranger to arrive. Presentation was vital. She placed objects in front of the hearth so they cast shadows just so across the room. The phantom shapes flickered as the flames licked the wood, as if the shadows were alive.

"He's here," Avery said, not lifting his head from the table, where he lay on his back.

The witch cast a nervous glance about the cottage to

make sure everything was in place. She hated surprises. She would have liked an extra few minutes to prepare herself for the encounter, but hurried to the door. Avery's hearing was far superior to her own, but even she could soon discern the footsteps on the path to her door. They stopped. The stranger paused to steel his courage, and just as he raised his arm and was about to knock, the witch flung open the door and cried, "Come in, come in. I've been expecting you." She turned away and left him to follow her into her intentionally-darkened abode. In her mind, she examined his image, she'd been expecting someone larger, she realized. No, not really larger, but older. She had been expecting Trent, is all. But Trent would never come back to her. Not now. Not after she . . .

She put him out of her mind and turned to the boy who had come to her for help. "Now, for a love potion, you'll need to bring me some of her personal effects." He can't be more than fifteen summers, the witch thought. Younger than usually dared come to her for this sort of spell. "And they won't all be easy to come by, I warn you. I'll need a lock of her hair, which should be little problem to obtain. But I'll also need her blood, and not just any blood, but the blood from her menses. You'll have to find a way of getting some. It doesn't matter if it's dried, if you can get ahold of her rags, so long as there's enough of it. There's just no making a love potion without it. And I'll need—" The witch stopped. The boy had not been looking at her, and he seemed . . . not exactly distraught, but something similar perhaps. She was used to people being fearful when they came to her, but this was different. "What *is* the matter?" she asked impatiently, for she had an image to maintain and she felt herself going soft around this boy for some reason, as if her desiring Trent had become displaced as concern for this boy. "You did come here for a love potion, did you not?" Could Avery have been wrong? she wondered. He was so good at reading omens, but there was a first time for everything.

"It's not for a girl," the boy said, quiet but firm.

The witch laughed. She tried so hard to intimidate her customers by knowing beforehand their desires. Their fear made them obedient and generous and kept her from worrying overmuch that she'd awaken one night to her cottage being burned by ignorant peasantfolk. But this time her assumptions had gotten the better of her.

"Can you make me one?"

The boy was so earnest, the witch felt her heart going out to him. I'm definitely getting too old for this job, she thought to herself. Or perhaps she had simply been living alone for too many years. Since Trent left her . . .

"Yes, I can. It'll cost more, though, since I'll need to do extra research. I don't get much call for those, you understand."

The boy nodded. "I am willing to work for as long as is necessary to pay for it."

The witch regarded him again, and it almost took effort to not allow her surprise to show. Why did she keep underestimating him? He had no money, which should have been apparent. He was obviously a farmboy with that sun-dyed skin, his cornsilk hair, and bright blue eyes. He was still young, but already the muscles of his work were beginning to show on his light frame. She had bartered before, but usually with produce or livestock or objects, not labor. But she liked him, instinctively, and she was impressed with his courage and determination. It had been many years since she'd had an apprentice to help about the place.

"I'll expect you tomorrow at sundown, then, and every evening until I've decided you've paid the debt."

The boy looked at the witch for a long moment, not

frightened, but not cocky, not bravado, either. Judging, perhaps. At last, he nodded and turned.

The witch smiled after he had gone. She imagined the boy would be less taciturn as he got to know her better. It would be nice, she thought, to have someone other than Avery to talk to.

"You're in a fine mood today," Avery complained.

The witch considered the cat's comment for a moment and realized she was anxious about the boy's return. She bit back a retort to Avery and busied herself about the cottage, creating small messes for the boy to clean and repair.

"Why bother? There's work enough to be done as it is."

The witch ignored the cat, as the cat so often ignored her. She wanted the boy to start off on the right foot, without being lazy. She couldn't go about teaching him anything if he weren't willing to devote himself. And she also had an image to maintain; she didn't want him telling stories back in town about her personal life and effects.

"You understand," she told the boy, when he'd arrived at the cottage exactly at sunset, "that everything that goes on in this house is not to be spoken of—to anyone. Not your parents, not your friends. Not even," she said with a smile, "your prospective boyfriend." He turned scarlet, even his neck flushing low into his tunic.

She did not want to breed a too-easy familiarity too soon, and thus teased him mercilessly, and was bossy. She was testing him, measuring his capacity to think and to learn—and to obey, for in dealing with magic, it would at times be vital that he follow her orders unquestioningly, despite the rational seeming of the situation, lest a spell go awry and destroy them both. Faith was often half the battle. Especially in the case of a love potion.

It was more simple to create the desired aphrodisiac than she had let on, but the witch had been so taken aback by the request, or rather by her having been wrong in her assumptions, that she continued in her elaborate pretense and delayed giving the boy the potion, which she'd already completed, assigning him various quests to obtain hard-to-find materials she needed for other projects, or those which would throw him into contact with his intended love, to begin establishing a connection between them.

The boy performed each request without complaint. Every evening, just before sundown, he arrived at the cottage, presaged the first week by a warning comment from Avery, but soon even the cat came to accept his presence as unquestioned and the boy set to work on one task or another before the witch had noticed his presence.

She asked him questions often, about life in the village, and especially about his boyfriend. His replies were mostly a terse yes or no. Not out of fear of her, it seemed, but because he always spoke simply and directly, and chose not to speak at all when he did not have anything to say. His answers soon became more elaborate as the romance blossomed:

"He kissed me today."

"We held hands last night, when I left here, and sat talking beneath the elm at the crossroads and watched the stars."

But he never volunteered this information without first being asked. He seemed too shy, too bashful, even though the witch thought he felt comfortable around her and in the cottage. He was thoughtful and kind, and often took care of things she had not asked him to, simply because he had noticed they needed repair: bringing water from the river for her; mending the broken section of the fence that surrounded her cottage; transplanting the windowsill herbs.

The witch quite enjoyed his company, and the fact of having company about the cottage once again, but she nonetheless stopped keeping him so late so that he would have time to spend with his boyfriend. That was, after all, the entire purpose behind his presence in her life, what he had come to her for. It seemed wrong, somehow, to deny it to him now, though she would be within her rights to exact such payment, should she so choose. The witch hardly regarded his presence about the cottage as payment any longer; he was, she realized with some alarm, a friend. She had not opened herself up, emotionally, to another person until Trent had been so cruel to her . . . Until she had chased Trent away . . . She felt vulnerable.

The witch resolved to be merciless, to hold the boy at arm's length with taunts and work as she would any apprentice. But when she tried, she found that she could not do it, and instead listened eagerly to the boy's tale of last night's romancing. The two boys were now inseparable when not working, and very much in love, it seemed. The witch was quite pleased with her handiwork. And her boy was so happy she couldn't bear to shatter that joy and innocence by suddenly holding him at arm's length, and for no reason at all. She intensely missed Trent each time the boy spoke of his blossoming love affair, but she was also happy for the boy, and took consolation in that. Definitely too old for this job, the witch told herself, as all her suppressed maternal feelings exploded to the surface.

And as all mothers must, there comes a time when she must push her young out of the nest. "You're welcome to continue to come to the cottage. I am, in fact, eager for you to continue to do so. But if you come, it must be of your own free will. You have now long fulfilled your obligation for the potion."

The boy looked thoughtful, and the witch felt her stomach churning with emotions. She knew, instinctively, that he would now leave her, and though she had meant to push him from the nest, she had never really expected him to fly away from her.

The boy spoke slowly and carefully, and managed to look at her the entire time. "Thank you for the offer. However, we will now be moving to the West, where my love has an estate that his father gifted him. We plan to live there, where we hope to be free of the prejudices we have found in town, where people do not acknowledge our love."

The witch felt betrayed. After all that she had done for him, grooming him to be her apprentice and learn the secrets of magic she could unlock for him, and he would leave her now. She was glad that she had not had children of her own flesh and blood. She imagined it must be even more painful to bear when it was time for them to leave the nest.

The witch felt herself pulling back into a tight emotional knot from which she resolved never again to leave. One must open oneself to the risk of pain in order to feel happiness, she knew—and she had been happier these past few months since he began coming to the cottage, happier than she had felt in many years—but it was hard to not instinctively lash out at the boy, for being, unwittingly, the cause of her pain and for not acting in the fashion she had assumed he would. But, then, when had this boy ever acted as she assumed he would?

"Well, I'm glad to hear that my potion was so successful and that he is so very much in love with you."

The boy looked away and did not say anything.

"It would be appropriate to say thank you at this point."

"I ... Um ..."

"Whatever it is, you can tell me. You do know that, don't you?"

He gulped in a deep breath and said, "I never gave him the love potion, I dropped it before I had a chance to use it." He blushed, his neck and face turning red in his embarrassment.

A hundred thoughts and emotions crowded the witch's mind and heart. She ignored them and tried to think rationally. "If you didn't use the potion, then why did you come work for me all this time?"

"You had performed your half of the bargain, and I felt it was only fair that I uphold my end of our arrangement, even though I did not, through my own fault, get to use what I had bought."

"And you never told me that he fell in love with you on his own!"

"You never asked. And I didn't know how to tell you, without you being angry, since you'd said it was so difficult to prepare the potion and I'd wasted it. You'd always assumed he fell in love with me because of your potion, and it was easiest not to correct you." He looked at the floor for a moment, then back up at the witch. "But, in a way, I'm glad," he said at last. "That I didn't use the potion, I mean. This way, he fell in love with me because of who I am. He wasn't coerced into it by a magic spell. I know that he truly loves me."

The witch was intensely jealous, constantly comparing this boy's success to her own aborted love affair; how, no matter whatever happened, everything seemed to fall into place for him.

No, not everything. They would face prejudice and hate and misunderstanding for the rest of their lives, similar prejudices to those she had experienced, being feared and misunderstood. Even Trent, she admitted to herself for the first time, even Trent had not understood or trusted her, and she had never allowed herself to earn his trust. This pair seemed perfectly suited to each other, and she was glad that they had found each other to cling to, to face the rest of the world.

"Very well, then," she told the boy, letting him go because she knew she must. "You must follow your own destiny. I would ask one request of you, though: I would like to meet him, before you go." See this boy who is stealing you away from me, she left unsaid. She forced a smile, and the boy smiled back at her and nodded, and in that moment the witch knew that there had never been room in this boy's heart for anyone but his love, certainly not an old witch who had chased away everyone she had ever loved.

SALVE, REGINA

by Melanie Rawn

Her bones were numb with kneeling on cold stone. On the cobbled floor beside the beds of her fevered children; on the broken pebbles beside the graves of her parents and her sister and her sister's sons and her friends and her own dear husband; on the rough flags of the Church, before the altar and the candles—she knelt and tended and wept and prayed all this long winter until her bones were numb.

The priest stood upright beside the deathbeds, beside the graves, before the altar, intoning the sacred incomprehensible words of the Faith. He called to Christ for surcease of famine and disease, for deliverance from poisoned water and dying cattle and withered soil. He stood upright amid the Holy Relics and the Holy Water, the candles, and the chalice her own dear husband had fashioned with worshiping hands and Monseigneur le Baron's gift of silver.

Excepting the priest's, all heads in the village bowed heavy with repentance for sins committed and sins imagined and sins unknown. The miller's wife flogged herself bloody; she died four days later, so it was obvious she had not repented enough. The baker's weakling newborn daughter did not cry out when Holy Water drenched her brow; she died the next morning, so it was obvious that her silence meant the Devil had not flown out of her at Baptism. All that winter there were ashes and offerings,

vows and Masses. The dying confessed, were shriven,
tasted Wine and Wafer one last time. The living begged
God the Father and Christ the Son to save them, have
pity, reveal to them their sins so that they might mend
their ways so the horror would cease.

The horror continued.

Worse than cold and hunger, worse even than her husband's death, her children did not know her. Their small
bodies burned with Hell's own fires (and why, for surely
such little ones had no sins upon their sweet young
souls). Her own body was numb, and her heart and mind
as well, the endless horror burning away all that she was.

Only last summer she had been plump and pretty, her
husband the envy of the village for her pink cheeks and
sunlight hair and bright laughter. Only last summer she
had quickened with her sixth child that this winter had
been born too soon and lived too briefly even to be
baptized. Now she was gaunt and hollow, gray and
empty. There would be no more children, and the five
that were left her would soon be no more if she could
not give them fresh water and nourishing food and certain cure for the fever.

She knew no medicine. There was no food. The water
in the village well was fouled, and she dared not use it
even to soothe the heat from her children's skin, for who
knew but that it did not soak fever demons into their
bodies? But water there must be—somewhere, somewhere, clean and pure. Water obsessed her. She remembered its coolness that slaked thirst and washed small
hands and faces clean for Sunday Mass. She remembered
how her children waved pink fists when Holy Water
drenched their brows and consecrated them to Christ
(but for that last baby, born too soon, whose soul would
forever wander—and why, for surely there could be no
sin on a newborn child).

She had no medicine and no food—but surely some-where, somewhere, there must be water.

She bade her husband's sister, whose husband the cob-bler was dead, to come sit with the children while she was gone, for the promise of sweet water to drink when she returned. She took up her cloak and two wooden buckets with fraying rope handles, and walked. Past the village well, past the Church, past the graveyard, past the dying apple orchard and the unplowed fields. She felt her cold numb bones come back to aching life, but when her heart and her mind threatened to awaken like her body, she said the word *Water* over and over and over again, a talisman like a Holy Relic against fear and thought and pain.

Water, water, water.

And then, deep in the forest, she could smell it. Not trapped in stone, like the water in the village well, or plate-smooth like the water in the font, but wild and free and swift-running over rock and moss.

Water.

She was deep in the forest, and did she allow herself to think, she would know she was hopelessly lost. Did she allow herself to feel, she would be terrified. But she smelled water, and walked deeper into the forest, where no daughter of the True Faith should ever go alone, for within lurked forbidden caves and mysterious groves and strange standing stones no man could pull down, stones that at each turning of the year were said to rise up and dance by white wicked moonlight.

And then she heard water, its soft laughter so like her children's laughter of only last summer that she cried out and ran. No root or vine or fallen log tripped her on her way, no bush or bramble or branch waylaid her. She came to a broad stream of clear, laughing water. Soft moss cushioned its banks like the fat pillows on Madame la Baronne's chair. Bright flowers nodded above its rip-

ples like Madame's daughters in their lovely gowns. Old
oaks and graceful willows whispered just like Madame's
ladies gossiping around the great hearth that always
blazed with fire. She had seen these splendid things, for
she had been in Madame's service before her marriage.
But all the comforts and colors of the distant Chateâu
were as nothing to the sumptuous miracle of water.

The moss gave gently beneath her aching bones as she
fell on her knees to drink. *Water, fresh water, such as she
had not tasted in months—* She scooped handful after
handful into her mouth, over her face, tore off her dirty
scarf and cap and unpinned her hair to rinse the winter's
sickness and grief away.

When her emptiness was filled and her hair spread wet
and clean down her back, she lifted her eyes to the white-
gold sunlight and murmured a prayer of thanksgiving—
not to God the Father or Christ the Son, but to the
Blessed Mother whose compassion was surely responsible for this miracle of water.

And a woman's voice answered her.

"You are most welcome, daughter."

The woman's voice was low and gentle and warm, like
a breeze returned from last summer. She turned, still on
her knees, to behold a woman standing beside an ancient
oak. Neither young nor old, dark nor fair, smiling nor
solemn—and yet all these things at the same time. Her
beauty was of face and form, but also of spirit that
gleamed in her eyes that were all the colors of the forest:
earth-brown, willow-green, sun-gold. She wore simple
robes of white, gathered at waist and shoulder. Around
her throat coiled a necklace of gold, and at her wrists
wrapped matching bracelets.

All the numbness and all the pain were gone. Covering
her face with her hands, she bowed low to the Blessed
Mother.

"What is your name, my dear?"

For all the water, her mouth was suddenly parched dry. She swallowed hard, bit her lips, and with her face still hidden in her hands she stammered, "Berthilde, Lady."

"Ah! Bright One—doubtless for your lovely golden hair. This is one of my Names, also." There was a smile in the warm soft voice. "I have so many!"

The words tumbled from Berthilde's lips in spontaneous joy, for here was the Lady for whom they were meant: "Queen of Heaven, Mother of God, Mystic Rose, Seat of Wisdom, Blessed Virgin, Lady of Light, Health of the Sick—" She caught her breath and dared peek from between her fingers. She *was* smiling now, with great sweetness and even a little humor.

"Lady of the Mountains, the Beasts, the Forest, the Lake," she said, nodding. "Quite a list! Add to these the Names Gaia, Isis, Hera, Ashtoreth, Brigid, Inanna, Britomartis, Car, and a thousand others that would mean even less to you, Bright One."

Her hands fell shaking to her knees and suddenly she was afraid. "Lady," she whispered, "never have I heard such sounds, not even when the priest speaks the Holy Mass."

"They are Names only. Those who know me know who I am." Pausing, she shook her head. "The priest does not."

"But—surely he serves you!"

"Not he. Few in this land serve me now."

Berthilde hung her head with shame. "We have sinned, Lady, I know this. Else why would there be this blight upon our land, and this sickness that kills even the strongest among us? We are unworthy of the sacrifice made by your Holy Son—we have not followed God's Laws—"

"On the contrary," the Lady replied, brows arching, "you have followed them all too well."

"I am only a woman, I do not understand such things—but I beg you, Sweet Lady, help my children! Free them from the fever that is killing them and all our village!"

"This is why you have come here, daughter. Such will be *your* doing. Bring water to your children, and to your village, and to the cattle starving in your byres and the fouled well and the weary earth of your fields. Take this water, pure and clean, and give back thanks for it."

"I do thank you, Most Blessed Lady—"

"But *not* like that!" she exclaimed. "Groveling with your face in the dirt displeases me. Stand upright! Lift up your hands to the warmth of the sun!" Berthilde did as bidden; the Lady smiled. "Much better. Now you show your gratitude with joy, not fear. Take the water, Bright One, and return as often as you have need. The water and I will always be here."

Berthilde dipped her two buckets deep into the stream. As she turned to say her thanks again, she was alone but for the sighing of the summer-memory breeze in the willows and the dance of sunshine on the water.

She walked swiftly, light of step and heart for sureness that soon her children would be well, the grass would grow, the orchard would bloom, the crops would flourish, the cattle would fatten and give sweet milk. These first two buckets would be for her children, then the sickest of the village and, of course, the priest. After that, the rest of the people and then the animals and the land itself would drink, and be healed.

Still, as she passed the withering apple trees, she could not but stop, and set down her buckets, and cup in her hands water for one tree that was special to her. Beneath its branches, heavy with spring leaves and white blossoms and the promise of sweet fruit, her husband had kissed her for the first time. She sprinkled the dry earth at its roots with water, and stood back. She waited, holding her breath.

The apple tree quivered, seeming to shake off the blight and the cold. Tender green shoots appeared. She cried out in wonder and snatched up the buckets, hurrying home anxious to watch the miracle occur to her children.

Yet caution slowed her steps as she neared the village. Last moondark, the tanner, trudging the long miles home from the Château, was set upon by cloaked men who stole the flour that had paid him for repairing Monseigneur's favorite saddle. If people saw this fresh water, would she, too, crawl to her doorstep bruised and bloodied—and lacking something even more precious than flour for a single loaf?

She could not risk it. She was sorry to be suspicious of anyone, but she must think of her children first, and the bloom of health that would replace the hectic fever in their cheeks. So she took the long way around the village so that none would see her. None did, and she crossed her own threshold at last.

The children were alone. Their father's sister had not stayed as she promised. Berthilde was angry for a moment, then shrugged, for it did not matter. Swiftly she took a cup—their wedding cup, made by her husband of good pewter polished to silver's gleam—from the shelf above the cold dead hearth and dipped it into the water.

Margot first, she was the youngest. Madeleine. Arnaud. Anne. Jean. Standing beside their small beds, she lifted her weary hands and gave wordless thanks to the Queen of Heaven as their breathing eased and their burning skin cooled.

Anne stirred, opened her eyes, and whispered, "Maman?"

Berthilde wept and laughed and hugged her children to her breast. After a time, when they had fallen into healing sleep, she picked up the buckets and started for the blacksmith's home; he was ill, and his family were close to death, they should have the water first.

The smithy was beyond the Church. As she neared the gray stone sanctuary, she knew she must give the water first of all to the priest. He was God's Voice in the village, a sincere and holy man, not like his long-dead predecessor who had always reeked of ale. Père Jerome went to every house every day, to comfort and hear confession and give the Last Rites. He would be wiser than she about whose need was greatest.

Accordingly, she carried the buckets up the three steps (symbolizing the Holy Trinity) and under the lintel with its carved wooden Virgin huddled beneath the eaves. As she passed below the Lady's sight, she looked up. Although this stiff, sorrowing face was nothing like the warm loveliness of the woman she had seen in the forest, she fancied she saw a smile curve the corners of those lips.

The priest was at the altar, but in a pose Berthilde had never seen before: prostrate on the floor, arms flung out, fists clenched and face hidden against cold stones. Shocked, she stood mute at the back of the nave, listening as he cried out and beat his fists on the flags for anguish.

"No," she heard herself say, and set down the buckets, and hurried to him. She bent, touched his shoulder. "Oh, no, you must not, Père Jerome! You must put away your despair, we are saved!"

He scrambled to his feet, a tall, thin, ascetic man in brown cassock and rope cincture with a fine ivory cross on a leather thong around his neck. He dashed tears from his face and stared down at Berthilde.

"Saved? When only today three more have sickened, and two others have died? What else is there but despair when there are too many bodies for the ground to receive?"

"There will be no more deaths." She tugged him by the arm to the back of the nave, and showed him the water. "I found it—no, I was led to it by the Blessed Lady, and I *saw* her, Père Jerome, I saw her and she spoke to me and—"

"You—" He choked on the rest, and stood back from her. "Berthilde, where did you find this water?"

"I will tell you everything, but first you must drink. You are not well, I can see the fever beginning in your face. Drink, Père Jerome. Please."

He cupped a handful of water, sniffed it warily, but did not drink. "Tell me where you have found fresh water in this blighted land, and then I will decide whether or not to drink."

So she told him of the forest, of the stream, of the Blessed Lady, of the water, of the apple tree. All the while the precious water dribbled between his fingers onto the stones. His dark eyes grew darker, and grim. At last, when she was finished, he crossed himself and murmured many of the Holy Words she did not understand.

Fixing her with a stern, worried gaze, he said, "Berthilde, there are things I wish to make clear in my mind. Questions I wish you to answer. Will you do this?"

"Of course, Père Jerome!"

"This woman you say you saw. Was she wearing a blue mantle?"

"No. She was dressed all in glowing white—finer even than Madame la Baronne's finest clothes."

"Was there a light about her? A nimbus?"

"I do not understand this word, Père Jerome."

"A halo, as you saw around Christ in the Château's chapel window."

"No. But the sun shone warmly around her, as if in her presence it was always spring."

"Did she carry a book? Or a lily, perhaps?"

"No, but she wore a necklace and bracelets of gold, all twined around itself."

"Did she speak with reverence of the Lord God and His Son Jesus Christ, and say that she had Their blessing to show you this water?"

"N-no," she said more slowly now. "But she did speak of God's Holy Law."

"And what did she say?"

"That—that we had followed it only too well. And that few in this land serve her now, or know her for who she truly is."

"You say she spoke many strange names to you. What were these names she used of herself?"

"I do not recall them, Père Jerome. I am only a simple, ignorant woman. I have no learning—" She hesitated, trying to remember the sounds, then said shyly, "She *did* say that my name means Bright One, and that this was one of her own Names as well."

"Was one of them—" And here his voice fell to a hush. "—Ashtoreth?"

"Yes! Ashtoreth—and a word like my daughter's name, Anne—"

The priest crossed himself several times and spoke very rapidly in the Holy Tongue. Then he took Berthilde by the shoulders and gazed with awesome intensity into her eyes.

"You have been cozened, seduced by frightful powers of evil. I give thanks to Almighty God that He has sent you here to His Holy Church before your simplicity could lead you into direst peril of your immortal soul."

Berthilde's heart thudded with terror. "Père Jerome," she breathed, "what have I done?"

"It is true that you are ignorant, thus easy prey. This

is my fault for not instructing you more strictly." He bowed his head, the small circle of his tonsure pale and naked at the crown of his head. "What priest, becoming shepherd of so gentle a flock, would believe his sheep capable of any but small everyday sins—let alone of being led so far astray? I spoke no harsh warnings, I saw no need. And I was wrong." Looking at her once more, he went on, "I repent of my sin and will remedy your ignorance. It was not the Blessed Virgin you saw, but a spawn of Satan."

"No!" she blurted. "She was not, she could not have been—"

"I tell you that it was. Had you truly seen the Mother of God, she would have worn a blue mantle, for blue is her color. Her head would be surrounded by a blaze of light, for she is the Queen of Heaven. She would have held a book, as she did when the Archangel Gabriel came to her, or the lily he gave her as symbol of her blessedness among all women. She would have told you that of her compassion she had pleaded with God and Christ to let her help you by giving you water. Instead—"

She trembled, not daring to breathe.

"She wore glowing white, as bright as the star Lucifer was before he fell into the Pit. Did she not say that Bright One was one of her own names? And the necklace and bracelets of gold—were they not like snakes twisting about her throat and arms? The names she called herself—oh, Berthilde, the name Ashtoreth is a word damned and damned again in the Holy Bible! As for the seeming miracle of the apple tree—do you not recall that it was this very fruit in the hand of a woman that led to banishment from Eden? You did not see the Blessed Virgin, you did not hear the words of the Mother of God! You saw and heard the Devil!"

Reeling with fear and confusion, she cried out. "But— but she was so beautiful, so kind—she smiled at me—"

"And do you believe that Satan cannot assume any shape he pleases, to trick and betray foolish women? How much wicked pleasure you gave, kneeling at the Evil One's feet instead of to God!"

"She bade me *not* to kneel, but to lift up my hands in joyful thanks—"

"Which only proves that she was *not* Holy Mary! Before her, all people and especially all women should go down on their knees, for she alone among you is without sin!"

"No, Père Jerome—please, no—"

"You have consorted with the very author of all our misery! When we turn our hearts from God, who is waiting to seize us? To torment us? To make of our lives on earth a foretaste of the Hell that awaits us for all eternity?"

Struggling, the air clogging in her throat, she protested, "But—but my children—they are well now, they sleep peacefully and without fever—the water cured them—"

"The water is accursed," he intoned, and with his bare foot kicked over both buckets over onto the stone floor. Crossing himself, he said, "It cannot harm consecrated ground."

Berthilde moaned. "It will save us—the people, the animals, the crops—it saved the apple tree—"

"The tree must be cut down, for any fruit of it is accursed. You and your children, having drunk of the water, are accursed until confessions are made and penances given. Perhaps even an exorcism is needed." He fixed her with dark eyes that burned. "Kneel, and give thanks that Almighty God has brought you to His Church in order to save your soul."

Berthilde shook like a willow in the wind. Her knees quivered—but she did not fall upon them. She could not.

"On your knees, and beseech the Lord to forgive your sin!"

She could not.

Through the thin worn leather of her shoes she felt the water, pooling in tiny lakes on the rough-hewn stones, soaking into the skin of her feet. She remembered how clean it had tasted on her lips, how bright it had felt on her face and in her hair.

It was not evil. It had not come from the Devil. It had revived the apple tree, *her* apple tree. It had cured her children.

She did not feel accursed. And she could not kneel.

She ran, out the door beneath the stiff unsmiling wooden statue and down the three steps, across the churchyard and through the village. She ran past the apple tree and the blighted fields, and deep into the forest.

The Lady was waiting for her.

"Your children are well now."

Wordless, Berthilde nodded.

"Then why are you distraught? Like me, you are a mother, and the first joy of a mother's heart is to know her children safe and well."

"Lady—" Breath caught in her throat. "Lady, the priest—"

The lovely face changed subtly. "Ah. Yes. The priest. Tell me, Berthilde."

"He says—he says you are evil, that the water is accursed, that you caused our land to sicken—"

Suddenly all warmth and sunlight vanished. The golden necklace seemed to writhe about the Lady's throat, the bracelets twisting about her wrists. Berthilde stumbled back from her terrible wrath.

"I?" she exclaimed. "Have I plowed the land until it bleeds, and never given back to it a single drop of the blood that poured from its flesh? Have I slaughtered trees for the burning, for clearing more land to feel cold and soulless teeth of iron? Have I fouled the sacred wells? Have I done any of these things? Have I?"

Wind shuddered in the old oaks, whirled across the water. Yet as quickly as it came, it departed, and with it the Lady's anger. The gold stilled around her neck and arms, and with wise, sad eyes she gazed at Berthilde.

"And yet this priest does me homage, though he knows it not. Had my other Names not been forgotten and denied, perhaps even priests would understand who I truly am."

Berthilde asked humbly, "Please—I am too ignorant to understand, but I would at least truly know you so that I may truly serve you."

"I am the Mother of the Sacred King who is slain. I am She of Eternal Sorrow, for my beloved Son must die so that the earth and all else may live. All life begins and ends in me. All peoples are my children. I am She who gives life, and She to whom all life returns to be reborn. I am the Maiden, the Mother, and the Old Woman of Wise Blood, the Trinity, the faces of the Moon."

She felt her arms lift, her hands open, not to ward off these words but to gather them to herself as the truth she knew they must be.

"My Breath spoke the Sound that began the world. The difference between me and the priests' god is that I will never speak the Sound that ends it."

In an awed whisper, Berthilde heard herself say, "For—for a mother's joy is to see her children safe and well. . . ."

The Lady nodded. "You see, you *do* understand. Go now, daughter, and be a mother to your children. You have been a Maiden, as I am, and served me with your dancing and your laughter. Now you are a Mother, as I am, and you may best serve me by tending your children. Women who are old, as I am, serve me in yet another way. Go now, daughter, and serve me by keeping your children safe and well."

She never saw her children again.

When she returned to the village, past sere fields and her apple tree, the priest seized her with his own hands, for no one else would touch her. The blacksmith, though hollow-eyed and reeling with fever, had yet made iron shackles for her wrists and her ankles. What little kindling was left after the long cold winter was piled up in the square, and someone brought the fresh green wood of the slaughtered apple tree, and at eventide she was burned as a witch and heretic.

The smoke rose, stinking of scorched human flesh and greenwood, to blacken the sky. And the horror continued, and the blight, and the grief. More in the village sickened, and more died. But not the priest.

For when Berthilde fled, in a moment of weakness—*Water, fresh water, such as he had not tasted in months*—he fell to his knees and touched his hand to the pooling water. The droplets on his fingertips were almost near enough his lips to taste when he realized the temptation to which he had nearly succumbed. He prayed for a long while, and at last, his Faith assuring him that all the Devil's handiwork had vanished, once more he touched the water and let it touch his lips. It was as sweet and clean and wondrous as Berthilde had promised. Of all the village, the priest alone did not sicken, and in due course this evidence of purity and holiness made him bishop, archbishop, and cardinal.

One Sunday many years later, as he lifted his hands in exaltation before a cathedral altar, a vision appeared before him. The woman was neither young nor old, dark nor fair, smiling nor solemn—and yet all these things at the same time. Her beauty was of face and form, but also of spirit that gleamed in her eyes. She wore a mantle of blue. One hand held a book; the other, a lily. About her head was a nimbus like golden sunlight, as if in her presence it was always spring. About her throat coiled a necklace of gold, and at her wrists wrapped matching bracelets.

His heart thudded in his chest at sight of her. She gave him a wise, sad smile, murmuring, "And do you know me now, priest?"

With his hands raised and trembling, his voice rang through Notre Dame de Paris:

> *Salve, regina, mater misericordiae,*
> *Vita, dulcedo et spes nostra, salve!*

"I suppose that must do," she said.

*　　*　　*　　*　　*

"Hail Holy Queen, Mother of Mercy, our Life, our Sweetness and our Hope, hail!"

TREES OF AVALON

by Elisabeth Waters

The dryad Eliona was dozing peacefully in her tree when the magician barged in to the central trunk without any ceremony whatsoever—not even the simple courtesy of knocking on wood and calling her name. Or, if he didn't know her name, a call to "the spirit of this tree" would have demonstrated a knowledge of the rudiments of manners. After all, the protocol for addressing a dryad wasn't *that* difficult. And anyone with the slightest claim to magical power knew that one did not enter a dryad's tree uninvited.

Coming reluctantly to full wakefulness, she opened her eyes and looked at her uninvited guest. It was the Merlin—who certainly should have known better.

The present holder of the title was still a fairly young man, dark-haired and slightly built, and one of the most gifted bards of the last three generations. Eliona had always admired him, until now.

"Lord Merlin," she said, blinking the sleep out of her eyes. "This is an unexpected honor." At least that sounded better than *What are you doing here and why didn't you knock first?*

The Merlin appeared even more startled than she was. "Who are you? Where am I?"

"I'm Eliona," she replied, puzzled, "and you're in my tree."

"You're a dryad."

Something was seriously wrong here. "Yes, of course I'm a dryad—what else would you expect to be living inside a tree in the Sacred Grove?"

"The Sacred Grove." He repeated her words in a dazed voice, looking around him as if he expected to see something in particular. Of course, the only thing to see at this level was the inside of the tree trunk. The knotholes which gave a view of the world outside the tree were all higher up.

"How did I get here?"

Eliona shrugged. "I was asleep when you arrived. I would assume that you simply walked in on your own, but I have no idea as to why." *And I do wonder* ...

"No." The Merlin shook his head. "I was having dinner with Nimue. Maybe I did have a bit too much wine, but wine doesn't make me wander around bumping into things. Too much wine just puts me to sleep ..." he frowned in concentration, "but I definitely didn't have that much wine." He shrugged. "I'm sure there's some explanation for this, and someday I'll find it. In the meantime," he bowed slightly to her, "please accept my apologies for my inadvertent disturbance of your rest. I shan't bother you again. Lady bless."

"May She bless you as well," Eliona replied formally as the Merlin turned to leave, took two steps, and was stopped in his tracks by the inner bark of the tree.

"That's odd," he murmured, trying again with the same results.

It was more than odd, as Eliona well knew. The Merlin should have been able to walk through every tree in the grove, one after another, without disturbing any of the inhabitants. Tree bark shouldn't even slow him down, let alone stop him.

"Maybe I'm more tired than I realized," he said in a dazed voice. "By your leave, Mistress," his voice trailed off as he sank to the floor, sound asleep.

Eliona knelt over him, disentangled his harp from his shoulder, and straightened his body so that he wouldn't wake up with his joints all awry. She set the harp carefully to one side, then slipped through the bark of the trunk as if through thin air, moving to the world outside. She couldn't leave her tree for long, but she had a very strong feeling that she needed to speak with Nimue.

She found the sorceress without difficulty. Nimue was sitting at the edge of the sacred well, gazing into its depths. But she heard Eliona's approach and looked up as the dryad joined her.

"Lady bless, Eliona," she said with a smile. "What can I do for you?"

"You can tell me what you did to the Merlin," Eliona replied, skipping the formalities.

"Don't you like having him as a house guest?" Nimue asked archly. "I was so sure you would—you've had a crush on him for years."

"I never invited him into my tree," Eliona pointed out. "And he seems to be ill; when he tried to leave, he couldn't get through the bark."

Nimue giggled. It should have made her sound like the innocent girl she was in outward physical appearance. It didn't. "He won't be able to leave, Eliona, dear. He's yours now, for all time."

"What?"

Nimue contemplated her fingernails, then began pushing back the cuticles on one hand with the little fingernail of the other. "It seems that he did something that got the Lady very upset, and it was decided to get him out of the way, someplace where he couldn't interfere anymore."

"So you shut him up in my tree? Permanently?" Eliona still didn't quite believe it.

"Quite permanently, dear. He's all yours." Nimue smiled brightly at her. "Lady bless." She turned her back on Eliona, returning to her contemplation of the water. Eliona briefly considered pushing her in, but thought better of it and returned to her tree.

She found the Merlin awake and up among the branches. Half a dozen birds flitted to and fro, listening to his voice. As Eliona floated up to join him, they all flew away, except for one raven, which ostentatiously tucked its head under its wing and feigned sleep.

"Ah, Eliona," the Merlin said, smiling at her. "You're back. I was a bit lonely here with you gone, but as you can see," he gestured to the birds, now scattering in all directions, "a few of my friends dropped by."

Eliona considered the implications of that statement carefully. Virtually every animal in the forest could be considered the Merlin's "friend" if the term friend encompassed all the animals he could summon at will. Visualizing that crowd camped around her tree was enough to give any dryad the shudders. Birds, with their bird-sized brains, would sit too many on a branch until it broke. Deer would nibble first leaves, then new shoots, then the very bark of the tree as high as they could reach. Too many of Lord Merlin's friends could easily kill her tree—and her along with it. Would that free the Merlin from whatever Nimue had done to him? And, more importantly, did he believe it would? She had better nip that notion in the bud.

"I went to speak to Nimue, Lord Merlin," she said. "That is why I was not here when you awoke."

"Why did you want to speak to Nimue?" the Merlin asked.

"I asked her if she knew why you were unable to leave my tree," Eliona replied. "She tells me that you have offended the goddess and that you have been shut up in my tree so that you can't do whatever it was you did again."

"For how long?" the Merlin asked.

"Forever," Eliona replied. "And if the tree dies, so do you. And so do I, if that's of any concern to you," she added sharply.

The Merlin looked around the inside of the tree. "Dear me, I had no idea. . . ." His voice trailed off. "I meant it for the best, but I fear that the priestesses did not understand."

"I do not believe that any of them is going to come here looking for an explanation, either," Eliona said. "Unless you manage to get us both killed, we're going to be together for a long time to come."

The Merlin looked at her, finally registering the fact that she was upset and realizing why. "I am sorry, Eliona," he said. "I would not willingly have inconvenienced you in this fashion. I promise you that I shall do my best to fit in here and not disturb your life any more than I can help."

"And you will respect my tree?" Eliona asked, trying to hide her anxiety.

"As if it were my own," the Merlin assured her.

Eliona decided against telling him that, in a very real sense, it *was* his own.

Maybe the Merlin was trying to be a considerate and unobtrusive guest. Eliona didn't know. She know only that he—and his friends—were driving her crazy. The tree was never quiet; the normal soft rustle of the leaves against each other was drowned out by the birds landing on the upper branches at all hours. The Merlin spent so much time climbing up and down the inner trunk to talk to them that he was wearing footholds into the wood— a change which Eliona did *not* consider an improvement in her interior decoration.

She had to chase away deer at least once a week. So far they had done little damage, nibbling only at the new green shoots that her tree put forth every spring. But when winter came and they started in on the tree bark ... Eliona shuddered. *I don't want to die,* she thought. *I'm too young to die. And it isn't fair. Whatever the Merlin did to anger the Lady, I had no part in it!*

The Merlin still didn't seem to understand the problem. But then, he *was* a human, even if he was—or had been—a powerful magician. Humans couldn't be expected to understand the life of a dryad, the days and months spent in dreaming, being at one with the tree, growing peacefully during the long summer days, sleeping through the winter....

It was only three days past the Longest Day, and Eliona was deathly tired. She hadn't had a decent spell of rest since the Merlin's arrival; she had to be constantly on guard against things that would damage, if not kill, her tree, and the Merlin never stopped talking!

If he wasn't talking to the birds, or the squirrels, or, Lady forbid, the deer, he was talking to himself. He also talked to the priestesses, as if rehearsing an explanation for his actions to justify them to women who would never come to listen.

And when he wasn't talking, he sang and played his harp. Eliona had never before realized just how many hours a harper spent tuning his harp for each hour he played it in tune. Nor had she realized how often harp strings broke when being tuned. The first string to break was one of the long ones. Normally it would have sounded a low note, but now it snapped with a sound like a medium size dried-out branch being broken, whipped sideways away from the harp with considerable force, and gouged a furrow up to an inch deep in the inner bark of the main trunk. Eliona's scream, a combination of startlement and pain, drowned out the Merlin's comment on the occurrence, but he was definitely put out.

Not, unfortunately, by the damage to the tree—apparently he couldn't even feel that. He was annoyed that his harp was now missing a string, which limited the songs he could play upon it.

So much for his promise to treat the tree as if it were his own, Eliona thought angrily, still in pain from the wound to its inner skin. The Merlin was still complaining about the broken string and about the certainty that more of them would break, leaving him with an even more limited repertoire.

Eliona considered the damage more breaking harp strings would do to her tree. Now she understood why so many old harpers were blind. *This tree isn't big enough for both of us.*

The moon was full that night, and all of the priestesses came to the Grove for their ritual. To Eliona's surprise, Nimue stopped by her tree and politely requested entrance. Curiosity alone impelled her to grant the request, although perhaps she harbored a faint hope that Nimue would release the Merlin. But, no, it seemed that she had come to gloat.

"You look dreadful," Nimue informed him gleefully. "Who would have imagined it: the Merlin, the Arch-Druid, the most powerful man in Avalon, brought down by a woman's wiles like any simple shepherd boy. I didn't even need to use my magic to trap you, and now I have all of yours for my own use as well!" She left the tree and the Grove before the Merlin could gather his scattered wits to say anything to her.

"*She* has your magic?" Eliona asked. "How did that happen?"

The Merlin was obviously trying to remember. "She must have taken it when she put me here."

"How?" Eliona demanded. The Merlin's magic could be very useful in solving their mutual problem if they could get it back. "You said that the last thing you remembered was having dinner with her, and drinking wine—"

"No," the Merlin said. "I remember a bit more after that. We were lying together and I fell asleep after—and when I woke again I was here."

Eliona opened her mouth to ask "after what" and then realized what he was talking about. "That would give her access to your magic, all right," she remarked. "I hear that men frequently forget all else in the throes of passion."

The Merlin groaned. "Don't remind me."

"Remind you?" Eliona said. "I'll bet you couldn't remember the details if you tried. Men have so little at stake in these matters, it's the women who bear the children. A man's part is over quickly and his energies return—"

"Not this time," the Merlin snapped.

Eliona ignored him, "—but a woman's energies go to nurture the child in her body, which takes a great deal of energy and about a year of time."

"How would you know?" the Merlin said bitterly. "You're not human; you don't bear children."

"Growing a tree takes much longer," Eliona pointed out. "And during several stages of a tree's growth, it takes incredible amounts of energy. I'm still young; I hadn't planned to start a new tree for at least another decade or two."

"*Hadn't* planned?" The Merlin looked at her suspiciously. "What are you planning now?"

Eliona smiled sweetly at him. "Would you like your magic taken away from Nimue—and maybe some of hers as well? That link she's gloating over *does* run both ways."

"Go on," he said. "I'm listening."

In the early fall, Eliona's tree dropped one perfectly formed acorn. A helpful squirrel buried it nearby at just the right depth, and Eliona used dryad magic to be certain that both it and her tree would be undisturbed throughout the winter.

In the early spring it sprouted, and it grew at an unprecedented rate.

It's amazing what one can do with combined magics and extra energy, Eliona thought, complacently surveying her offspring.

By late spring the tree was quite a respectable size, and no one would suspect that it was less than a year old. And after a good winter's rest and a season of having her tree to herself again, Eliona had recovered her old health and spirits. She even felt well enough to leave her tree and visit the sacred well.

Nimue was lying in the grass by the well, her head propped on a tree root, sipping water listlessly from a silver cup. She looked pale and weak.

"Lady bless, Nimue," Eliona said politely. "You look tired; is something wrong?"

"Nothing a dryad would understand," Nimue said dismissively.

"If you say so." Eliona could see that Nimue hadn't the slightest idea what ailed her, but she decided not to explain. The Merlin's tree was growing well and would continue to grow for centuries. It would be interesting to see if Nimue figured out what had happened to her before she died of old age. Eliona suspected that she wouldn't.

SPARROW

by Esther Friesner

The boy staggered through the forest, doing his poor best to keep up with the men who fled before him. He had been given charge of the horses, but the horses had run away that first night—all but Bedwyr's. Still wild-eyed and skittish after the clangor of battle, they were none of them the king's own, bred to face blood and the clash of steel as bravely as any warrior. No, these were only mounts hastily scrounged from masters either too afraid of Sir Bedwyr's murderous words, face, and blade to speak a word of protest, or taken from men stretched cold and still on the field, now well beyond all mortal speech.

No time to learn the true mettle of these mounts, no time to do anything but fly as if ten thousand demons were at their heels. Indeed, the horses themselves seemed to see those very demons the instant that the little ragtag band of human remnants took refuge in the forest. They tore their reins from the boy's weak grasp as he struggled to tether them for the night. They galloped away, shrieking as they plunged blindly through the underbrush into the bellies of waiting wolves. Only Bedwyr's mount remained, standing still and stolid, as hard-mouthed and empty-eyed as his master.

Fortunately, none of the king's arms had been borne off on the panicked beasts. Not so fortunately for the boy, who received a sound beating and the news that he

was to supply the horses' place and carry the cursed
heavy things instead.

"And don't think you can run off, too," Sir Bedwyr
said severely. "You're nowhere near as fast or as clever
as a horse. Try it and I'll hunt you down. You're less
valuable than any horse I ever rode, too, so it's your
hide I'll hang over my shield-arm if you try breaking
your oath to our king."

The boy wanted to say, *What oath? I never swore any
oath. It was my father.* But he knew that Sir Bedwyr
would cut short all his protestations with the clean, simple argument of a leather-sheathed blow across his face.
So the boy, who was almost as smart as any horse, kept
still, picked up the king's arms, and made his way behind
the men as well as he might.

He was nearly the age of manhood, but he was poorly
grown. Therefore the other pages all bullied him, calling
him Sparrow—dirty and helpless and small—instead of
his given name. In the court at Camelot, where right
supposedly outweighed might, no one had bothered to
bring that news to the pages' dormitory. And so by virtue
of brute force alone, the name stuck to the boy like
horseturds to a man's boot sole. His father was dead,
slain in the service of his king, and now it seemed as if
his king, too, was about to die. Bedwyr said he'd gotten
his death-wound at Camlann.

Sparrow remembered little of the battle, knew nothing
of what passed on the field of Camlann. Men gossiped
that it would last for days. He was only a page, not a
squire, and so he had been left behind among the other
servants to tend the camp for however long it might take
Arthur to bring his bastard son to heel, or to death. The
fighting reached him as a faraway rumor of steel on steel,
the faint screams of men and horses.

Once there came a lull in the distant tumult, a strange
silence that made the camp-bound prick up their ears

more anxiously than all the pandemonium that had gone
before. It did not last long enough for any to learn its
cause, and when it ended, the battle seemed to have
gathered breath for a howl of havoc to make all that had
gone before seem trifling.

The battle was scarcely reborn before Sparrow was
almost trampled as a fine white beast, its sides streaked
with blood and foam, came galloping riderless through
the camp, insanity in its eyes. It charged straight on,
never minding obstacles, until it fouled its foot on a tent's
guy-line and pitched forward, breaking its neck. The
cook skinned it and cut it up for stew. The other pages
forced Sparrow to kiss the gray, velvety lips of the animal's severed head. His stomach revolted and he spewed
up all he'd eaten as soon as they took the poor, pitiful
relic away.

And then the great news: Modred was dead! All cheer!

And then the grim news that followed: Arthur, too,
was slain; Modred's orphaned force was on the march to
avenge their lord.

The cheers crackled and shattered into little cries of
alarm. The camp became a nest of uprooted field mice,
all a-scurry to save their provisions and their pelts.
Armed men returned from the killing ground, some on
foot, some mounted. Those whose hurts were not too
severe turned all their efforts to snatching up as many
of their belongings as their horses might carry, and more
besides. The goods of dead men were divided coldly
among the living, and sometimes the goods of the living,
too, were portioned out, when the living were too frail
to defend what was theirs.

Hunched into a little ball of terror in the lee of Sir
Bedwyr's pavillion, guts still shaking every time the dead
horse's face rose in his mind's eye, a weakened Sparrow
saw a wounded knight dragged back from the field on a
litter by his servants. They were grown men, brawny

things, yet they laid their lord's sore hurt body most tenderly upon a pile of cloth-draped straw. They then proceeded to despoil him of everything save his shirt. When the man by main effort raised himself on one elbow to protest, to name them outlaw curs, the taller of the two gave him a casual glance and just as casually rapped in the side of his head with the butt of a finely-made spear. The skullbone crumpled as simply as an egg knocked against the lip of a pudding bowl.

Sparrow must have uttered some sound then—a mew of horror or pity, perhaps—for the servant turned his stone eyes in the boy's direction and regarded him with that same vacant look he'd given his lord just before giving him his death. It was a look that as good as said: *If you die here among so many dead men, what will it matter?* Saying so much, it did not need to add: *Keep silence and keep life.*

Sparrow kept silence. He was so small, so helpless, that he clung to whatever weapon would best save his skin, even if that weapon was only a tongue that knew when to guard stillness. The chaos of the camp surged up around him on all sides, like a great rock breaking up in the midst of a ravenous sea. He only hugged his knees closer to his meager body, buried his head beneath bony arms, and prayed to become air and shadow.

At last the din subsided. Sparrow raised his head. He was alone in the midst of desolation. A clinging mist was rising from the earth. Broken tent poles became the shattered bones of monsters, rags of silk fluttering from despoiled pavilions were the wagging tongues of hungry ghosts. Sparrow slowly unfolded his gawky limbs and clambered to his feet. Turning, he beheld a miracle: The king's own tent, which he and the other royal pages sworn to Arthur's service had been left to guard, was whole. Spectral and glorious as the apparition of the

Grail, the gleaming sides rose up untouched by the reivers' passage.

Sparrow took a hesitant step forward, trembling hand outstretched to raise the entry flap. A chill ran from shoulder to fingertips and his arm dropped back to his side. There was something uncanny about the survival of the king's tent. His mind painted ghastly things behind the silent silken walls. Surely there was some reason behind this sole survival. If Arthur were dead indeed, perhaps the king's spirit had flown to invest his body's latest habitation. What manner of shape or substance would such a ghost assume?

Sparrow shivered and shut his eyes tight, but his mind's eye was a lidless thing opening on one horrible imagining after the next. The other boys had delighted in telling ghoul-tales in Sparrow's hearing, knowing well that of all their number, his was the mind most given to possessions and hauntings. His nightmare-ridden screams always were a source of entertainment for them.

"My lord—" Sparrow hesitated, eyes still closed but hand now rising once more, fingers touching silk. Against all that his mind had absorbed of heaven and hell from the priests' lessons until his too-brief childhood's end, his heart still felt the need to beg pardon of his dead master before trespassing here. "My lord, with your permission, I—"

A sharp buffet to the ear sent him tumbling sideways. A deep voice well-rooted on the near side of the grave bellowed, "Damn you, boy! What's this foolishness? What are you up to, eh? Trying your hand at theft, are you? And from the king's own tent! I'll slash your head from that twig you call a neck!"

Sight reeling, Sparrow blinked until his blow-starred vision solidified the form of Bedwyr looming above him. The armored man was helmless, his mail and leather blotched with dirt and blood. Sparrow stammered his

excuses down the length of the notched and battered
sword now leveled at his throat.

Sir Bedwyr smiled, a sallow sliver of broken teeth
glimpsed between the black bramble of his whiskers. He
meant no kindliness by it. "Faugh! What a stink of cow-
ardice. You witling, I but jested! You've held your post
and kept our lord's possessions well—though now I wonder whether I owe the thanks to you or to mere circum-
stance. I can't see you standing strong against a crippled
beggar, let alone a looter bound on his task. Never mind,
you'll do me." He sheathed his sword and rubbed his
chin in thought. "Yes, it may be you'll do me better than
a lad with more liver might. Come."

And that was all. Bedwyr summoned and Sparrow
scampered. He was told to go and fetch the knight's
mount and lead it back to the tent while Bedwyr himself
entered and considered which of the king's possessions
were worth the taking.

Sparrow did as he was told. Motherless, now fatherless
as well, his gentle birth had done little to shelter him
from the knowledge that disobedience brought beatings.
Those meted out for his own good (as he was frequently
told) hurt no less than those given for no other reason
than that it suited the giver's fancy to strike out at one
weaker than himself simply because he could.

The mist was thicker now; evening was coming on, and
with it the crisp and winey air of autumn. But this day's
vintage reeked more thickly of blood than of apples.
There was a rumor of many voices that grew stronger.
As the sound waxed, Sir Bedwyr's calm waned percepti-
bly, until his round face was as pale and dewy as a new-
made cheese.

"Damn! Modred's men," he muttered. "At least they
had the backbone to keep faith with their master even
after he was slain. They've given him good burial and
now they're marching here, to take back his blood mea-

sure for measure in ours. Too cursed many of them, and trained the Roman way. I told the king he'd do better to make our men learn that drill, but he—!" Bedwyr's laugh was bitter. His glimmering, small eyes fixed themselves upon Sparrow. "Do you know what sort of a fool your king was, boy?" he demanded.

Sparrow's lower lip felt like jelly. The knight was staring at him, silently commanding him to reply by the sheer brutish force he embodied. Sparrow's loyal heart fought against his fragile spirit, the one refusing to grant any measure of complicity to one who named his beloved king a fool, the other trembling in terror over what his fate might be if he did not tell Bedwyr what Bedwyr wished to hear. Bedwyr was right: He was only a boy.

"I—I don't know, my lord," he said, and hated himself.

Again Bedwyr's laugh crackled over his head. "Then I'll tell you, but not here. Modred's men are coming, and they'll be less than pleased to see what crow's pickings we've left them in this camp. Come. I'll do better than tell you, I'll show you. Hop!" Sparrow jumped at the word, but not fast enough to avoid a painful kick from Bedwyr's boot.

The knight led the way and the page followed. Already Sparrow could hear behind him the sound of Modred's troops approaching the nigh-abandoned campsite. To his quivering mind their coming sounded like the roar of a hellmouth spewing out its complement of demons. He had seen enough of mortal man's evildoings, these few hours past, to dread what excess wickedness demons might heap upon the helpless.

And yet it had not been always so, this raw brutality he had witnessed in the camp. A shimmering vision of Arthur's court rose before his eyes, a seeing that swam through the curtain of tears now half-blinding him. Oh, life in the pages' quarters had been rough and blunt and hard, but as soon as he left those boisterous rooms behind him, he entered into the dream: Arthur's dream.

He could still see him, the great, good king who had brought the obstreperous lords of Britain to heel under his rule. Powerful? Yes, Arthur wielded power; no king could hope to rule this land without some show of strength. But once his point has been made, once the lesser chiefs had been made to see that deference to Arthur's rule meant prosperity for them all, he never resorted to the sword to subdue a man when a word of good counsel might suffice.

Sparrow remembered those few precious times he had been chosen to wait on the king himself at table. It was a singular honor, one for which the pages contended jealously, but Sparrow did not cherish it for the status it gave him. He took greater pleasure in the chance to be near his king, to see Arthur on his throne: regal, noble, strong, yet always with the look of kindness on him. Not even Guinhwyfar's pale, luminous beauty could kindle a flame half so warming as that welcoming glow of benevolence which radiated from the king's own presence. Love-hungry, Sparrow basked in it, immersed himself in it, dreaded the time when he must leave it to return to his own small, harsh world. It bound him to his lord as no mere oath ever could.

"Here, boy!" Bedwyr's voice shattered the dream into a thousand sparkling splinters. "Come here, look, see what a burden we're to bear!"

The knight stood at the verge of the thicket of berry briars. Gems of juice-swollen fruit gleamed black and tempting amid the thorns. Sparrow's mouth watered.

Then it went dry. Something moved in the shadow of the prickers. A manshape sheathed in battered armor, streaked with darkening blood, crawled from beneath the thorn-starred shelter, groaning. Beard a white rag, eyes hollow of all save horror, Arthur dragged himself into the fading light of day.

His eyes, gray as winter sea, fastened their gaze to Sparrow's face. "M-Modred?" A scarred, shaking hand reached out for the boy.

Sparrow's guts knotted and sealed themselves with ice, but he was powerless to move. The king clutched at him, used Sparrow's frail body to haul himself unsteadily to his feet, as if the boy were a beggar's staff, a cripple's crutch, a leven-struck tree. He leaned heavily on Sparrow's shoulders, and the reek of death blew strongly from him as he spoke.

"My son—my boy—why this battle? I tell you, it was an accident made my man draw steel! You know as well as I, we were treating for peace when it happened. There was a serpent in the grass, it stung his heel, he drew the blade to kill it—" The king's voice failed, broken on the coughing fit that racked his body and brought a fresh stain of blood to his lips. All around his mouth his beard was crusted brown. "Mordred, my child . . ." His strength left him when his voice did. He crumpled to a heap at Sparrow's feet.

"He lives," Sparrow breathed, hardly knowing that he spoke his thoughts aloud. "I thought he was dead, we all thought—"

A slap from Bedwyr fetched his attention. "Well, he's not. He's still got a turn to serve. Help me horse him. Don't just sit there, you bastard, *move!*"

With much grunting and cursing, Bedwyr divested his king of the heaviest and most cumbersome pieces of his armor. He slung Arthur's body across the back of his own horse, then commanded Sparrow to hold the beast still while he found other mounts they might employ. He did this swiftly, efficiently, with only a thin line of fresh blood shining along the edge of his sword when he returned.

Then they were off, the king, the knight, the frightened boy.

Sparrow was not a horseman. He had never cherished any dreams of knighthood for himself, even if his father had. He held on with knees and heels and hands and desperately grasping fingers, with no desire to cut a fine figure, with only the desire to stay on the beast's back and not suffer a sudden backward bite from the monstrous teeth. To make matters worse, Sir Bedwyr had taken another horse to carry their supplies and the king's arms. It was a hasty job of packing, poorly done. Sometimes the great sword Excalibur slapped against the packhorse's flank, making the creature skitter sideways. Bedwyr bawled at Sparrow to get down and lead both the packhorse and his own mount. Sparrow was relieved to feel earth underfoot again, but he soon came to forget his relief as he struggled to make two half-spooked horses obey. While they kept to the road it was bad enough, but when Bedwyr imagined Modred's men might yet be on their track at eventide and decided they'd do better to take to the forest, all hell broke loose and the horses with it.

And that was how it happened that Sparrow found himself trudging behind Sir Bedwyr and his king, his skinny back bent under the weight of Arthur's arms. Bedwyr himself carried their scant foodstuffs in a pack that shared space across his horse's rump with the unconscious king. Of the two, he treated the supplies with more reverence. At this season, in this place, the wild yielded little sustenance.

"Run off now and you'll starve," Bedwyr told the boy, grinning like a wolf. "Unless I gut you first."

At least there was only the sword and the shield and the crowned helm to carry. Bedwyr himself had seen to disposing of the bulk of the king's arms as soon as he reckoned they'd put enough distance between themselves

and Modred's reivers. He did it the very night the horses
bolted. Deep in the forest they had found the ruins of
an abbey, sacred to none knew which holy brotherhood.
Oaks and their sister ivy vines had split the stones of the
house and brought them down to the dust, but the well-
shaft still stood. Bedwyr wrapped the burden of leather
and metal in his own cloak, weighted it with rocks, and
sank it deep in the well's gaping throat. If Sparrow had
any word of protest to utter, wisdom stifled it. Arthur
raised a feeble objection, but soon enough lost consciousness once more.

Unluckily for Sparrow, Bedwyr was the sort of man
more likely to take amiss too much silence than too many
words. His black scowl made the dark beyond the campfire seem bright as broad day by comparison.

"What do you stare at, boy?" he snarled, and cuffed
the page. A small whimper of pain escaped Sparrow's
lips. Bedwyr smiled as if it were a word of love and gave
the boy a second blow, and a third. "Maybe that will
teach you wisdom," he said, satisfied at last.

Sparrow touched the sticky trail of blood leaking from
his split lip and crawled deeper into himself. To save his
life, he could not say what manner of wisdom was taught
by such blows, unless it was the wisdom of fear. That
lesson he had learned long ago, and well.

Bedwyr awoke with the chill gray dawn and came after
Sparrow. Gruffly he bade the boy take up his freight
again and follow the knight's horse. There were woods,
black branches hung with the tattered banners of the
night's retreating mist, and shadows that held either
wolves or wonders. Sparrow fell into a steady, plodding
pace behind the mounted men, letting his thoughts carry
what little was left of his old self to a place of dreams,
a place beyond Bedwyr's heavy reach.

He was jerked from the shelter of reverie by a sudden
to-do up ahead. Sparrow's eyes grew wide. Could this be

merely another vision, one born of his heart's own wishes? The king! The king no longer slumped across the rump of Bedwyr's mount but had slipped to the ground.

To the ground, yet to his feet also. He was standing— *standing,* for a miracle! Standing and not dead, might God be praised! His garments were stained with lost blood, his face was ghastly pale, but still he found voice enough to speak in the clear, unmistakable tones of command that had once rung throughout the great hall of Camelot.

"Bedwyr! Where are you taking me?" he demanded. He clung to the knight's leg and harrowed his soul with a scowl of fire.

Oh, what wizard's spell had fallen over Sir Bedwyr? Sparrow could scarcely keep down the glorious gloating that now bubbled up in his hollow chest. Bedwyr cringed in his saddle, turned chary eyes to his lord, his *living* lord.

"Sire," he said, voice whispery as a drift of dead leaves. "Sire, I was but fulfilling your desires. You said you wished to be taken to—"

"And did I also say I was to be taken there like a sack of flour slung across a donkey's back? By heaven and the hidden ones, why did you not take me to the abbey of Inys Witrin first, so that they might look to my wounds? Or did you hope the journey would finish the work Modred began?"

"My lord—" Bedwyr's thick lips moved over a dozen excuses, but he lacked the liver to voice a single one. All he could stammer was, "My lord—" and yet again, "My lord, I—"

Arthur spat. He turned his back on Bedwyr, and for the first time took notice of the boy standing there, bent beneath the weight of sword and shield and helm. "Joseph?" He called Sparrow by a name the boy had not heard for so very long. "What has he done to you?"

Sparrow was mute, afraid that if he spoke he would

break the spell whose magic had reached to the very
borders of the otherworld to pluck his beloved king's life
back from the dark margin of the grave. Arthur took a
few unsteady steps nearer, his ungloved hand outstretched. The sword-hardened fingers gently touched the
bruised face, the still unhealed lip. Against both will and
knowledge, Sparrow flinched away.

"What has he done to you?" Arthur repeated, and this
time it was said in heart-deep pity touched with
indignation.

Arthur's face became flint. He summoned Bedwyr to
dismount and attend him. Words flew. Sparrow saw Bedwyr's face go from white to whiter under the berating
Arthur gave him. The king's own visage had the un-
healthy cast of curds, and yet he managed to sustain the
illusion of strength. From time to time a grimace of pain
flitted across his features. When this happened, Sparrow
thought he caught the flicker of a smile dance over Bedwyr's lips; a phantom, there and gone. For all that, it
haunted his heart. Dread pooled inside him as the king
mounted Bedwyr's horse and the knight, with a look to
turn the fires of Hell to frost, roughly relieved Sparrow
of his burden.

Bedwyr would not carry as great a load as Sparrow's;
Arthur would not have it. The king's sword was now in
the king's keeping once more. Bedwyr's hands caressed
the hilt of Excalibur a moment before handing it up to
his lord. Arthur's heavy shield was all that Bedwyr would
shoulder, besides his own weapons. The king's helm, with
its distinguishing circlet of gold above the brow, was left
in Sparrow's keeping.

It was a different road they walked now. Arthur led,
and Bedwyr and the boy had to do their best to follow.
"I know the way," Arthur said. "Though I've no notion
what you meant by taking the path you did, Bedwyr. A

few days' march more and we'd have reached the Saxon shore. What then?"

Bedwyr made some few small, badly phrased excuses. Arthur heard these out with one eyebrow raised, his skepticism plain to see. "An honest mistake, hm? Not a hint that your intent might be to give the enemies of Britain my corpse for their comfort and my sacred sword for a trophy? And the boy for a slave. No, Bedwyr; I do not think you were born to sell your soul to the Saxons."

"Lord, I swear on all holy, I thought the road led to the lake!"

"Yes, if you truly believe the sun rises in the north-lands." Arthur sighed. "Let it pass. You are all the men left me, Bedwyr; for a time. I must reach the lakeshore, get counsel, consult the visions of the water. She will heal me of my hurts better even than the kindly brethren of Inys Witrin, and then I will be hale enough to find my scattered troops once more. Modred is dead, who pacted with the Saxons. Let his fate lesson you, Bedwyr. No man can ever hope to build a realm in Britain unless the stones of its foundation are men of the land, the blood and life of Britain." He drew the great sword Excalibur from its sheath, though the branches of ancient oaks dipped low to tangle themselves around the shining blade. "I will show them this thrice-blessed steel, and its power will call them back to life."

Sparrow thought he heard Bedwyr mutter "Babbler," but he could not be sure.

That night they made camp within the smell of water. Sparrow performed the chores of the night willingly, for once, not driven by fear of Bedwyr's heavy hand but by the renewed strength of spirit he had gained from his true lord's presence. He gathered wood, made the fire, and used the last of their water to form the contents of the meal-pouch into cakes for the baking. Arthur watched him wearily.

"You are prodigal, Joseph," the king said. "What shall we do for drink?"

"There's water nearby. That way." Sparrow gestured through the shadowed trees in the direction from which a potent tang of half-rotted reeds wafted. "Can't you tell?"

Arthur gave a small laugh. "Of course, of course. It is the lake, my lad; her lake, the one I've come seeking."

"Her lake?" Sparrow echoed.

Arthur did not seem to hear him. His eyes wandered, coming in and out of focus, as a man who, waking, still dreams. "I have fallen out of blessing," he said. "She touched me once, and by her touch I was made a king, and more than a king. If I had only been satisfied with her blessing, I might be king yet, and the realm safe. But I sought more. The acclaim of men comes to the man who can show them that he is master of more possessions than they: Arms, treasure, land, fair women. The riches of the soul ... these they do not—cannot—choose not to see. And so I made my conquests for the sake of men's praise when by rights all the benison I should have sought was hers."

Sparrow blinked, troubled. "I—I do not understand you, my lord," he dared to say.

Arthur's smile was gentle. "How could you? You are only a boy. Yet perhaps that is a better thing to be than a man. Your understanding comes not from words, but from the heart, and I—I gave up my heart's dream long ago. That is why I have come back now, to this place, to her care, in the hopes I may recover it. In the domain of love, is anything ever truly lost?"

Sparrow did not know how to answer this. Instead he groped for the empty gourd and said, "I will fetch fresh water." He stole out of the leaping, fire-cast shadows and plunged with relief into the tangle of trees.

It did not take him long to find the lake. The trees themselves seemed to pull aside their branchy veils from its margins. It lay like a toss of cloth-of-silver over the breast of the land, an unblinking eye whose pupil was the moon.

Sparrow knelt and dipped the gourd into the water. It sang a gurgly carol, an oddly jolly sound in this lorn place. The boy's self-appointed task was quickly accomplished. He set the gourd aside carefully and splashed some water over his bruised face ...

... and gasped to feel not the cold clap of water, but the warm caress of a lady's hands.

The lady's face was there the way the world is there when a sleeper opens his eyes. Her eyes were a more brightly minted silver than the lake, her hair a paler frost than the distant moon. Sparrow's throat closed; he threw himself backward, away from the apparition. The gourd toppled, water spilling out, soaking back into the spongy marge of the lakeside.

"Boy, are you afraid? Of me?" Tall and splendid beyond lost Guinhwyfar's poor play at majesty, she wore mists and the green rustle of lake reeds for her garments. Sparrow stared, willing himself away or awake or—if he but had the courage—embraced by those same delicate arms from which he now shied.

"Has he sent you?" the vision inquired. Her voice rippled, wind and water and dreams. "I see his mark upon you. Tell me, is he near? Will he come?"

She named no names, but Sparrow knew. All the talk of the early court had been of how Arthur took his sword from these same white hands now coaxing Sparrow calm. The blade, symbol of a king's main might, bore a second message for those with the wisdom to read it: That Arthur's reign was sanctified by more than human agencies. Sparrow had thought it nothing but a fine tale.

"Y-yes," Sparrow replied, slowly picking himself up, rising only as far as his knees. To do more in her presence would be blasphemy. "My lord is here. There. Be-

yond the trees. He—" He did not know if he dared to
say more, to tell her of Arthur's hurts. He feared that
he might somehow bear the blame for them. No matter
what the truth was, the lady did not need to accept any
fact but her own whim. So it had always been with Bedwyr, and she had more power in her glance than that
knight ever owned in all his pride of body.

"Tell me, Sparrow," she said, and this time the simple
sound of his name from her lips washed over him with
the tenderness his starved soul craved.

He did not question how she came to know his name.
His faith encompassed it. "He was wounded, my lady,"
he said. The sturdy sound of his own voice surprised him.
"Grievously hurt in battle against his traitor son, Modred. But he's better now," the boy hastened to add,
seeing sorrow abruptly strike the lady's face. "And he'll
be better still once you've healed him."

The lady only shook her head and turned away. Now
Sparrow saw that she stood not upon dry ground, but on
the very surface of the lake. Her dainty feet were solid
enough to kiss the face of the water with rippled halos.
Other rings starred the waters around her, too: marks
like the scattered fall of rain, of tears.

"My lady, why—why are you crying?" Sparrow rose
from his knees, unable to do less, and came toward her
as if he, too, owned the enchantment to glide over the
face of the water. He did not, and his feet made clumsy
splashing sounds as she drifted farther from the shore
and he followed.

Only when the cold lapped him up to his waist did she
stop and turn. She gave a little cry when she saw how
closely he had dogged her path, understood that he
would have followed her into the depths of the lake and
drowned just as willingly. Her slim hand flashed and he
found himself beside her on the shore, soaked, shivering.

"Child, what possesses you?" she asked softly. This

time, when she reached out to him, he did not pull away. Her body held the thousand fragrances of the springtime and her hair enclosed him like angels' wings.

Giddy with so much beauty, Sparrow felt his breath almost fail him as he replied, "You were weeping. I could not bear it. I wanted only to comfort you, if I could."

Her smiled pitied him without making pity something a man should shun. "So ill-used, and yet you still cherish compassion? You are a wonder." Her fingers stole to the lacing of his tunic, touching the talisman that hung there. It was a cross, simply carved of oakwood. "You serve the white god. Is it his teachings that have given you so sound a heart?"

She held the cross in the palm of her hand. Sparrow marveled at this, for he had been taught that creatures of the otherworld could not bear the power of the cross, and shunned it for the sake of preserving their soulless selves. She read his thoughts in his face and laughed.

"Love is love," she said, letting the cross fall back. "Love to those who serve it under any sign. Once I knew the worship offered your white lord. Now the hallowers of my name have dwindled to a faithful few. It is of no consequence. There were many who served me falsely, used my name and power to justify things that are anathema to me. Better a new god with servants who will keep heart-true to the good teachings than a multitude of false servitors crowding my altars."

Sparrow bit his lip. He touched the carved pendant and imagined it glowed with a ghostlight where her hand had cradled it. "It was my mother's," he told her. "She left it to me. My father never taught me much of the white god, or of any god, but—but I have heard the priests teach at court, and I have attended the queen to Mass, and there were pictures painted on the chapel walls—" He took a deep breath and yanked the cross so hard that the thin twine binding it to his neck snapped. He offered it to her. "My lady, I would serve only you."

The lady would not take the offering. She held up her hands, and the cross twinkled from Sparrow's grasp. He drew a short, sharp breath to feel it back around his neck once more. "For the love your mother bore you, serve her god, whose teachings are also mine. If the water is pure and good to drink, what does the name of the wellspring matter?"

"Water ..." Sparrow echoed. The image of his lord flashed before his eyes. He grabbed the lady's hand without thinking. "He—my lord Arthur—he is your true servant," Sparrow said. "He needs you now. You must come!"

The lady sighed, her eyes straying back to the lake. "The moon casts many shadows on the water," she said. "I, who am bound to this place, read far and near in the images they give me. Dear child ... dear, loving, loyal heart, do you know how much may happen in the time it takes a boy to fill a watergourd? Do you know how much more than water may be spilled in an instant?"

Her words pitched black terror into Sparrow's bones. He shook his head, knowing and not knowing what she was saying, trying to push it all away. Her hand clasped his. She helped him to his feet. Still he shook his head dumbly, like a dog.

"Poor child," she murmured. "All this is too much for you. The sorrow is that you must yet bear more. Little Sparrow ..." She drew him near and pressed her lips to his brow, her fingertips to the cross that hung over his heart. "By this be blessed: Whatever more you must bear, bear the light."

And she was gone.

Sparrow lay flat on his back, the waters of the lake lapping against his heels, the moon a mask riding the night sky overhead. He sat up slowly, blinking like a daylight-startled owl. Hands groping to steady himself, he brushed against the gourd, filled to the lip with water. He got to his feet, picked up the gourd, and started back to camp.

Bedwyr was there alone, the sword Excalibur across his knees. He was cleaning the blade, his face dark with the greedy, all-possessing love of an old man who has taken a beautiful young wife, with or without her will. His enraptured eyes stroked the surface of the sword more tenderly than his ministering hands. Sparrow might as well have been a dead tree stump for all the attention he could draw from Bedwyr. The oatcakes smoked untended, half-charred and half-raw in the ashes.

Sparrow's darting glance searched the shadows, but there was no sign of his lord's presence anywhere. Every clue to point to Arthur was gone, vanished, even to the king's shield. "I brought water," the boy said at last, hearing the silly words tinkle weakly in the midnight silence.

Bedwyr looked up. A transformation terrible to see passed over his face. "There you are," he said. The words fell like drops of quicksilver, heavy and chill. "I am glad to see you, boy." Sparrow's wide-eyed stare betrayed too many doubts for the knight to do anything but laugh. "Oh, yes! Don't goggle so. I mean that with all my heart! Although I think you'll come to regret not having been here sooner. Your dawdling has cost you the benison of witnessing a miracle."

"A ... miracle?"

"Sit," Bedwyr directed. The sword Excalibur turned easily in his grasp. He used the holy blade to indicate a place beside him, hard by the campfire. Reluctantly, Sparrow obeyed. As he sat, he saw the glint of a battered gold circlet in the grass between Bedwyr's feet. "I will tell you what happened."

I will tell you what happened ...

A great hall, many men-at-arms filling the air with their clamor.

Stone walls giving back the dance of firelight, the rafters holding in the smell of burning logs, roast meat,
spilled ale.

In the high seat, the place of honor, Lord Bedwyr sat
with the sword Excalibur across his knees, receiving a
fresh delegation of chieftains whose former allegiance
had been to Arthur. "I will tell you what happened," he
said to them affably.

I will tell you what happened ...

The words filled Sparrow's head with fire, brought
back the sights and smells and awful revelations of that
night. Standing beside the throne at Lord Bedwyr's right
hand, his slim body neatly dressed in his master's livery,
he held the great gold cup from which Bedwyr took his
wine. It was set all round the rim with gems of the finest
water, rubies red as blood, diamonds like a lake whose
waters give back the light of the moon, and a single huge
sapphire of a clarity dazzling and all-encompassing as the
eye of God.

"It happened thus," said Bedwyr to his newcome
guests. "I rescued my lord King Arthur from the battle
against his traitor son and at his command brought him
to the shores of the holy lake. You know the place? It
was from those same waters Merlin summoned the Lady
who gave him this very sword you see, a blade of un-
earthly power, token of his kingship."

The men murmured assent. They knew the tales.

"He was very weak, alas," Bedwyr went on. "Too
weak to keep his feet. Is that not so, boy?" He called to
Sparrow for confirmation the way another man might
whistle up a hound. "He was with us, that boy," Bedwyr
paused to explain.

Sparrow felt the weight of the men's eyes upon him.
This was not the first time he had known that burden.
Ever since he and Bedwyr had emerged from the doings
of that lost night, the knight had retreated to his ances-

tral lands, sending out messengers to all of Arthur's former allies. The Saxons raged in the east; men who
squabbled over the bones of broken Camelot turned
their eyes together to face a common enemy. They were
ready to hear a single voice in their ear once more, and
Bedwyr had the wit to make sure it would be his.

The wit, the proof, and the tale.

"I made my lord the king as comfortable as I might,
with the boy to tend him," Bedwyr said. "Then Arthur
spoke. His voice was weaker than a whisper. He commanded me to take his sword, the holy blade Excalibur,
and bring it to the lakeside. He said I was to throw it
into the water and then come back and tell him what I
saw. Then he fainted, for his wounds were mortal and
he had lost much blood."

The man murmured louder—all save those who were
already Bedwyr's sworn vassals and had heard this tale
before. If Arthur had commanded Bedwyr to throw away
the blade, how did it come here? All knew it on sight;
they had followed its bright beacon many times into battle. What magic was hidden, yet to be told?

"I must obey my lord." Bedwyr sighed. "Conscious or
no, I must obey him; though I confess, I toyed with the
notion of simply *telling* him I'd obeyed his command.
Such a shame, to throw such a sword away! But I could
not do that; he was my lord. And so I did as I was
bidden, whirling the blade three times above my head
and finally letting it sail free over the lake. The boy is
my witness. Is that not so?"

Sparrow nodded. Bedwyr's face, now clean-shaven in
the Roman style, all rosy smiles, was a mask overlaying
the creature that had once clutched Sparrow's shoulder
till bone grated against bone, a creature with foam-
flecked jaws that snarled: *Don't tell me what you think
you saw in that bog, boy! I'll tell you what you saw, and
you'll tell it that same way, again and again, whenever it*

pleases me for you to speak. Make me a fool in sight of my men and I'll give you worse than I gave your precious lord!

Bedwyr nodded, too, well pleased with the boy's biddability. He continued: "Both of us thought to hear the splash. None came. Instead we saw her, the Lady. She rose from the waters of the lake, the sword held fast in her hand. She was clad all in white samite, fairer than the daughter of any earthly king, and when her gold-shod feet touched the shore, roses blossomed."

The lady's true image rose from the phantom lake of Sparrow's memory, and mocked the false image lord Bedwyr's words had made.

"She came toward us and we knelt in homage to her beauty. Then she said, 'Arise, Sir Bedwyr! Arise and take what is yours by right. Shall this good blade rust beneath the waters while Britain stands in need? Shall this metal crumble away while there remains one fit to wield it?' And she gave the sword to me." He settled his spine against the high back of his throne and a beatific look bloomed over his face.

Someone spat. "Prove it!"

Bedwyr's face darkened at the challenge. He had heard its like before—more times in the past than of late, when he was just beginning to rally men to his standard—yet each time he greeted it with no less killing wrath in his soul. He sprang forward, hands gripping the armrests of the throne as if these were clay to be gouged with his fingertips.

The one who had spoken so was a chieftain, big-bodied, strong in arms and men. Bedwyr damped his wrath as swiftly as it had kindled, though Sparrow saw the coals still smoldering in his new lord's eyes. He would speak softly to this cynic, but he had marked the man. He would use what words he needed to win him over, but he would not forget. At the first chance—a battle, a tourney, even a dark turning of the castle stair—Bedwyr would see to this man's death. That was what Bedwyr did best.

"You see here the sword," Bedwyr said smoothly. "You are free to examine it as long and as thoroughly as you like. Surely you were one of my lord's closest companions, certain to know Excalibur on sight?" This last was the tickle of a whiplash; Bedwyr and the chieftain both knew how minor the man's rank had been while Camelot still stood.

"I know it," the man grumbled. "Just as any good smith might know it well enough to forge its twin."

Bedwyr was untroubled. "I see you are not disposed to hear my words as truth. Whose will do?" His head turned almost casually in Sparrow's direction. "A little child shall lead them," he purred.

Relics were brought. The doubting chieftain, by his own lights a devout Christian, made much of reminding Sparrow of the torments of hell awaiting those who forswore themselves on the bones of saints.

Sparrow glanced at his master. Bedwyr's smile was stiff now. This was the first time the boy had been made to testify on martyrs' bones. Bedwyr knew that Sparrow wore the white god's sign around his neck; he could not know that it was holy to the boy only for the touch of two women—his mother and the Lady—now both lost to him. Sparrow knew he had lost the Lady's grace the first time Bedwyr called on him to back the false knight's tale and he yielded up the truth as a sacrifice to his fear.

I am no hero, my lady. I am only a boy. Bitter tears stung Sparrow's lashes. *I could not bear what he would do to me if I did not lie. So I have betrayed you; so I have lost you forever.*

"Do you understand me, boy?" the chieftain demanded, siezing Sparrow's hand and crushing it to the reliquary.

"I will be damned for eternity if I lie," Sparrow replied. Gems and worked gold bit into his palm. "I understand."

As much as he could step into the boy's skin and rule him by terror for his life, Bedwyr could not step into Sparrow's mind. And so, not knowing what the boy's solemn expression might mean for him, Bedwyr quickly said, "Let us hope he truly does understand! For I confess, he has always been a little weak-minded, and the wonder we both saw at the lakeside was not an easy one for a hale man to behold and still claim full possession of his mind. Sometimes he rambles, and sometimes—"

"I will hear what he has to say," the chieftain gritted, his back to Bedwyr. To Sparrow he said, "Speak now, boy! You know the oath you've sworn. I will not doubt your words."

Sparrow drew a breath; Bedwyr held his. Then: "I saw the Lady of the Lake. The sword Excalibur is my lord Bedwyr's."

"And?" The prompting word came from Bedwyr and the chieftain both. Sparrow looked to his new lord, and a sigh escaped his lips so subtly that only he knew of it.

"Then there came a great black barge, hung all with draperies of the finest silks. Three queens sat in the prow, and it was steered and poled by no man. They came and took my lord King Arthur aboard and laid him gently on a bier. Then the great barge went away, and the three queens mourning."

Sparrow spoke the words without heart. Bedwyr had cared only that he know them well enough to recite them letter-perfect when occasion demanded them. All up and down the length of the great hall men were whispering among themselves. Most of them had heard the tale already, some of them were such old allies of Bedwyr that they could recite the words in their dreams. A few had heard the tale so frequently, from Bedwyr's lips as well as Sparrow's, that they had conjured up new ornaments to hang upon it, for their own amusement. They assured their boardmates that the three queens were women of Faerie, that Arthur had boarded the barge a living man, that the three had taken him off to Avalon, to heal him of his hurts, to restore him to the lordship of the land when again Britain might need his conquering arm in her service.

Until that day, men such as Bedwyr would have to do. If Bedwyr knew of the new embroideries to his story, he did not seem to mind. A throne was a throne; he did not need a legend to wrap around himself. "This satisfies you?" he asked the chieftain, leering.

The man of might said nothing, but knelt before Bedwyr and did homage.

The taste of falsehood was acrid in Sparrow's mouth. "My lord, may I go?" he whispered. Bedwyr's nod was curt; he, too, was satisfied. Sparrow removed himself from the hall with the perfect poise of a well-schooled page. Only when he was out of sight of the revelers did he break and run.

There was a well in the forecourt, a circle of yellow stones that made a low lip to keep night-wanderers from tumbling down the shaft and to ward the path of silly sheep. Sparrow flung himself across this slight barricade and stared down into the well. All was darkness. No moon rode the sky this night, no light could steal into this throat of hell.

Yet for Sparrow, the black water held a hundred clamoring mouths that named him coward, and his eyes alone had the power to see the well-beloved face of his true king floating just beneath the surface.

My son, my son, why have you betrayed me? The ghostly cry did not go out to Modred; Sparrow knew it was for him.

"Boy! Hey, boy, come here! Our lord wants you!" A

hand descended to Sparrow's shoulder with almost enough force to plunge him over the lip of the well, into the black water. *Better it were so,* he thought, still seeing the king's face rippling slowly from his sight, sinking deeper into the darkness. *Better if I had followed him; better I follow him now.* But his longing went unheeded. Instead the hand seized him in a merciless grip and hauled him to his feet.

"What in the devil's name are you doing here?" The servant's breath stank of rotten teeth and stale beer.

"He—my lord Bedwyr gave me leave to go," Sparrow replied. The servant was squat and square, a troll of a fellow, with all of a troll's coarseness and crudity.

" 'Gave me leave to go,' " the man mocked, imitating Sparrow's soft accent, culled from his time of service in the king's court at Camelot. He shook Sparrow by the scruff. "Well, he's changed his mind! You're to attend him at once. That northcountry bullhead who doubted our lord's tale but heeded *your* telling of it had further business to bring."

"I don't see—"

"Who cares what you see?" The man gave Sparrow a shove back toward the castle portal. "All you need to know is you're wanted, I'm sent to fetch you, and you'd best scamper back double quick or it's my skin, too!"

Mindful as a kicked dog, Sparrow scampered. He left the loutish servant breathing his dust as he raced back into the great hall.

What a transformation met Sparrow's eyes! Before, the atmosphere of the hall had been fragmented. On the one hand there was the air of sleek and solemn diplomacy lapping Bedwyr as he stretched his wiles to win over a fresh batch of allies. Beyond this compass, those who were already his sworn men held themselves apart, merry enough, but at the same time on guard. New allies meant new internal rivalries; no need to fret about these until the alliances were firmly made, yet wise to be alert to each new shift in the powers surrounding their lord, Excalibur's heir.

Now there was no such division. An air of high hilarity lit up the hall. Servants hustled back and forth, trundling barrels of ale, mead of the Saxons' brewing, and the smaller casks of wine from the far shores of Gaul.

"Here, boy! Here! Attend me!"

Sparrow's head snapped up. Bedwyr had risen from his throne and was summoning him. He stood in the straw-strewn open space between the two long rows of trestle tables that filled the great hall. A priest stood by him—old and wrinkled as an autumn plum—a book of holy writ in his gnarled hands. Sparrow ducked beneath the nearest table and was at Bedwyr's side with thought's speed.

"Good, you're here!" Bedwyr seemed to give the boy's cheek an affectionate pat, but Sparrow's long hair concealed the fact that his lord had grasped his ear and given it a sharp twist. He knew far better than to cry out with the pain. He knew the forfeit there'd be to pay if he flinched under one of Bedwyr's little "gifts."

"What would you have of me, my lord?" he said, as bravely as the smart would allow.

"Your goodwill, my lad. And your eyes to witness. I'm being wed this night!" Bedwyr chuckled, then stooped so that his words were for Sparrow's ears only. "Our friend the doubting chieftain has been won over better than I'd hoped. He has a daughter, an only child who'll bring her father's lands to the marriage bed. He's offered her to me in token of his remorse for ever having doubted my story. May God bless all such Christian niceties of conscience!" To those watching, Bedwyr's exultant laughter might have been over some jape his scrawny little page had uttered, though in truth no one believed the sad-faced boy capable of mirth.

"Wed ..." Sparrow tried to fathom what this change might mean for him. Would a lady's presence soften the austerities of Bedwyr's household, mitigate the casual cruelties broadcast over the weary days?

"Wipe that donkey-look from your face, boy!" Bedwyr growled. "Drop it or I'll knock it loose for you. She comes!"

Sparrow heard a cheer mount the air from the massed men to either side of the trestle tables. The Christian chieftain had entered the gauntlet at the far end of the hall, and with him came the slight, small, veiled figure of a girl. They walked with dignity between the ranks of Bedwyr's men, the girl with eyes downcast beneath her all-shrouding veil, the father acknowledging the shouts of bawdy goodwill with curt nods to left and right.

When they reached the priest's place, the chieftain took his daughter's hand and placed it in Bedwyr's blunt paw, then stood aside. Bedwyr gazed at the bowed head—fair hair a tantalizing hint beneath the veil—and smiled like a fox about to dine. The priest opened his book and began the sacrament.

"Wait!" Bedwyr held up his hand. "If this lady is to be the foundation of my royal house, I would have my men see her face now."

"What?" The chieftain was irate. "That's neither seemly nor modest. My daughter is an honorable virgin and—"

"I do not doubt your word on that," Bedwyr said easily. "Although you doubted mine. They say that the wise-women and wizards of the countryside can read fertility in a person's face. Certain signs reveal how fruitful a bride will be. Arthur's rule fell because his queen was barren. I owe this to my loyal men, that they may be assured that what we fight for will outlast a single generation. I say they have the right to see her face! If you quarrel with that, you quarrel with them, not me."

Bedwyr's men saw the chance for good sport in the chieftain's discomfiture. They set up a mighty roar demanding to see the face of the bride. Some drew daggers and set these on the boards in token of how far they'd go to defend a right they hadn't known they possessed until Bedwyr mentioned it. The chieftain's face flushed crimson, but he saw where he stood.

"So be it," he grumbled, and turned away.

Bedwyr grinned. "You heard it from her father's own lips!" he told his men. And he raised the bride's veil.

Sparrow's heart stopped. He must be dead, and all his short life flashing through his mind in the final agony. That was the only explanation. For there, under the veil that until this moment had concealed the chieftain's daughter, was the face of the Lady.

No! he cried out in the lone places of his soul. And again, *No! It cannot be!* The great hall bled away around him. He stood in a place of desolation and howled his despair into the empty sky.

But it is, Sparrow. Her presence filled his mind even as the priest's dry liturgy filled his ears, coming from a place now far, far off. She was with him as she had been with him by the lakeside, standing less than a stone's throw away. *It is because it must be; don't you see? Arthur's day is done, the holy blade has fallen into worse than rust. My champion is dead, and the light has gone out of the land.*

She did not move to join him, or to hold out her hands. Sparrow felt a greater fear than any he had ever known slowly creep up to possess him, body and soul, as he saw the fetters at wrists and ankles, the chains that rooted her to the earth. *Better to give yourself to the Saxons than to Bedwyr!* he cried in anguish.

Better yet to give myself to none, the Lady replied. *But I am what the age makes me. What I am now cannot hope to survive without a champion, one strong enough to take up the sword in my name.*

Sparrow's spirit fell to its knees. *I will be your champion.* He spoke as one who believes.

Her sigh gusted through his mind like the breath of winter. *I thought you were.*

He heard the blighted hope that underlay her words as surely as he had heard his dead king's voice rise from the depths of the well's dark water to accuse him. It hurt him more deeply than any blow of Bedwyr's. *How can I defend you without a sword?* he pleaded. *How can I serve you rightly until I'm grown? I am only a boy, but if your magic can make a man of me, if you can set the holy blade in my hands, then—!*

My magic cannot trespass on your own. My enchantments are powerless before your birth-given powers. How can I give you what you already hold? The Lady's image was fading, dwindling, but losing none of its light. *You are my champion, but only if you will champion yourself.*

I don't— He stared at his hands, still empty of any weapon.

Free the prisoner, my lord! she cried. *In mercy, seek him out and set the captive free! This is the only true quest of a champion.*

The captive . . .

We are all captives, child. She spread her hands to the limit of her chains. *Only a few of us find the strength to reforge the bars of our cages into the strength of a sword.*

Her presence shrank in upon itself, becoming a bright, white dove. It tried to fly away, but the chains still held it fast. It beat its wings against the darkness until its heart broke and it fell at his feet. He stooped to pick up the small, shattered body and saw that all he held in the palm of his hand was a dirty, dead sparrow.

"NO!"

Silence surged back over Sparrow's shout with the

force of a great wave breaking on the shore. The priest's words snagged in his throat, the chieftain's head swung around with the unwavering, uncomprehending gaze of an ox, the bride's features melted from the Lady's mask to the vacant, pleasant, timorous face of an ordinary girl.

If Sparrow saw this last transformation, it made no matter. He was speaking, voicing all the hidden truths he knew, loud and clear, one hand clutching the cross at his neck, the other leveled at Bedwyr. He felt as if he were two beings—one soaring far above the throng of stunned and stricken gapemouths filling the great hall, the other a boy whose piping voice sang out, tearing away the lies, bearing the light.

Time stretched taut as a bowstring. At first it thrummed with only the sound of Sparrow's voice, then by degrees it buzzed with threads of other voices, Bedwyr's men whispering, whispering, whispering . . .

"—dead?"

"By *his* hand! All that story of the lake, the queens—"

"Horseturds! The boy saw the body. There was a bog. Bedwyr'd sunk it there, shield and all, but they had to pass by it as they left the lakeside and the boy saw—"

"—*says* he saw. And said he saw the queens as well! Are we to believe him then or now?"

"Lord Bedwyr says the boy's not fully right in the head."

"*Your* lord. No lord of mine! The filthy murderer . . ."

"What proof, beyond the boy's words?"

"Proof enough, that he said the words at all! They'll be his death."

Time fell back into the normal pace of seconds, minutes, lifetimes. Bedwyr loosed a growl. "Curse you, you toad, I'll crush you for this!" Excalibur leaped from its scabbard to his hand and fell like judgment on Sparrow's head.

Metal struck metal, shattering the blade in Bedwyr's hand. The man stared, dumbfounded, at the notched and

blood-blackened sword he'd carried from the field of
Camlann, the weapon he'd used to kill his king.

Not dead, untouched, Sparrow looked up to see the
holy blade gleaming in the withered hand of the priest.
Before his mind could accept this mad vision, he saw the
sword's enchantment spread over the old man's image in
a spate of light. It washed away all seeming of the priest,
leaving behind a tall, magnificent warrior whose face
bore the deathless cast of the Fey and whose breast bore
the badge of the Lady: from out of a shining lake a white
arm arising, bearing a sword of miracles.

Time froze. Sparrow looked around him and saw that
of all those massed in Bedwyr's great hall, he and the
Faerie knight were the only two still capable of movement. Bedwyr's men were stone, their expressions of
anger, betrayal, outrage spelling out a litany of vengeance to be taken, accounts to be paid.

"They will kill him," Sparrow breathed, and marveled
inwardly at the fact that even so, for all Sir Bedwyr's
evil, he still felt a pang of pity for the man.

"What they will do is their path to choose," said the
Faerie knight. "You ride another, if you will." He was
no longer afoot, but mounted on a steed that shone like
the dawn star. "Faithful page, will you serve your lord
still, until he come again?" He gestured, and there was
a second mount, riderless, waiting.

Sparrow stared and then, knowing more with his heart
than with his mind what it was he did, he nodded
consent.

Bedwyr's hall blew into dust behind them as they rode
out, leaving stone men to fight and vie and struggle over
trifles. The tumult of their squabbling faded from Sparrow's ears. He sat his steed with the ease of a prince
born to the saddle. All fear and all pain fell away from
his soul like the brittle shell that yields the butterfly. He
turned his face to the light as they rode on to Avalon.

THE SPELL BETWEEN WORLDS

by Karen Haber

The morning sun rent the fog, spearing particles of vapor on golden beams, seizing motes and setting them dancing as the skies over the green enchanted isle of Avalon cleared.

Nimue, second high priestess of Avalon, knelt at the altar of the Lady of the Lake and touched a wand of juniper to the glowing coals in the carved brazier. Blue smoke spiraled upward. She inhaled its fragrance three times and reverently invoked the name of the Goddess.

"Please, Lady," she whispered. "Don't forswear your faithful servant. I've kept faith with you, Goddess, haven't I? Why, then, have you forsaken me? Why have you denied me? Three times over three nights I've invoked your visions at the scrying pond and three times you have refused me. Why? Why?"

She waited, scarcely daring to breathe.

All she heard was the sound of wind in the trees and the forlorn cry of a distant bird.

In wavering tones Nimue repeated her prayer.

The Goddess was remote, silent, immutable.

Nimue felt tears sting her eyes and a sudden surge of anger. "Are you even there, Goddess, or are you attending to some other more favored daughter's prayer just now? I know I was taught that you are everywhere and your will is inherent in all things. What, then, is your will for me?" She was silent a moment. "Is anyone listening?"

She received no answer, nor did she expect any. The Goddess worked in her own ways and in her own time. But Nimue's next attempt at scrying would come tonight. She had hoped and prayed for a sign before then.

Grimly she doused the firepot and got to her feet. There was no use invoking one who would not come. She left the stone temple, took a deep breath, and gazed up at the azure patches peeping through the clouds. She thought of the deep blue bowl of the sky over Camelot, of Merlin's ancient sapphire eyes beseeching her mercy, and she was laden with a heavy sense of longing and dread.

Dear Goddess, she thought. Avert and spare me. Memories are the worst curse known to humankind, surely.

Nimue would not let herself think of the mage of Camelot nor how she had brought him low. She forced herself to stare at the green curve of land until her vision blurred.

"Nimue! Why aren't you resting?"

The voice was as pointed as a needle. Miriame, her cousin, stood scowling before her, dressed in a mud-colored shawl and robe.

"You mean I should be preparing myself for the evening's ordeal?" Nimue said sharply. And regretted the barbed tone of her voice almost as soon as she had spoken.

Of late worry had honed the edge of voices all around Nimue: the voices of her sister priestesses, of the initiates, of her cousins, of her nieces. All of them had seen her try and fail at the pond, once, twice, three times. Each one of them wondered what would happen tonight.

Their piercing concern gave Nimue an aching head.

Were they so very blind, her sisters of Avalon? Why

didn't they use the senses that the Goddess had given them to see and understand? Was regret such a foreign country? Surely the Old Ones who had forged the cult of the Goddess had journeyed there once. Surely.

She smiled an apology at Miriame. "After a cold night spent casting in vain for portents in the scrying pond I wanted a walk in the sunshine to warm my blood."

"Sunlight draws us all to its healing powers," Miriame said. Her thin, dark face softened in sympathy and her features, which hearkened back to those of the Old Ones, seemed almost pretty for a moment.

Nimue's tall blonde fairness gave strong contrast, virtually a rebuke, to Miriame's pinched and somber looks. Some of the less charitable initiates in Avalon had been known to whisper that Nimue's veins carried a strange changeling blood.

They had said the same of Merlin.

And they had cursed him, the servants of the Lady of the Lake, had cursed Merlin for betraying the Goddess and the Old Ways. Hadn't he mingled the Lady's sacred regalia with the tinny decorations of the Christian god? Nimue had been sent to Camelot to seduce and entrap the venerable sorcerer, to wring him dry of spells, and to force him to return to Avalon to face the Lady's justice.

Nimue thought of Merlin now and felt the cold knife of conscience enter her soul. My spells go awry, she thought. My scrying yields nothing. And you are all coming to fear me, my sisters, to fear my failure and your need of me. You need a high priestess to take old Raven's place.

A shadow flickered across the sun. Nimue glanced up, but there was nothing in the sky, nothing at all.

"Are you ill?" Miriame said. "You look pale. Here, let me help you to a seat in the pavilion."

"No, please, I'm fine." And again a moment of darkness, a quick flicker overhead. Nimue knew that she had

felt the tremor of the Unseen dancing along the edges
of her consciousness, a warning of things to come. "I'm
just a bit fatigued," she said. "That's all. Perhaps I should
go meditate." Again a flicker and the world turned up-
side down, then back again.

Miriame nodded, her satisfaction evident. "I'll bid you
good day, cousin."

All around Nimue the air sparkled and shifted. Her
breath came hard, rasping in her chest. She forced herself
to smile and wave as Miriame took her leave. Only when
her cousin was out of sight did she allow herself the
luxury of quivering in fear and anticipation. She needed
a safe and private place, quickly. There. A grove of trees
not far from the path. Half-stumbling, she thrust herself
between two wide brown trunks and into the pungent
shelter of the thicket.

None too soon, for the vision came down around her
with smothering force and she fell to her knees, swooning
upon the mossy ground.

She is six years old and she hears the wondrous singing, smells the sweet incense, sees the sacred, dancing
light and the smiling lady all aglow in blue and white—
a queen, perhaps?—beckoning her up the steep stairs of
the temple. How big everyone is around her! How unfamiliar the fragrant perfume of the woman whose arms
enfold her! She is gathered in; and she hears her own
mother's voice, loudly protesting, fading as the chorus
swells higher and higher.

The scene slides and subtly changes. She is twelve,
long-legged and coltish, wearing the robes of a novice.
The temple stairs are no longer so steep. When she
thinks of mother, Nimue sees only the face of the high
priestess Raven, dark-eyed Raven, doyenne of the sisterhood, first servant to the Lady of the Lake.

"Be a good girl," Nimue is told, by which she understands that obedience will be rewarded by wonders. She enters the House of Maidens, a warm and fragrant space. A golden cup encrusted with gems and redolent of spice and wine is offered to her. She drinks deeply, closes her eyes, dreams. The images are peculiar, magical.

She sees a white-bearded stranger, his face seared by time. Lights and colors play across her mind and she hears maddened arpeggios, strange chords and screeches, sounds she has never heard before. She is floating like a bird upon the purple layers of the air, inhaling marvelous perfumes.

Switch! She is older, pledged to silence, never daring to utter a sound. Even as she receives the tattoo called the kiss of Ceridwen—a slender blue crescent at her right temple that marks her as a priestess and thereby binds her to the Goddess—she remains stoic, silent although the pain entreats her to cry out.

She falls ever deeper into the swirling mists, floating farther into the mysteries. She is wandering in a strange dark land, lost between gray hillsides, her features obscured by a spell. She wants to walk, but her feet won't move. She is caught in boggy ground, immured within a circle—no, not a circle. A pentagram. Caught within another's spell. A spell against wandering demons. But she is no demon! Or is she? She struggles, desperate to pull off her mask, but it is fixed tightly to her face. She tries to call out, to beseech Merlin to come back, come back, please, and help her, forgive her, but the spell has stolen her voice as well.

With a choked cry Nimue awoke. The sending had left her dizzy and confused. She was curled upon the damp ground, her undyed woolen cloak stained green by the grasses she had crushed. High above her loomed the great dark crowns of the oak grove, the heavy limbs raised in scallops against the sky. The sound of peaceful waters lapping the shores of Avalon came to her. She shivered and pressed her hands to her face. Her head swam and the light hurt her eyes.

What could the vision mean?

The sending had reawakened Nimue's childish awe of the temple and the Lady. Once again she could feel the pinprick ache of the tattoo and the holy sense of mission that accompanied it. She had been righteous, strong, and brave, possessed of the Sight and consecrated to service of the Goddess.

Somewhere she had lost that ennobling sensibility. Had it been when she first glimpsed the white-bearded Merlin? Or when she had come to know him, to know his kindness, his wisdom, his sad humor? Perhaps she had lost it when she had sent the doomed mage across the waters, back to the arms of the vengeful priestesses. Seen his pitiful bound form curled in the bottom of that rocking boat which, lacking rudder and sail, nevertheless had found its way between worlds to the shores of the enchanted isle. Nimue had wept in silence where one could see, but what did that matter? The deed was done.

And now, was this particular vision a sign? Had the Goddess restored her favor to Nimue?

She remembered the shifting lights, the eerie sense of floating alone between layers of air, between worlds. Wandering alone and lost. And then to be trapped within a pentagram. What had that meant? Was it a warning, a reminder of her pledge to the Goddess? A sign that the Lady felt she had strayed in her faith?

"Not so," she whispered. "Goddess, not so. I've remained true." But a small voice in her head said, you have dared to question and doubt.

She got to her feet, knees shaking. Slowly she made her way back along the winding processional, all the way up to the Temple of the Sun. Behind her on the lake swans glided in and out of the purple reeds.

The stone walls of the temple were pale gray and ancient, visible only to her and to those who, like her, followed the Old Ways. If any stranger were to stumble by chance upon this shore he would see only a pale green hillside, a tor topped by a crumbling ancient tower. But no one ever came here by chance.

Beyond the temple sat the sacred spring that fed the mirror pool where all scrying was done. At the thought of it Nimue tensed. The evening seemed a long way off. Only when the moon was a pale silver sliver reflected back at her from the sacred pool could she bring the four elements together to petition the Goddess. Wind, water, earth, and fire would open the Sight once again to her questing gaze. The Goddess granted only certain visions. Others had to be summoned after long, sweaty travail. And Nimue had lately found the effort taxing almost beyond endurance.

These months past she had walked the island that had been her home for so many years and found herself a stranger. Before, she had been content to stay within the limits of Avalon's boundaries. But Merlin had shown her more, so much more. Could it be that her encounter with the mage had fundamentally changed her?

As a child, Avalon had been all the world to Nimue. She had watched the priestesses at work among the apple trees and at the scrying pond, and longed for the day when she would take her place among them.

But Merlin had shown her the moon and the stars. He had taken her inside a thrush's body so that she could feel its beating heart, and into a river pike where she had counted its slow aqueous thoughts.

She had felt herself opening, deepening, embracing great truths and marvelous facts.

He had taught her how kings are made, and how they are brought down. How wars can be won. How castles can be summoned, stone by stone, from empty air. How the great, wide world worked.

Knowing all that, how could she be content now with only the pond and the orchards?

A bird threw itself out of a silvery-gray tree and into the wide blue sky. Nimue watched it unfurl dark wings and, beating them against the air, swiftly become a speck in the distance. She recalled Merlin's rasping voice telling her how to change herself, to become a fish, a bird, a forest creature. To leap into the air and fly away. It would be so very easy. . . .

A sudden chill prickled her skin, brought her back to herself. The sun cast long shadows across the grass toward her.

Become a bird? Nimue thought. *What can I be thinking of? I'm a priestess of the Goddess, in line for the greatest of honors, to become high priestess of Avalon. Raven has anointed me. That's life enough.*

A group of young novice priestesses awaited her counsel and instruction. She hurried toward the temple: the maidens and their youthful enthusiasm usually buoyed her spirits.

Eagerly Nimue climbed the curving stairs and entered the room to find the girls arrayed and waiting. A pretty sight, she thought. The young faces, smooth skin, hair pulled back in neat loops and coils. So serious. So determined to learn and master all the varied mysteries.

So had she been, and so had she learned. And now she would pass along what she knew so that others would take her place at the appropriate time. Give and receive, give and receive, the reassuring cycle of ritual and continuance.

Nimue greeted them and told them to gather around her. The room was nearly dark, lit only by a sputtering firepot, and the air was dank and chilly. Nimue saw that the girls, clad only in their thin maidens' robes, were rubbing their hands together and shaking with cold.

"Here," she said. "I'll show you how to do a simple warming spell."

Nimue took a deep breath and spoke musical words as softly as the rains fall upon the ground. A small bright spark leaped to life between her outstretched hands and danced nimbly from fingertip to fingertip.

The girls smiled and giggled. The youngest clapped in sheer delight. Nimue felt her mood lift as she handled the glowing sparklers. "Hold out your hands," she told the maidens. "Yes, you try. It's simple."

They stretched out their fingers, eyes shining.

The dancing sparks moved from hand to hand, spreading a warming glow throughout the room.

But something began to go wrong. As Nimue watched, the spell slipped sideways and the sparks combined, fanned into a fire imp, malevolent and powerful.

The thing had baleful eyes of deep red, while its flesh, if flesh it could be called, was a constant ferment of blue and green and yellow. It was no bigger than Nimue's hand. But as she watched it laughed in monstrous delight and seemed to grow, to expand in all directions, exuding a terrible stench. It was pure evil.

The thing fell upon the youngest maiden, grappling with her while the girl shrieked in pain and fear.

Dear Goddess, what had gone wrong? Nimue felt stunned and yet she must move, must stop this horror. Quickly she whispered the spell for unmaking.

"Fire, be still!
Congeal and submit!
Bite no more,
Grow cool and yield—"

The fire imp clambered up the girl's robe as the others, gasping, drew back in fear.

Nimue whispered the spell again. No use. The Goddess's magic was not working. Desperately she rummaged through her memory but could find nothing that would avail. She fell upon the child, trying to beat the fire imp down.

A wild voice, made of thunder and howling winds, filled the room, chanting in the Old Tongue.

The imp froze.

Suddenly Raven, the high priestess, was there in the room with them. She seemed to float in midair, her age-withered face pale as ice, her eyes alight, her hair standing on end. When there was extreme need, Raven had the ability to travel somewhere instantaneously. Her voice, great and terrible, railed once more against the invading spirit. The very walls of the room shook with it.

The fire imp slid down to the stone floor, pooled there, a shining puddle, and trickled toward the firepot. The fiery liquid climbed the sides of the blackened brazier and doused itself upon the coals.

With the danger past, Raven seemed to sag into herself, to deflate and compress. The light in her eyes went out.

Nimue cradled the youngest girl in her arms. "See? There was no damage. No harm. The thing is gone."

Wordlessly Raven held out her hands and the girl ran to her, hiding her face in Raven's dark skirts. "Go to your rooms," she said, her voice flat, her expression weary. "I would speak with Nimue alone."

The girls filed out silently. Raven poked at the firepot, and for a long moment neither woman spoke.

Finally Nimue could bear it no longer. She looked up in anguish and said, "I don't know what happened."

Raven turned and faced her. Her eyes were bottomless pools. "You summoned the thing."

"The spell went wrong. I wanted merely to amuse the girls and warm the room."

"And what spell was that? I never heard of such a thing."

Nimue could not meet the old woman's eyes. "One I learned from Merlin."

"The blasphemer? You dared to use his magic here?"

"It was a harmless jest," Nimue said.

"Not harmless enough. And where did that horror come from?"

"I don't know. What do you think, that I brought it in here clinging to my apron?" The words slipped out before Nimue could stop herself.

Raven's mouth twitched in what might have been cold amusement. "Perhaps. Certainly I have no better explanation."

"Nor do I."

"Perhaps you should meditate upon it, then." Raven gestured brusquely in dismissal and, as if to drive home her point, walked stiffly from the room rather than relying upon any incantation to speed her way.

Nimue stared after her. She treats me like a child instead of the heir-apparent, she thought. Yet I know magics of which she has no inkling, incantations which Merlin taught me.

Back came the mocking thought: Yes, but what good are these great magics if you can't control them, and if they harm the very ones you love?

Again Nimue had no answer. She put the cap on the firepot and sought the seclusion of her tiny room.

Nimue rested upon her hard mattress and waited for the sun to set. The mishap in class had left her edgy and unhappy.

She closed her eyes, calmed her thoughts, and began to count her breaths.

One.

Two.

Three.

The image of the scrying pond popped into her mind. She shook it away, told herself to concentrate.

Four.

Five.

Her left foot itched. She ignored it.

Seven.

Eight.

Hopeless. Sighing, Nimue opened her eyes. Meditation availed her nothing, merely adding to her disquiet.

She did not attend the evening meal but supped in her room on bread, cheese, and the dark mulled cider made from the apples of the orchard below the hill. Tonight was her last chance in this lunar cycle. She could only attempt to foretell the future under a waxing moon.

Just before moonrise she arrayed herself in a deep blue gown, pulled her hair back, and tied it. Several long breaths cleared her lungs, calmed her mind. It was time for the scrying.

As Nimue approached the temple, she saw the novices kindling the torches and candles. The sky above was deep purple, flecked with the cold light of stars. The horizon glowed as the moon rose above its darkened curve.

The scent of burning sage, pungent and smoky, greeted Nimue. The pool awaited, placid silver in the moonlight. She knelt before it, feeling again, as if for the first time, a thrill of wonder at its mystery. Here the Goddess revealed what would be.

The novices, pale maidens in their green robes, fell on their knees beside her. Raven knelt among them, her blue-dyed gown looking nearly black in the candles' glow. Nimue felt she could read her thoughts.

Raven would be thinking, "Sister, bring the Goddess back to her rightful place in the world of men. You will be first among us. She will work through you."

Nimue knew what they all desired, novices and old priestess alike, knew only too well. They wanted—and expected—Nimue to become the Lady of the Lake, the living incarnation of the Goddess's will. Keeper of the sacred pool. Defender of the Old Ways against the incursions of Christians. Raven was old, too old, a dried apple doll with bright raisins for eyes in a withered face. She lacked the strength to attempt such work much longer.

As Nimue saluted the four elements and pressed the hazel branch to her head, she thought, *I was chosen. Chosen for this work. Chosen to deliver up Merlin to his fate. Gave my maidenhead in return for his magic.*

I only did as I was told. I was chosen. Or was I cursed?

Nimue shuddered and put down the bough. Raven's eyes cut through her.

The maidens quivered like taut bowstrings, like saplings in the wind, but there was no wind.

Nimue told herself to concentrate. She would succeed this evening. She must. She reached for the silver pitcher of sacred water. The curved handle was cool to her touch.

Raven blinked, relaxed.

Slowly Nimue poured a trickle into the pond. The spreading ripples distorted the reflection of her face and, behind her, the faces of priestesses-in-training. Nimue watched and felt a strange fear ticking in her stomach.

She calmed herself. *I will see whatever the Goddess wills.* She whispered the words to invoke a vision of the future.

The ripples spread thinner and thinner until they were no more. The pond remained silvery and placid. Nimue saw only her own wide blue eyes staring up from a face gone ashen. Nothing more.

Behind her, the maidens were murmuring. Raven stared, shock and dismay in her dark eyes.

The pond was tranquil. The spell had failed for the fourth time in as many nights.

Nimue felt alarm move through her in ever-widening circles. Again the Goddess denied her. What did it mean?

Warring magics were roaring within her spirit, shattering her focus. She struggled to regain her composure. Again. She would try it again.

She closed her eyes and breathed deeply. Saluted the four elements. Poured the sacred water. Whispered the sacred words.

Nothing.

Once more. She would put everything she had into this attempt. She reached for the pitcher yet again.

A hand closed around her wrist.

Nimue turned to meet Raven's glittering dark eyes. "Perhaps another night, sister." The old voice was a breathy whisper, but it carried the weight of ancient authority. The pitcher rang like a bell, tolling a deep, mournful note as Nimue put it down.

She saw all around her the shocked eyes of the novices. Raven, too, stared at her with an accusatory glare. The thought, unspoken, was obvious: What have you done to bring the disfavor of the Goddess upon you?

Muttering apologies, Nimue fled the eyes and murmurs, fled the pool and the hillside for the safety of her cell-like room. There she paced out the long hours of the night, reliving the failed attempts at the pond and the awful incident with the fire imp. As she paced, she felt that her soul was in torment, contested for by rival forces, by the Lady and Merlin.

Just before dawn, Nimue came to a decision. She rebraided her golden hair, gathered her blue cloak about her, and strode out into the corridor. Each stone she passed seemed an old and dear friend and she drew her hand along the smooth timeworn walls.

At the end of the hall was a wide, iron-braced oaken door. Despite the hour Nimue knocked firmly.

"Come." It was a voice heard in her head rather than her ears.

The hinges creaked as she pushed the door open.

Nimue saw Raven sitting upon a hardbacked chair, fully dressed, as though she had been awaiting a visitor. The small, dark woman nodded, rose, and beckoned Nimue into the tidy space. Fresh-cut reeds rustled beneath her feet.

"Sister," Raven said. "What would you?"

"I must leave this place. Right away."

A look of pain crossed the old face before Raven veiled her emotions behind an impassive mask. "I see. And where will you go?"

"I don't know."

"You don't know?" For a moment Raven seemed to grow larger, to become once again the frightening mother-priestess whose tongue had lashed any novice who dared to falter. "What kind of plan is this? We do not require anyone to stay here against her will. But to leave without giving me good reason or good plan ..."

Nimue said, "I have a good reason. Something has gone wrong with me. Somehow I've been defiled. Contaminated."

"Contaminated? By what?"

"By Merlin's magic. That's why the scrying pond won't open to me."

"Don't be silly. You're overwrought. It's understandable, or course, after your ordeal. You need rest."

"Oh, Raven, please! I can see it as plainly as if you had grown another nose. Strange spells fill my head. I sleep poorly and dream of Merlin."

"You suffer from guilt? Ridiculous. He deserved his fate."

"Nevertheless, I can no longer participate in our sisterhood. And you're the foolish one if you try to ignore this fact. I failed at the pond. Again. You were there. You saw." Nimue bent her head in despair. Tears stung in the corners of her eyes, but she forced them back.

Raven's voice was surpassingly gentle. "Perhaps it will go better next month."

"Will it? I don't think so. No, I must go forth and somehow cleanse myself."

"You're suggesting a pilgrimage?"

"What else?" Nimue's resolve wavered and she was suddenly uncertain, a small girl again, grasping the homespun hem of Raven's garment. She fought down her panic. "I never wanted this."

"Nor did I." Raven's eyes were soft upon her. "You have been much like a daughter to me, Nimue, the only daughter I'll ever have. I can't pretend to take your leaving lightly. But whether I will it or no, you must go. I wondered, when you came to me with this, if you were sincere. But yes. Yes. *You must go.*"

Nimue's feelings were a jumble of sorrow and relief. "Who will take my place?"

"I'll do it until an appropriate novice can be trained."

"But—"

"This is no longer your concern." Raven's eyes held both grief and farewell. As Nimue watched they seemed to mist over until she doubted that Raven could see her at all.

And so she came to the road.

Behind her the temple pavilion and maidens' quarters dwindled and vanished, obscured by fog.

Nimue shivered in the cold wind.

Am I to be set outside the sacred circle, then? she thought. *For ever and always? And is this really my choice?*

She turned back to stare once more. In the distance

the fires of the settlement gleamed, beckoning, bidding her return. She longed suddenly to be welcomed within the circle again. To walk amidst the groves of oak and fruiting apple trees. To do the Goddess's bidding, unquestioningly.

I could unmake this path, turn and hurry back to the sacred sisterhood.

No. Her decision must stand. There was something prideful, unbending in her, that would not let her return. She must go forth and rid herself of whatever darkness had entered her spirit.

She stood with riven soul, forces pulling her this way and that, drawn one moment toward Avalon, the next toward Merlin's Britain.

The path before her led down to the shore of the lake and the other world beyond. She whispered the words of passage and stepped off firm ground into a spirit boat. Gray mists closed around her.

The space between worlds was no safe waiting place. No place at all, really. It was deep, of a peculiar dark colorless nature, suffocatingly hot and as cold as a tomb, filled with mist and the deepest loneliness Nimue had ever known. It was a killing loneliness. If she lingered she was done for. But the veil of the world of men would not give easily. Always before she had slipped through, her chant and the boat leading across the lake and out. Now she pushed hard, then harder. She was battering her way, and yet still the other side would not open to her. Nor could she go back. Avalon, behind her, was sealed. She would be trapped here forever to languish, unliving, undead, as the winds of loneliness seared her soul.

She would end as Merlin had, neither alive nor dead, imprisoned between worlds.

Fear made her strong, gave wings to her unbalanced

powers. She uttered the spell of naming to learn what
had snared her.

"In darkest night
and brightest day,
show me the spell
that bars my way."

A line of runic script appeared in midair before her,
glistening and pearly. A small, foreign charm, forged of
unfamiliar magic, was caging her.

It was quick work to croon the charm of unmaking.
The mists cleared. The barrier gave way and Nimue's
spirit boat sailed on. With a gasp she broke through into
Britain and the world of men.

Nimue had time enough only to see that she was nowhere near Camelot. The land was gray-green and
craggy, ugly and unfamiliar. Castle walls loomed up in
the distance, the outer curtain of some grand keep.

She stumbled and fell within a circle of firelight. To
her horror she realized that she had trod within a pentagram. A sound buzzed and gnawed at the perimeter of
her senses.

"Witch!" A wild-haired woman with raddled features
shrilled at her. Her eyes were dark green, her stance that
of a seeress. "Eater of spells! Begone! Back to the hell
that birthed ye."

Gathering her wits and dignity, Nimue stood,
smoothed back her golden braids, and said, "I beg pardon, sister. I am no witch. Merely a humble traveler lost
in the night."

"A traveler, eh?" The voice was mocking. "With no
eyes in your head? Can you not see a pentagram, vaga-
bond? Do you know what a spell weaver is?"

Nimue remembered suddenly the last vision the Goddess had sent her. Was this to be her fate? In her confusion Nimue heard herself reply, "I am a spell-weaver."

The sorceress glared sourly at her. "You? A ragamuffin straggler, more likely. Spell-wrecker is what you are." She spat at her feet. "That for your charms."

Nimue opened her mouth to summon a wind of changing to stop the mouth of the impudent witch, but suddenly a hoarse male voice broke through her concentration.

"Hah! So, Mara, you promised me a diversion, a spectacle. Is this it? A woman in Druid blue?"

The speaker was short and muscular. He had a wide face rimmed by a reddish beard, a gap-toothed smile. He spoke with an odd, lilting accent. Despite his size he radiated authority.

"Halan, this is not what I intended," the sorceress said. "Let me kill her for her interruption."

"Kill? If it were killing I'd wanted, I would have called for games. No, she's far too pretty to be killed." Halan inspected Nimue, walking around her as though she were some prize horse at market. A sly look came into his green eyes. "And didn't I hear her say she was a spell weaver? If it's games you want, Mara, I've got a game for you. A contest. Spell caster against spell caster."

Part of Nimue wanted to protest, but a larger part longed to hurl the woman Mara right out of the clearing. "Fine," she said. "I accept."

Mara glared at her. "You take a great deal upon yourself."

"No more than I can manage."

The antagonists stared at one another with clear hatred.

"Good!" Halan roared. "It's settled, then. A better diversion by far."

The two women sized each other up. Nimue could hear Merlin's voice whispering the spells to her: this one to cast illusions, that to make the spell of invisibility. These thoughts will shape-change. These gestures bring weapons from the air and forge chains no man can break.

Were such fabulous magics intended for cheap display? Surely not. No matter. Nimue would set this upstart in her place.

Dust kicked up from the center of the pentagram, billowing clouds of red earth, powder-fine, coating Nimue's face.

It should be blue, she thought. Druid blue. And suddenly her smoldering anger against the unfairness of her fate blossomed into soaring flames with the stranger, Mara, at the center of the holocaust. Always, always she had done what she had been told, even when it had caused her anguish. And her fealty had been repaid with confusion, pain, and now exile. Never before had she felt such fury, such agony of spirit. Was this the test that would cleanse her soul or kill her? She welcomed it.

Mara circled to the left.

Nimue moved to counter her progress. It was a slow and graceless dance. She tested Mara, probing with a spell of dizziness and nausea.

Her opponent grimaced and, leaping back, sent a screen of counterspells whirling at Nimue. But Nimue deflected them with ease.

Then, with a fierce cry, Mara summoned a burning spear from the depths of the fire and set it spinning toward Nimue's heart. Only at the last moment did Nimue manage to step aside, feeling the sizzling heat of the thing upon her face as she jumped to safety.

Nimue called forth chains of ice for Mara. Steel blue links whistled out of the air to circle the witch from mouth to toe. But before the chains could completely solidify and bind her, the woman uttered a sharp oath which shattered them to a wintry powder.

Nimue wondered where Mara had learned her spells. There was a strange wild quality to this magic.

She summoned a spell of silence, to deprive Mara of her sorceress's arsenal. She saw by the woman's stricken expression that she had succeeded. But she hadn't anticipated that Mara knew hand magic, and as she watched, the woman made sharp, vivid gestures, baring her teeth.

The spell broke, ricocheted, and turned back upon Nimue. Only by the greatest exercise of will did she destroy the enchantment as its boundaries closed around her.

Mara laughed. "Devil's spawn! I'll send you back where you came from."

Nimue was shaken. The woman was far more powerful than she had thought. By the Goddess, where had she learned her skills?

In a deep guttural voice, Mara chanted:

"Elder magic,
Heed my call!
Smite this false witch.
Rend her flesh
Grind her bones.
Send her to
the place of worms."

In horror Nimue felt strength draining out of her limbs like water from a sponge. A thickening of the air above her coalesced into a giant horrid spider with long crystalline legs. As Nimue watched, it clambered through the air, spinning a dark web that floated down toward her.

Nimue began to sink into sleep. How tempting to dream away her life forever, sleeping just as Merlin slept. Everything around her grew misty, the fire a faint gleam, the eager faces watching the contest turned to grinning skulls, fading, fading. Only one bright spot, one shining star, remained. Was it an ember from the fire?

No. No. It was the Goddess, the Lady herself, her shining aegis gleaming.

The Goddess, yes. By the Goddess, Nimue would defy them.

Above her the spider spun on.

Words ran through her mind like sand through a sieve and different voices chanted many spells, one male voice louder than the rest. Dreamily Nimue started to chant along with the chorus. With Merlin.

No. She had come to cleanse herself of Merlin's magic. Only the Lady could save her. Only She would redeem her. She would use the Goddess's magic or none at all.

Nimue struggled back up to wakefulness, hacking at the bonds that ensnared her mind. A supreme act of will forced her mouth open, gave life to her voice. She cried:

"Sacred Goddess,
Send your winds,
Sweep through this world,
and blow evil from my path.
Send me your sword of truth,
Let it be
Mine to wield.
Oh, Lady,
Yours is the only truth,
The only way.
Sacred steel,
Come aid me now!"

The onlookers gasped as a glowing puddle appeared in the center of the pentagram and spread to cover its boundaries. A sword tip, razor sharp, broke the surface of the water, emerged straight and true, glowing white-gold with strong magic. All along its length runic letters curled and danced. A slender female hand glad in golden chain mail grasped the jeweled hilt.

The hand flexed and the sword flew up and up, springing through the air, arcing down upon the magical web. It sliced neatly through the tangled skeins and the web's many-legged occupant. The hovering spell dispersed like dark mist upon the wind as a sound like a great gong being struck by a clapper split the air, terrible to hear.

Nimue covered her ears, gasping at the pain of it.

The sword plunged down, down, to be caught by the hand. It was drawn steadily back into the puddle as an explosion of light commenced within the circle, sweeping both Nimue and Mara into its fury. Nimue did not know whether she lived or died, if she burned or froze. The winds of time seemed to sweep through her body, her mind and memory.

When the enchantment had cleared, Nimue alone remained standing. The sword, the hand, the puddle were gone.

Mara knelt witless upon the ground, blinking open-mouthed into the fire, smiling vacantly.

The only sound was that of indrawn breath. Obviously Halan and his minions had not expected Nimue to win. But win she had.

She felt clearheaded and thankful, cleansed. The Goddess had saved her. Merlin's magic had been expiated. She was free, free!

"Ho, missy." Halan's face was pale and a river of blood vessels stood out livid against his cheek. "Quite a show. I wouldn't have given a copper for your chances. Of course, Mara wasn't much of a spell caster. Still, you trounced her fairly and well. You've proven yourself a strong sorceress indeed. What would you?"

Nimue realized that she had no idea what she wanted, what she would do, or where she should go. Her thoughts turned toward Avalon, toward home. She shook her head, uncertain.

"Stay with us, then. We have need of a strong sorceress." Halan's tone was wheedling, but Nimue saw fear in his eye. Plainly he wasn't sure that he could control her. She would never be safe with him.

"No safety in this land or any other. Rely on no one save yourself."

The words were Merlin's. Nimue heard them as clearly as if the old mage had whispered into her ear just now. So she wasn't free of the sorcerer's legacy. Not this quickly, no. Her return to Avalon was not yet within her grasp.

Stay here, though? This grim land, these half-civilized people? That held little appeal for her. But would she go? She thought again of the lofty castle in the clouds that Merlin had once shown her. For a brief moment she imagined that Merlin was there and, with a word, she could visit him. A lovely fantasy. But she was in the world of Christian kings. There was no room for airy castles here.

She had learned much from her time with Merlin. Therefore she had much to unlearn before she could remain in any one place and belong there. Her pilgrimage was not yet finished.

"I would go," she said, "where the wind wills."

And as the chieftain Halan and his minions watched, open-mouthed, Nimue transformed herself into a falcon, unfurled powerful wings, and rose high above them into the lightening sky.

The gateway to the shores of misty Avalon lay somewhere to the West. Nimue turned and, with a haunting cry, flew East toward the rising sun.

THE STONE MOTHER'S CURSE

by Dave Wolverton

In the days when clouds were just learning how to fly and therefore often wandered the earth on soggy feet, at the end of a long dirt road near the cliffs at the edge of the world was a village called Pretty Weed that sprawled among jagged mountains atop the ancient Graveyard of the Gods.

The villagers of Pretty Weed built their homes from massive stones, so that even the simplest peasant lived in a monolith, and the inhabitants of this land kept their noses in the ground all day as they mined adamant from the petrified bones of gods.

Merchant caravans sometimes took the winding trek to Pretty Weed through forests infested with shadow giants and the ravenox, but few others dared. Huddling beside campfires in faraway lands, storytellers whispered that the simple folks of Pretty Weed had become like stone themselves—cold, unyielding, oblivious to the beautiful hills around them that were all covered with wildflowers. Some said that the poor folks had become victims of their own greedy magic, that in order to shape the adamant into scimitars or medallions, they had to become harder than the stone they worked. Others feared that by drinking from springs that percolated up through their quarry, the villagers had poisoned themselves over generations—having partaken of adamant, the villagers therefore had become like adamant. But everyone agreed that whatever the cause, a horrible curse was on the land, and nothing good would come of it.

So it happened that shortly after the death of her husband, Bronwythe, Queen of Pretty Weed, gave birth to a daughter. In the pain of childbirth the queen begged the midwife to take the princess and offer it to one of the villagers, for she could not bear to look on something that reminded her of her dead husband.

But some time in the night, Bronwythe woke to the persistent cry of a teneriel peeping outside her window. The queen stirred in her bed, found her breasts swollen, dripping with new milk. She listened to the nightbird and realized that the sound came from the bassinet under the windowsill. *So, they have left the child,* Bronwythe thought, *and my breasts have learned my daughter's cry before I have.*

Bronwythe rose and went to the bassinet. An ivory tallow candle beside it had burned down to the stub, yet in its light she could see the child: Chestnut curls, like her father's, and the girl's dark eyes carried the blue of the twilit summer sky. The child became silent, looked up. *All this day without food,* the queen realized, *yet the girl did not cry. She will be easy to raise. I should name her Teneriel, for her voice carries the song of the nightbird.* Bronwythe lifted the child, gave her the nipple, and as the infant suckled, Queen Bronwythe held her daughter close and wept. It had been three weeks since the king had died in the mines, and for the first time Bronwythe cried for the husband she had lost and for the daughter she had gained.

And if it is true that Queen Bronwythe's people seemed cold and hard of heart, then it is also true that when they loved, their love often ran deeper and stronger than the roots of mountains. Certainly no one doubted that Bronwythe's love for Teneriel grew ponderous and unyielding, like a stone.

* * *

While the people of Pretty Weed dug holes and trudged through their tunnels, Teneriel was raised in a black tower thick with dusty tapestries and rusting armor. Winters were bleak, cradled between the arms of mountains and blanketed under snow. As a child Teneriel suffered through the dim months waiting for the brief passionate spring to stun some life from the ground.

Teneriel's mother worked the mines, using the magic of her resonant voice to cut and shape the black bones, and in time became the greatest of adamant stonecutters. Through the long summers Teneriel ripened like wheat. Because Teneriel loved the earth, the earth loved her in return and bestowed its beauty on her. Once in spring when fragrant wild roses erupted along the stone walls beside her mother's castle, Teneriel touched one to her face, and its hue permanently clung to her cheeks. It took only a simple glance of admiration at the deep-blue mountain orchids for them to present her with a new shade for her eyes. By watching how the summer sun set in a blaze of glory, she learned to lure light from her chestnut hair until it grew so lustrous that Queen Bronwythe commanded her to never cut it again.

Even as a child, Teneriel's voice resonated like her mother's, but she never used it to carve adamant. Since the plain folks of Pretty Weed did not sing for pleasure, Teneriel learned no music but songs she heard from meadowlarks darting among hedges or the nightly chorus of crickets in a new-mown field. She memorized the liquid tones of water spinning over smooth pebbles, spring rain hissing upon grass, the moan of wind as it whips leaves among alleyways.

Sometimes Teneriel would raise her own voice after the shrill light faded from the winter's day, cold and lonely, timorously singing words that seemed whispered by her bones, and villagers trundling home from work would hesitate outside her bedroom window in the tower and still their breath to listen, heads tilted, almost wishing their hearts would stop in mid-beat.

When Teneriel reached the age of eight, gypsy traders traveled the far road to Pretty Weed. They were much like all the other grasping folks that came to Queen Bronwythe's village, fingering her riches and pinching all the chickens to find the tenderest. Queen Bronwythe knew nothing about them, but the gypsies plied her with compliments, so she liked them. Bronwythe invited them to dine in her castle so that she might display her most valuable treasure of all—her daughter.

After the gypsies had entertained the queen with magic tricks, the servants pulled the candelabras from the table and brought little Teneriel, set her above the platters of roast pig and black bread, and the whole crowd gasped in amazement. The queen had made a necklace for Teneriel to show how its rubies seemed lusterless and dead as rust next to her wavy chestnut hair all wrapped in a crown.

The leader of the ragtag band, a toothless crone named Mama Cecesceau, stared up at Teneriel and gasped, "Look at all that wilderness in her eyes!"

The queen proudly stood next to her daughter, took the girl's hand. Teneriel removed the golden combs and shook her hair, and as it touched the tabletop, the full glory of her hair shocked the crowd so that they sighed and cried out, and Teneriel sang an innocent, heartfelt song of welcome to her mother's guests.

Queen Bronwythe looked over the ragged multitude. Mama Cecesceau was weeping openly, and others sat with their hands over their mouths, and Bronwythe smiled to see how her daughter's beauty could break people's hearts.

But that night after the gypsies drove off in their brightly painted wagons, a giant owl flapped a twisted path across the moon and perched in the tower window where Teneriel slept, and the next morning a cry of outrage rippled through Pretty Weed like a mounting wave as one after another the villagers learned that Teneriel had been stolen. Bronwythe stormed from the castle, grief and rage warring in her eyes.

Everyone in the village grabbed knives and hammers and rushed over the mountains, and for many weeks they did their best to chase down the thieves. During the hunt, the ravenox carried off three villagers in its talons, and the whole town could only curse the monster as it flew away with their companions. Yet anger strengthened the survivors, drove them forward, so that no matter how fast the gypsies fled, the villagers managed to dog their trail.

When at last Queen Bronwythe overtook Mama Cecesceau, both the queen and the old hag were only tattered, half-starved apparitions of themselves. Bronwythe found that the gypsies had not only stolen her daughter, they had taken many fine chickens and much of her gold. For stealing her chickens and gold, she had her soldiers cut off the gypsies' hands; and for kidnapping her daughter, Bronwythe personally cut off Mama Cecesceau's head and, grabbing the old woman's white hair, hurled the head into the woods alongside the road.

Then Bronwythe went to the painted wagon where her daughter waited, locked in a cage, and she pulled open the bars and held her dear Teneriel so that the girl buried her face between Bronwythe's breasts.

Teneriel cried, "Mother, Mother, you came! I prayed you would come. I prayed that you would save me! Even when the old witch cast hastening spells so that we darted over the ground like foxes, I still hoped."

Bronwythe wept and pulled the child close, and said, "I promise, I promise: No one will ever take you from me again!" A hush fell over the crowd, and a change came over Queen Bronwythe. Something in her hardened, so that she looked like a woman who might never smile again. Her voice caught, and she said, "I ... I'll make certain that no one ever takes you."

Bronwythe gave Teneriel to the care of the captain of the guard, and made the good man swear on his life to take Teneriel home. The captain asked, "But where are you going?"

Bronwythe lowered her head. "By magic my daughter was stolen, so I must find a magic that can hold her." Then the queen set off down that long dirt road alone through the dark forest, and brooded, heedless of the shadow giants and the ravenox. For many weeks she rode through drenching fog, for the clouds had not yet learned how to fly. At long last she reached a stark desert where she found the tent of a sorcerer rumored to be the spawn of a houri and a desert whirlwind, an old wanderer named Farouk al-Hassad.

Bronwythe stood in the wind outside the sorcerer's billowing tent at sunset and pleaded for help. At first Farouk spurned her, "I cast my spells for a hefty price. I suspect that a beggar woman like you could not afford them." Farouk turned to go back in his tent.

"I am Queen Bronwythe, and I own all the quarries of adamant. I've walked many days to find you."

Farouk raised an eyebrow, turned, mumbled a spell, and touched Bronwythe between the eyes to ascertain if she told the truth. When he was satisfied, a closed look entered Farouk's eyes. "Few spells are as powerful as the one you seek, Your Majesty—able to withstand magic both black and white. Even the strongest spells can be broken by those who wield certain talismans. But if you want to hold your daughter, I can encase her in an amber stone so heavy that none may carry it. There you could view her beauty forever, and none would be able to bear her away."

Bronwythe covered her mouth with her hand. "But she would die!"

The sorcerer shrugged. "I would keep her alive within the amber. Trapped, but alive, only to be set free on the day Allah calls you to his bosom."

"But I would never be able to touch her, to feel her hand or hear her voice."

The sorcerer knelt and began drawing pictures in the sand with a stick. "There are no other spells strong enough to hold her," he said, and Bronwythe's hope died. She turned to leave, and Farouk added, "But ... I could cast an illusion upon her, a glamour, so that all who see her face will think her ugly and avert their eyes in horror. No one would think to steal her then, and she would be all yours. To touch, to hold."

"You have not seen the beauty in my daughter's face," Bronwythe said. "Are you sure your spell could mask it?"

"It's a small thing," Farouk insisted. "She would appear so ugly, that even her own pup would not lick a scrap of liver from her shoe. I can curse her so."

"Not her hair. Leave her something of beauty. I would not want you to curse her hair."

"If you wish," the sorcerer said.

"And if I ever want to break the curse?" Bronwythe asked.

"Once I cast the curse on the wind, you must call your daughter twice a year and, gazing into her eyes, tell her that she is hideous to look upon. As long as you continue this, she will believe she is ugly, and all others will see her so. As for breaking the curse, it can only be broken by one who truly loves her, by one who can look into her eyes and tell her that she is beautiful, believing it to the core of his soul." Farouk looked up from the sand where he had been writing strange symbols—eyes and owls and daggers and a woman holding scales. "But no one will ever love her. No one will ever be able to gaze at her face."

Bronwythe swallowed hard. "But . . . I will always love her," she said, her jaw trembling, trying to firm her resolve. "I would always love her, and I could break the curse."

The sorcerer smiled sadly, and his dark eyes glittered in the fading light of a crimson sunset. "Can you be sure? Can you be certain that you will look into the monstrosity of your daughter's face and still remain firm in your love? I warn you: it will be hard."

But Bronwythe remained certain, for she was strong-willed, as were all her people, and Bronwythe's love for her daughter had grown ponderous and unyielding, like a stone.

Long before Queen Bronwythe reached home, a strong south wind blew a plague of smallpox to the village of Pretty Weed. Many fair men and women found their faces horribly scarred for life, but upon none did the plague wreak such havoc as upon the tender child Teneriel.

The maid had set the plates just inside Teneriel's door, then fled again. Teneriel did not mind. She had grown accustomed to it. No one could look upon the horror of her face, six years after the onset of the illness, six years after she had thrown all her mirrors away.

As Teneriel drank her tea, she stared into the depths of the black ceramic cup, tried to gaze at the reflection of her own face without gagging or turning away. It was hard, impossibly hard. She peeked over the rim of her cup at her ravaged face. The boils and red puckers had never really retreated, leaving her swollen, misshapen, so that her bulbous nose twisted to the side. Even the clear whites of her eyes had yellowed like an old man's tooth, as if she suffered perpetual jaundice.

Teneriel stared at the face, strained mightily to look upon it, and felt almost as if an invisible hand wrenched her head aside so she would not have to bear her reflection. She closed her eyes and wept.

The maid knocked on the door again, "Teneriel?"

"Yes," Teneriel cried.

"Your mother has guests from out of town. She wants to show them your hair, tonight after the feast. Will you need your mask polished?"

Teneriel's heart thumped wildly, and she looked over to the dresser. The silver mask rested in its blue satin case, lips twisted into a permanent party smile, gleaming. "No. I won't need it polished," Teneriel said.

The maid's footsteps retreated from the door, and Teneriel resisted the urge to throw herself on the bed and weep some more. Another extravaganza she would not be invited to attend except as some grotesque object whose hair would be ogled by barbaric merchants. Another feast. *I wish,* she thought, *that just once, I could eat alone with my mother.*

But Queen Bronwythe seldom asked Teneriel to dine with her anymore, and on those few occasions when she did, she'd look upon Teneriel's twisted visage in pity and remind the girl how ugly she had become, and Teneriel would long for the days of her childhood—the soft warmth of Bronwythe's body as they hugged, the way her mother's hair tickled Teneriel's forehead. Teneriel craved her mother's affection, craved the affection of almost anyone, yet she could not bear the way the queen made her feel . . . loathsome.

Teneriel wanted to throw herself on the bed, as if she were a child, but she knew that more weeping would not help. *My feasting days are over,* she told herself, *and rightly so. No one can look at me. Tonight as they eat, I must resist the temptation to hold the mask out too far from my face. I mustn't force them to stomach even the slightest glance.*

Teneriel went to her window, opened it. The evening sun slanted in, blushing pink, highlighting dust motes that revolved like worlds in her bedroom, her hideaway, her prison. The milk cows wandered green fields on the hillsides, and smoke coiled up from the villagers' cooking fires. She let down her chestnut hair and began brushing, careful to keep her face in the shadows lest any townspeople happened to glance up.

Trevor's back ached from too many days riding his old mare, and he held himself a bit stiffly. He had traveled for years now, looking for a place to settle and farm, and here, he decided, he had found it. Village of Pretty Weed, right at the edge of the world. If he rode for another day, he'd fall right off. It seemed a good place to stop.

But God, it was beautiful: Pure silver brooks running down mountains, wildflowers blooming across the land, every beggar's house as big as an Irish castle, and red chickens running about, plump and tender as a nursing mother's full breast. He had heard rumors of how the townsmen all mined adamant beneath the earth, like freakish moles, never sticking their noses above ground, and the streets were so empty he judged the rumors to be true. *God, this town must be filled with ignorant buggers,* he thought.

As Trevor passed beneath a shadowed tower, his horse clomping on cobblestones, a strange thing happened: A hair fell from heaven. As he rode, he saw it descend from the sky, chestnut hair glimmering in the setting sun like twelve feet of fire and spun gold. Trevor swallowed hard, for as the hair draped itself over his reins, he thought. *Only an angel would have hair that beautiful, and if you dare to look up, Trevor O'Brien, you'll see an angel flapping her wings through heaven, and God will have no choice but to strike you dead for spying something so Holy, and then what kind of fix would you be in?*

But Trevor did look up. He saw something flying very high, with vast white wings, but decided after a moment that it was either a small albino griffin or a pegasus. No angels. Then he looked in the window of the tower, and combing her hair was the most ravishing woman he had ever seen—or at least, there was the torso of the most ravishing woman he had ever seen. Her face was shadowed, but she moved with grace, her bones fawnlike, and she had all that stunning chestnut hair—enough to lend to ten maidens by the look of it, and still have enough left over to weave a gown.

Trevor happened to be both a simple man and a single man, and with his breath short and his heart clapping like a dinner bell in the hands of a child, he decided he should get to know this woman. Though his rough tunic was stained from the road, he slicked back his long red hair and shouted the most pertinent question on his mind, "Are you married?" The maiden stopped brushing, froze, as if listening for his voice.

"You, in the tower: Are you married?" The girl stepped back into the shadows. "Young lady, I'm going to sit here on my horse and ask until you answer: Are you married?"

"No," she said, then closed the curtains.

Good, Trevor thought. *Good answer.*

Teneriel never meant for it to happen. She didn't really want to lead this mad peasant boy on, but that night after Teneriel's mother forced her to display her hair in the feasting hall, just as she had since Teneriel was a child, Teneriel returned to her room and looked out in the starlight. There he was, sitting beside a small campfire that he'd built right at the edge of the street next to the tinker's shop, roasting a chicken, and he wouldn't go away.

Teneriel ordered the boy to leave, and he asked, "By whose command?" obviously hoping she would betray her name. She told him she was royalty and he objected, "Princess to the freakish mole-people? What kind of royalty is that?" She told him she was ugly, and he said, "Right, well, every young maiden thinks she's ugly. Put on a new dress, Princess, and you'll feel grand enough even for the likes of me!"

Sometime in the night, she found herself laughing at his jokes. He told stories of faraway places—of battles he had won and fortunes he had nearly won. She could see that Trevor was a braggart, but at least he was entertaining. They talked long into the night, and sometime in the darkness she heard the roosters begin to crow and realized that Trevor had become more than just a mad peasant camped on the street. He had become a friend. She bid him good night, and he begged for her name— and the privilege of speaking to her again the next night.

She hesitated a long time. "My name is Teneriel. And I really am ugly. My face is horrible. Ask anyone in the village. They will tell you."

Trevor smiled up in the half light before dawn, trying the name on his tongue. "Teneriel. A beautiful name. With a name like that, I can't imagine that your face would frighten any flies off a honey dish," he teased, trying to make light of her tragedy.

She forced a laugh. Teneriel knew he would ask around. She knew he would probably never speak to her again.

Yet Trevor came the next night and set his campfire beside the tinker's shop. He stood on the street with his hat in hand, waiting. "I talked to folks in town," Trevor said when she opened the window, "and I've heard that what you say is true—about the horrible pox on your face and all, and I've been thinking: Even if you're not pretty in the face, it really doesn't matter, because after last night, I still want to be your friend."

And that is how their love began, yet that is not how it ended. Each night, as the brilliant stars wheeled into the sky, Teneriel crept to her windowsill to speak with him in the anonymity of darkness, and sometimes she would sing for him. Each dawn, as the pink blush of sunrise touched the face of heaven, she pulled away from the windowsill praying that Trevor would return.

As she lay in bed each day, she'd sift each word Trevor had spoken, scrutinizing every innocent phrase. For example on the third night when he left the window with the words, "Pleasant dreams, sweet maiden," did he mean to say she was *sweet,* or was it a passing phrase, the kind of thing he would have said to any girl? Or again, when Trevor told her that he had dreamt during the day that Teneriel had lain beside him, softly singing in his ear, did she really hear a thrill of longing in his voice?

A few days later, as Trevor prepared to leave at sunrise, he said the words she both hoped for and dreaded: "I love you, Teneriel." Trevor waited a moment for an answer, then added, "Please, stay at the window a while so that I can see your face. It cannot be as bad as you say."

"If you love me," she answered, "then my face should not matter." She closed the curtains, her heart hammering, and threw herself on the bed, crying into her sheets. Trevor called to her, but she didn't answer. When he returned that night, she spoke to him briefly. "Please go away!" Teneriel begged. "I've done something terribly evil!"

"What have you done?" he asked.

"I've let you fall in love with me," Teneriel cried. "I did it only for selfish reasons. I . . . I didn't think it could happen. I—"

Trevor stopped her. "Is it so hard to think someone could love you?"

Teneriel thought of the children who sometimes called her "troll-face," and of how she could not bear to look in a mirror. Most of all she thought of her mother, grown icy over the years. "No one could possibly love me," she said.

Queen Bronwythe labored in her shadowed chamber, far beneath the earth, grasping a long chunk of adamant in her sinewy, thin hands. This piece was heavier than usual and resonated in an abnormally low pitch—perhaps because it was the tip of the index finger of a god, and therefore had been petrifying for millennia, far longer than the other bones.

The peasant Trevor waited nervously by the door, shifting from foot to foot. The guards seemed to frighten Trevor so much that he would not even clear his throat to get the queen's attention. *Let the fool boy wait*, Bronwythe thought. *The cheeky upstart. Caught in the act—the very act—of wooing my daughter.* Bronwythe raised the old bone to her chin, resting her lower teeth against the cold blackness, and sang loud and low until she felt the bone hum in response. Bronwythe gazed into the bone and visualized where to carve. The bone split cleanly, as if cut with a saw, and Bronwythe set aside the smaller piece, continued working. She watched Trevor as she worked, and wondered what to do.

Part of her wanted to kill the boy, as she had Mama Cecesceau, but if Teneriel loved Trevor, Bronwythe could not kill him outright. The boy gulped when he realized that Bronwythe was carving a sword, yet to Trevor's credit, he did not try to run.

When a crude sword gleamed in Bronwythe's hand, she swung it through the air and said, "Come here, boy." Trevor gulped and stepped forward, more boldly than Bronwythe liked. Brash, that's what he was. "You were caught promising my daughter your love. It's a cruel jest—don't you think—telling a wretch like her that you love her?"

"I do love her, Your Highness," Trevor whispered.

Bronwythe could hear sincerity in Trevor's words. "Really? For that answer, I shall spare taking your manhood." With that, Bronwythe thrust the blade of adamant into the stone floor. "But, tell me, how did this come to be?"

"I saw her in the tower one afternoon, and I've spoken to her often. I know her face is marred, and it is said that no man could love her, but . . ."

Bronwythe felt dazed. "You mean you've looked at her face, and you still love her?"

"No," Trevor admitted. "She stays in the shadows—speaks only at night. I have begged to see her face, but she refuses—"

"I suppose you want to take her off my hands, as if she were a sick cow?"

"I never thought . . ." Trevor said. "I . . . I wanted to speak to you, and I'm glad for this opportunity. . . ."

Bronwythe looked at the boy, dripping sincerity as a willow drips sap. He was worse than a whole army of gypsies. The boy frightened Bronwythe, froze her to the core. Such a boy could break the glamour, or such a boy could break Teneriel's heart. Bronwythe wanted to drive him from the castle. "Loving someone so marred can be a terrible burden," Bronwythe found herself confiding. "It requires tremendous resolve. You have not seen her face. Believe me, she is hideous."

"Perhaps I've been blessed," Trevor said, "for in the darkness I learned to see the beauty beneath her face."

Bronwythe sighed. The adamant sword glittered in the floor. She pulled it free, turned it over and over. "This sword is rough," the queen said, "but in a few days I can make it beautiful, and men will consider it to be of great worth. It takes time to make a thing of beauty—patience, hard work, discipline—whether the thing made is a sword, or a daughter. I am making this sword for a king. It could never be yours.

"You are right about Teneriel. Beneath her mask of flesh, she is beautiful, in part because I forged her, helped make her beautiful, I hope to give her to one more worthy than you. Someday, I shall give her to a prince—not a commoner."

"Though I have no claim to title or land, the blood of Irish kings runs through my veins," Trevor countered. "I am not common."

The queen waved her hand in dismissal. "It is said that in Ireland, one cannot toss a stone without having it sail over two or three kingdoms, the holdings are so small. And your kings breed like cats in heat, without discretion or temperance. Why, it is said that one can go to any flock and find that every ewe there . . ." she paused, held her breath, "is herded by some boy with the blood of an Irish king in his veins."

Trevor's face reddened, but he did not rise to the queen's bait. "But I have heard," Trevor countered, "that none may bear your daughter's presence. If she is so hideous, won't you have difficulty finding someone who will truly love her? And if this is so, I beg you, let me prove my worthiness! I love her more than life itself."

Bronwythe sagged into a chair, holding her head. She could not kill the boy outright, yet the thought of letting him live was frightening. When it came down to it, Bronwythe had been frightened a long time. She sometimes worried that the old sorcerer had played her foul, that perhaps Farouk had put no curse on Teneriel stronger than a pox, and if that were so, the girl could never be restored to her beauty. The best she could hope for was someone like Trevor, a sappy lovesick boy, sweeter than a confection.

Yet Bronwythe feared more than that: At times the horrible swellings on Teneriel's face oozed pus or moved as if worms had burrowed beneath her skin, and the horror—the sheer psychic pain Bronwythe felt when she gazed on the girl—the guilt for what Bronwythe had wrought, the fear that she might not be able to break the curse—it weighed heavily.

And yet, Bronwythe told herself, *I did it to protect Teneriel. No one has tried to steal her from me again— until today. I am tired of it. Tired of loathing her face, tired of loathing myself for what I've done. I want it to end. Death for the boy, or death for my guilt. Either way, it will end somehow.*

"I will send a messenger to Teneriel," Bronwythe told Trevor. "If she loves you, I will name a suitable task so you can prove your worthiness. I warn you, it will require great courage and resolve—traits you will need if you hope to love an ugly woman."

For six days Trevor rode west on his old mare, trailing rumors of the shadow giant. At last in a barren land of rolling green hills and white monolithic stones carved with ancient runes he came upon an old toothless goat-herd who lived where none other dared. Trevor camped with the man for the night, and as the goats huddled in circle around a large bonfire, the old man spoke. "You must never let your fires dim so near the giant's lair. Many other men have lit fires against it, but still the beast stalks from the forest on a moonless night, taking those whose untended campfires dwindle to hot ashes. If you will battle your giant, you must do it at night, with the fires at your back."

"Have you seen the creature? Can you tell me something of it?" Trevor asked.

"Oh, yes, I've seen it many times," the goatherd answered, "prowling outside the circle of light shining from my fire. Some say it is a spirit that haunts the Graveyard of the Gods, but the thing I have seen is not as big as those ancients. Others claim that it guards the edge of the world. I think they are closer to being right. I think it lives on the other side of the world in the daytime, when all is dark there, and then it hunts here at night."

"Why do you think that?"

"I knew a young man once, who went to the edge of the world and spit off. That night, the shadow giant came and took him. Now, even in far lands, fools believe that spitting off the edge of the world angers the giant. As for me, I think the giant saw him there, from a distance, and stalked him."

Trevor didn't speculate on what the creature might be, but at dawn he rode to the cliffs at the end of the world, and at midday he stood looking down at the endless red stone cliffs, streaked white with swallow dung. He gazed at the stars on the dark side of the earth below, and watched millions of emerald swallows darting about in the half-light, like glittering seeds blown in the wind. Trevor spit over the edge.

Then Trevor retreated to some abandoned fields near a forest where pale stones marked the graves of hapless shepherds. The woods were strangely dead: blackberry vines hung clotted with ripe berries, but no bears or birds or even foxes had fed from them. No deer cut splayed tracks in the soft ground at the forest's edge.

Instead, the dark trees, shrouded with old man's beard, were silent, and the place felt cold even when the sun shone on the broad hillsides.

Trevor slept during the days. Stark fear kept him

awake nights while the moon was down. He set no fire, for he could not hope to kill the giant unless it drew near.

On the second night, the shadow giant came wading through sixty-foot pines as if they were ferns, and it made a soft shushing sound from miles away, as if it were a burst of wind sighing through the trees. It was also heralded by the unmistakable crack of wood, the creaking of whole trees as it bent them aside.

As the giant neared, Trevor leaped to his mare's back, pulled out an ax, and listened to the rushing wind as he watched the sky. At last the pinprick of stars darkened above Trevor, and a shadow blotted part of the River of Heaven, a black silhouette against the midnight-blue sky. The giant stooped, considering Trevor, its outline only roughly humanoid, and at the touch of the giant's breath, the ground froze at Trevor's feet. His old mare neighed in terror, and reared up on her hind legs like some young stallion as she sought to run madly.

But Trevor swung his sturdy axe, shouting in deprecation at the giant, "Hah! Mother warned me that you were big enough to swallow me whole, but I see she lied! You're not so big! Prepare to meet your end!" and Trevor charged.

The giant strode forward. In the vast blackness, Trevor secretly fingered the sulfur box in his pocket. Just a little closer, just a little closer, and he figured he could strike the sulfur, wield the fire as his weapon.

Trevor never saw the hand snake out, knew only that one moment the giant's crushing hand pinned his arms, lifted him high in the air in a world where he could discern the pinprick of stars, the slap of wind, and the next he was worming down headfirst through a narrow freezing channel, pushed along by a ring of gut muscles.

The air inside the shadow giant gagged him with its acidic fumes, and it took Trevor several seconds to retrieve the sulfur box and flint from his pocket, took well over a minute to get his hands above his head, and by then his mind was reeling. He imagined fairy lights ahead of him, and he seemed to be spinning down, down, ever toward them. He managed to open the lid with one hand and feebly struck his flint against the steel box, struck it again and again, till suddenly the box flared as the sulfur caught.

The flames raced through and sliced the giant just as lightning will slice the bark and limbs from a tree. As fire gutted the giant, Trevor dropped into some brush, landing on his shoulder.

Trevor lay dazed, unable to move his right arm. The shadow giant towered above, waving its hands in the sky, huge flames leaping through insubstantial flesh, burning as if it were a cloth bag that had been soaked in pitch. The giant staggered among the trees, setting their tops afire, and reeled. It cried out, and its voice was the voice of great rocks tumbling in a quake, so that earth and heaven seemed to shake at its cry, then it stumbled, reaching for Trevor, and fell only a few yards short. Trevor rushed for the giant, and with his left hand drew a knife, slashed a piece of shadow skin from the giant's outstretched fist, then rolled the flesh in his cloak to protect it from the light.

Fire took the giant then, took it whole and clean, burned both its flesh and everything beneath—trees, stubble and soil—so that by dawn, all Trevor could see on the ground was a huge man-shape of ash, eighty feet from head to outstretched foot.

Queen Bronwythe was surprised to see Trevor again, was more surprised that the folks of Pretty Weed trumpeted the news of his return. People thronged the hall below the earth, crowding and shoving to see Trevor. As Trevor unwrapped the dark matter folded in his cloak— spreading the ragged piece of skin from the shadow giant—the good folks of the city drew breath in admiration, and Bronwythe's guards cheered. Bronwythe hated the guards for that, but since the shadow giant had killed over a dozen of their ilk, she forgave them.

Bronwythe stepped down from her throne and touched the flesh—almost freezing her fingers—and held it up: The skin was heavy and slick like any hide, so black it seemed to be a hole in space, soaking all light. For a moment she held the abominable thing, then the lights of the guttering torches in their sconces in the far corners of the hall overwhelmed the insubstantial flesh. It smoked and burst into flame. No one could doubt that Trevor had indeed killed the shadow giant. And as Trevor told how he had tricked the giant into swallowing him whole so that he could strike a fire within the beast, he proved that he'd shown courage and resolve—more than any man in the kingdom. Trevor finished by saying, "I killed the giant. I pray, Your Highness, give me Teneriel's hand in marriage."

Bronwythe bowed to hide her flushed cheeks, thinking, *I sent you to your death, and you bring me a scrap of giant flesh. But I only gave in at a moment of weakness, I can break the spell without you.* "My daughter is not to be sold so cheaply," the queen said at last. "I value her above all my kingdom. You have proved yourself bold and cunning, but it will take more than that to love my daughter. Go now, prove yourself patient and faithful: Climb the mountains to the Throne of Wonder, and bring me the wings of the ravenox!"

The whole crowd muttered in dismay—for the ravenox fed on men as magpies feed on maggots—and Trevor looked the queen in the eye and said "No!"

"What?" Bronwythe asked in shock. "Are you telling me 'no?'"

"We had a bargain, and I've won my bride," Trevor said. "I've heard that the queen of Pretty Weed is a cunning trader, a ruthless negotiator—but I have never heard her called a liar or a cheat. Give me your daughter's hand, now, as you promised, or everyone in this room," Trevor waved at the knotted crowd behind him, "will bear rumor of your betrayal!"

Queen Bronwythe licked her lips, looked over the crowd. Liar. Cheat. Traitor. No one had ever called her such things before. No one dared such impudence. If there hadn't been so many witnesses, Bronwythe would have had her guards cut the boy down, but she thought of a better punishment. Bronwythe shouted, "Very well! Take the hag if you can stomach her! Take the vomit! Guards, bring Teneriel!"

The guards returned to the room only moments later, long before the queen's rage had a chance to subside, and Bronwythe realized that Teneriel must have heard the commotion and been on her way, for she had dressed in a magnificent gown of white that accented her graceful figure, and her long chestnut hair trailed out behind like the train to a wedding dress, flashing in the light. She held her silver mask before her face, its thin lips upturned in a delicate smile.

"Come," Bronwythe told her, and the crowd parted. The princess stood beside Bronwythe, took her hand. Bronwythe raised her daughter's hand to Trevor. "Come see the horror you have won!" Bronwythe shouted, ripping away the silver mask.

The crowd moaned as one and many fell back, shielding their eyes, and the most fainthearted collapsed. Bronwythe reached up and stroked Teneriel's face, the red blotches, the infected pustules, the swollen nose. Trevor wept, and could not move forward to take her hand.

To watch a stranger suffer would have been horrific, but to watch the woman he loved, to behold her like this, made the young man feel faint. He sagged, holding the wall for support.

Bronwythe laughed. "You are an ugly thing, my child," Bronwythe told Teneriel. "You ugly, pitiable thing."

Teneriel tried to put the mask back up, but Bronwythe slapped it away so that it clattered to the floor. Teneriel tried to cover her face with her hands, but Bronwythe fought her, grabbed the girl's face and held it up like a medusa's head. "Look in her eyes, and break this curse if you can!" Bronwythe shouted at Trevor. "You say you love her to the core of your soul: Then look in her eyes and tell her she is beautiful like the dawn, glorious and streaming! Tell her if you can; tell her if she is suitable for your sick devotion! Come, you noble young man, kiss the sow-faced thing! Kiss it!"

Bronwythe could sense the spell working, could feel Teneriel growing uglier moment by moment. Townsmen covered their faces, and something tickled the queen's palm: As she watched, a faint green worm—the color of a young apple—wriggled its head from Teneriel's chin, looked upon the crowd, dropped to the floor. Trevor turned away in revulsion and scuttled backward like a crab.

Teneriel moaned and fainted in Bronwythe's arms. Bronwythe held her, and one brave guard rushed forward to catch the princess, his arms knotted like cords.

When Bronwythe looked up again, Trevor was fleeing up the stairs toward the sunlight, shouting in dismay, staggering blindly into the walls in his haste. Bronwythe was tempted to hurl some insult at the retreating boy, but what purpose would it serve?

Bronwythe had the guard carry Teneriel from the throne room, and the crowd moved away, people muttering, "Ah, God, the hideous thing!" "Poor wretch!" "Bless her!" Bronwythe saw tears in children's eyes, tears of horror and pity, and everyone moved away, as if afraid Teneriel's ugliness might catch. None could bear to look upon her face.

Up the dark stairs they went, and Teneriel began heaving, her chest jerking in spasms. Bronwythe realized the girl had wakened, and she was sobbing at the core of her soul. "Shhh. Shhh, my sweet princess," Bronwythe said. "Don't weep." The guard stopped, and the queen came, took her daughter's hand.

"Mother, kill me, please. . . ."

"No, I am saving you. Someday, you will marry a prince. I have been saving you for that day. No one will ever steal you away from me again."

"No one wants me!" Teneriel cried. "Please, I can't stand it. Kill me!"

Bronwythe wanted it all to go away then, the ugliness, the guilt. She realized that she had been rough with her daughter, overpowering the girl in the struggle, forcing her chin up. *I should not have treated my daughter so,* she thought, and Bronwythe wanted more than she wanted her next breath to receive forgiveness. She hugged Teneriel close, looked into her face. It was hard to believe anything so ugly could even speak, hard to believe that such silver tones could issue from the girl's throat. "No one knows it but me, my sweet daughter, but you are beautiful, Teneriel! I love you—I've always loved you like adamant. I know it's selfish. It has been selfish to want you like this." Bronwythe looked into Teneriel's yellowed eyes, rough as parchment, "But you are beautiful! So beautiful! And I could never bear the thought of losing you!"

Bronwythe kissed her. Teneriel kept her eyes open, and the queen scrutinized her daughter, searching for a sign of change. *I've spoken the right words while looking into the girl's eyes; I love her and crave her as always. If the curse can be broken, it will break now.*

Bronwythe watched to see if the mask of ugliness would dissolve.

The wormhole in Teneriel's chin seemed a bit bloody, and the queen waited—until at last she could stand her daughter's revolting face no longer, and was forced to turn away. *The sorcerer lied,* Bronwythe realized. *Teneriel will be marred for life.*

It took all Bronwythe's strength to escort Teneriel into her room.

Teneriel knelt by her bed, an adamant knife in hand. The moon cast golden rays into the room, adding to the light of the single candle she had placed on the floor. Teneriel fingered the black knife, tested its razor edge against her throat. *There are no dull knives in this palace,* she realized, and she wondered. . . . For the first time in six years, her mother had kissed Teneriel tenderly, just as she had done when Teneriel was a child. That moment made her heart soar—yet Trevor had run off. It seemed that the one small victory with her mother should help offset that greater loss, but it didn't. It only underscored her loss.

I shall never have a lover, Teneriel realized. *I was a fool to think Trevor could love me. I'm a fool to hope,* and she wondered, *Is it worth it to live one more day? To prolong my hope for one more day?*

The answer was no.

I must not cry out when I make the cut, she thought. The queen had posted a guard at Teneriel's door. *It wouldn't do to make any noise while bleeding to death,* she thought. *The guard might rush in and save me.*

She heard a fluttering behind her, saw an ugly brown moth colored like a dead leaf, on its back, thudding its wings against the stone floor beside the candle.

"Don't get close to the flames," Teneriel said, "they burn you every time."

The moth batted its wings, and Teneriel reached out one finger, righted the creature. It jumped into the air and began circling the flame again, unable to move away. Teneriel caught it in her hand, carried it to the window, tenderly tossed it into the air. It fluttered clumsily, climbing toward the full moon.

"Teneriel," Trevor's familiar voice called softly from the street.

"Yes," she whispered, stiffening.

"Will you marry me?"

She poked her head out the window, letting the light shine full upon her face, and she saw his eyes glinting up in the moonlight. "Are you sure?"

"I've been thinking all afternoon," Trevor said. "I came to apologize. I ... don't know what happened today. I went lunatic. I've wandered all day, thinking of you. I ... I thought of my grandmother when I was a child. She was old and her face was as wrinkled as last year's apples, but I remember how she would make the best bread in town and then spread it with butter and honey and set me on her lap while I ate. I could look in her eyes, and I never doubted she had always been beautiful. She was just a beautiful person in an old woman's body, and I thought, 'no matter who you marry, that's how she'll end up.' So, I had to see you again. I had to see you."

Teneriel looked in his eyes. He was weeping. "Teneriel, you're beautiful. I just saw what you did for that moth. You are a beautiful person where it counts. I love you, and I'm sure. Yes, I want to give myself to you. I want to marry you."

Teneriel stepped back from the window, and a glowing feeling stole over her, as if she stood in a gentle summer rain that increased in power until it became a cascading waterfall. It filled her with wonder and a sense of peace she'd not known in years. She circled the room three times, trying to catch her breath, wanting to cry out in joy. Dimly, Teneriel recalled the guard at the door. She looked out the window. It was a thirty-foot drop, and she had no way to climb down. Then she thought of using her hair as a rope. Her beautiful hair was nearly twelve feet long, she hoped she could leap the last few feet without harm.

Teneriel took the knife and stood a moment, recalling her mother's oft-repeated words, "Teneriel, Teneriel, let down your hair, that the world might bask in your beauty fair." It was the only thing of beauty she had, and she worried about how Trevor would feel. She recalled her embarrassment at the public feasts, the humiliation. *Well,* she thought, *since this is all my mother ever seemed to love of me, she can have it.* She took her knife and cut her flowing hair with a soft snick, then tied it to the post around the window.

She stole out over the windowsill, climbing down the hair as if it were a rope, taking nothing from her mother's kingdom except the clothes on her back. When she dropped, she fell into Trevor's arms. He stood, holding her a long moment, looking into her face as if pleased and surprised, and he did not turn away. "You know," he said in wonder, "you look better with short hair," and they jumped on Trevor's old mare and rode till sunrise.

That day, after a brief fever, the swelling on Teneriel's face eased and her nose came back in line. Within the week her red pox faded away, and Teneriel was shocked to see that after six years of illness, she had no trace of scars.

When Queen Bronwythe learned of her daughter's disappearance, she did not send her men after the girl. Bronwythe simply frowned, and joy eluded her. In time, Bronwythe's frown deepened, forming permanent grooves around her mouth, as if her face had turned to stone.

In later years, after Teneriel had borne three children, her beauty won her fame. Wherever she walked, people's eyes would light on her face, and they would not be able to look away. Sometimes troubadours traveled to the ends of the earth—to a green valley where wildflowers grew beside a silver brook—to look on Teneriel and write a song of it. Yet always the troubadours left in dismay, for her beauty was ineffable, and none could compose a song to do her justice.

Sometimes Teneriel would grow her hair to her waist. Always before cutting it she'd ask Trevor which he liked best, long hair or short. Trevor would take her hand, letting the flames play in the ruddy light of her hair, and he'd gaze in the clear depths behind her blue eyes, and say, "Love, I don't even care."

Then Teneriel would smile and say, "I know."

APPRECIATION

by Paul Edwin Zimmer

I was only six when my sister Marion married Robert
Bradley and moved from upstate New York to Texas. I
grew up reading not only the new issues of her fanzine
Mezrab, but the careful preserved second and third issues
of her earlier fanzine, *Astra's Tower.*

Until I was ten I was not allowed "upstairs"—the second floor of what Marion described as "an old Lovecraft-
ian farmhouse." In my early teens, poking around in
rooms walled and ceilinged with bare lathes, filled with
old trunks and old pictures and old books, was a pleasant
alternative to wandering in the woods—and sometimes,
especially in the room I later learned had been hers, I
found precious things.

Few could have been more precious—or more fate-
ful—than that first, hectographed issue of *Astra's Tower.*
The fifth page bore the heading "Saga of Carcosa," and
after quoting the first two verses of "Cassilda's Song,"
began:

"CARCOSA!

"There is witchery in the name ..."

Any reader of my *Dark Border* will see at once how
these evocative two pages—mostly juxtaposed quotes
from Chambers, Beirce, and Lovecraft—haunted my
imagination. I was fifteen.

What I did not know—then—was that Marion herself had written her own "Carcosa-Mythos stories"—the "Merdinian" stories that she later transferred to "an imaginary planet called Darkover. . . ."

IONTIOREN'S TALE

by Paul Edwin Zimmer

Grieving, the King of the Forest came to the western edge of the Wood to gather his father's bones.

The day was bright, though to the north the Mountain Onontajiwak was capped with dark clouds. Halladin was sunk in his own thoughts, for the week that had passed since he felt the old man's death had not dulled the pain. At first he paid little heed when the trees whispered of a stranger in the Forest.

Then he saw the tracks. Not the soft moccasin-scuff of the Men Made of Corn, but the hard-edged heeled prints of Outland boots. He hurried then, but the other was far before him. When Halladin raced into the blackened area of ash left when the need-fire locked in his father's sword consumed both the Demon and the man who fought it, he saw a man in Outland garments kneeling beside Halamon's skeleton, examining the tarnished silver band that bound the skull.

With a shout the king sprang forward. The stranger looked up. Although he wore Outland robes of rich velvet, white and red, and a small beard, the eyes in the stranger's dark face were the black eyes of the Men Made of Corn.

"Do you not know me, Turtle?" he asked in the Secret Speech. Halladin stopped, staring at this man who so casually used the childhood name he had not heard in years.

"Iontioren, the Splitter—" whispered Halladin. Tears blurred the king's sight, as he remembered bright-colored days from their childhood, long ago—before his cousin had left the Forest, before the Dark One came. . . .

"So your father named me," said Iontioren, "and now the time has come to earn that name." He looked down at the skeleton and shook his head. "I stand in awe at his wisdom. He knew, somehow, that the Dark Things would come again, and he guessed that this old sword might serve as a weapon against them." He lifted the glowing hilt-shard of the Sword of Halladin. The broad blade was broken a foot from the hilt: the squared end seemed shaped, until you looked close and saw the jagged marks of the break.

"And most amazing of all, he even guessed at these stresses and knew that the sword might break, not from a blow or from any weakness in the steel, but from the force of its own inner fires." Iontioren pointed to the ground, where, dull and leaden, other pieces of the sword still lay.

"See how the break is scored where the ruined steel splintered? The very metals were transmuted to quench the blade's flame! But that untouched part of the sword scorned to be joined to such foul stuff! Or, perhaps the transmuted metal could not transmit the power, and so burst from the force." He shook his head, staring at the long splinters of dead metal.

"Your father sent me to study with Hastur's grandsons, so that I might reforge the blade if it did break. I hope his trust was not misplaced. I have forged many swords in the last few years, but this will be my masterwork, I think."

"It will be difficult, then?" Halladin asked.

"Somewhat. I think I can hammer the hilt-shard out while keeping the spells in it intact—otherwise I must uncoil all its separate wires and braid all the spells anew.

But if I can keep the spells intact, I can use that as a core to weave new spells around. Also, there is this—"

He held out a tiny piece of something that flared like glass in the sunlight. Halladin took it, and realized it was metal—but a metal transparent and self-luminous.

"What is it?"

"It is a fragment of the Sword of Hastur, one of the few that were not sucked back into the Dark World with the Lord of the Eight, when Eallal fought him and lost both himself and the Sword."

Halladin nodded. He remembered only too vividly the day when Hastur's grandson had battled with the greatest of the Dark Things—so huge that it had nearly covered the entire range beyond Mount Onontajiwak—and the great wind of their passing had flattened trees and killed most of the birds in the Forest.

"Hastur's grandson, Narsil, thinks that he will be able to anneal it—no fire I could make would be hot enough. If he can, it can be stretched into a wire and bound around the core, and add its spells to those in Halladin's Sword. If so, Halladin's blade will be more potent than before. Then it will be a matter of weaving charms of steel and silver around them and shaping the spell into a sword. It sounds easy when I talk about it. I wish it were as easy in the forge!" He laughed, and Halladin, looking at the skeleton beside him, winced.

He knelt and opened the bag he had brought to carry King Halamon's bones back to the Heart of the Forest, to mingle them with the soil which held the bones of the other kings of his line. Through the eyes of a curious weasel that watched from an unburnt bush nearby, the King of the Forest saw how the wizard pressed his lips together, with pain in his eyes. A savage, chill, childish satisfaction leaped inside him, and then he heard his father's voice: *He mourns, too, my son, but in his own way.*

Tears blurred the bones before him. Even his numbing

grief could not mute the pain of the singed roots of burnt flowers and trees. Reverently, he began to gather up the charred bones and place them in the sack he had brought. The ashes of the burned bones would sweeten acid soil where the pines grew thick. . . .

But there was something wrong with the bone in his hand. Blinking the tears from his eyes, he saw that its end was not charred by fire, but turned to dry gray metal powder that began to flake and fall away as he lifted the bone from the ground.

"What shall I do?" he cried aloud in his distress. "My father's very bones have been poisoned! I cannot take this poison to the Heart of the Forest!" The violence of his heartbeat frightened the crows into flight: the weasel crouched trembling in its thicket. Even the trees were startled.

Iontioren reached out with a tentative finger, and again, Halladin felt that strange mind probing into the mineral and organic patterns of bone and ash, to feel atoms twisted awry by the same force that had broken the sword, locked into deadly angled dances through tortured space. . . .

Iontioren drew his finger back with a little shudder. Flakes of gray ash fell from the bone's end.

"As I thought," he said somberly. "Give me the poisoned bones, Halladin. Narsil Hastur-Smith has already transmuted some of this stuff into earthly metal—just such metals as I need for the sword. Do you think that your father would like his bones to be part of the Sword? It seems fitting."

Fitting indeed! Halamon's ghost exclaimed in his son's mind. *I do wish that—and I have earned it!*

Halladin nodded. "Take the bones," he said.

From the breast of his robe, the wizard brought forth several small, metal phials, and silently began to fill them with the ash-flakes from the bones, while Halladin sorted the clean bones into his sack.

Part of the skull had been eaten away: Halladin took only the jawbone. Iontioren lifted from the skull the band of pitted silver with its dark stone, which Hastur had taken from the earth to crown the first Halladin, a thousand years before.

But the silver circlet was broken now, the wire above the transmuted section of the skull melted and blackened as though by fire.

"This, too, must be repaired," the wizard said, "but I can make it far more powerful than it was. This spell is very simple."

"It served my fathers well enough as it was, and so did the Sword," Halladin said.

"Your fathers left the Sword in a cave for a thousand years," Iontioren grimaced. "But that was before the Dark Things came."

Five years ago, thought Halladin, staring at him unhappily. For a thousand years the kings of his line had ruled, their minds linked to the Forest, each in his turn inheriting his ancestors' memories. For a thousand years that had been enough to preserve the Forest and the tribes that lived there. But everything was changing now.

Iontioren considered the broken band of blackened silver. "In truth, this Crown is far closer to the kind of work I have been doing these many years. It is only since the Dark Things came that I have forged many swords. You will be seeing some of them, long before you see this one again, when the assembled host of the Orders of Croyterre reach this land."

"What?" Halladin asked sharply, bristling instinctively at the thought of hordes of strangers in his land.

"Did you not know? The heads of the Knightly Orders of Croyterre have taken oath to march to these mountains, as part of the penance for their defiance of Hastur. They had turned aside—"

"What you are talking about?" Halladin cried.

Iontioren blinked at him. "I had thought sure the whole world had heard the tale by now. But I had forgotten how isolated these woods are."

"We have not even heard the names here, and if our isolation is to be violated, it were best for me to learn by whom—" Halladin fought for control.

"Croyterre is—or rather, was—far to the south and east, beyond the southern tip of the Sea of Ardren and the land of the Takkars. The peoples whom Hastur placed there, south of the Mountains of the Star, were fighting when he found them, and enemies they remained. One group, the Croyterrans, founded many little kingdoms with names like Defianza, Poulainia, Verterre, and the like. But the greatest power in these lands was not any of these kingdoms, but the Orders of warrior-priests devoted to keeping alive their ancient religion.

"They have a strange mythology of a sacred city that they must reach, where their god, Iesucri, lies bound to a cross, tormented by their enemies. Since Hastur, by bringing them to this world, kept them from rescuing their god and his city, they declared Hastur to be evil and allied to their enemies.

"They did not change their minds until Narsil, the master-smith and grandson of Hastur to whom I was apprenticed, helped Prince Toustin defeat the Knights of Croyterre in order to regain his throne—just a year before the Dark Things came. The war was long and terrible, but in the end, the great wall of the last fortress of the Order was brought down upon its defenders by the power Narsil had forged into Toustin's spear. Even then, the survivors might have chosen to go down fighting. But suddenly a voice, louder than thunder, cried out that here had been enough bloodshed, and called on the Knights of Croyterre to lay down their arms.

"And Narsil appeared, floating in the air between the armies. An aura of light like sunfire blazed about him, and men fell to their knees, shielding their eyes.

"The walls that remained boomed with Narsil's voice. For too long, he said, had the Children of Hastur suffered the defiance of the Knights of Croyterre. Never, said Narsil, had any of his kin quarrelled with Iesucri. But Iesucri, said Narsil, had never been friend to injustice or oppression, and must be ashamed of these false followers who had forgotten his teachings, but still used his name to mask their own cruelty and greed.

"And at these words a sigh swept through the kneeling, steel-clad ranks, and many wept. Toustin and his men sat like statues on their horses, staring. But I felt a stir of Power behind me, and turning in the saddle, saw a huge block of stone rise into the air.

"Hastur's grandsons, Eallal and Erluin, stood on either side of the stone, staring at the block as their minds lifted it. While Narsil spoke to the knights, his kinsmen were searching the shattered ruins of the wall, clearing away the fallen stones from pitiable, broken wrecks who had stood on the wall and laughed when Toustin charged with his spear."

Iontioren paused, frowning and thoughtful. No breeze moved the new leaves, and so many birds had been killed when Eallal fought the Lord of the Eight that the few who remained left vast parts of forest in songless silence.

"How they screamed, those poor men!" the wizard said abruptly. "I hear them still in nightmares. But they were lucky. The boundless compassion of the Hastur-children numbed their nerves; the power of their minds guided the splinters of shattered bone back through the torn flesh and welded them back in place. They wove new the tattered skein of veins and arteries, and spliced and soothed the soft red shreds together again, like—like mere clay! Mended! Miracle of mind!" The wizard's eyes were bright with awe, and he shook his dark head in wonder.

"Their traditions make much of penance, and so the Masters of the several Orders asked Narsil for some deed to do whereby they could redeem themselves."

"And well they might," Halladin exclaimed, "but why should the Hastur-kin set them to do it here?"

Iontioren shook his head. "They did not. Narsil said he would consider the matter, and the Hastur kindred were still discussing it months later, when Rethondo the thief stole Hastur's Brooch. When he pried the jewels from their settings, he destroyed the spell that held the Dark Lords from the World. The city to which he had fled with his plunder was obliterated: Hastur's other city was wrenched from the World—"

"But what about the Knights of Croyterre?"

"When garbled word of these events first reached Croyterre," Iontioren went on, "the Masters of the Orders assembled not only the Knights, but also the Orders of Women and unarmed priests, who all together make up what they call the *Eccles Militawn.* When the heads of the Orders meet, their assembly is called the *Crusat,* and it was they who voted that as penance they would march to the aid of the Hastur Kindred.

"They had no real conception of what it was they faced, having heard only confused stories. So the great march began, the march of the Iron Men that still goes on, though often checked and turned aside. Do you think them unworthy, or is it that you feel no need of allies? Until you have heard their story, how can you decide?"

"While they were still marshaling their host, one of the Dark Things appeared upon the height that marks their border with the Takkarians. The knights marched, but their first battle was a disaster, for weapons of plain steel, however finely forged, are useless against the powers from Outside.

"The Hastur-kin drove the Dark Thing out of the World before the Host of the Order could be completely destroyed, yet the shadow-larvae that it shed killed many. But Narsil gave several swords to the knights.

"Narsil had rekindled the fires in the volcano *Ignis-del-bonn,* and then made his forge in the crater of the mountain, and brought metals up, fresh from earth's hot heart, to weave with his mind into strong spells of steel and silver and other, rarer, metals from the depths of the earth. And some he shaped into Swords of Power, attempts to make anew the Sword of Hastur that had been lost with Eallal, and others were made into weapons of a different kind.

"He sent then for me, because he knew that I had long pondered Hastur's Sword, comparing it in memory to this blade here—and I had learned mortal smithcraft, and hammered layered steel before I ever tried to shape spells with my mind. We labored then together for a year, forging ever finer swords, with ever stronger spells. But Hastur's secrets eluded us—and they elude us still.

"But while we labored thus, all the *Eccles Militawn* were disposing of their castles and their lands and withdrawing from the southern parts of that realm and gathering in Verterre in the north. The vanguard of the host had already crossed the mountains to the Central Plain, planning to march around the northern end of the Argendarean Sea. Had they followed that plan, they would have been here long since. When Narsil and I came down from the Mountain, with half a hundred of our new swords, we found those to whom we had meant to give them gone. Their capital was deserted save for a handful of merchants; barracks, nunneries and monasteries all lay empty and forlorn. I am told it is completely forsaken now, and falling into ruin. We had to journey all the way to the mountains that mark the borders of Adlerheim before we caught up with their rearguard."

He shook his head in wonder. "Imagine it—a whole people on the march, chanting ancient songs of praise for Iesucri. Thousands upon thousands of ox-drawn wagons, and millions of black-clad men and women marching on foot, and at the rear, great orderly blocks of horsemen, the Knights of the Hospital, sweeping up stragglers and tending to the sick even as they guarded. With them we left the Swords we had brought. When at last they stopped for the night, all the land was filled with great tent cities, and their fires stretched northeast to the horizon and beyond.

"It was then that I decided—or rather, *we* decided, Narsil and I—that I should march north with the Orders, that I might forge new Swords as we journeyed, and also teach my skills, as far as they could be taught—or those I journeyed with could learn. So I have journeyed for these five years with their Hosts, and learned much of them. They are a strange folk, vowed to poverty and chastity in the service of Iesucri. The women live in separate orders and avoid the men, except for nursing the sick, and when they are chosen by lot to breed children to restore their numbers.

"For centuries, that, and the adoption of orphans and recruiting from the populace have been enough to keep their numbers stable. During the march the custom was changed, and now, each year ten Knights are chosen, from a different Order each year. Also, human nature being what it is, the vows are not always kept, and under the conditions of the march they have found it even harder. And so, many children have been born upon the march, and this is good, for many, many others have died upon it."

"You said they would have been here long since if they had followed their original plan," said Halladin, bringing him back to the subject. "Why did they change it?"

"It was only a little while after I had joined the march. Word came down the line from the vanguard that they had met refugees fleeing south, who said that one of the Dark Lords now crawled upon the Plains of Tierra Nielmo. An emergency meeting of the *Crusat* was called, and I was permitted to attend, for I could speak to Narsil or the other Hasturs, and my own visionary powers could see afar.

"The Dark One had appeared in the Leontierra and crawled north and east, into Sardis. It left behind it miles of bare stone, and swarms of its shadowy spawn. And now a second Dark Thing had appeared farther to the north, crawling south, and the first one had turned and crawled to meet the other, so that the fleeing population of the destroyed lands were now between them, driven like sheep toward doom. And the Children of Hastur had to divide their forces between the two.

"After much discussion, the Council resolved to divide the Host. The Templars and the Knights of Malta, who made up the vanguard, and had already reached the Sea of Argendarean, would march along its eastern shore as planned, but instead of turning west when they reached the northern shore, they would continue on into Tierra Nielmo, and march east, toward the monsters.

"The main body of the Host, meanwhile, would seek passage through the Mountains of the Star, asking the Emperor of Adlerheim for guides and safe passage, and pass due east through the Mountains into Leontierra, and then march north in the Dark Lord's track.

"But the Knights of the Hospital, taking with them all the sick and wounded, and three of the Orders of women that marched near the rear, were to turn back and march along the barrier cliffs almost to the Sea, and sail north to Heyleu in Seynyor, and march from thence to Carcosa to seek the guidance and protection of the Hasturs. The combined Host would assemble again at Carcosa."

Iontioren was silent a moment: out of the distance came hoarse cawing, where crows harrassed an eagle that had flown too near their nest. The heavier bird flapped clumsily near the treetops, trying to escape as his more agile tormentors dived and darted, pecking at his eyes and neck and head.

"I rode with the main host—partly so that I might join the embassy to Adlerheim and add Hastur's authority to their pleas, and partly because these folk had the most need of swords. The vanguard Knights of the Temple and the remnants of Malta had the blades Narsil had given them after that first disastrous fight. The rearguard had the swords we had brought from *Ignis-del-bonn*. Only five of these swords had been given to the Knights of the other Orders, with whom I rode.

"Hundreds died crossing the mountains—for it was now winter, and we had to force our way through snow-blocked passes—and many women, old men, and children perished from the cold. Many more had to remain behind and were taken in by the people through whose country we passed.

"The king and the people had at first been hostile, for despite their mountain barrier, they had some experience of the arrogance of the Orders. But as word spread of what it was that brought the Orders into the high mountains, the people of the land rushed to aid with food and fuel—otherwise we would have lost far more.

"And when we came down from the passes and marched into Leontierra, many warriors and young men followed us, begging leave to join our army, though not enough to replace all those who had died in the mountains. But now we were come into a land that swarmed with homeless refugees, and all the food given us in the mountains would not have sufficed to feed even a tithe of them. Beggars swarmed around us. Many were orphaned children, and the Sisterhoods took them in, thinking so to replace those lost in the mountains. But most ran away a few days after.

"At first, we—the Brothers of the Orders, I should say—attempted to feed and clothe all who came. But it soon became apparent that there were far, far more than our dwindling stores could support—even had we some other source of food for our own needs. But as we pressed on, the beggars dropped away, and when, on the third day of the march, we reached the edge of a vast blighted area of dead trees and withered grass and great swathes of grey dust, none were left, save a few men mad for revenge, who joined one Order or another as time passed.

"Here night brought the demons, rising like black ghosts from the ground. We ringed our camps with great fires, and Knights with torches patrolled them, and even so, many died. It was only the handful who carried the swords that I had made that protected us for long enough to kindle the fires.

"There was little time for working at the forge, but now my skills were needed as never before, and so I labored through the night while demons howled around the camp. And the smiths, and many Knights, stayed up to watch me and to learn.

"In the morning I rose early, and set out at the head of the line, dozing in the saddle even as I pushed my horse to stay ahead. We halted well before sunset to make camp. Knights scoured the empty land for anything that would burn, while I set up my forge and went to work. And some of the smiths understood enough of what I was doing that I could set them tasks, and we labored on through the night, and then all the next day while the host marched past us, and when the rear came up they stopped and camped around us and we worked on through the night. And by dawn two more swords were finished, and others begun.

"But all that day I slept in an ox-cart, and woke bruised and sore from the jolting that had not awakened me. If I dreamed, no nightmare was as bad as waking.

"For while I had slept, the host had passed over a vast waste of gray dust and come down onto a great floor of polished stone, set between steep banks of dust, that stretched away to the north as far as the eye could see, and was more than ten miles across from east to west. And there were deep gouges in the stone—like the marks of terrible claws.

"Before I woke, the host had moved out onto the stone and made camp there. It looked safer than the dust. But it was not long before we realized that we were in a deadly trap. Our scant stocks of fuel were nearly gone. There was no grass or water for horses or oxen. There was nothing on the stone that would burn except what we had brought.

"Soon the entire host was huddled in the center of a ring of fires, while the ox-carts were being broken up and added to them. The eight knights who carried the swords I had forged stood guard at gaps in the ring, and other knights held sticks ready to plunge into the fires. I worked with the smiths at another of the fires, trying to finish another sword. The women and children were at the center of the ring.

"I tried to call for aid from the Hastur-kin, but they were locked in terrible battles with greater Dark Things in the north, and there was no help there. Demons wailed around the fires all night long, and some tried to cross the flames and burned. Panicked horses trampled several people, and some broke loose and stampeded through the flames and fell on the other side. In the morning there were only bones—or rather, gray dust in the shape of bones.

"Thrice demons leaped the flames and came in among the people and ate many, but each time the Knights set fire to them, or slew them with one of the swords. And one demon took to the air, and flying above the circle, came down in the middle among the women and children, and many were eaten, and more were trampled in the rush to get away: but one Knight was able to throw a torch into the darkness, and the demon burned.

"Then the priests went round the circle, blessing the fires, and that made a crude magical barrier around the camp that was just strong enough to make the demons hesitate; and I, cursing myself for a fool, went around the camp myself and added power to the ring. Toward dawn the wood was gone, and the fires, smoldering coals, but the barrier held them off until dawn drove them back under the ground.

"It had been a harsh and a costly lesson. We got ourselves off the stone as quickly as we might, and through the gray dust into the blighted band of land that edged the Dark Thing's track, and there we buried our dead and gathered wood for the next night.

"Some still urged that we hurry north to aid the Hastur-kin in their fight against the Dark Thing in whose track we had all so nearly died. But most now realized that such a task was far beyond our strength, and that if we could rid this land of even a few of these lesser creatures, we would have done more to aid Hastur's family than we could by wasting lives in a futile attack upon the living mountain of death that had left its track in the bedrock behind us.

"So, at last, my counsel prevailed. The host halted while I labored with the hammer, forging sword after sword, and teaching my skill. The Knights of the Essuit Order had their own mental training techniques, and so were the quickest to learn to send their will, through concentration and visualization, into the inlaid patterns braided within the metal, and though their first few swords were powerless and had to be reforged, it was not long before they learned to work together, focusing their choral will as they chanted at the anvil to kindle the powers in their swords.

"Now we changed our camps only as the stocks of fuel became exhausted. We moved slowly, so, to the north. Soon fewer demons howled around our fires, as the knights hunted and slaughtered the shadows that haunted the waste.

"In the lands beyond, men stared at those sent to buy food from them, and wild legends spread. Soon bold men—and foolish boys—came flocking to join the Orders, and smiths and sages and learned men came to learn to forge the swords that would slay the Shadows.

"Meanwhile, far in the north, the vanguard had reached the Sea of Aguadorado, and turning, came out of the west to where the Dark Lord crawled upon the plain, and more than two-thirds of the Maltese Knights died in an ill-considered assault. And even more would have died, but Hastur's grandson Thyron died to save them. Then Narsil and Erluin, in great wrath, drove the survivors away and bade them march south to join us.

"Two years then, we spent beside that barren strip of stone. Slowly we cleaned that land of the night-walking demons, and the people flocked to us. For we had proven that ordinary mortal men could face these lesser Dark Things and live—although only the Hasturs could deal with the great ones. But with fire and with the swords I had forged, men could not only defend themselves, but hunt down the demons and destroy them—or at least drive them from the world.

"Do you begin to understand?" His gaze fixed Halladin suddenly "It was the same battle your father was fighting here. He, though only one man, could do much, because he had this—" he gestured toward the shards of the Sword of Halladin. "But you will have no such advantage, until it can be reforged!"

Halladin nodded, and after a moment Iontioren remembered his story and went on.

"Still we moved slowly north. Word reached us that the monster on whose track we marched had been driven from the world, and later, that the other one farther north was gone. But, of course, by then others had appeared. The Hastur-kin were continually rushing from one side of the world to the other, locked in long struggles against the Dark Lords. It seemed that the lesser spawn of the Dark Lords would be left entirely to mortals.

"Then, one night, men saw a great light, far off in the northern sky. I was roused from my bed to divine what this might mean, and sending my thought into the darkness, I touched the minds of Narsil and Erluin. They rode upon one of the new weapons Narsil had forged in Ignis-del-bonn, a strange frame of tubes and crystals, hanging in the air; and from it radiance poured deep into the dust and the earth and the stone beneath the earth. And before them the demons fled—southward, toward our camp.

"So warned, we built high our fires and stood behind them; rank upon rank of flaming swords, while the rest of that steel-armored host huddled behind. Soon, wailing waves of cold black ghosts rolled down upon us out of the spell-lit north. As they hit us, our fires flickered and failed and Knights died, blades shattered, need-fire quenched in the black tide. Then, suddenly all that wall of demons was aflame.

"Narsil had come.

"No doubt some few of the Night Things escaped, flying east or west to haunt some hidden corner of the land, but men will hunt those lonely few, for many men of Leontierra had come to learn my art during that time, and forged swords for themselves and learned to forge more for their neighbors and kin.

"But at last our path lay clear to Carcosa. It was now the fourth year since the Dark Things came, though it seemed longer because our lives had been so changed. Before that was a different age, a different world: it all seems so long ago.

"A hero's welcome met us in Carcosa, for we alone of mortal men had stood against the Dark Things in battle and lived to—"

"Not true!" Halladin interrupted sharply. "By that time my father had slain several demons, and the monks of the Dorjie Kang stood up against the great Darkness that walked upon the mountains there, and halted it for a time. And many of them still live."

"Hah! Is it so?" exclaimed Iontioren. "I shall have to speak with them, or perhaps more to the point, have Narsil or some other of Hastur's kin look into their minds to find the basis of their power. For such secrets are important now. We are building a school at Carcosa, assembling sages and wise men from different lands to determine what powers may be learned by mortal man. The Hasturs work with us when they can, but that is seldom, now.

"I spent my time at Carcosa, teaching men to forge swords of power, while the host rested from its march. But the Hospitalers of the rearguard, and the wounded and sick in their care who now were well, envied those who had been tempered on that nightmare march. Having sat in peace for so long, they were eager to depart. When men came from Galdor, begging for aid, they clamored to be gone, and the Templars, as well as that handful of the Knights of Malta that remained—for they still smarted, it seemed, from the words that Erluin had used when he ordered them south after Thyron was

killed. And some who had newly joined the Orders eager
to prove themselves.

"Both the north and the south of the land of Galdor
were scarred with the marks of the Dark Things' passage,
and each night, demons hunt. So the *Crusat* was called,
and after long debate resolved that the Orders should
march, but that now the Hospital should lead the vanguard, and the main body divide into two hosts, the first
of which, made up mostly of those women and sick who
had spent these last three years at Carcosa, would march
under the guard of the Templars and the surviving
knights of Malta. The other half would follow, and the
Order of Essuits would be the new rearguard. So the
Hospital was able to march at once, while those who had
taken the brunt of the fighting and the hunting of demons
were able to rest at Carcosa.

"At first I thought to remain behind and teach my
skills at the new College, and so, for a time, I did. But
I grew homesick for my own land. In dreams Our Father
the Forest called to me, and your father the king as well.
At last I resolved to march with the host after all, for
by now I had trained others who could teach in my stead.
So, when the first half of the main body left, I joined
them and marched with them across the plain to Arlath."

"*Arlath?*" Halladin exclaimed, startled into sudden
homesick memory a thousand years old. "Tell me, how
stands Arlath?"

The wizard, unaware that Halladin was remembering
their common ancestors' wanderings, could not help but
stare, and it took him a moment to gather his wits to
answer.

"The ancient city still stands," he answered at last—
startling Halladin in his turn, who remembered Arlath
as the rough-built, still growing town where that first Halladin had lived for many years.

"Miles of the great outer wall are down, crushed or

eaten by the Dark Lord; and many houses in that outer circle were smashed and broken before Hastur's Children could drive it away, and demons laired in the deserted houses. The inner wall had been rebuilt before we arrived; it had barely been touched, we were told. Now knights hunt night-haunts through the stone shells, or ride abroad to cleanse the countryside. The inner city is untouched.

"Galdor is now the only nation in the north whose civilization is intact. But the fields and farms at the foot of the mountains, where most of their food was grown, were destroyed. Nothing remains but poisoned dust and polished stone. Every rose garden has perforce been resown with vegetables or grain, and they are terracing the mountains behind the city to make new fields. And even so, they starve. One of the chief duties of the Knights has been to escort caravans across the blighted region to the south, to Vaqueria, Yonerossa, and Seynyor, to barter all the treasure the Galdorian kings have amassed over a thousand years for cattle, and for wagonloads of grain.

"Many men of Galdor have joined the Order of Malta—so many that they have almost regained their original strength. And many have come to me to learn to forge enchanted swords, and so I spent my time at the city—until I felt the King's Sword break. . . ."

He paused, as though groping for words. Halladin fought to subdue his own memories of that moment by directing his attention to what he saw through the myriad eyes of the Forest. Through the long ears of a hare and the smaller but still sensitive ears of the weasel who hunted it, he listened to the wailing of a newborn child, and the strange-toned lullaby that its exhausted mother sobbed, twenty miles to the south. She was part of a ragged group of refugees that had staggered down the mountain, fleeing from the terrors on the heights.

Swift thought leaped through the Forest to a village where monks chanted in strange tones like wolf-howls that rang with shimmering echoes roused inside their own heads, while the masked shamans of the Men Made of Corn listened in respectful silence. The Forest spoke, and a shaman and a priest arose, and set off down the trail to meet the fleeing refugees and guide them through the wood. Distant thunder muttered in the north.

"I felt the Sword break," Iontioren said. "I had pondered its steel for many years. I felt my uncle's thought touch me, and then felt the Forest cry out as he died. I felt his death. . . ."

As did I! Halladin could no longer withstand the rush of terror and triumph that had been his father's dying, reexperienced in memory, and the dizzying spiral of expanding awareness as the full consciousness of the Lord of the Forest was added to his own. Overwhelmed by his own sensations, he could no longer deny that the other man, in some part, shared his pain.

"I called to Narsil then and Narsil came," Iontioren said harshly. "None saw him, I think, when he came to the wood and added his need-fire to the flames of the torches that your people threw. But the king was already dead.

"Narsil returned to me. I gathered my tools together, and then he brought me here. He has taken them yonder," he pointed to the north where storm clouds above the mountain Onontajiwak loomed tall against the sky.

"Narsil will meet me there, when he can. Another Dark One has broken into the world, and all Hastur's kin must go to battle once again. But they are becoming ever more skilled at defeating them, and he hopes to meet me today or tomorrow to help set up my forge."

"But what of the Orders?" asked Halladin. "You said that I would be likely to see other blades of your forging before I saw this one again. Are they so close, or will it take you so long to reforge the blade?"

"Truly it will be a long task," said the wizard. "For this blade contains spells infinitely more complex than any that I ever learned to weave. I will need Narsil's help even to begin to anneal the steel. The spells on the Sword of Hastur are more complex still. If I tried to hurry the forging, all those spells would be lost. I expect to spend at least a year, perhaps more, weaving the spells together.

"As for the Orders—that is hard to say. They are still gathering in Galdor and helping to protect the city and hunt demons down. But Narsil has been able to help with that, and some are already talking of moving on. They could come in a year, or another five years. The *Crusat* will decide, when next they meet. But after so long a march, after having come so far from the lands where they were born, many now look forward to ending their journey, and finding new land where they may build new homes and settle to rest."

"Not in the Forest!" Halladin snapped.

Thunder drowned the wizard's laughter as he answered, shaking his head. The storm was moving down from the mountain, and dark clouds were launching themselves from the lightning crowned peak.

"Indeed not," the wizard was saying as the thunder died away. "The flat land of Korhandol's plains would no doubt be more to their tastes, but they will try to occupy land to the mountains to fight the Dark Lords of the Shadow yonder. They plan to take only land from which others have fled, so you need not fear for the Forest. After all you have heard, can you not welcome them as allies?"

Lightning flared again, and thunder cut off his voice. Black clouds were spreading south from the mountain, scudding rapidly before a high wind, shutting away the sunlight. But the darkness which was filling the sky was nothing to the Shadow that threatened the world. He saw now that even as his link to the Forest expanded his awareness of some things, it was also a limitation. Like the Forest, these newcomers, with their strange ways and their stranger religion, belonged to this world and must be accepted.

Now a thin rain began to patter on the dust and ash around them. The Forest Lord could see, through the senses of the Forest, the widdershins whirl that was the essence of the storm, the webs of power between ground and cloud, moving swiftly south.

"It's going to be wet," Halladin said. "The village is only a few miles that way." But the wizard shook his head.

"I have been wet before," Iontioren said, smiling. "It is good to be home. But it will be a long and hard climb to the heights of Onontajiwak where Narsil is to meet me." He rose, wrapping up the shards of the Sword, and began to move away.

"Tell your Iron Men—" said Halladin, and Iontioren turned. "When they come, the Lord of the Forest will welcome them—and their swords."

The wizard's teeth flashed white in his dark face. Then he turned away and trudged into the teeth of the storm.

WINTER TALES

by Adrienne Martine-Barnes

Tante Matilde watched the children grow more and more restless as the brief winter day drew to a close. She sighed and reflected upon the burdens of her life. She had never wed but had remained in her childhood home to care for her widowed brother and his five young children. At the moment she was stranded in the gatehouse of a ruined chateau with all of them, due, as usual, to the follies of her brother Phillipe. A broken carriage wheel had interrupted their journey homeward. Their luggage had been left behind when they had departed in one of Phillipe's rages. The gatehouse where they had taken shelter was cold and drafty, and there was nothing to eat and only some melted snow to drink. Fortunately, she was of a serene disposition, and very little disturbed her for long. She tucked up her lacy mitts and continued her knitting.

The eldest of the girls, her niece Jennifer, was peering out the mullioned window at the falling snow, her starched fontage drooping a little in the clammy air of the room. With her fichu drawn across her bosom she looked forlorn and chilly. One window of the gatehouse was broken, and Jennifer had insisted that her own traveling cloak be used to cover it, while her brothers and sisters were clutching theirs across their young shoulders. Of all her nieces and nephews, she knew she loved Jennifer the best, as the daughter she had never been blessed with.

Matilde did not blame her in the least for looking sad. They had gone to the Comte de Nantes to sign the wedding contract, and nothing had gone right from the start. One of the horses had gone lame and delayed their arrival. The Comte had taken umbrage at their tardiness and been insulting as only the very wealthy can be. Jennifer had taken an immediate aversion to her betrothed, an ill-favored and pimply youth with the manners of a pig for all that he was extremely well born. Phillipe had tried fawning and toadying, then lost his temper. He had bundled Matilde and the children into the decrepit carriage and set off with his usual volitility, abandoning luggage and servants without a thought. Was there ever a more maddening man?

"Tante, I am bored," Jean-Phillipe announced for perhaps the twentieth time. He was seven, and a charming child, when he was not pulling his sister's hair or finding other mischief.

"I am hungry." Antoinette announced unnecessarily. "When will Father return? I hope he remembers to bring some supper." She was just ten and plump as a pullet.

"We must count ourselves fortunate if he returns at all," Jennifer answered, turning from the window. "He will likely send an ostler while he stays in some warm inn and drinks."

"What a shocking thing to say," her sister Marie said very severely. Marie, at fourteen, was a sober young woman, destined for the Abbey Michele unless the family fortunes were reversed.

"Why?" Jennifer tried to pull her fichu closer to her drooping shoulders and shivered.

"He is our father and we must treat him with respect."

"He is a gambler and a wastrel. If he had been otherwise, we would not be here." No one could deny the truth of Jennifer's stern words, and an uneasy silence followed. Matilde hated to see her seventeen-year-old niece so unhappy, and she wished she could think of something to do. It was clear to anyone who bothered to look that Jennifer was not ready to marry, and certainly not that nasty son of Nantes.

"I am tired," Antoinette whined. "There is nothing to sit on. We will freeze to death in the night, if we do not starve first."

"Sit on the floor," her brother Paul advised. At twelve he was already like his mother, steady and reliable and a little dull. It had been he who had found wood for the ancient stove, the snow bucket and a dipper to drink from, and the single chair upon which Matilde now perched somewhat uneasily. One leg was shorter than the rest, and the back of the chair creaked ominously whenever she shifted her weight.

"On the floor? It is filthy!" Antoinette, shocked, pointed to the hem of her dress that was streaked and soiled.

"Unless you intend to sleep standing," Paul replied, "you will have to get to know it sooner or later."

"Sleep? Here? Are you mad? I could not close my eyes for a moment!"

Matilde gave her youngest niece a fond glance and thought it was a shame that the girl could not become an actress. She had such a natural ability for drama—much too much like her father. But it was unthinkable. She would have to marry, or enter the convent, or dwindle into an aunt. Matilde had a great deal of trouble imagining Antoinette as an aunt.

The wind, which had fallen in the brief afternoon, began to rise, rattling the roof tiles of the old gatehouse and causing the windows to quiver in their frames. A draft blew under the warped door and through the broken window. The branches of a tree outside made a nasty, scraping noise, as if someone were scratching at the walls. The little stove was a circle of warmth and light as the rest of the room grew dark and shadowed.

Matilde peered down at the knitting in her lace-mitted hands and wondered if she could manage to complete the row before it became too dark to see. She felt old and tired and useless, and as much as she loved the children, she longed for the comforts of her rooms in the dilapidated chateau they called home. A glass of mulled wine, a poached hen with fine herbs, some bread, and her bed, clean and warm and sweet-scented with lavender—a vision worthy of heaven, to be sure.

Marie made a face, then tucked her skirts beneath her and sat on the floor beside her aunt's chair. "Perhaps if you will tell us one of those histories you are always scribbling at, Tante, it will help to pass the time."

Matilde gave the girl a sharp look. How had she discovered them? Had she been spying? The older woman frowned, then thrust her knitting aside. Trust Marie to be practical.

"A story? I am too cold and too hungry to listen to tales," Antoinette began, her young voice shrilling. She was dreadfully spoiled, for she had been a sickly child, and no one but Matilde appeared to have noticed she was now quite robust. "I want my dinner and my bed and . . ."

"If you fly into one of your fits of pique just now," Jennifer interrupted sharply, "I shall slap you silly and push your head into the snow." She pulled her skirts about her and plumped down beside Marie in a single graceful movement. She smoothed her apron across her lap, folded her hands and smiled. "Please Tante, tell us a tale."

"With a dragon who eats naughty girls," Jean-Phillippe suggested, his young eyes alight with mischief.

"Dragons? Pah! There are no dragons," Paul sneered. "Let there be wolves and brave knights instead."

"And a fair maiden to be rescued," added Marie in an unexpected show of fancy.

"And a good feast," Antoinette put in, quite forgetting her own objections of a minute before, and entering into the spirit of the room. She plopped down between her sisters, and Jennifer put an arm around her waist, drawing her close. Antoinette snuggled close and spread her cloak so it covered both of them.

"And you, child," Matilde asked her eldest niece.

"I will let you choose," Jennifer answered, "but perhaps a treasure would be good."

"Very well!" Matilde tried to find a comfortable position on the rickety chair as she ordered her thoughts. She drew her black shawl about her, folded her hands in her broad lap, and nodded so vigorously that her fontage cap fell forward. She pushed it back as her charges struggled not to laugh—as if she did not know what a foolish figure she presented.

Outside the wind rose furiously, howling around the little building, making it shudder and shake. Jean-Phillippe looked alarmed and sat down beside Matilde's chair on one side, while Paul added another log to the fire in the stove.

"Did you notice the ruins of the chateau on the hill," Matilde asked. "Before that was built, there was a castle there, which belonged to the Chevalier de Breon."

"When?" demanded Jean-Phillippe. His sisters hushed him.

Matilde drew a long breath. "A long time ago, on a day like today, when the snow lay thick upon the ground, and winter kept its guard. The Chevalier de Breon was a cruel fellow, and known for his greed. He had buried two wives, both heiresses, and now he sought another. And there was a young woman with a goodly dowry and

an old and honored name. He invited the family of the
girl to come to Breon for the Christmastide, and after
some consideration, they accepted."

"What was her name," Antoinette demanded.

"She was called Melissa."

"That means 'honey' in Greek," Paul said, eager to
demonstrate his learning.

"Oh—do be quiet and let Tante tell the story!" Jennifer's eyes were gleaming in the light from the stove, and
her brothers and sisters settled down at her words.

"It was the feast of St. Lucy and . . ."

Melissa de Montalban stood beside one of the narrow
windows of the castle of the Chevalier de Breon and
shivered. She hated the cold halls of the place, the faded
tapestries, and the smell of rotten rushes upon the floor.
The servants had made little effort to tidy the place, and
they were surly and rude as well. Her mother was quite
impressed with the size of the keep, and her father by
the Chevalier's title, but Melissa was in despair at the
idea of remaining there for the rest of her life. The thick
damp walls made her throat choke closed, and the pro-
posed bridegroom made her skin crawl.

It was nearly dusk, and the guards were preparing to
close the bridge across the wide moat when a figure appeared. Melissa watched it because she was bored and
cold and, she knew, very frightened. She was afraid that
when the drawbridge closed, she would be trapped inside
forever. Her throat tightened, and she could hardly
breathe for a moment. She brushed a strand of dark hair
from her brow and straightened her shoulders. She was
a Montalban and that meant she must be brave and do
her duty.

An ancient woman tottered across the heavy boards
and between the clanking wheels. She wore a tattered
cloak, all motley, a patchwork of black and white frag-

ments of old cloth, and the sight of it made her smile just a little. One of the guards made a rude gesture at the odd figure, but another whispered something and he stopped. Not even the surly servants of the Chevalier were foolish enough to annoy one who wore the magpie robe of the wandering tale tellers.

Melissa knew something of their history from her grandmother. They came from the south, from the places where the Church had slain many heretics, and they told wonderful stories, and had the power to curse if they were angered. Whenever anyone said "I heard this from a magpie," the hall would still, and all would listen eagerly, certain of a treat. She had never seen one of these wanderers, and had always wished to, so she felt a certain excitement.

The girl hastened down the narrow stairs, drawing her heavy skirts away from the dirty stones, and reached the entrance just as the woman walked in. The hood of the cloak shadowed her face, but Melissa could see a face wrinkled with years and weathered by the elements. Her hand, where it gripped a strangely carven staff, was gnarled and twisted. Beneath the cloak the garments were ragged and filthy, and the smell that rose from them made even the Chevalier's brute dogs draw away. While Melissa hesitated, the crone pushed her hood aside, and gazed about with night-dark eyes, clear and sharp as glass. They were the eyes of a much younger woman, and they seemed to see everything.

The two women looked at each other, and Melissa felt something stir in her breast. She knew, in that glance, that the old woman was not quite what she seemed. There was something mysterious about her, something even magical. So, while the servants tried to decide what to do, and the brute dogs whined, the girl stepped forward and offered her strong, young arm to the stranger.

She led the wanderer into the great hall and seated

her near the enormous fireplace, to warm her old bones. The old woman nodded, smiled with great, yellowed teeth, and peered around with her sharp, black eyes. Melissa followed her gaze, to the rafters hung with rotting banners and festooned with spider webs, to the crushed rushes strewn over the cold stone floor. Together they watched the servants set up the warped trestle tables and spread them with food-stained linens. Slatternly kitchen women slapped down trenchers, then platters of meat, custards of Lombard, and trays of grapes rolled in fine sucre. Their aprons were soiled and their hands thrust into the food. It was so unappetizing a sight that Melissa felt her gorge rise once again. How could she eat?

The Chevalier stomped in, his face rosy with wine, his tunic still soiled from the previous day. He barely noticed her, but staggered past to his high-backed chair and called for more drink. Melissa's mother appeared, her eyes anxious, and plucked at her daughter's sleeve, drawing her away from the fire and toward the table.

The feast began, as it had for the previous two nights, but Melissa could not take her eyes away from the old woman by the fire. The hall grew dark, even though the torches blazed around the walls, and the food grew cold. Grease congealed around the many meats, and the custards in their coffins were watery and unappetizing. Their crusts were so tough they nearly broke the teeth, and Melissa noticed that her mother was dropping them onto the rush-strewn floor. The linens smelled of mold, and the rushes stank of dog piss and old bones. It seemed to go on forever, and Melissa wanted to cry. All the while the old magpie woman supped from a shallow bowl of boiled gruel, lifting a wooden spoon to withered lips, chewing for a long time, and pausing in between.

Outside, the wind howled, and something else resounded. The wolves were singing to each other, as they had on each previous night, and some of the servants cringed at the sound. The Chevalier did not appear to notice. He ate and drank and made lewd jests, and Melissa's father matched him goblet for goblet, until both men lolled against their chairs, half asleep. Up in the gallery, the musicians strove to lend some air of gaiety with their shawms and viols, but they too were uneasy.

At last the boards were cleared away. The Chevalier roused enough to give an enormous belch and pulled his tunic down with grease-smeared fingers. A jongleur came forth and bowed, then tossed his brightly colored balls in the air, as the guests watched dispiritedly. Melissa shifted in her chair. The wind seemed very loud tonight, and the wolves seemed to be very close by. She tried to be glad she was not out in the darkness, but at least the wolves were honest beasts, unlike the Chevalier.

Melissa's mother cleared her throat and everyone turned and looked at her, except those too drunk to hear. "Perhaps La Mere Pie would favor us with a good tale," she said. Melissa's mother had descended from kings, and she had an air about her which commanded the room. The rest of the guests nodded, for they had already seen the jongleur and heard all the music, and they were bored.

La Mere Pie regarded Melissa's mother with a curious look, grunted, and straightened on her stool. She pulled a small pouch which hung from her rope belt into her lap, and put a withered hand inside. After a moment she drew out a scrap of stuff and looked at it for a long time. It was the color of the sun, and it glowed like an ember in her fingers. Melissa could see it was a small bit of fine embroidery, old and rubbed, but still beautiful, and she wondered what it meant.

The great hall grew quiet, except for the cracking of the fire, the howl of the wind, the singing of the wolves, and the snores of the Chevalier de Breon. The guests waited, watching the ancient woman by the fire. After a few moments, La Mere Pie nodded over her bit of finery and began to speak in a surprisingly strong voice.

"Once, long ago, in another land, there lived a man who had three daughters. Each of the daughters was pretty enough, and each was quite accomplished, but the wonder of the daughters was that they had all been born at the same moment, so none of them was eldest. This made the father, who was not a rich man, nor a poor one, troubled, for he only possessed a dowry for one of them, and he could not choose. His wife, who might have aided him, had died when the daughters were born, and he had never taken another. He loved each of the girls, for he was a very fair man, and he never favored one over the other, and thus matters stood when a fine suitor approached him for the hand of one of the young women.

"Which of my daughters will you have?" the father asked.

"Whichever one is the most accomplished, as they are all equal in beauty and wit," answered the suitor, so the father was no better off than before.

After a time the father bethought himself to set the daughters to some womanly task, to discover which was the most accomplished between them. One fine spring day, he led them to their spinning wheels and told them to make fair garments for their beds. The young women spun and wove through the green days of spring, and each made a fine coverlet. And one daughter wove a green coverlet, light but warm, for spring nights. And one wove a coverlet the very color of the summer sky, cool for hot nights. And the last daughter made a thick and heavy blanket as white as winter, and warm to the touch. The father and the suitor rubbed them with gentle fingers and shook their heads, for each was a fair piece, and none could choose between them.

In summer, when the days grew long and hot, the fa-

ther set the young women to make him some new shirts
and they plied their needles with a good will while the
sun made the fields rich with golden grain. The young
women did not complain of the work, though in truth it
was a weary way to spend a golden season, and if they
eyed one another's work a little, there was no malice in
it. They were sisters true. One sister made a shirt al
broidered with green leaves, and was soft and cool and
a delight to eye and hand. It was a shirt for the summer's
heat, and the father wore it gladly. The next sister cre
ated a shirt with many birds in gay colors, and it was
soft and warm, and a delight to eye and hand. It was a
shirt for the crisp days of autumn, and the father wore
it gladly. The remaining sister made a fine shirt all broi
dered with golden flowers, and it was soft and heavy
and a delight to hand and eye. It was warm, a shirt to
brighten the days of winter, and the father donned it
gladly. But none, not even the best needlewomen, could
choose between the three shirts.

The father was at his wit's end, and the suitor was
becoming impatient, for the winter was upon them now
and he wished to wed and return to his home. It was a
cruel winter that year, and the wolves came down from
hills, and the snow fell in great drifts. Tempers were
short and wood was hard to come by, so the house was
cold. The daughters, who were usually good-natured
young women, snapped at each other and tried not to
hear the cry of the wolves and the howl of the wind.
Most of all, they tried not to think of the suitor or the
dowry.

It was the time of the festal nights of winter, and the
father bethought himself to set each daughter to prepare
a feast for himself and the suitor and the other guests
who had come. Surely the kitchen was a woman's su
preme place, and this would decide the matter. He was
a fair man in all things, and he made lots, and the daugh-

ers drew them, to see who would begin the festal season,
who would make the middle feast, and who the last.

The daughter who drew the first lot was fond of all
manner of sweet things, and she took honey and apples
and spices and made fine cakes. She took flour and sugar
and made fair loaves which gleamed like the sun when
they came from the oven. She spun syrups into great
ships and palaces for the long table, and as she worked,
she nibbled and tasted, and her heart grew hard and
brittle, like her confections. Her rosy cheeks grew round,
and her waist strained at the seams of her gown, and her
blue eyes almost vanished, so plump did she become.
She tucked sweetmeats on heaping trays and placed
sugar plums in baskets spun of sugar, and felt, in her
heart, that at last matters would be decided in her favor.

When her father and the suitor and the rest of the
guests entered the eating hall, they gasped. It was indeed
a splendid sight. The candles glowed and the napery
shone and the trenchers gleamed while the board fairly
sighed under the weight of the viands. With great appetite, they began to drink and dine. They ate all the pies
and sweetmeats. They stuffed the scented breads into
their mouths. They ate woodcocks stuffed with dates, and
flayed peacocks and swans, and hares, and all manner of
delights. The sister who had cooked the feast lifted her
eyes from her trencher and looked at her sisters in
triumph.

The candles were not half burned when the guests
began to push their trenchers away with discontented
faces. No matter how much they ate, it did not seem to
satisfy them, and the sweetness was wearying. Everyone
agreed it was a fair feast, fair enough for even a prince,
but something was amiss. The suitor fell silent and the
father frowned, and the remains of the great feast stood
upon the board untouched. The daughter wept quietly

and waddled away from the table in defeat. She could
not believe that she had failed.

The next daughter was of a more abstemious nature
and she entered the cookhouse in her rather sober way,
her head coiffed in a white kerchief, her apron gleaming
like the breast of a swan. She peered into the larder and
found flour and salt and yeast and sugar, and set plain
loaves to rise. There were coneys and plump ducks and
a whole sheep to be cooked. She set to work with a good
will, heartened by her sister's failure to please the guests.
She cooked and she cooked and not a morsel passed her
lips. As she worked, her rosy cheeks grew pale and wan,
her coif turned gray with ash, and her gown no longer
hugged her waist. She piled trays of breads and platters
of fine meats onto the long table and waited.

When her father and the suitor and the guests entered
the eating hall, they smiled. It was indeed a splendid
sight. The candles shone and the linens were as white as
the snow without, and the board nearly moaned with the
heaviness of the feast. They fell to with eager appetite,
putting slabs of roasted meats upon their gleaming trenchers. They dipped the good bread into the juices which
ran from the meats, and ate and ate, and they gulped
great draughts of warm ale, for the food was as salty as
the first feast had been sweet. The father and the suitor
noticed that the cook sat without eating, her eyes watching each mouthful as the guests ate. And only the remaining daughter noticed how spare her sister had
become, how dull and brittle her hair seemed in the
flickering light, and how the bones in her folded hands
seemed barely covered with flesh.

The candles were not a quarter burned when the
guests began to cease to eat. Everything tasted of salt,
as if the sea had washed across the board, and stomachs
growled and grumbled and the feast remained unfinished.
The father frowned and the suitor scowled and the

daughter wept quietly and slipped from the table like a ghost. She had given everything to the feast, and somehow she had failed.

The final sister went into the cookhouse the next morning with a heavy heart, for she loved her father and her sisters, and she was weary from being set against them. Of the suitor she had no opinion, for he was neither good nor bad, neither handsome nor ill-favored, but only a man who desired a wife who could cook and sew and give him children.

She peered into the larder. The spices were much depleted, but many herbs remained, and there was still a good amount of yeast and flour and salt and sugar. She found carrots, still yellow and bright, and apples yet full and round. The huntsmen had brought some fishes frozen in the brook, and a few foolish pheasants hung from the rafters, their feathers dull. There were eggs still warm from the hen house and the milk still frothy from the dairy. She took dried apricots and raisins from warm summer days, onions with golden skins, and carrots and parsnips and turnips. There was a beef which had somehow been overlooked by her two sisters, and thick bacon, and an old rooster fine for stewing.

First she mixed bread and set it to rise, and as she kneaded it before the fire, a tear fell from her eyes, she thought of her sisters, one so plump she nearly burst the fine seams of her gown, the other so spare her dress hung without shape. Then she cut carrots and onions and meat and the knife slipped, and a drop of her blood fell into the meal before she set it to stew. She spitted the pheasants to roast, and as she leaned into the fire to start them turning, the dew from her brow spattered onto the crisping skins.

As she worked, adding sage here and rosemary there, sprinkling savory on the fishes baking in their coffins, she sang a little cradle song, and brushed her brow with her sleeve and praised the generous earth which provided them. She stirred the stews and basted the pheasants and soaked the apricots in wine until they grew round and plump, then baked them with apples in a fair crust. She tasted as she cooked, a little here, a little there, until the feast was ready.

When the father and the suitor and the guests entered the eating hall, they nodded. The candles flickered and the linen shone and the trenchers were polished. The board was well laid, neither groaning and sighing, and the chamber smelled of good things. The bread was broken, the stews were ladled, the fish in coffins cut. The guests ate and drank, made jests and told tales, and the candles burnt low in their sockets. When they could eat no more, they sighed, for everyone agreed it was quite the finest meal they had ever eaten.

The father looked at the suitor, and the suitor looked at the father, and they smiled at each other. At last the matter was resolved. The father was relieved and the suitor looked forward to such good and simple fare, and everyone was content, except perhaps the other daughters. They knew they had lost the dowry, and were doomed to be old spinsters, but they loved their sister enough to be a little pleased for her.

The father looked around for his daughter then, but her place at the board was empty. He sent a servant to the kitchen, but there was no one there but the scullions washing the pots. He sent a maid to her chamber, but it was empty as well. They searched all over the house, from the root cellar to the garret, but no trace could be found. The now-fat daughter peered into her sister's chest, and discovered the fine coverlet was gone. The lean sister looked among the clothing and found the warm, broidered shirt was gone, as well as a cloak and some goodly boots.

The daughters looked at each other, and went to the

igh window and looked out. The snow was falling and
he moon had risen, but they could still see the deep
ootprints left by the goodly boots. They held each other
.s the cold seeped into their bones and the cry of the
wolves rang across the low hills and the footsteps van-
shed in the falling snow. And they knew that she had
gone and would not return. But they did not know why.

The suitor departed in a rage, and the father took to
drinking too much wine, and the two sisters remained,
dwindling into old spinsters. And whenever a wolf
nowled in the night, they looked at each other and wondered what had happened to their accomplished sister.
And they are wondering still, if they are not dead yet."

The voice of La Mere Pie dropped, and several of
hose who were still awake and listening looked puzzled.
Melissa's mother gave a frown, as if to say that this was
not a proper tale at all. The Chevalier de Breon was
snoring away, and Melissa's father was drowsing beside
him, and no one seemed to know quite what to do. Then
he musicians began to play again, and the guests yawned
and stretched, and some began to go to their chilly chambers overhead.

Melissa felt as if she had awakened from a dream, and
she tried to keep the memory of it, because it was important. The old woman looked at her again, with the
sharp, dark eyes, and nodded at her. The girl rose from
her place and went to the old woman very quietly. She
bent forward and thanked La Mere Pie for her story,
swallowing the questions which rose to her lips. A servant came close, but Melissa waved him away. Once
again she offered the old woman her strong, young arm,
and once again she found herself in the grasp of a
bony hand.

She drew the old woman out of the great hall and up
he narrow stairs toward her own small chamber, unno-

ticed in the crowd of guests returning to their rooms. She could hear the wheeze of the woman's breath as they climbed up the stairs, a labored sound, as if it hurt to breathe. She felt the tremble of the ancient hand in her own, and within it, she felt something soft.

Melissa thrust the soft object into her pocket as the old woman seemed to collapse halfway up the stairs. The girl gripped her closely, then lifted her up. The body was surprisingly light in her arms, and she carried it with very little difficulty into her own room. She placed the ancient on the bed and drew the coverlet over the bony body. She could smell the filthy old woman, but unlike the scent of rotting rushes, it did not disturb her. Instead, the girl tucked the woman in as warmly as she could, drawing the black and white cloak across her over the covers, and rubbed the cold hands to warm them. She knew that La Mere Pie had told her last tale, and she knew it had been told for her, somehow.

Melissa wondered what it meant as she took off her overgown and climbed beneath the covers in her chemise. She listened to the wind around the castle, and the singing of the wolves, and the rattle of breath beside her. La Mere Pie did not stir as the night passed, and Melissa did not sleep, but thought about the Chevalier de Breon and her father and her mother and her duty as a daughter. And in the night the sound of breath was stilled, and she felt the old woman perish beside her, slipping away quietly.

In the gray light before the dawn, Melissa rose and put on her thickest hose and her warmest gown. She thrust her feet into her traveling boots hastily, then tied a white kerchief over her dark hair and pulled the magpie cloak across her shoulders. Then she remembered the thing she had put into her pocket, and retrieved it from the gown she had worn the night before. It was the small pouch La Mere Pie had worn on her belt. Melissa peered within it and found pebbles and feathers and small pieces of old embroideries. It was an assortment that made no sense, and yet she knew that somehow the old woman kept her tales in those oddments.

Melissa bent down and kissed the withered cheek of La Mere Pie, now cold and still. Then she arranged the covers so the body was hidden, knowing that what she was about to do was undutiful. At the same time she knew that if she did not seize this opportunity, she would end up in the graveyard with the first two wives of the Chevalier before the next Christmastide was celebrated. And she did not wish to die.

The girl drew the black and white motley cloak around her and pulled the hood up over her head so the shadow of it hid her face. She found her shabbiest old gloves and put her hands into them, trembling all over. Without a backward glance she left her little room and crept down the stairs, wheezing like an old woman, and clutching the damp castle walls as if she were eighty and not eighteen. She found the carved staff of La Mere Pie in the entrance hall, and she leaned against it heavily.

As soon as she heard the clanking of the drawbridge being lowered, Melissa began to cross the wide court-yard. It was still half dark, and very cold. The cold stung her cheeks, and for a moment she hesitated. She had no food, and no money. She had stolen a cloak from a dead woman and gone against all custom by leaving La Mere Pie in her own bed. She was a Montalban, the daughter of a proud house. What was she thinking of? And a voice within her said Live!

Melissa stooped her shoulders and crossed the snowy yard in the faltering steps of a beldame, leaning on the staff and moving cautiously. The sleepy guards hardly noticed her as she passed beneath the portcullis and stepped onto the wooden boards which now spanned the moat. Her throat was so tight she could hardly breathe, and when she did it sounded as wheezy as the real owner of the cloak had sounded. In a hundred paces she was outside the castle of Breon, and in a thousand, she was lost to the eye, her magpie cloak vanishing in the snowy landscape."

There was no sound in the gatehouse except the flutter of the fire, the fading rustle of the wind, and the even breaths of four sleeping children. Jennifer looked at her aunt and stroked Antoinette's head which lay in her lap. In the shadows of the room the black of Matilde's gown and the white of her fichu and apron seemed to stand out. She was thinking of the girl in the story, in her magpie cloak as she looked at her aunt.

"There were no dragons, Tante, and no treasure, but that was a fine feast you told. It has left me with a great appetite. I will be whining like Antoinette soon." She gave a nervous laugh.

"No treasure? Are you certain, child?" Matilde looked maddeningly smug, and Jennifer frowned, wondering what she had missed. "What did you feel about the story, Jennifer?"

"I am not sure. It seemed to say that one's duty was not to one's father."

"Does that thought disturb you, child?"

"Yes, Tante. I have tried to be a good daughter, but truly I cannot abide the sight of Armand de Nantes, and the thought of him touching me is disgusting. But I must marry, mustn't I? I cannot grab my cloak and wander away into the snow like the girl Melissa. But if I do not wed, what will become of me? I am not fit to enter the convent, and Father needs me to marry."

"That is true. At your age I thought much the same. But you know perfectly well that if you sacrifice yourself for duty, my brother will not be in the least grateful. He will not cease from gambling and drinking and being a fool."

"Why are you telling me this?"

Tante Matilde picked up her knitting and continued her interrupted row. She was weary, bone weary, and she did not know herself why she had chosen that tale to tell. It was almost as if the spirit of La Mere Pie had settled on her plump shoulders. She gave a little sigh and ignored the empty feeling in her own middle. The story had given her an appetite as well.

"Because I wish you to be happy, child. We both know you could never be happy married to that scion of Nantes. He is a disagreeable youth, and he will doubtless grow into a disagreeable man. We both know you are not suited, as Marie is, for the life of the convent. And you are not the sort of person to go to Paris and engage in the slipshod intrigues of the court of the king."

"What else is there?"

"That you will have to decide for yourself."

"Tante, have you been happy, living with my father, taking care of us and being alone?"

"Alone? Child—I have not been alone. While your mother lived, I had her for a sister, and we loved each other dearly. Then, I had all of you, and Philippe, of course. But I have lived a good life, and I have no regrets."

Outside there was a shout, a man's voice, and then the snort of a horse and the faint jingle of a bridle. Then came the rumble of cart wheels. The door of the gatehouse opened, and Phillippe came in, brushing snow from his cloak and looking red-cheeked from the cold. He waited to be greeted, and when his daughter and his sister just stared at him in silence, he had the grace to look a little shamefaced.

"I have brought the wheelwright," he announced. When neither his daughter nor his sister praised him,

Philippe began stripping his gloves off his hands. He stepped toward the stove and picked up a fresh piece of wood. Then he opened the stove and thrust it into the fire. "And I brought some food. I was sure you would be hungry."

"That is very thoughtful of you, Philippe," Matilde answered dryly. "We have had a lovely night, listening to the wind and the snow, shivering with cold." She gestured at the still-sleeping children. "They will, no doubt, be delighted to see you."

He gave a nervous laugh. "It is no wonder you have never married, Matilde. You have an uncanny ability to make a man feel like a worm. I had better see to the horses. I will have the food brought in, if you will wake the children up."

When he had gone back outside, Jennifer looked at her aunt again. "He is not worth the sacrifice, is he, Tante?"

"I cannot make that decision for you, my dear."

"No, you cannot. No one can choose my life except me." Jennifer was silent for a moment. What a shocking thing to have said. "Tante, what happened to Melissa after she left the castle?"

Matilde smiled over her knitting, content. She had done something, had gotten her dear niece thinking. The rest was up to Jennifer. "That, child, is another story."

DARK LADY

by Jane M. Lindskold

I

"Wren, when you've finished undressing, I would like to speak with you. It's important."

"Yes, Mr. Shakespeare," I said, staring wide-eyed at the playwright, my wig dangling from my fingers. "I'll hurry, sir."

"I shall be out on the stage."

He exited and I struggled out of Bianca's gown, wondering what I had done wrong. *The Taming of the Shrew* was an unqualified success and I had thought that I was playing the role of Katherine's deceptively meek sister according to direction. As I hurried onto the stage, I was trembling despite the pleasant warmth of the late afternoon sun.

Mr. Shakespeare was talking to some men about freshening the paint in the heavens and I huddled on the edge of the stage, looking down at the mess of crusts, apple cores, and sweatmeat ends left by the groundlings. I barely dared to look up as the sounding of footsteps on the boards announced that Mr. Shakespeare was done with his business and had come for me.

"Good of you to wait, Wren." he smiled and my heart sped up with dread. "Come along with me over to the White Horse Tavern, lad. I'm famished and we can have our talk over a couple of meat pasties as easily as out here."

"Yes, sir." I tried to find something intelligent to say. "Uh, thank you, sir."

At the tavern, Mr. Shakespeare greeted most of the hangers-about by their Christian names, but he took us a private booth. When the serving wench had taken his order for ale and meat pies for both of us, Mr. Shakespeare turned his stern gaze on me. I cringed despite myself, awaiting the rebuke.

"Wren, you've been doing bit parts with my Players for some years now—isn't that right?"

"Yes, Mr. Shakespeare. Walk-ons mostly, sir, though I did speak the young Duke of York in *Richard III*—before the plague closed the theaters, sir. And now Bianca, sir."

"Yes, that is how I recall events." He took one of the mugs of ale the serving wench had set down and shoved the other to me. "I still recall your father coming to me a few years ago. 'Will,' he said, 'I've seen the book for your latest. I'll be happy to play the Keeper of the Tower, but how about giving my boy one of the children's roles?' "

I sipped my ale, waiting still for him to chide me for some flaw in my performance.

"Then Bianca," he continued. "I had my doubts about casting you for such a large role. You're rather young for so many lines. How old are you, exactly, lad?"

"Thirteen, sir."

"That young?" He reached out and gave my hand a fatherly pat. "Well, you are doing well, Wren. You have made a study of Bianca. I particularly like how you deliver her rebuke of her husband in the final act."

"You do, sir?" I blushed. "I mean, thank you, sir."

The meat pies came and we spent several minutes on tearing through the flaky lard crust and blowing on burned fingers. A meat pie was a real treat. Normally, I would have savored every bit, but this afternoon I was so nervous that I could barely taste the pork and pot herbs.

"Wren, I'm working on a new play—*Two Gentlemen*

of Verona. One role calls for an actor who can play a girl pretending to be a boy." He paused. "Do you think that you can do it?"

I blushed from my collar to the tops of my ears, pretending to chew until I could find my voice.

"Oh, yes, sir. I think I could. I'm sure I could."

II

". . . and if you could find your way back to London in time for casting and rehearsals, Mr. Harper, I am near completed the book of a new tragedy: *Romeo and Juliet*. My hope is that your son, Wren, will agree to read for the female lead. It is a substantial and thoughtful role, designed in part by recalling the sensitivity and wit that he brought to Julia in *Two Gentlemen of Verona*. Respectfully Yours, William Shakespeare."

Father set the letter on the washstand in our room at the inn, staring at it as if it might fold itself wings and flutter out to join the pigeons roosting in the eaves.

"D'you hear that, Wren!" he crowed, squeezing my shoulders until they ached. "William Shakespeare himself all but begging you to take a part in his new tragedy. That ends thought of wintering here. We'll finish this run of *Two Gentlemen* and head for London, hang the expense and the plague alike."

I raised the letter and read the script myself. Father had read every word as true as a clerk: William Shakespeare wanted me for a lead role. My head spun and I sat heavily on the bed.

"But, Father, what if he . . ." I drew in a breath so deep that my ribs ached. "What if he learns about me?"

Father groaned and sat down beside me. "Wren—Peggy, lass—how would he learn? You've learned to be careful where you undress, where you piss . . ."

"Aye," I interrupted, "and the other lads think me a

proper fop for it. Playing a boy was well enough when I was small, but I'm near marrying age, now. My body— it's changing. I . . ."

"Wren, I never knew our little deception would come to this. When your dear mother died . . ." Here he bowed his head as always, the simple motion so poignant that I resisted believing it studied. "I had no wish to leave you to relatives, but taking a wee lass on the road was a chancy thing. No one would notice if a lad was dirty or poorly clad. How was I to know that you would take to the stage as you have? Never did I believe that it would go beyond a bit part or two. Now, now though, you've acted with the Lord Chamberlain's Men and with this invitation you could become one of them!"

"The Lord Chamberlain's *Men*," I said, tasting the irony, "except that I'm a girl."

"Take it, Wren," he pleaded, "you are filling out, but your mother was small-figured. It could be that no one will notice a change. I have no dowry for you. We'll put by from what you earn and, if you wish, when the play ends Wren Harper will vanish and Margaret Harper can find a husband in some distant town."

III

"Wren, lad, a word."

The White Horse Tavern was a-bustle with a crowd just fresh from the afternoon's performance of *Romeo and Juliet*. Fresh-scrubbed of the tints that left roses on my cheeks, I was drinking with a few of the younger lads, including the handsome fellow who played Tybalt and whom I rather fancied. One voice still had the power to cut a crowd for me and I was on my feet, excusing myself to my friends even before William Shakespeare had reached me.

He held a sheaf of foolscap. Ink stained his fingers and

sleeve. With a smile, he gestured for me to join him at
a corner booth.

"I hope that today's performance was satisfactory, sir,"
I said.

"Today?" He thought for a moment. "Ah, yes, quite
well."

I was somewhat miffed at his lack of enthusiasm, though
that was hardly fair. In the past year, I had learned that
for William Shakespeare a play ceased to be important
once it was in production. He lived for the next challenge—
a good thing since the Lord Chamberlain's Men were increasingly in demand and new material was always needed.

"Is this the new play?" I asked, touching the sheaf at
his elbow.

Amazingly, he colored, sipping his ale rapidly down. I
politely looked away and when I looked back he was his
calm, gentlemanly self.

"This is not the play, but a few poems—sonnets—I
have worked on between times. I had hoped to share a
few with you, but this tavern is too noisy. Could you
come by my home?"

I knew he meant his rooms in the city, not the house
in Stratford he shared with Anne Hathaway and their
children. After a moment's consideration, I agreed.
When we arrived at his rooms, he served us sweet wine
and agreeable jam tarts. Seeing I was comfortably settled,
he pulled out the foolscap.

"My handwriting is fair," he said, "but if you would
suffer my reading aloud ..."

I readily assented. Many poets have thin, reedy voices,
but Mr. Shakespeare was an actor before he was a playwright and his voice was deep and resonant.

He began:

"A woman's face with Nature's own hand painted
Hast thou, the master mistress of my passion;

A woman's gentle heart but not acquainted
With shifting change as is false woman's fashion;
An eye more bright than theirs, less false in rolling,
Gilding the object whereupon it gazeth;
A man in hues all hues in his controlling,
Which steals men's eyes and woman's souls
 amazeth.
And for a woman wert thou first created,
Til Nature as she wrought thee fell a-doting,
And by addition me of thee defeated,
By adding one thing to my purpose nothing.
  But since she prick'd thee out for woman's
   pleasure,
  Mine be thy love, and thy love's use their
   treasure."

Panic's flush rose to my cheeks as I heard those first
lines, but as the sonnet progressed, I became calmer.
That William Shakespeare had conceived a passion was
clear; that the passion was me his blush and swift breathing confirmed, but that he did not suspect that Wren was
lass not lad was also bitterly certain.

William Shakespeare took my blush and silence for
approval, but I heard nothing but the opening conceit
of his next sonnet, "Weary with toil, I haste me to my
bed . . ."

I played audience as the bard spun out for me his
heart in elegant poems, my mind a wild tangle. I had not
been without admirers—male and female alike—but this
man was the first I dreaded hurting with my rejection. I
found a response as he set the sheets aside.

"They are lovely, Mr. Shakespeare," I said sincerely.
"For whom are they intended?"

His eyes widened in shock and he searched my features for evidence of dissembling, but never but for one

role have I played my part better. I could see him decide that I was a dear innocent.

"I meant them for you, sweet Wren," he said gently. "Near since you were a lad of twelve, spouting off York's lines with brazen confidence have I been watching you. Now, despite all inclinations otherwise, I am pricked to make my devotion."

"This is sudden, wondrous, and strange," I managed. "Please, fault me not as green if I need time to reflect over these sincere protestations."

Disappointment flashed over his features and then vanished. He schooled himself to patient lines. "I forget. A life is not a play. You need time to decide. I will wait, but mayhap you will tarry with me anon." He shifted aside his poetry and fetched out a heavy manuscript. "I have my new work here—meant for a wedding this midsummer. I have in mind a change for you from these young women—a mystical queen of the fairy folk called Titania."

IV

"The play was well-received, I think," William Shakespeare said to me as we walked along the riverbank outside of the Earl's estate.

Behind us, the wedding revels in the tented pavilions could be faintly heard. Most of the Players had mingled with the throng, commoner status overlooked by the noble guests in favor of their novelty. The weather was oppressively hot and Will had asked me to walk with him in the woods that bordered the estate.

Despite my continually putting off his polite advances, Will and I had become friends. Since Titania had less stage-time than Juliet, Will had asked me to help him with the business of managing the show. Given the complexity of the production—with the elaborate costumes for the fairy-folk and Bottom—I could accept that he needed assistance. However, I suspected that he also desired an excuse to seek me out and be alone with me.

"I thought Father did Bottom to a turn," I said, smiling at the memory. "He even managed that clumsy ass's head without tripping."

"Indeed," Will chuckled. "I had begun to despair of the results of my own cleverness. This stretch of riverbank looks enticingly cool, Wren. Come and sit with me."

He sat and unlaced his boots so that he could trail his feet in the water. Seeing no harm, I did the same. We sat thus for a time in companionable silence, me covertly studying Will from the corner of my eye. He was well-fed, though not heavy, and a shade pallid from too many hours at the writing desk. His hair had thinned of late, but there was a dignity about him that was more noble than I had seen in many of the so-called noble wedding guests.

"Shall I compare thee to a summer's day?" Will said with a mischievous grin, "Thou art more temperate . . ."

As he continued his recitation, I leaned against a tree, my eyes closed, listening to the words and reveling in the caress of the cool water against my feet. I was completely unprepared when he finished the sonnet, leaned over, and kissed me squarely on the lips, his probing tongue slipping into my mouth in a fashion not unpleasant, but distinctly startling.

My eyes flew open, showing Will leaning over me, his expression quizzical but pleased. He moved as if to kiss me again, but I rolled clear.

"What is this, Wren? I thought you were fond of me, lad."

"I am, sir, but . . ."

I stopped, for I could not tell him the truth and I could not lie and say that I found his attentions distasteful. To be honest, I had dreamed of little else since he had read me that first sonnet a year before. I stuttered instead, crawling for my shoes. In my haste I misjudged and, amid a shower of pebbles and greenery, I splashed into the river.

The water was not overly deep nor swift, but in no time at all I was thoroughly soaked. Will stood on the bank, his hurt vanishing as he chuckled at my predicament.

"Give me your hand, lad, and I'll pull you up."

He extended his hand, then halted, his expression blank with astonishment. His gaze rested where my soaked tunic now clung to my figure. Father had been correct. I had grown as small-breasted as my mother had been, but small breasts are quite different from none at all and the wet fabric revealed two distinctly female breasts.

Dumbfounded, he helped me onto the bank, alternately staring and averting his eyes. I sat sullenly, wringing the water as best I could from my trousers and shirt and waiting for the world to end.

When Will spoke, at last, his voice was husky with astonishment. "Wren, you're a lass!"

"I know," I replied, "as I have been all my life. Father thought it a lark, nor did we ever mean a serious deception, but Juliet was too good a role to pass up, and then you offered me Titania, a chance to learn management ..." I trailed off, my voice dropping to a whisper, "and your affections. I could not vanish to some small town and let Margaret Harper find a groom."

"Margaret?" He paused. "That is your Christian name?"

"I prefer Wren. It is what I have always been called." I bit my lip. "What will you do now, Mr. Shakespeare?"

He tugged at his beard, distraught. "I am in a muddle. There is no time to rehearse another Titania—your understudy is ill-prepared because you are so reliable. And I wrote Portia specifically for you. No one else can play her and *Merchant of Venice* cannot go on without her."

I stared, unbelieving. "Is the play then the only thing that concerns you?"

He turned and confronted me. "No, but speaking of a broken heart is not seemly, is it?"

"Must it be broken?" I said softly. "I am still Wren. 'What's in a shape?'" I misquoted Juliet's speech. "'A Wren who is a lass might be as sweet.'"

He studied me with confused intensity. "Can you still play the lad, Wren, even if I know the truth? I don't want to see Wren go away from my life, yet a girl cannot be one of the Lord Chamberlain's Men."

"It is my best role," I assured him. "I have played it for most of my life."

V

"Wren! Wren! Hurry here," Father came chugging up, still costumed as Old Gobbo. "Will has had a letter from Stratford and the boy who carried it said that Will read the note, wailed like one mad, and then tore off to his rooms. I pray, go to him!"

I left Portia's dress in an untidy heap and, grabbing Baltazar's trousers and my own shirt as the closest respectable clothing, ran from the tiring house and to Will's rooms.

He was a wealthy man, now, had bought a fine estate called the New House in Stratford where his wife and children resided, but in London he still kept rooms near the theater. This suited me, for Anne would never visit an area so near the stews, gaming pits, and rougher pubs.

I was safe to meet with him there and we did, often, cultivating a relationship that twined his genuine love around his vague disappointment that I was not a boy. I had resigned myself to his feelings, realizing that his confusion was more social than sexual. If I had been a boy, Will would never have felt himself in breach of his contract with his wife, but as long as he loved me as a man did a woman, he felt a danger to his rising social status.

None of this was foremost in my mind as I hurried in the door of the boarding house, up the stair, and to Will's closet. Boldly, I did not even knock, but opened the door and went inside. Will sat on the edge of his bed, weeping.

"Will?" I said, touching his shoulder. "Will?"

He looked up at me blankly, then grasped my hand. "Oh, Wren, Hamnet's died! I just had the letter. An illness came—not plague—and slew him in a day. There was no time to send for me, and now my dear boy is dead and his father will never see him again!"

"Oh, Will!" I knelt and put my arms around him and let him sob into my breast.

Will's children were little more than names to me, though they had sometimes attended a private showing at Blackfriar's Theater. For all his scholarly habits, Will loved them dearly and Hamnet was his father's heir and pride. I held Will until his sobs lessened then dared a question.

"The girls, Susanna and Judith, and their mother, are they in good health?"

Will nodded, "Anne writes asking me to come home direct for the boy's funeral."

A lump barred my throat, that at this of all times I could not be with him. I steeled myself. "I will enquire after a coach," I said bravely, "and pack a trunk for you. You rest. Do you have any wine left from the other night?"

"Below the washstand," he said, mutely accepting the glass I poured for him.

He left a few hours later. The Players were well rehearsed. Indeed, once a play was past its first few performances, we directed ourselves so that Will could concentrate on our next venture. Most hardly missed him. I was distraught, but hid my feelings from all. I had much practice in this.

Will returned a changed man. I went by his rooms carrying a bottle of good French and a loaf of bread. He answered his door when I knocked—my hands were too full to open it myself. He did not return my shy smile but motioned me in coolly.

"Will?" I said hesitantly when he neither embraced me nor offered me a seat.

"Margaret, I must speak with you," he said, sitting but leaving me standing. I was so astonished by his use of my Christian name that I did not protest. He continued, "During my visit home, I had ample time to meditate on this liaison we have perpetuated. It came to me that Hamnet's death was God's punishment for my sin with you."

"Will?" I gaped and he motioned me to silence.

"Just as the country suffers if the king is corrupt, so the home suffers if its head is sinful. I have resolved to have naught to do with you further. My next play is a history—a celebration of Henry IV. There is no strong female role." He handed me a folded sheet of foolscap. "Your father requested, some time ago, that I license a few plays to him so that he could form a traveling company. This sheet gives him the rights to *Romeo and Juliet* and the *Merchant of Venice*. As these contain two of your greatest roles, no one will question your departure from London."

"Will, how could you?" my voice broke. "I thought you loved me!"

"Good day, Margaret," he said, picking up a sheet of foolscap and his quill.

I stumbled out, the wretched paper in my pocket.

A single bottle of wine is not enough on which to get really drunk.

I went out and found a tavern where no one knew me and drank cup after cup of cheap sack. Somehow, my father found me and carried me home.

VI

We were gone from London the better part of two years and never in that time did I speak Juliet's paean to love or Portia's invocations of justice and mercy without the words curdling sour on my lips.

The news from the Globe was not heartening. Will had indeed returned to history for his themes. *Henry IV,* the first part, was the classic story of the riotous youth who makes good. I had to admit that there were clever lines—I even wondered if Will had begun writing with the part in mind for me. However, in the end, only Falstaff shone. Its sequels, *Henry IV,* the second part, and *The Merry Wives of Windsor* were weaker yet. Nor was I encouraged by Hal's blunt rejection of his old friend and revelling companion. "I know thee not, old man," haunted my nightmares.

Needless to say, I was surprised to receive a letter from Will. I had heard naught from him but by hearsay for over a year, but I knew his hand.

"Wren," the missive began promisingly, "I hear good things of your productions. Perhaps, however, I can woo you back to the Globe. My newest play, *Much Ado About Nothing,* weeps for your deft touch and the female role I intend for you is my best since Portia. I enclose a brief sample and await your reply. Ever yours, Will."

My heart pounded so that I could not stand but must sink onto a chair. With nerveless hands, I unfolded the sample. The character—Beatrice—was witty, acerbic, and clever. I ached for the role from the first. The play's title, too, was promising. Could it mean that all was forgiven?

As I was refolding the sample, I became aware of a second sheet. Unfolding it, I read:

When to the sessions of sweet silent thought
I summon up the remembrance of things past,
I sigh the lack of many a thing I sought,
And with old woes wail my dear time's waste;
Then can I drown an eye (unus'd to flow)
For precious friends hid in death's dateless night,
And weep afresh love's long since cancell'd woe,
And moan th' expense of many a vanish'd sight;
Then can I grieve at grievances foregone,
And heavily from woe to woe tell o'er
The sad account of fore-bemoaned moan,
Which I new pay as if not paid before:
    But if the while I think on thee, dear friend,
    All losses are restor'd and sorrows end.

Grabbing for quill and ink, I scrawled my reply: "Dear friend, We shall return to London. . . ."

VII

Sack, song, and too many afternoons on windy stages finally did for my dear Father. He took ill while playing Verges and died before the week was out. Will was at my side at the funeral.

"You have no family now but the Players," he said as we walked to the White Horse Tavern with the other mourners. "I hope you will be inclined to stay and that sorrowful memories will not drive you to the road."

I wiped away a persistent tear. "Do you have a new

role for me? I am not certain that I can play in *Much Ado* right now."

"I'm certain that I can find a place for you," he said.

I took the role of the Chorus, a role for a single actor despite the name, in *Henry V* and studied for a new comedy entitled *As You Like It*. Will and I continued as lovers, partners, and friends despite some bitter fights on the publications of two rather cutting sonnets—one that opened with the lines "When my love swears that she is made of truth/ I do believe her, though I know she lies" and a second that played on the conceit of a woman as a corrupting force on an innocent boy.

Will pleaded that both had been written in the heart of his melancholy, when he sought to resolve his love and his guilt, and had been published without his knowledge. I forgave him, remembering how I had once longed for his mercy.

The years passed, swift and productive. I played my last young girl as Hamlet's mad lady, Ophelia. The play was such a hit that I continued with it as Will spun out four more comedies. Will did convince me to take a role in *Measure for Measure* which we played before King James as His Majesty's Servants.

As *Othello* was being written, we faced the fact that though I remained as beardless and sweet-voiced as a boy, members of the Players could count my years. Lest my secret be guessed, Will cast me as Emilia, the sharp-tongued but wise and noble friend to Desdemona. I thought the role better than the weak-willed if virtuous wife and took it happily. Equally, Regan, one of the wicked daughters in *King Lear*, fascinated me more than gentle Cordelia. Talking this over with Will one night, we together conceived the character of Lady Macbeth as my role in his next tragedy.

The play ended up shorter than many, but pleased King James, who appreciated the use of witchcraft as a

motif nearly as much as the celebration of his lineage.
Following one afternoon's production, Will put his head
into the tiring house where I was changing.

"Wren, when you're done undressing, I would like to
speak with you. It's important."

I met him out on the stage where he was inspecting a
blot on the heavens caused by the smoke from the Weird
Sisters' cauldron. I expected that he wanted to discuss
his next writing project, so I was surprised when we took
the road to his rooms.

"Margaret," he said when we were alone and he had
sat me beside him, "have you ever considered relin-
quishing your masquerade and living as a woman?"

"Not for nearly ten years," I said. "I have grown fond
of this life. I don't believe I would be happy settled in
as some man's goodwife."

"Not even mine?" he asked, squeezing my hand.
"Margaret, I have thought long on this and I realize that
I want you always by me. My daughters are married and
there is little to hold me."

"What of Anne?" I asked.

"King Henry introduced divorce," Will said. "I have
gently queried at Court and believe that one would not
be impossible. What do you think?"

I was too surprised to even frame words. Once my
dearest wish would have been this very proposal, but
now—what I had said to Will was true—I was settled in
my role. I liked being Wren the player. I did not wish
to be a goodwife, not of anyone, not even Will. I was
satisfied to meet him as a lover, to have a rest from him
at times, to play my role.

"No, Will," I said as gently as I could. "This would
not do. It would be unfair to Anne, to you—have you
considered what a divorce would do to your social standing?—and to me. If Wren becomes Margaret, I will never
act again, and I could not bear that."

"Have you considered that if you cross me, you might not ever act again, in any case?" Will retorted, hurt and angry.

"Oh? Is that how you propose, William Shakespeare?" I replied sharply. "Then let me tell you that I can find acting work without your patronage. Just this day past a man from the East India Company was by asking who might be interested in taking a job performing for them!"

"I know," he said sadly. "Their representative came by today for licenses. Please, Wren, say you'll marry me and never go away!"

I cupped his face in my hands. "Will, surely you know that you can't keep another person prisoner just because you love her. I cannot give up my life to comfort your worries. Nor can I let you ruin yourself."

"You're going, aren't you?" he said.

I hadn't realized until he said it that I had made up my mind. Will's intensity moved me and I feared that if I remained he would persuade me into a choice that I would regret for the rest of my life.

"Yes," I said, "I'm going."

VIII

We did *Hamlet* and *Richard II* off of the coast of Sierra Leone and at other ports where the English were establishing colonies. Even when we returned to England, I avoided London, taking roles with smaller traveling companies. My work with my father and Will served me well and in time I founded a company of my own.

Though I avoided London, news of London and the London stage could not escape me. Will's new play was *Anthony and Cleopatra*. I could see myself as the Egyptian queen of "infinite variety," but I could also hear Will arguing with me in its theme of love versus duty.

Some time later Thomas Thorpe published a volume

of Will's sonnets. The dedication: "To the Only Begetter of These Insuing Sonnets, Mr. W.H., All Happiness and that Eternity Promised by Our Ever-Living Poet Wisheth the Well-Wishing Adventure in Setting Forth" brought tears to my eyes. The sonnets themselves alternatingly made me weepy and furious.

A few who had known me in my London days asked if I might be the "W.H." of the dedication, but I assured them not, suggesting that William Herbert, third Earl of Pembroke, was a more likely candidate. All knew that Will was certainly not above flattering potential patrons—as *Macbeth* had showed—and this answer satisfied everyone who asked.

I avoided London for the better part of five years, then homesickness overtook common sense. I sold my interest in my traveling company and with a fair sum in my pocket wended my way to London. Familiarity rather than any intelligent impulse took me to Will's old rooms. I knocked and heard a familiar voice call, "Come."

I opened the door and stepped into a room that seemed little changed from years passed. Will sat at a table by the window slowly scratching out lines of dialogue onto a much crossed-out bit of foolscap.

"Just set the tray on my footstool, Mistress," he said without looking up. "I will attend to it anon."

"Will?" I said. "I fear it is not your supper—only me."

The quill made a great arc across the page, spoiling a large part. Will looked up, not noticing his hand's work. He was much as I recalled, his hair thinner, his eyes more shadowed, but his smile was the one of my memories. In a trice, he was on his feet, his arms around me, his lips on mine.

"Wren! Tell me you're not a vision or evil sprite come to haunt me!"

"I'm no spirit or goblin damned," I said, embracing him in return, "but your own friend."

Will helped me from my traveling cloak and sat me beside him on the bed.

"New bed," I remarked playfully.

"My best," he said. "Anne has the second best in Stratford, but I needed a new one—even if it has been empty without you. Five years, you evil creature, five years without hardly a note! Every shipwreck ripped my heart lest you be on it. I asked after you from every traveling player until they must have thought me mad. Tell me all of what you have been about!"

We talked and suchlike until the sun set and after. Dawn was pinking the horizon when Will mentioned his latest project.

"I have a play in mind about a nobleman exiled on an island who is permitted to confront those who have wronged him in a place where he—not they—is the absolute arbiter of not only law, but even of reality and illusion." Will frowned. "I have been reading many contemporary sailors' accounts, but the play resists taking form."

"Let me see it when there is more light," I suggested, "but for now, come and kiss me."

Come day, Will read me his beginning notes and after we had talked over them, I left him to his business, promising to return late that afternoon. I wandered about seeing the sights, ending by taking in a production of Will's newest, *A Winter's Tale*. I was brought to foolish tears by Leontes's reunion with the wife he had wronged and believed lost to him.

After, as promised, I returned to Will's rooms and found him writing as before, but now his eye was bright and his quill could scarce keep up with his hand. I waited and at last he paused and came to me.

"Wren, I have come to a decision."

"Yes, Will?"

"I shall take the stage again and play the lead, Pros-

368 *Jane M. Lindskold*

pero, in my new play. He is a gray-haired scholar—I believe I am yet active enough for the role."

"I see no reason why not," I agreed, recalling the night before with a grin.

"Wren, would you consider taking the stage but one more time for me?" He grasped my hand. "I have a role that cries for your touch—that of a spirit of air called Ariel. Prospero found the spirit imprisoned by its former mistress—a foul witch—for refusing to do her evil bidding. He releases it and it serves him well and faithfully."

"I am not certain," I said guardedly. "I am not certain that I care to play a servant. I am not yet so far come down."

Will smiled, knowing my unspoken hesitation, "And to play a prisoner after earning your freedom would be a grave indignity. Nay, Wren, when I said that this role cries for you, it does. Ariel desires his freedom above all, but Prospero denies it. At the last, Prospero realizes that he is wrong to have refused Ariel his wish and to have sought to keep an equal as a slave."

"Do I hear a change of heart, dear friend?" I asked. "Will you take me back—as Wren?"

"With sincere and noble intent," Will promised. "Can you forgive me for my foolishness? Can we begin again with this behind us?"

I took his hand, "As you from crimes would pardoned be, let your indulgence set me free."

THE LILY MAID OF ASTOLAT

by Laura Resnick

I have no body servant, having come in such haste from Astolat. The King, whose eyes are so sad, has assigned a squire to help me prepare for this joust. Though I am a younger son, and though my father is only a minor baron of little wealth, the King has accorded me great courtesy. I thought he would hate me, after the way I made the Queen cry, but he has been most kind.

I am sorry for him, that he must lose his greatest knight today.

We did not know who he was, when he rode out of the gold-drenched western sky and came upon the Castle of Astolat. We were surprised by the approach of an unknown rider, for Astolat lies far from the well-beaten thoroughfare, that hard and heralded road which leads to many-towered Camelot. And we have few visitors at Astolat; my father leads a retiring life in these peaceful times, and his fame is a long-dead shade of the distant past.

My brother Lavaine and I, practicing our swordplay at the end of the day, ceased our thrust-and-swipe antics when we were told of the stranger's approach. Curious and excited, we joined our father as he stood before the castle and awaited the rider.

Even simply-clothed as the stranger was, we knew him instantly for a great man. Wealthy and well-fed he certainly was, for no one becomes that tall and broad without meat and cheese aplenty in his growing years. Nobly bound in hard muscle and graceful sinew was his body, and even tired and befuddled as he so clearly was, he rode with the erect pride of a man who bows to none save one he *chooses* to.

He was a knight; no doubt of that, even without the shield he carried before him. His destrier was a grand beast, easily worth more coin than most men collect in a year of hard labor. He had used the warhorse badly today, though. As the stallion drew near, we could see he was covered in heavy mud. He was soaked with sweat and blowing like the northern wind. Foam frothed around his mouth. I looked up at the knight, wondering what had driven the man to drive his horse so madly.

My father spoke to the stranger, reciting an ancient formula of greetings and proud welcome, for the men of Astolat have long and noble bloodlines. In olden days, this friendly habit of hospitality was more honored in the breach than the observance, but these are golden days under King Arthur, and now no village, farm, or castle with men in it need fear a stranger's approach.

"Astolat?" the stranger mumbled. "Where ... where is this place?"

"Less than a day's ride from Camelot, on a good mount," my father replied. "Do you go there?"

The stranger laughed, a sad and bitter sound. "No, my lord, I have *come* from there."

"Camelot!" I cried, too excited by the revelation to remember my carefully-taught manners or the hard-won dignity of a young man. "You've come from *Camelot*? What is it like there? Why did you leave? Are you going back? Have you seen the King himself? Do—"

My brother's sharp elbow stopped the flow of words. My father, never a strict man, chuckled at us both and tousled my hair. Now I could blame my offended dignity

on *him,* and I cast him a look that let him know it. I
have nearly sixteen years—well, more than fifteen, any-
how—and am too old to be treated like a puppy.

"Your pardon, sir knight," said my father. "My sons
are young and eager to see the world. Astolat is a dull
place for the young, and perhaps I have been too selfish
in keeping all my children here with me."

The stranger murmured a vaguely polite comment. His
accent sounded foreign. His face was gray with fatigue.
Recognizing this, my father invited him to dismount and
enter the castle with us.

"My son Torre will take your horse to the stable and
see that he is properly attended. Please, come inside and
let us offer you food and drink. You cannot go on in
this condition."

"How did you come here?" I asked the knight as he
slid heavily off his mount. "Are you lost?"

"Lost?" His gray eyes clouded with sorrow. His face,
once handsome but now scarred and aging, crumpled
with some terrible emotion. "Yes," he whispered, "I am
lost . . . lost . . . and do not even truly desire my own
salvation."

I stared at him in naive shock. He must be ill, to say
such a thing. "*All* men desire salvation," I explained to
him. "There is a priest here, an excellent kind man. Perhaps you—"

His snort of amusement stopped me. I felt my face
flush. Though young and inexperienced, I am not a fool;
I shrugged with embarrassment and turned away from
the weary knight, knowing myself as yet unworldly and
somewhat awkward.

When I returned to the castle some time later, I saw
that the knight, like his mount, recovered quickly from
physical hardship when given a little proper care. My
father had seated our unexpected guest in the hall's best

chair, offered him an extra cushion, and was refilling his cup with ale when I joined them.

My brother Lavaine appeared a moment later, carrying food for the stranger. I smirked at Lavaine, recognizing his awe of the knight, for though we do not stand upon ceremony at Astolat, it is still the work of servants to carry food from the kitchens. Seeing my expression, Lavaine finished serving the knight, then turned and discreetly kicked me when no one was looking.

My father's long experience as a parent has given him eyes in the back of his head, though. Without even turning to look at us, he absently admonished, "Enough, you two."

The knight never told us how he came to be wandering the hills and valleys around Astolat, and my father was too well-mannered to press him for an explanation. A man of honor, my father had often told me, may keep his own counsel. Forced by this selfsame father to confess all my mischief, shirking, petty fights, and wicked pranks on a regular basis, I had once finally asked him when I would become a man and entitled to keep my own counsel.

He said only, "The day will come, too soon for me and not soon enough for you, I daresay. The day *will* come, though, and we shall both know it."

One had only to look at this knight to see that he had left behind the strictures of his boyhood long ago; but the demands of manhood weighed heavily upon him. Even I could see that.

After convincing the knight to stay the night at Astolat, for it was already growing too dark to travel, my father asked, "Do you return to Camelot soon?"

The knight stared into his cup and sighed. "Yes, my lord. Tomorrow, I suppose."

"You seem less than pleased at the prospect," my father observed. "Why not tarry in Astolat a while, until your heart desires you to return to Camelot?"

"My *heart*." For a horrible moment, I thought this great knight would weep, right there in front of us all. "My heart lives only at Camelot," he whispered into his cup. "And there it dies a little each day, too."

"Is that why you left?" I blurted.

My father frowned at me, his silent gaze suggesting that I cultivate a little tact before speaking again. My brother stepped on my foot, making me wince.

"I left for sanity," the knight said wearily. "I go back for honor."

"And must it be tomorrow?" my father asked.

Coming to some sense of himself, the knight said, "Yes. There is a great tournament tomorrow, and I have sworn to the Queen that I would be there for it."

"The Queen," I breathed in awe. "You *know* the Queen?"

He smiled slightly. "And the King. And all others, too, who make their home at Camelot."

"Camelot?" repeated a soft, womanly voice. We all turned to see my sister enter the hall.

"Elaine, come meet our visitor," my father said, holding out his hand. He has always been so fond of his only daughter.

Out of courtesy, the knight rose to greet Elaine as she came forward. I saw his face lighten with interest, as so often happened when men beheld my sister for the first time, for God gifted her with beauty and grace in abundance. Her long hair was the color of honey, her eyes the warm brown of freshly turned earth, and her skin was white and pink and perfect. Though older than me, older even than Lavaine, she was still unwed. With my mother gone for so many years, we had no other woman in the family. My father was reluctant to part with Elaine, and in this, I shared his selfishness. It would have been different, of course, had Elaine announced she wished to marry; but she seemed content to tend her father and scold her brothers through the green and golden days of our life at Astolat.

"My daughter Elaine," my father said proudly, "the Lady of Astolat since my dear wife's death ten years ago."

The stranger greeted her in courtly fashion, and Elaine's pink cheeks turned red, for she was not accustomed to such flowery compliments. After a moment's silence, she said shyly, "And you, sir? May I not know to which great knight of Camelot I am being presented?"

He hesitated, then said quite simply, "I am Lancelot du Lac."

I gasped even as my brother gripped my arm in excited astonishment. My father guffawed with surprise, then coughed. Only Elaine remained calm, staring into the knight's eyes as fixedly as he stared into hers.

When she finally spoke again, her voice was rich and full of promise. "Yes," she said. "Yes, you could be no other."

My brother and I could not contain ourselves, and after a few gruff reprimands, my father stopped trying to make us do so. The greatest, most famous knight in all the world was taking his ease in our humble castle! We couldn't believe our happy fortune! A mere knight from Camelot had been wonderous enough—but Lancelot himself! Questions tumbled from our lips faster than our tongues could form them. We asked about jousts and tourneys, lords and ladies, damsels in distress, feats of dashing daring, and great battles. We demanded stories about the Round Table, Merlin, Morgan Le Fay, and Prince Modred. But mostly, of course, we wanted to hear stories of King Arthur himself, the brave young king raised in obscurity who had claimed his crown in adversity and changed this land for everyone, forever.

"And what of the Queen?" my sister asked at last,

nterrupting another of Lavaine's questions. "Tell us bout the Queen."

Lancelot's eyes met hers again, as they had been wont o do so very often throughout the conversation. A trange silence fell upon us all which I did not under-tand. I saw Elaine bite her lip as she watched his face.

"A great and honorable lady," he answered at last. 'And one to whom I must keep my promise."

"To fight tomorrow?" Lavaine asked.

"Yes." Inexpressible emotions washed across his face, ll sternly forced aside, until at last a smile came upon im. His eyes sparkled with what might be called mis-hief in a less formidable man. "Yes. I have promised he Queen I would ride tomorrow. But I would like to o as a stranger, the way I came here."

"But how can you?" Elaine asked. "Are you not well-nown there?"

He looked down at the engraved shield resting beside is chair. "Yes," he said slowly. "Easy to identify, car-ying my own shield and riding my own horse. But with *nother* man's . . ."

My father chuckled. "I see what you are about, Sir ancelot. Your opponents now fall off their horses at the nere mention of your name, but if you were to appear s an anonymous knight—"

"You would win," Lavaine cried, "and your glory vould be yours all over again!"

"And would the Queen be pleased to honor an un-nown champion?" Elaine asked Lancelot.

"Tomorrow I ride not for the Queen," Lancelot said vith sudden force, "but for my own honor."

"We can give him Torre's shield, Father," Lavaine aid. "It's blank enough, to be sure."

I hit him.

"Enough, you two," my father said absently. He ex-

plained to Sir Lancelot, "Torre was hurt in his first tilt
and—"

"Father!" I was appalled. "Surely this does not inter
est—"

"Never be ashamed of falling honorably," Lancelot ad
monished, turning to me. "No man is undefeated, and
most are hurt in their first joust."

"Even you?" I asked doubtfully.

He grinned. It was the first time he had looked genu
inely happy. It made his face almost unrecognizable.
smiled back. "Oh, yes," he assured me. "Even me."

And then, without the slightest hint of embarrassment
he told us the story of his first joust, of how young and
vain and inept he was. We all laughed. All except Elaine
who looked upon the rest of us with a soft smile o
womanly tolerance. The look she cast upon Lancelot
though, was quite a different thing.

"Very well, Sir Lancelot," I said at last. "Since I do
not need my shield, I will allow you to use it tomorrow.'

My father laughed again. "I will rename you Sir Churl
young Torre! Is that the way to speak to the greates
knight in the world? You will *allow* him!"

I felt my cheeks burn and tried to stammer an apology
This time it was Lancelot himself who tousled my hair
I did not mind it so much, coming from a knight of such
great fame.

The leather tunic, a gift from my father, is new and
stiff. I have worn it only once before, in the joust where
I was hurt this spring. The squire helps me with the pad
ded, quilted shirt I will wear over it, to protect myself from
broken pieces of chain mail being driven into a wound.

I only wear it to honor my father's brokenhearted re
quest, for I have no fear of festering wounds.

No, for I will not leave the field until one of us lies dead

* * *

We left for Camelot early the next morning, we three—Lavaine, Lancelot, and myself. My father, still concerned about the injuries I had sustained at my first joust, forbade me to take part in the tournament. But since Lavaine must go with Lancelot, who didn't know where the road to Camelot lay, my father hadn't the heart to refuse my request—or, rather, my *demand*—to go with them.

"Why don't you ask to come, too?" I urged Elaine as she helped me choose my clothes for my first visit to Camelot. "Father would let you. With both Lavaine and I there, it would be proper."

"Come to Camelot?" Her voice was hard, surprising me. "Why? To watch him with the Queen?"

I blinked, confused. "Who, Lancelot? He's not going to joust with the *Queen,* silly girl!"

She looked beyond me and murmured, "Yes, he is, little brother. Yes, he is."

I tugged on her long braid and teased her for her foolishness. Then, fully dressed, I asked, "How do I look?"

But she didn't answer, having already turned and hurried away in that purposeful manner women have. And like any man, I didn't know whether or not I was properly dressed for the occasion, without a woman to tell me so. But I knew something else had captured my sister's attention, so I joined Lancelot and Lavaine in the courtyard, where we mounted our horses and took our leave of my father. He had given Lancelot use of his own fine mount, keeping the knight's destrier hidden in our stables until Lancelot should return for him.

My father was still giving me worried advice about what to avoid and whom to greet when Elaine came running out into the morning sunshine. In her hand, she carried the right sleeve of her best gown; its thick red material was soft and finely broidered. Breathless and flushed, she asked Sir Lancelot to carry her token that day.

He hesitated, looking surprised. "I . . . have never carried any lady's favor." Seeing her expression, he added, "I mean no offense, Lady Elaine. It is simply not my habit. Ask any man who knows me, and he will tell you—"

"Then, sir, will carrying mine not help to conceal your true identity today?" my sister challenged, her cheeks darkening at her own boldness.

Lavaine nudged me, but I only scowled at him, not wanting to embarrass Elaine. A woman may be taken with a great warrior, just as we were, after all.

With a wry smile, Lancelot agreed and accepted the favor with courtly grace. In return, he asked her to guard his shield well, until he should come for it again.

"I will take it to my tower," she promised, "where no one ever ventures but myself, and sometimes my brothers. I will guard it as my own honor, sir, and no man shall take it from me but you."

I took his shield from her tower room, and I will carry it today. God grant that its magic does not turn against me, and that my own shield, which he carries, does not shield him from me.

There is little need to speak of Lancelot in his glory, for who has not heard the tales of his skill? Well concealed in armour, with a horse and a shield no one recognized, the mysterious knight was the talk of the tournament. No man was proof against him, and word of the stranger's skill and courage spread quickly through Camelot that day; he was even compared to Lancelot! Lavaine acquitted himself well, too, and I tried to follow my father's teachings and overcome the envy I felt,

watching him gather his own measure of glory as he
fought at Lancelot's side in the *mêlée*.

But then Lancelot's opponents, afraid of his extraordinary prowess, all fell upon him at once. Though a brilliant fighter, he was not proof against the sudden attack
of so many men, not even with my brother valiantly trying to help him. One of the knights drove a lance into
his side, and there it broke off. Lancelot fell from his
horse and lay in the dirt.

A woman screamed terribly, so terribly that I lifted
my eyes from the horrible sight before me and sought
her out. It was the Queen herself, and after that one
fearsome wail she went as still and silent as death, poised
in an animal crouch upon her throne, staring with such
intensity of pain in her eyes, it was as if *she* had been
wounded. Or as if she had somehow guessed that Camelot's favorite knight now lay bleeding in the dirt. The
King was beside her, trying to comfort her. He looked
older than I had expected, but then I hear so many tales
of the wars that I often forget how long ago they were.
He was every inch a king, though, and all of Camelot
held its breath when he turned his attention to the *mêlée*
as if he might call a halt to it right then and there.

And then Lancelot grasped Lavaine's arm as my
brother bent over him, and started hauling himself to his
feet. I grunted loudly with surprise. No one could see
Lancelot's face as he slowly climbed back into his saddle,
but my own face—and that of each man in the crowd—
reflected the expression which must undoubtedly be on
his; for surely it was pain beyond what any ordinary man
could endure.

They will still be singing songs and telling tales about
that day when I am a very old man, for he fought like
a lion then, with the broken lance-head still sticking out
of his pierced armor. I would not believe it if I hadn't
seen it with my own eyes, but he drove back his oppo-

nents with brilliant fighting, seeming more like a young
man fresh from his bed, rather than an aging and desperately wounded one who had been fighting all day.

And yet when the day was over and he was proclaimed
the unparalleled champion of the tournament, he turned
away from glory, prizes, and the cheers of the crowd.

"My prize . . ." he said wearily, "is death." His breath
rasped so heavily beneath his helmut that even I could
hear it. "I go hence . . . and I charge you all . . . follow
me not."

He turned away from the King and Queen, spurred his
horse, and raised dust as he rode past me. My brother
followed him.

"Get your horse, you idiot! We're leaving," Lavaine
shouted as he galloped past me.

*My armor is old-fashioned, being mostly borrowed
from my father. He intends to have my own made for me
in another year or two, after I have stopped growing. It
is his wont to study my long legs and dangling arms, then
laugh and say perhaps I will* never *stop growing.*

We took Lancelot to a boatman's hut, a place we knew
of because our father had sheltered there long ago. Once
there, he ordered us to pull out the lance-head. I was
afraid to, knowing he would then surely die. But Lavaine,
after arguing, finally obeyed him.

Oh, the blood. How he bled! It burst forth in a thick
red river, blackening the earth around him and seeping
across my feet. The pain made him faint; I was glad, for
seeing him suffer was more than I could bear with
dignity.

Knowing that he would die without better help than
we could give him, I left Lavaine with him and rode out
beneath the setting sun, toward Astolat. I had never ridden at night, nor had I ever been alone so far from home

before. Demons gibbered at me as the shadows sighed and shifted between gnarled and waving trees. The way became unfamiliar, and many times I stopped and circled my horse, looking for a landmark, for some sign that I was going the right direction. My teeth chattered, for I was not dressed for nighttime riding, nor for the mist which rose to chill and confound me.

So slow was my progress that it was dawn by the time I reached Astolat and roused my father and sister from their beds.

"He's *hurt*," Elaine whispered fiercely, before I could even tell her what had happened, "isn't he?"

I nodded, trying to catch my breath.

She closed her eyes and grabbed her side, as if she, too, felt a lance-head pierce her flesh. *"There."*

"Yes." I stared at her in astonishment. "How did you know?"

"The shield," she said, dressing quickly in the thin light of dawn.

"What?"

"The shield . . . knows his fate."

"How can—"

"I think it is enchanted," she interrupted. "You must take me to him. I can help him."

"Yes," I agreed wearily, too exhausted to care about this womanly nonsense about an enchanted shield. I had come for my sister, and now I must take her with me. Since before I was born, she had spent long days learning the art of healing. She tended the sick all around Astolat and knew prayers to help barren women to become fertile and babies to be born healthy. I knew of no one else who could help Lancelot fight Death.

So Elaine gathered together her herbs and medicaments as I hungrily broke my fast. My father ordered fresh horses to be brought up from the stables, and he watched us ride away with a worried gaze. Someone must

remain at Astolat; now, for the first time ever, my father
was there without any of his children.

*I am glad of the squire, for my wits are strangely fud-
dled today, and I think I might dress myself in the wrong
order if he were not here to help me. But he is calm as
he helps me don the hauberk. I hope he does not notice
my hands shaking.*

It was Elaine who saved his life. Also Elaine who bore
the brunt of his violent brain-fever, his demanding delir-
ium and haunted dreams, his churlish insistence that he
didn't need anyone's help, his pained embarrassment,
and his sulking. A man like that does not respond well
to weakness and helplessness. But he learned, in the end,
to respond well to my sister's care. With the passage of
days, his gruff courtesy fled, to be replaced by a tender
warmth which flowed between them. She had a way of
soothing him which I scarcely understood, but which
seemed to lighten the heavy burden of sorrow that lived
in that aging face.

Lavaine saw it differently. "She tells me not to tire
him with questions, tells me he needs his rest, tells me
he has no strength to keep telling me stories and giving
me advice about my jousting.... And *then* she sits in
that hut and talks with him for hours!" he complained
to me as we hunted one afternoon.

Elaine would make good use of our kill, preparing
broth for Lancelot and roasted meat for us. I missed
my father's table, however, and was pleased that Elaine
thought Lancelot would be well enough to return to Astolat with us in another day or two—as long as we rode
gently, she cautioned me.

"She comforts him," I said mildly, more interested in
finding fresh game than in this conversation.

"That's a sly word for it," Lavaine sneered. "She wants

what every woman wants, but why she should choose a wounded and helpless man as her—"

"Oh, do shut up! Your bellowing is chasing all the game away!" I snapped, offended by his criticism of Elaine and getting hungrier with every passing moment.

It was late when I returned to the boatman's hut, but the fowl we had caught would make a good meal. Lavaine was stoking the fire outside as I entered the hut to tell Elaine we had returned. As she rose to come outside, Lancelot kissed her hand before releasing it.

The breastplate is stiff and heavy, but my father begged me to wear it today. I agreed, for I have seen how vulnerable the heart is.

The ride to Astolat took us more than a day, so slowly did we travel. I was relieved to finally be home, surprised at how much I had missed it. For the first time, I began to understand why my father had settled into such a quiet life after the end of the wars.

Elaine insisted we house Lancelot in her tower room. He readily agreed, despite the effort it cost him to walk up that long flight of tightly curving steps.

"This is ridiculous!" Lavaine protested, red-cheeked with anger. "Why should he not sleep in my chamber? He would be much more—"

"I can care for him more easily in the tower room," Elaine said firmly, "where I keep all my herbals and charms. Besides, he needs more peace and quiet than he would get in—"

"Oh, is *that* what you think he needs?" Lavaine challenged.

"Please, my friend," Lancelot intervened wearily, "Lady Elaine saved my life, and I would not be so ungracious as to dispute her advice."

Lavaine gave in with ill grace. My father diplomatically suggested we all eat and retire early.

The King's herald arrived the next day. The entire court by now suspected that the mysterious knight of such great skill was indeed Lancelot in disguise. Concerned that he had ridden away after being badly wounded, the King's men were searching the countryside for him. My father welcomed the herald and offered him food, drink, and rest. Although Elaine insisted that Lancelot was still too weak to be troubled by visitors, she gave the herald a good account of Lancelot's improving health.

The Queen's messenger came the following day. He brought a gift which he offered to Elaine with a courtly speech; the Queen presented this small, unworthy token as a symbol of her gratitude to Elaine for having saved the life of Camelot's most noble knight. To everyone's surprise, Elaine politely refused the Queen's gift, saying that Sir Lancelot's growing health and peace of mind were the only gifts she would ever want or expect in payment for her skills.

After that, the Queen sent a messenger to Astolat almost every day. Sometimes he would merely inquire after Lancelot's health. Occasionally he would deliver a letter from the Queen. After reading these letters, Lancelot would keep to himself, and Elaine would roam the castle, tense and hollow-eyed.

Lavaine and I returned to our daily regime of studies and swordplay. As Lancelot regained his strength, he began coming outside to watch us and offer advice. After a fortnight had passed, he was even well enough to demonstrate his suggestions. Though much older than us and still somewhat impaired by his wound, he could disarm and defeat either of us—and sometimes both of us at once!—with effortless grace. But even fiercely proud young men couldn't resent defeat at the hands of the greatest knight in the realm, particularly not when he was so gracious and good-humored in his victory.

Elaine was tolerant of our antics, though she watched Lancelot with evident concern when he began entering into our swordplay. His wound reopened on one occasion, and she wouldn't let him touch a sword for the next three days.

I don't know what they talked about in the privacy of the tower room, but they seldom spoke to each other at all in the hall or the courtyard. Not that there was any coolness between them. On the contrary, even I could see that Lancelot had developed a great affection for my sister. But it was as if words were unnecessary between them, for they seemed to speak to each other with their eyes.

The gauntlets are old and comfortable. I flex my hands, then grasp the heavy sword, testing its weight in my grip. He will have better armor, better weapons, and a better horse than I, but I feel confident as I finish preparing for the joust. For I know that God is on my side.

I was sorry to see him go, but I had always known that he would someday leave us and return to the sky-reaching towers of Camelot. No man who had sought his fame at the king's side all these years could forever be content with our quiet life at Astolat. To my astonishment, Lavaine asked to go with him. I tried to talk him out of it, for I knew how it would hurt my father to see his eldest son ride away from Astolat; but Lavaine wanted his share of fame and glory, and my father said he could not deny him that.

Elaine was inconsolable over Lancelot's leaving. She was too proud and brave a woman to let us see her tears, but I knew by her red-rimmed eyes that she had shed them aplenty. Pale and fragile, she bore her sorrow with dignity as Lancelot rode away, his own shoulders stooped with a kind of wretchedness.

The days dragged by after Lancelot and Lavaine had gone. My father had little time and even less energy to help me with my swordplay, so I began helping him with his many duties. Still, time often weighed on my hands, for my brother had been my constant friend, foe, and companion, and I missed him more than I had expected. And so, one rainy afternoon, I found myself climbing the steps to Elaine's tower in search of companionship.

She sat on the cold floor, her hair unbound, her arms wrapped around herself as she rocked back and forth. Her back was to me, but I did not need to see her face to know that she wept. I would have knelt to comfort her, but then I saw what she gazed at with such rapt attention that she had not even heard my approach.

He had left his shield ever in her care, and now it leaned against one stone wall. A parting gift, I supposed, staring at it in wonder. A piece of expert craftsmanship, it now glowed with something other than the usual luster of fine polished metal. There was a radiance to it, an inner light that spoke of sorcery and enchantment. As I watched its shimmering surface, Lancelot appeared before my very eyes.

It was sunset as he rode through the gates of Camelot. He was dressed for hunting, and he rode alone.

Horrified, I tore my gaze away and stared at Elaine's back, at the tangle of golden hair that hung past her waist, at the bereft posture of her trembling shoulders.

What had she said about the shield—that it knew his fate? I had been tired and worried at the time, too impatient to listen to one who had always been older and wiser than I. Had she been watching him like this ever since he had left Astolat? Did he know? By the blood of Christ! Is that why he had left it with her?

My gaze flew back to the enchanted shield, and in it

I saw Elaine's heart mirrored in Lancelot's lovesick gaze. What a fool I had been! How could I not have known? True, I was a stranger to the ways of a man and a woman, but how could I have missed the naked yearning in my own sister's face whenever she gazed at Lancelot? It was the same agonizing expression I now saw painted across his scarred, weary features as he gazed at another woman. I recognized her as the Queen.

A sob tore from Elaine's throat. Oh, by the Blessed Virgin, I finally understood! And I felt more like a mere boy than ever before. Did no one else know? Was my father too steeped in duty and mundane family concerns to see that his daughter had fallen in love? Was Lavaine too wrapped up in his blind admiration of Lancelot to understand the source of his own jealousy?

And Elaine, poor, sweet Elaine. Why had she borne this suffering all alone? Did she think I wouldn't care about her broken heart?

I stared at the mirror with sorrow-misted eyes. Lancelot's face twisted in anguish, torn between desire and shame, as he stealthily slipped into the Queen's bedchamber after dark. When he took her in a carnal embrace, I turned away, unwilling to bear the sight, and unable to bear any more of Elaine's sobs in silence.

"No!" she cried. "No, you said you loved me! Don't go to her! Not *her*! She can't give you ... give you ..." She rocked forward and collapsed facedown on the floor.

"Elaine!" I knelt down and scooped her into my arms, even as she gasped and fought me. "Elaine ..."

"Oh, Torre!" Her voice was shrill with shock and misery. "You saw! You saw them!"

"Shhh, yes, I saw. But how is it possible? The shield—"

"A mirror of his life, his heart ... I don't know. Some sorcery. The King's wizard, perhaps."

"I'm so sorry, Elaine. I never knew, never guessed.

How could I have not known?" I shook my head in wonderment. Had I been so young and foolish only yesterday? "I wish you could have come to me. I wish—"

"You're a boy, still," she murmured. "It wouldn't be right to burden you with—"

"I'm a man," I insisted quietly. "And it's my duty to protect you."

She turned her head to look up into my face. Her tears slowed for a moment as she studied me. "A man?" she breathed. She touched my cheek, searching my face. At last, she nodded slowly and said, "Perhaps the day has come." She sighed and burrowed against me. "Oh, Torre, Torre. What can I do?"

I shook my head. "I wish I knew. At least you won't have to bear this alone anymore."

She stiffened. "But I bear something else, little brother, and I bear it alone."

It was like receiving a hard, unexpected blow. I sucked in my breath and asked foolishly, "Are you sure?"

"Quite sure."

"When did it happen?"

She almost laughed. "I'm not *that* clever a midwife. It could have been almost any time since we returned to Astolat."

"God have mercy." I lowered my head and whispered, "Won't he marry you?"

"He doesn't know about the baby."

"Then you must tell him."

"No."

"Elaine—"

"No!" She pushed me away. "I begged him to make me his wife. But he wants *her*."

"She already has a husband," I pointed out. "And you're going to have his—"

"No. If he ever comes back, he must come for *me*. I

will not sleep next to him night after night for the rest of my life knowing that he dreams of *her*."

"But Elaine, surely the baby is the most im—"

"No!" she snapped. "He must come for *me*, or not at all."

But the months passed, and he never came, never even sent a message, for he was as entranced by the Queen as Elaine was by him. And by the time Elaine's shame could no longer be hidden, her heart was too broken for her to care about frowning priests, whispering villagers, and public disgrace. I thought for a while that love for the child she carried might comfort her, but the daily torment of the mirror stole her mind in the end. And so when the pain and bleeding came upon her, long before her time, she, who had helped so many others, seemed not to know what to do. My father and I begged her to tell us how to help her, but it was as if some strange curse had come upon her, for she only wept and sang bits of old songs from our childhood.

And so she died, taking with her the last glimmer of the happiness we had known at Astolat.

All of Camelot has come to watch today's contest, though the crowd is somber and quiet. I thought they would cheer when Lancelot rode into the arena, for he has ever been a hero in story and song, but they are nearly silent when he appears. I sense hostility around us and realize, with considerable surprise, that it is meant for him. *I am unknown here, after all; but he has inspired envy and jealousy for years in Camelot. Perhaps, I begin to think, perhaps I will do him and everyone else a favor when I kill him today.*

He tried to refuse my challenge when I came to the King's court. There was a terrible scene when I arrived at Camelot with Elaine's body, floating downriver by boat from Astolat. She was pale with blood loss, and her snowy gown made her look even whiter. The Queen wept when I told the story. Lancelot seemed to grow twenty years older in those few minutes. And the King ... how sad Arthur looked.

My brother's tears for Elaine dried when I spoke to the court. When I was done, he flung himself at me as if we were still boys in my father's courtyard, pummeling and struggling to best each other. "You lie!" he cried as the King's men pulled him away from me. "*She* lied! He is the noblest knight in the world! He *never* would have—"

"He did," I said, my heart burning with hatred. "Ask him!"

"I don't need to ask him! Elaine lied, and if you fight him, he will prove it by killing you!"

The court burst into furious shouting and arguing, and only the King's repeated commands stifled the uproar. Then Arthur implored me to reconsider, for nothing could be proved by combat, he said, and nothing could bring back my sister. Lancelot said nothing, would not even look at me; but when I refused all course of action save that of honor, he finally accepted my challenge quietly and turned away from us all.

Before following him out, Lavaine promised me, "If you survive this fight with him, then I will kill you myself!" He gripped my arm to pull me closer as he snarled, "How could father have permitted this? You will not live to return home, Torre, so you had better write to him tonight. And when you do, tell him I will *never* return to Astolat! You have all disgraced me!"

I shook him off and told him he was no longer my brother. The green and golden days had ended with Lancelot, and Lavaine would never be welcome at Astolat again; even if my father would forgive him for this, I never would.

I looked into the mirror that night as I polished the shield in preparation for combat. Lancelot was there, and so was the Queen. He turned away from her, and I saw that there would never be peace between them after this.

His destrier is as splendid and powerful as it was the first time he rode into Astolat, the day we welcomed him with open hearts. His armor gleams beneath the autumn sun, and his hands hold the reins with the steady grasp of courage and experience.

My own hands tremble, and I feel sweat trickle down my back under the weight of my armor. I have never killed a man. He will be the first.

I blink away the mist of my fear, grasp my lance, and commend my soul to God.

APPRECIATION

by Jennifer Roberson

I met Marion Zimmer Bradley where all authors wish to be met: in a bookstore. Not in the flesh—Marion herself wasn't present—but in the spirit, in the words, and was summarily bespelled by a brand new world.

In those days of little money and less time, it was a task to make do: to buy such books as I could afford, more often in used bookstores, and to lose myself for a while, forgetting altogether what time it was, what day; to be caught up in the magic of someone gifted enough— and generous enough—to share a world with me.

As such moments are only rarely remarkable, I thought nothing beyond hoping I would enjoy the book. I certainly thought nothing of other books set in the same world, or of other characters who peopled other volumes. I just wanted a good read.

The book was titled *The Spell Sword,* and was remarkable primarily, at first glance, for its battered appearance—and for the Chinese take-out order jotted down on the inside cover. I have always detested people who abuse books in this way, and it annoyed me that I was buying something clearly unloved, but I bought it anyway. And loved it.

Some twenty years later here I am, paying tribute to a author who has done so much to encourage my own career, and to found a genre.

Marion was not the first. She was not part of the early

years, the Golden Age, the days of Campbell, Kornbluth, Howard, Moore, Brackett, and others. She was part of the second wave, if you will, or third; part of the tide of authors who, so inspired by and enamored of the fictions of those before them, chose to create their own worlds and people them with characters readers cannot ignore.

Marion was birthed by this thing called science fiction fandom in the true sense, but transcended it by becoming one of its icons. She remains so to this day. Her work, and her influence, her support and enthusiasm, is part of the fabric of our genre; without Marion, without her work and generosity, many of us would not be published today. The genre, though constantly mutating with an influx of new talent, new ideas, new technology, is nonetheless *what* it is because of authors like Marion who popularized it to the point that others were sucked in— and came out the other side with literature of their own to share with subsequent waves.

Marion herself would never be so arrogant to claim as personal possession any part of this genre, to count herself a progenitor of modern science fiction and fantasy. But those of us who have read her work, ranging from YA adventure stories, through the novels of Darkover, to ambitious masterpieces such as *The Mists of Avalon,* know very well how much we owe her.

As readers, we are grateful for what she has given us. As authors, we can but pay tribute to, to celebrate, a professional who made it a little easier for us all, who has given of time, money, health, and influence in order to support those she believes in.

It's not my place to analyze Marion's body of work; I leave that to academics and reviewers who are better suited to it. It's my place only to thank Marion for opening so many minds to the possibilities some of us have explored, that others *will* explore. And to pay tribute to a woman who has, in her personal life as well as her fiction, permitted and encouraged authors to be free with their own, despite the times, politics, and prejudices that might otherwise argue against such frankness. But Marion has never been a coward or "politically correct," nor is she a fool to let others tell her how to think. She is what she is.

And the genre is better for it.

GUINEVERE'S TRUTH

by Jennifer Roberson

I am not what they say I am, these bitch-begotten myth-makers so adept at patching together occasional truths, and falsehoods into a wholly improper motley. They were not *there,* any of them, to say what did happen. Or also to say what did not.

They call it a tragedy now. I suppose it is; I suspect it was even then, when none of us knew. When none of us thought beyond what two of us imagined might be enough to preserve a realm. To preserve a man's dignity.

They make of it now a sacrament, some of them; others name it sin. To us, it was merely what *was.* We were never prescient, to know what would come of the moment. We were never wise, to consider consequences. We were what we were. Nothing more than that.

More, now, they would and will have us be. Great glyphs of human flesh, striding out of stories, tidbits of tales of others such as we: kings and queens and knights . . . and the follies of the flesh.

Was it folly? No. Not then. Not now. Was it flesh? Oh yes. Entirely the flesh. Wholly *of* the flesh, though they would have it be more: sacrament, or sin. The anvil upon which a realm was sundered, despite the tedious truth.

A man, first. A woman. A binding between them, magicked and ill-wrought, yet enough to get a child. And that child, bred up to be a king despite his bastardy, was made to *be* a king—be it necessary, be it required that he kill another king to gain the crown. To break what was built of heart, mortared together by blood.

And yet they blame me.

Seductress? I was not raised so, nor was given to believe it could be so; men wanted me for what I was, not who. The daughter of a man judged to be of use, of some small power in the chess game of the realm, the patchwork of a place that was not, until he came, a nation in any wise.

But he came. Was born to come. Bred to come, to take up a people as he took up the sword, to preserve what might otherwise have fallen before it was truly built; bred and brought up to stitch together out of the fragile patchwork a whole and well-made quilt resilient enough to guard the limbs of his lady, his one true lady, his steadfast Lady whose name was Britain.

A man who is king needs nothing of a wife but that she be his queen, and bear him an heir.

Whore? Some name me so. And would have burned me for it.

Yet I will burn. The priests tell me so. Afterward. God will not tolerate an adulteress in His realm.

If that be so, if it be true of men as well as of women, then surely we will play this out again, this tragedy, this travesty, this humiliating dance. And none of us wanting it.

If that be hell, we have lived it.

Such stories, in their conception, in the truths of their births, are infinitely simple. Ours was no different. But they make of it now a grand entertainment, fit to cause people to weep.

We none of us wept.

It was what it *was,* not this great sweeping epic, not this literature of the soul, binding others to it. There was no immensity to it, no bard's brilliant embroidery to win him a month of meals. Our tapestry was naught but a

square of clean, fine linen, hemmed on all the edges ...
only later was it used to sop and display the blood of
Britain's broken heart.

His one true lady, undone. His wife, the queen,
unmasked.

Seductress. Adulteress. And worse yet: barren.

Ah, but it *was* my lack. His seed was proven, though
unknown by any save the woman who was his sister. His
seed was sowed, was born, was bred up to be a king,
even if it be necessary to kill another king.

Well, it is done.

All of it is done. And all of it also *un*done; there was
no wisdom in the bastard who was inexplicably son and
nephew, to see what might come of it. To see what has.

Lies. So many lies. The truth, you see, is plain, is pro-
saic beyond belief, and therefore tedious.

A man, and a woman. Stripped of all save the flesh,
and the flesh freed of such constraints as crown, as
armor. And the hearts stripped of all things save compassion for a king who needed a son, yet had none of his
queen.

We did not know, then, what we came to know: that
the king had bred a son. We knew only there was none
and no promise of it, and a man growing older with no
son to come after him, to lift the great burden and don
it himself, like the hair shirt of priests. It was known only
that Britain had need of an heir, and that the king's wife,
after so much time in the royal bed, offered nothing to
prove his manhood.

It was a solution, we thought, that might prove least
painful to a man who was king, and was of himself well
worth the sacrifice: his wife and his liege man would
between them, in his name and the name of his realm,
make a child. And call it the king's.

But no child came of it. Only grief.

It is easier, I know, to make a myth of it, to commute

us to legend. But the truth is small, and of less glory than what is sung: what we did was to comfort the king. To save what the king had wrought.

Practicality. Not undying, tragic love. Not this travesty of the truth.

But it is prettier, I admit, what they have made of it.

Such a small story, ours. And a world wrenched awry.

Blame me as you will for the folly, but not for the intent. Any more than you blame the bards for making magic of what was nothing more than necessity as we viewed it then, for and in the name of a simple, compassionate man.

For king that was, and king that shall be.

THE CONTRIBUTORS

DIANA L. PAXSON has written more than fifty short stories and fifteen novels, specializing in Germanic and Celtic cultures. Currently she is collaborating on a trilogy about Fionn MacCumhal with Adrienne Martine-Barnes. She lives in California, and has been featured in every volume of Marion Zimmer Bradley's annual *Sword and Sorceress* anthologies.

ANDRE NORTON is one of science fiction and fantasy's most prolific and beloved authors, responsible for dozens of popular novels, collections, and anthologies. She has been cited by the Science Fiction and Fantasy Writers of America as one of its Grand Masters for her ongoing contributions to the field.

ELUKI BES SHAHAR is the author of thirteen novels and more than a dozen short stories. She lives in Poughkeepsie with a large collection of cats and books, and is currently working on an historical fantasy romance.

JUDITH TARR has published critically acclaimed fantasy and historical novels in addition to short fiction, and was a nominee for the 1994 World Fantasy Award for her historical fantasy, *Lord of the Two Lands*. She lives near Tucson, Arizona, with two dogs, two cats, and three Lipizzans.

KATE ELLIOTT is the author of four novels, and has contributed short stories to several anthologies. Recently she collaborated with Melanie Rawn and Jennifer Roberson on an upcoming fantasy novel. She lives with her husband and three children in Pennsylvania, and is working on a fantasy trilogy.

C.J. CHERRYH is the highly regarded author of many bestselling fantasy and science fiction novels, and has been awarded the coveted Hugo Award for both novels and short fiction. She lives in Oklahoma.

DEBORAH WHEELER is best known for her short fiction, which has garnered nominations for the Nebula Award, but she has also published two novels. Her first short story was published in one of the *Sword and Sorceress* anthologies, and she remains a regular contributor. She lives in Los Angeles with her family.

KATHARINE KERR is the author of a series of Celtic-based fantasy novels, but is also acclaimed for her science fiction. She has contributed short stories to several anthologies, and has also edited one. She lives in San Francisco.

DAVE SMEDS has published two fantasy novels and many short stories, as well as non-fiction articles. His short fiction is frequently recommended for awards, and is equally featured in the *Sword and Sorceress* anthologies. He holds a third-degree black belt in Goju-ryu karate, and lives with his wife and two children in Santa Rosa, California.

SUSAN SHWARTZ has written several historical and fantasy novels, has contributed to many anthologies and collections, and has edited several. She is a four-time Nebula nominee in short fiction, and has also been nominated for a Hugo. She recently completed a novel set in the 11th-century Byzantine empire, and is working on another about the First Crusade. She lives in New York City.

CHARLES de LINT has published more than a dozen novels, and is best known for establishing the urban-fantasy genre. He has also been a frequent contributor to anthologies and magazines, and his earliest work found a home in the *Sword and Sorceress* anthologies. He resides with his family in Canada.

LAWRENCE SCHIMEL is a prolific short fiction author whose work has been featured in many anthologies and magazines, including frequent appearances in those edited by Marion Zimmer Bradley. He is a graduate of Yale University, and lives in New York City.

MELANIE RAWN is best known for two bestselling fantasy trilogies, as well as a new science-fantasy trilogy. She has collaborated with Jennifer Roberson and Kate Elliott on an upcoming fantasy novel. "Salve, Regina" is her first published short story. She lives with a noisy cat in northern Arizona.

ELISABETH WATERS has won the coveted Gryphon Award, founded by Andre Norton, for an as-yet unpublished novel. That novel has since been published, and she has recently completed a second. She has also published short fiction. She lives in the Bay Area of California.

ESTHER FRIESNER is perhaps best known for pun- and fun-filled novels and short fiction, though she has also written serious fantasy as well, including the story in *Return to Avalon*. She has edited anthologies as well as contributed to them, and lives in Connecticut with her family.

KAREN HABER is the author of several science fiction and fantasy novels, and her short fiction has appeared in magazines and anthologies. She lives in California with her husband, Robert Silverberg, with whom she has edited several science fiction anthologies.

DAVE WOLVERTON has published several acclaimed science fiction and fantasy novels, but is perhaps best known for his *New York Times* bestselling STAR WARS novel, *The Courtship of Princess Leia*. He has worked as a technical writer, but now writes fiction full-time. He lives with his family in Utah.

PAUL EDWIN ZIMMER has published two fantasy novels, several short stories, a novelette, and co-wrote *The Survivors* with his sister, Marion Zimmer Bradley. He resides in California.

ADRIENNE MARTINE-BARNES has published several novels and many short stories, and has collaborated with Marion Zimmer Bradley and Diana L. Paxson. Her most recently completed novel is about the Holocaust. She lives in California.

JANE M. LINDSKOLD has sold over a dozen short stories and four novels, two of which have recently seen print. She has also published non-fiction, including a biography of the late Roger Zelazny, and holds a doctorate in English. She lives in New Mexico.

LAURA RESNICK is best known for her frequent short fiction contributions to anthologies, but has recently sold a hardcover fantasy trilogy. Two years ago she won the John W. Campbell Award for Best New Writer. She lives in Cincinnati, Ohio, above a dog kennel.

JENNIFER ROBERSON has published sixteen novels including two fantasy series as well as historical novels. Though now a frequent contributor to anthologies, collections, and magazines, her first published short story appeared in the first *Sword and Sorceress* volume. She lives near Phoenix with two cats and five dogs.